THE WITCH OF THE MEADOWS

THE WINDBORNE BOOK 1

Books by Laurel Wanrow

The Windborne Series ~ for young adults
The Witch of the Meadows

The Luminated Threads Series ~ for ages 15 & up
The Unraveling, Volume One
The Twisting, Volume Two
The Binding, Volume Three

Science Fiction Romance ~ for adults
Passages

THE WITCH OF THE MEADOWS

THE WINDBORNE BOOK 1

LAUREL WANROW

Sprouting Star Press

Laurel Wanrow/Sprouting Star Press
P. O. Box 2311
Reston, VA 20195
www.laurelwanrow.com

Copy Edit by Joyce Lamb
Cover Design by Deranged Doctor Design
Book Layout ©2017 BookDesignTemplates.com

Wanrow, Laurel
   The Witch of the Meadows/ Laurel Wanrow. ~ 1st ed.
   ISBN 978-1-943469-11-6

First Edition: March 2018

For those who love nature.

1

Late

Fern had most summer days to herself, which made arranging chores and babysitting jobs around her secret trips easier.

Today was not one of those days.

Inside their SUV parked in the driveway, she scooted the box labeled *wrens w/ bugs* and *Glass-Fragile* into place. She was about to close the hatchback when her mom came to the door of the garage they used as a glassmaking studio.

"How many boxes of flowers do I have?" she called in her soft Irish accent. Mom was ready to go, her curly brown braided hair trailing down the front of her blouse and hanging past the waist of the dressy jeans she always wore for art shows, but she turned back inside.

Fern squelched a groan. She had *one* day to finish Gran's projects—less if Mom didn't get going soon. But Mom didn't know that, couldn't know that. Fern ducked into the vehicle. She'd planned to leave by eight this morning. It was nearly eleven. Their inspection started tomorrow, at noon. Brush didn't cut itself, ponds didn't magically fill and wildflowers didn't sprout from nowhere. *I'll just have to work as fast as possible once I get to Gran's.*

"Wish you'd made a list," Fern muttered. *Like Gran.*

"Eighteen of flowers, thirty-seven total! Is that all you need?"

she called, trying not to sound too impatient. These were usual steps in Mom's show-packing process, but today, of all days, why was it taking *forever*?

Straightening, she hovered one hand over the hatchback, then pulled her phone from her cargo pants pocket, checked the sunrise time for Glasgow and set tomorrow morning's—Friday's—alarm for seven hours earlier.

A shadow fell across her phone, and Mom handed Fern the tool bag—which she never packed until the last minute—and closed the studio door. "Five hundred pieces should be enough stock for three days."

Fern let out a breath.

Finally. She put the tools into Mom's torch case, zipped it and then closed the hatchback. "Inventory and display stuff. Your demonstration supplies. Your cooler is on the seat, water bottle. Got the cashbox? Your purse—yeah, both are here. I think you're ready, Mom. Long drive to Colorado Springs. You should get going." She opened the driver's door.

"That anxious to get rid o' me, huh?" But Mom smiled up at her, her hazel eyes bright with laughter.

"Oh, you know that's not true," she started, but Mom put a finger over Fern's lips, a reach from her five-foot frame to Fern's height of six feet. She patted her cheek and brushed back strands of Fern's hair, the silky black so different from Mom's thick curls that people often assumed Fern was adopted. They mentioned that more often than Fern's light olive skin.

"I appreciate your help." Mom gestured to the studio, then pointed beyond it and across the bridge to their cabin half hidden in spruce and ponderosa trees. "Remember what I said about being careful, locking the door—"

"Seventeen, Mom. Remember?" Fern pointed to other cabins dotting the forested hillside of their small mountain town. "Neighbors we trust." She balled her fist and flexed her bicep. "Wrestling training."

Frowning, Mom clasped Fern's hand and pulled it down. "Unless you are in danger, do not physically confront a stranger. You never know what weapons people possess."

"Sure, have me haul all your stuff, but forbid me to take anyone down." Fern rolled her eyes, but Mom was only reiterating the team honor code. "Fine. I'll call for help."

"I'm happy you're spending time with friends," Mom said.

Guilt stabbed Fern. She forced herself to smile back, bent and hugged her mom so she didn't have to say anything. Mom had allowed her to skip helping at their booth for the weekend because she'd been offered a babysitting job one night for the boys she tutored and a sleepover at a friend's another.

What Mom didn't know was that Fern had said no to both invitations.

Three more days and the secret—and dreaded lying— would end. Fern drew a breath. "I love you, Mom."

"You're growing up so much, my meadowsweet, I wish..." Mom gave a watery smile and traced a design with her index finger on Fern's forehead, just as she always did when they parted. Then she kissed it, leaving Fern's skin tingling for a moment. "I love you, too." Mom gave her a last hug and climbed into the SUV. "Oh, my sunglasses!"

"Right here." Fern plucked them from her mom's hair.

She shook her head. "What would I do without you?"

And that was exactly why Fern had this secret. With no father in her life, she and Mom were all each other had, cut off from any other family *at all*...until a year and a half ago.

Some days Fern wanted to shout what she knew.

But there was so much more Mom refused to tell her—like what had happened to her dad and why Mom acted like she was in the Witness Protection Program. Gran was just as bad. Three generations of secret-keepers. Fern could wait through the weekend. By Sunday, Gran's strict community council would vote on their inspection, and she and Gran should—*would*—have the approval to keep their family land.

So Fern shrugged and said, "I don't know what I'd do without you either."

The SUV drove away, a cloud of dust rising off the gravel road, Mom not suspecting a thing.

———

Fern waited, without obviously waiting, by watering her flowerbed. Or at least she pointed the hose at it, one hand trailing a familiar path to the suede pouch she always wore, its leather laces looped around her neck and hidden beneath her favorite Earth Day T-shirt.

When she was sure Mom hadn't turned around because she'd forgotten something—and when she could stand it no longer—she locked herself inside their cabin, stuffed a can of pop and a candy bar into her cargo pants pockets and headed for the bathroom.

It looked ordinary enough, but their bathroom, and Gran's, held a secret. That secret allowed Fern to keep two promises this weekend—to Mom that she'd be safe at home and to Gran that she'd be there for their inspection.

Pulling out the pouch, Fern removed a glass piece on a fine chain. She had found the long teardrop among her mom's things and had taken it for dress-up when she'd been little, but she didn't think Mom had made this piece. The color-flecked glass wasn't one Mom used. And it did something no other glasswork of Mom's did.

Fern held the glass on her flat hand. "I wish to go to Gran's."

The glass glowed bright green and warmed her palm. A wind rose, circling her hand and then her, whipping her loose hair around her face. Light from the teardrop rose into the air, changing as it did. Bright green, to sage, yellow green, rusty brown, chestnut brown and back to bright green again. She braced her legs against the current until the light settled on the wall, swirling round and round in a perfect doughnut. The doughnut grew, nearly touching the floor and not quite reaching above her head.

Portal? Gateway? Wormhole? Whatever. Fern called it her rabbit hole. Secret passages were supposed to be in wardrobes, forgotten attics, the study—or was it the library?—with Colonel Mustard. But the bathroom? It was where she first discovered what the teardrop did, and because this was the only magic Fern could do in her otherwise mundane life, she used it there.

Ducking, she stepped one foot over the glow in their bathroom in Colorado's Front Range, through the rabbit hole and into Gran's bathroom on the Isle of Giuthas in the Irish Sea.

2

Deadline

The wind faded, and the rabbit hole shut down by itself once Fern closed her hand over the teardrop. She put the glass into her pouch, calling out, "Gran?"

No answer. Strange. Fern glanced into the open bedrooms along the hall and strode to the main room at the front of Gran's cottage.

Wheek, wheek, wheeeeek! came a shrill cry. Seconds later, Gran's guinea pig barreled around the old couch, her long gray and white hair brushing the polished floor like a dust mop. She ran straight to Fern, who bent and caught her up into a hug.

"At least you're home, Hilda. How have you been?"

Hilda burrowed under the hair that had fallen over Fern's shoulder, then poked her nose through the black strands. Her little eyes were barely visible under a shock of white fur, and when Fern brushed it back, Hilda licked her.

"Aw, thanks. I've missed you, too." Fern streamed her fingers through the chubby animal's soft fur. "I promise, soon there'll be plenty of time to pet you. But right now I've got to find Gran." She carried Hilda to the window overlooking the vegetable garden, scanned it, then the nearby wildflower patches, searching for a gray-haired, wiry, outdoorsy version of her mom.

"I guess she's started without me." It was nearly six o'clock, early evening. Fern had promised to arrive by three.

The guinea pig burbled a string of chirps, and Fern looked down to find Hilda's gaze locked on her face. Oh, great. Hilda had *that* look, sounded *that* way. Just like when Gran talked to her and Hilda "talked" back. Fern shook her head—

Something moved outside the window. A bird...yes, a small flock flew ahead of someone coming around the cottage. Several *someones*, including Gran.

Their gazes met, and Gran said something to a man at her side. Fern's breath caught. It was Sir Humus.

"Surely," Gran blustered loudly enough her voice carried in through the open window. "I can spend a minute with the lass now that she is here."

Only Gran had guts enough to antagonize the council representative who had threatened to take away her land if they didn't replant it.

Why is he here already? Had they got the start of the inspections wrong? *But we're so close to being done.* Fern's fingers started tingling in the annoying way they sometimes did, so she set Hilda down and shook them.

Gran burst through the door, her pixielike face twisted into a frown. The five songbirds that'd managed to enter with her circled the room and twittered furiously.

Fern bent to hug her. "Are we in trouble?" she whispered.

"No, but you were late, and I have to go."

"Mom ran late—oh." Gran was wearing an off-white linen dress, not her work clothes. Her long, wavy hair hung loose instead of in a braid. "You can't work this evening, then? That's okay, I can manage."

Gran patted her cheek. "Good, lass. I'm glad you're flexible, because I have some news: I'm on the council and have other inspections to attend to, not to mention they are sticklers about favoritism so don't want me present on my land for the judging. You must complete your trial on your own."

"What?" Fern gasped, her mind blank for a moment as she tried to keep up. "*You* are on... What do you mean *my trial?*"

"Aye. You asked me to stop keeping secrets from you and the time has come for that." Gran's brow creased, her bony fingers crushing Fern's. "Your work on the Meadows is a test to see if you can restore the land despite having no magic yourself. However, I didna tell them you have no magic. Nor that you are Heather's child. Keep it secret you are my granddaughter until you pass. Then we shall fix that, best we can. But your mother's blessing—do you have it?"

"Geez, Gran! I thought we'd tell her together." Fern's voice rose. *Stressed out much?* She clenched Gran's hand, although what she really wanted to do was throw someone to the ground. "And just how will I do these things? A magical place needs magic."

"*Shh.* I have but a minute, dear. I know you're up to taking charge. 'Tis clear you've inherited the touch and tha' is enough. They are seeing the lovely flowers you have grown and know it is all your doing, because I lifted the barrier that kept others out of the Meadows. But with the barrier gone"— Gran raised a finger—"take care if you see flickering along our boundaries."

That was why she wasn't allowed off the property? And never saw anyone else here either? "No nasty neighbors, then?"

"None," Gran said cheerily. "In fact"—she dropped her voice—"I've arranged some help for you, though I have no doubt you can complete our work. Stick to the rules."

The screen door creaked, and Sir Humus poked in his white-haired head at a height that matched Fern's. "Lark Fields, you know very well a minute is up. Come along now." He waved a small glass globe—tan—attached to his watch chain. "Good day, Mistress Fern." With a nod, he retreated.

Gran pulled Fern down, as if to kiss her cheek, but instead whispered, "I wish you hadn't been late, lass. Finish your list as best you can. Get your mother's blessing. And please feed Hilda," she added louder. Then she pointed at the guinea pig, said, "You be good!" and went outside, the birds with her.

Fern assumed the people on the porch would walk away, but as she watched, the air shimmered. Gran's birds alighted on her shoulders and disappeared with her and the others.

Fern smashed her fists to her forehead. *I will not freak.*

Seriously, Gran had arranged a trial for a nonmagical per-son—*her*—to take charge of magical land? Gran had said "the touch" was enough, but that was just Gran's old-time word-ing for a green thumb. That wasn't *magic*, not like the portal.

Gran had to keep her land. *If she thinks I can pass the test, then I will darn well try.*

The pressure was on, worse than finals. Fern opened the can of pop from her pocket and drank until the sugar refu-eled her. She trudged to the refrigerator and ran her finger down a worn piece of paper. *The List.*

Sir Humus had delivered this paper a year and a half ago in the winter, an attachment to a notice in legalese that said the Meadows habitat no longer contributed to the wildlands of the Isle of Giuthas. The council would seek replacement caretakers if Gran didn't bring it into compliance, which could be satisfied if she grew the plants on their list. After the no-nonsense Sir Humus left, Gran had stood on the front porch a long time, her jaw tight. Finally, she'd said, "Well, Fern? What should we do?"

There'd been no question in Fern's mind. All that old-fashioned talk about the land being a part of you suddenly felt real when told they might lose the land Gran's family had lived on for centuries. They'd researched the plants, plus added projects like raising partridge and repairing a pond dam to "put things very right," as Gran said.

Gran had hired out some clearing and ground preparation, but the rest hadn't been easy. Growing flats of seedlings and spending hours planting while sneaking around Mom and trying to keep up with her homework, wrestling team and tutoring left Fern wishing for magic.

None had appeared. And Gran's was all but gone, for some reason she wouldn't explain.

Most of the items had been crossed off, leaving *Cut oak saplings. Clear pond ditch. Put in pond plants. Grow ratna plants.*

Wheek! Hilda climbed on Fern's foot, nose sniffing at the refrigerator.

"You want a treat?" Of course she did, especially after Gran had said to feed—no, Hilda hadn't understood that. This was the guinea pig's usual behavior when demanding food. Fern got a carrot from the fridge. Hilda took it and trotted to her basket.

Fern swept her long hair into a band and covered it with an orange bandanna. If she wanted to knock one project off the list, she ought to cut those oak saplings before the rains that came most every evening.

Taking the rest of her pop, she pushed through the screen

door, grabbed a pair of loppers from the tool bin under the covered porch and walked into the surrounding fields. In the peak of summer bloom, countless pastel-colored wildflowers speckled the tall grasses. Flax and daisy, pennyroyal and teasel, yarrow and bedstraw. Acres of meadowland filled the shallow between two wooded mountains on the twenty-mile-long island in the Irish Sea, closer to Scotland than Northern Ireland, though Gran said they considered themselves Irish.

A bank of rain clouds was already moving up the valley. Hiking hard in long strides, Fern crossed several hillocks, dodged butterflies trying to land on swaying flowers and breathed. She filled her lungs and her soul with the perfumed mix of blooming flowers, pine and the faint hint of the sea. She exhaled, then inhaled even deeper. Just the scent of the island calmed her as much as digging in the dirt and handling plants.

She topped a rise and allowed herself a moment of *this*: the grasses brushing her hands, birds singing, the damp of the coming rain. This was totally not the dirty farm her mother claimed she'd grown up on. Their family land was wild and natural, and Fern loved it with a fierceness that sometimes hurt.

She scanned the rolling hills to find the right gully.

A birdcall echoed with the whistling wind, a different one than the usual sounds. *Weoo-weoo-weoo*, came the call again, and she spotted the reddish, hawklike bird. A red kite, rare here, hunted their property, even though it usually preferred the woods growing up the side of Mount Lookout.

She groaned. "If you're nabbing our partridge, Gran'll be sorry she left." Some of the two dozen birds they'd reared must be hunkered down nearby. She swung the loppers at the kite. "Hey. You. Get out of here."

The kite flapped higher, and she kept an eye on it while walking the low swale between several hills. The bird circled twice more before finally folding its wings and diving among the oaks. *Good.* No doubt her grandmother would run down the "Forest neighbors" and lecture them about controlling their kite. Gran called these neighbors by the land they managed, though likely they had other, *real* names. *Says the girl named Fern Fields.*

Taking another swig of pop, Fern skirted the hillside they'd seeded weeks ago with knapweed and came to the gully between two hills, the one filled with skinny oaks marked for removal.

The saplings weren't here. Their painted stake stood on the top of one hill, surrounded by their flowers. Had Gran cut them without telling her? Fern poked through the grass. Stubs of cut wood stuck up, the cuts fairly fresh. But where was the brush? It'd take a lot of effort for one little old lady to carry off dozens of saplings, and like Mom, Gran let Fern, with her broad, muscular shoulders, handle the heavy labor.

On the other side of the gully, a patch of grass lay flat. Fern picked up a lone branch, and its leaves whipped in the wind. Oak. Maybe Gran's promised help *had* shown up.

A faint trail of bent grass stalks led over the hill toward the trees. Fern followed it. She shouldn't be so fixated on this. The saplings were cut, gone, whatever. Yet, with their inspection this weekend, the last thing they needed was a complaint that Meadows' brush had been dumped on the neighboring property.

Raindrops began hitting her back. Great. She'd take a look

inside the woods, mostly because she was curious what she'd see now that Gran had lifted this property barrier. But if she didn't find the brush soon, she'd give up.

Halfway down the hill, she missed a step—or the ground fell off—and her feet slid out from under her.

Crying out, she landed on her rear, dropped the pop and loppers and skidded on her back until her flailing hands caught bunches of wet grass. For a moment, the ground tilted, and starbursts of light blinded her. *I didn't hit my head, did I?* Then the ground leveled.

Ohmigod. Lying facing the sky, she drew a breath. It had happened so fast. Her shirt and pants were soaked, chilling her skin, but she wasn't hurt. The rain had let up and somewhere close the kite's *weoo* resonated over and over like an echo. Above her...was that hollyhocks? And over there, sunflowers?

Fern rose on her elbows. They were. These weren't plants they grew in the Meadows. Non-native flowers sprang from carefully tended soil plots, like the one she lay in. Crushed plants surrounded her, delicate whorled leaves catching on her forearms.

"A kind of bedstraw?" Okaaay, a secret non-native garden had been behind Gran's barrier. But was it on the neighbor's property or theirs? She rolled over and pushed onto her knees. Where were her loppers? She straightened—

Lights blinked in pinpricks over the grass. *Oh crap, Gran warned me—*

The ground tilted. Fern crouched for balance. Everything shifted like her computer's whirling photo screen saver, the images framed in a murky light revolving like her rabbit hole's magic. The garden of hollyhocks and sunflowers cartwheeled away, and several scenes flipped by until two settled before her like an open card. On one side, rain pummeled the Meadows' hills in a thrumming she could feel through her heels, and on the other, a fresh leafy scent wafted from the interior of a deep woodland.

Those had to be other portals since the swirling magic was similar. The Meadows portal was farther away... *But that's where I want to be.*

She took a step. The ground shuddered, and a new image appeared inches from her feet. A yawning hole. A wave crashed up over the edge of it, wetting her shoes and salting her lips.

Fern recoiled, just as the strip of ground she was standing on fell away.

With a yelp, she leaped for the closer woods. The world canted, wind and rain thrashed her. Instead of clearing the dull, twisting light, she tripped across it and crashed to the ground. She grabbed a tree trunk and held on.

3

The Rip

Weoo-weoo-weoo. The kite's call sounded over and over while the ground slowly rocked to a halt. The bird, the lack of rain, the rough bark digging into her fingertips...even with her eyes closed, Fern knew she'd made it to the woods. Soaking wet.

So that part had been real.

Please let me still be on the isle.

She released one arm to swipe aside the strands of hair stuck to her cheeks and looked around. The murky magic was gone. The tree she clung to grew just inside the woods' edge, and—thank goodness—the Meadows lay back the way she'd come. The ground didn't look quite right, like puzzle pieces not aligned.

At least it wasn't dropping into the sea.

Fern tried pulling her feet free of some scrubby bush. Her right ankle was stuck and numb. It didn't hurt, but it was super cold, colder than the rest of her. She couldn't see what held her trapped, and a buzz of panic rose, intensifying her struggle. She put more muscle into it and felt something pulling on it, on *her*.

Fingers tingling, she clutched the tree, using it and all her strength to haul her leg free. It was like dragging a bag of mulch. Her numb foot was coated in murky slime. Strings of it stretched back to the bushes, pulling at her like a bungee cord.

She scrunched to the tree, got a better hold on it and looped one arm under her leg to hold it against the slime's pull. *I just need to lose the shoe.* No way was she touching the slime, so she dug her heel in and wiggled. The laces were tight. A stick to loosen them would help. She reached—

"He wouldn't be wrong, so she has to be here," said a male voice. "Keep looking for a gap."

Fern sat up fast. The slime yanked on her leg, nearly jerking her free from the tree. She held on. No one was in sight, but she heard erratic breathing between the kite's *weoo* calls. Leaves rustled from two different directions as something moved closer... A guy crawled into view. Her breath caught, and he pivoted, close enough to touch if her arm hadn't been around the tree. His rusty-red hair fell in curling waves around his face. Freckles dusted his cheeks.

"Hey, lass, there you be. Raven?" he called over his shoulder. "This way."

For a moment, she just stared, because—geez—one second she'd been alone, and the next here was this big guy. He looked in his late teens, with green eyes and an accent. Scottish, or Irish, she didn't know, but he wore some kind of traditional clothes, a pullover shirt with laces at the neck. He crouched on his heels, taking her in from wet hair to her slimed foot.

"Ach, that's nae good," he said.

She shivered. *Think. His arrival isn't so different from how I got here, so he's likely a neighbor of Gran's and not dangerous.* But her pounding heart didn't believe that. Despite what she'd promised Mom, she struggled to get both feet beneath her in case she needed to defend herself. The muck pulled back, harder this time. Her grasp on the tree slipped to fingertips caught on the bark.

The guy lunged and wrapped a large hand around her free wrist. "Do'na let the rip take you in!" He grabbed her other arm, too, and hauled against the slime.

An unstoppable tremble coursed through Fern, which had nothing to do with her wet clothes. She seized his wrists, found a root or something to brace her left foot against and shoved with everything she had toward this freckled stranger who had become her lifeline.

"Raven!" he shouted, fingers digging into her flesh as he struggled to hold her. "Help."

Leaves crushed right beside them. Someone invisible grunted. "Watch out," groaned her rescuer, just before a knee popped into sight between two trees and a body stumbled after it.

The ground tilted toward the bushes. Gasping, Fern lost her footing and thumped onto her belly, sliding—

"Ohmigod, no!"

The rescuer heaved backward and dug in his boot heels. She jerked to a stop, muscles straining. Above them, the new guy—Raven?—swayed off-balance, his hair swinging in a long, black braid. He flailed his arms—and wings. Huge, black wings.

Impossible.

The first guy yelled, "Rip energy's got her," at the same time Raven swore and threw himself right at her.

She flinched, expecting him to fall on her, to halt her slide. But she continued to lose ground while he—*is this really happening?*—hung suspended, half over her, wings sweeping up and down, feathers whacking her, the bush, the ground, sending sticks and leaves flying everywhere.

Blood roaring in her ears, Fern ducked her head, and when she dared to look up again, her rescuer was also sporting a pair of wings, rusty-colored like his hair. *Of course, that makes sense,* said a ridiculous voice in her head.

"Ready?" Raven grunted.

For what? Fern wanted to ask, but she couldn't catch her breath. Numbness was spreading up her right leg, her body was stretched to its limit, and her rescuers had wings. Asking stupid questions was low on her list of needs.

Hands clamped onto her right knee—Raven, it had to be him, though Fern didn't turn—and her leg warmed. He pushed his hands down her calf, driving away the numbness. The heat reached her ankle. Her heel. Over her foot. Her toes felt like a vise grip had them, numb and heavy. Fern strained to move, once more digging her free foot into the soil and clinging desperately to Rescuer Guy.

"Come on," he muttered, his face close but gaze looking past her.

Seconds stretched to a minute, and still her foot didn't come loose. Then, finally, she felt the pressure of Raven's hands squeezing.

Her foot popped free.

Rescuer Guy fell backward, and Fern landed with an *oof.* The ground rocked under them and tilted again.

"Go!" shouted Raven from right beside her head. He scooped an arm under hers. Rescuer Guy did the same on her other side, and they hefted Fern to her feet.

As she hurtled into flashing lights, the woods disappeared, and then the ocean reappeared between two flares of color.

Roaring filled her ears, the wind whipped her hair, and a giant wave crashed over her shins.

The water shot up colorful droplets that coalesced into a black mist. It spread, boiling inside out, becoming a whirlwind of brown leaves with the sound of flapping wings.

4

Flight

Fern opened her mouth to scream, but she could only gasp as her rescuers lifted her among oak and birch trees.

Ohmigod, ohmigod, ohmigod. The leafy ground dropped away, her stomach with it. "Lemme go," she screamed. "It's safe now. Look!" But last year's leaves blurred to dark patches. She flinched, and her arm slipped in Rescuer Guy's grasp.

"Nae," he yelped, at the same time that Raven shouted, "She canna touch the ground!"

The three of them lurched into a sparkling fog, snapping branch tips before they emerged with Rescuer Guy's arm hooked under her armpit again, his breath panting in her ear.

On her other side, Raven clenched her to his body. "Lass. I'd love to oblige you," he said, sarcasm edging his voice. "But you'd end up in the rip, and me dad'd have me head." He looked pointedly downward.

They'd risen above the trees. The oaks' tops mounded like green mushrooms floating in mist, a glowing murky line twisting through the undulating haze. Fern swallowed, thoughts of struggling dissolving. Whatever the rip was, it didn't look safe. Neither, her gut said, was relying on strangers. How had they known she'd fallen into the rip? And where were they taking her? And how did they fly like storybook angels, keeping their legs up? Hers were dangling like wet bedsheets pulled from the washer.

Come on! Why worry over that teeny bit of magic? Freaking *flipping* portals lurked at the edge of the Meadows, and Gran had mentioned only, "Take care if you see flickering," in an offhand way. What other impossibly crazy magic was out there to bite her in the butt?

At least she was still on the Isle of Giuthas. The same mountains rose on either side of the Meadows' cloud-filled valley, the familiar rock cliffs only closer now.

Squinting against the wind, Fern peered at the first guy, who was still panting, and then Raven, who scowled back at her. He was anything *but* an angel. She had to be reasonable, to sound reasonable. "Thanks for the rescue. I appreciate it. I'm safe now. Please—"

"Hardly," snorted Raven, the word snatched by the wind.

She sucked in a quick breath. *Nice. Be nice.* "Please take me to the Meadows."

"After tending," he grunted.

What the heck did that mean? "I'll be fine at Hillux. Gr— Lark Fields' cottage," she added in case they didn't know what she called it. She'd almost revealed Lark was her grandmother.

"No," he repeated, adding to her growing fury.

"'Tis a...downpour there," gasped Rescuer Guy, but he said it kindly. Both spoke quicker than her Irish-born mother or Gran, their accents thicker, yet Fern could understand them well enough.

It *had* been raining in the Meadows. But here, the clouds were high, way above the stony top of Mount Lookout. "Then how about—" she started at the same time Rescuer

Guy said, "We could land below—"

"No," Raven spat. "Her foot."

Nothing was wrong with her foot *now*. She peeked to make sure—ugh. She snapped her gaze up. Vertigo to the max. Dirty, that was all. Not glowing, not numb. Just wait until she got both feet on the ground again.

Raven jerked his chin. Ahead, the sun shone through a break in the clouds and lit a swath of evergreens on the mountainside. "The grove is...close. She's heavier than I realized," Raven panted. "And nae dropping weight."

Thanks for that, Mr. Too Big For His Boots. Working this spring and summer, she'd lost fifteen pounds and was slimmer than nice Rescuer Guy. Still, her hands balled into fists at the hated—and all too common—put-down. "I'm not big for my height," she snapped.

Raven ignored her. "Your place yonder," he said over her head.

Apparently, *yonder* was in the evergreens they flew toward. The ridge of oak trees gave way to a wall of pines spiking far above the regular trees' height.

"Wow," Fern whispered. "They're huge."

"Watch yourself," called Rescuer Guy. With rapid wing beats, they rose at a stomach-rolling angle, pulling her with them. Wide, prickly treetops blocked the way, and instead of going over them, they flew *between* branches, passing what looked like full-sized trees growing on limbs of other, more massive trees. Her legs dangled precariously low, the soles of her running shoes skimming needled branches.

A clearing opened up. Across it stood a huge trunk with a hollow among a thicket of branches. They zoomed closer. Burns scorched the edges of the cavelike opening. Dammit, they were going to hit it if they didn't slow down.

Fern didn't want to look, but she couldn't *not* look, and at the last second, they soared into the tree hollow and crashed to the floor, skidding as she screamed. They rolled over and into each other, scraping to a stop in what felt like crunchy dirt.

This place smelled of fresh pine, and the floor felt warm beneath her...though moving. In sharp gasps. Fern opened her eyes. She'd landed half on Rescuer Guy, and his chest was heaving up against hers.

She scrambled up so fast her head swam. She caught herself on hands and knees, pausing as dizziness blinded her and that weird finger-tingling started up again. Fern pressed a hand to her belly, feeling through her wet T-shirt for her pouch. Thank goodness—her teardrop hadn't fallen. Then she slid her hand along her cargo pants. Her phone was still there, if it wasn't dead from the soaking. The island had service, but Gran didn't have a phone, and if Fern had to call Mom—crap, for this, she would.

The lightheadedness passed, though the floor was still swaying—the big tree was moving.

Raven was already getting to his feet, his black wings folded.

Fern shoved up into a crouch and tried to stand, but promptly had to drop to a squat again. "What the—" *Be nice.* She ground a fist into her forehead and looked around. The hollow in this massive tree was bigger than her loft bedroom. The dim space held a cot, neatly made with blankets, and a chest. Several shelves lined the walls, with pegs mounted below, one holding a green woolen cape similar to the brightly colored ones Fern borrowed from Gran when the weather turned cold.

Her gaze found Raven again. "Why did you bring me *here*?"

He blew out an exasperated breath. "To fetch you help. In a place that's dry. Out there, it'll be raining in a quarter hour."

The other guy rolled to his side, eyes closed as he gasped. "Sometimes," he hissed, "you have the most harebrained ideas."

"I do not!" snapped Raven.

"I don't buy it either." Queasiness rolled through Fern—the weird portals, the muck, flying, the swaying tree. "Rain or not, I have work to do. Why couldn't we go to Hillux?"

Someplace she knew.

"Believe me, I'm askin' myself the same thing." Once again scowling at her, Raven stretched one pale-skinned arm and fluttered his wings. "My body will never be the same from hauling a full-weight lass, and a huge one at that."

Muscle memory from three years on the wrestling team kicked in. Fern sprang, wrapped her arms around his thighs and took him down. He landed on top of her, his wings flapping wildly and muscles tightening over a broad build that matched hers. She rarely had an opponent match her physique—since girls were allowed to wrestle only girls—and if she let go, he'd probably best her. Pushing with her legs, she rolled him to the side. The wings vanished before his back hit the floor.

Throwing a leg over him, she pinned one arm behind his back and the other with her hand in a well-practiced move, thanks to Mom insisting she take a sport. Wrestling was better than self-defense classes, as long as these guys weren't skilled in the same techniques.

Which reminded her to check on Rescuer Guy. He was still down, but likely not for long. Adrenaline spurred her to snarl, "Take me back."

"Try and make me," Raven spat, his hazel eyes growing oranger. He jostled under her, but couldn't budge.

Obviously, she couldn't *make* him take her back. A stand-off.

A chill ran over her. *It's not wrestling. It's not...it doesn't feel right.* She didn't feel right. Damn, she had reacted badly, in anger.

"Beri?" Raven grunted. "Some help here?"

Rescuer—Beri had propped himself on one elbow, still panting. Their gazes met, and he stared at her with an exhausted frown.

"Don't you dare move, or"—ohmigod, she had nothing to threaten these boys with, not if they had magic to fly—"you'll regret it." Scowling, she wedged her knee up to hold down Raven's arm and pointed her free hand at Beri in case she had to fend him off.

Beri lifted his hands aloft, like she had a gun. "Jus' calm down, lass. We mean you no harm."

"Are you for real?" she asked. "You rescued me, but instead of taking me someplace reasonable *on the ground*, you haul me into a tree, prevent me from doing my work and have the gall to tell me to calm down?" Her voice grew hard. "I want to know what's going on, and quick."

Beneath her, Raven grunted and rocked, freeing his hand. She slammed hers down, pinning his arm to the floor—or rather, to the bits of decomposed wood. He winced.

"He'd be more likely to answer if you weren't hurting

him." Beri sat up, eyeing her like a wild dog, and brushed his freckled hands slowly down his old-fashioned shirt. Also wearing brown canvas trousers, these boys looked dressed for work as colonial reenactors. "Sorry 'bout all this, lass." He glared at the other boy. "Raven. The rip zone was nae a place to argue, you ken, but Merlin'll have our hides for—"

"He won't. That foot needs tending."

"You couldna—" Squinting, Beri craned to peer at her right side.

"No." Raven pressed his lips together.

Fern nearly looked at her foot, too, but caught herself. It might be a trick. After all, Merlin? Like, the wizard? Seriously? These winged boys were trying to distract her. And her arms wobbled—no, tingled. She had good leverage on Raven, but all this was too freaking much.

"Willow," Beri said as if he'd solved the mysteries of the universe. "She can handle this. Then we won't involve—"

"Fine." Raven rolled his eyes, looking reasonable for the first time as his muscles relaxed under her hands. He pointed with his chin. "Use the cot yonder until we fetch you help."

She glanced around—a second's turn—but Raven rammed sideways. Fern threw her weight the same way. He fought harder than before, his brows knit above narrowed eyes that almost glowed. She tried to keep her face blank, her wrestling competition look. His arm was rising, and she shook with the effort of holding it down. Then, his fist balled, and flashed into *flames*?

Before she could move, Beri lunged, swatted Raven's hand and suffocated the orange-brown flames. "Come now, that's nae fair. She's nae like us. It's nae right to deal with her in that manner." He dropped to sit cross-legged a few feet away.

Fern didn't dare look up again. Beri didn't know her at all, but he'd helped her. She didn't even want to think about what Raven might have done with his magical fire. They were in a *tree*, dammit.

Raven snorted and heaved this way and that. They rocked, but he couldn't dislodge her.

Yet.

After a minute, Raven sagged to the floor, just as her arms would take it no longer.

She wanted to rub her aching muscles. Or her queasy stomach—did this tree ever stop moving? But she had to out-last Raven. "Give up and take me to Hillux. I'm on a wrestling team at Boulder High, so you're not going to win."

"Ressing? Boulder High?"

"Wrestling. You know a, er, fighting team. At school."

Raven wrinkled his brow. "Ye *learn* to fight in your school?" His gaze flicked to her hand on his wrist. "Of course you do."

"Extracurricular." At his blank look, she shook her head. "Never mind." She'd never met any kids on the island, just Gran and the councilman. The island was rural, but... "Surely you two attend high school?" Duh. Wings and all, probably not. Damn, she should just let him up. Confused looks passed between them, and she stole a longer glance at Beri. Would he continue to defend her?

"Nae, we are unfamiliar with this," Beri said.

"What do you do on this island? Tutoring? How do you learn things?"

His face lit up. "Apprenticing."

Beneath her, Raven said, "Merlin has taught me what I

need to know."

Fern froze. *Merlin* as a teacher. Wings. Fire at his fingertips. Beri had said, *She's not like us.* Maybe they weren't like Gran either.

"I apprentice to Sir Humus, Lady Lark and several other elders," Beri said.

What? Fern's gaze shot to him. Why did Gran need an apprentice? And why hadn't Fern ever seen him? Raw emotion bit at her. *Isn't my help enough?*

Oh, no. Were these the helpers Gran had promised?

"Aaaargh." Raven heaved and threw her off. She scrambled after him, but he gained his feet first and unfurled his wings at the same time. He darted to the opening, and she followed, arms reaching to grab—

He leaped. And when his wings spread, she remembered *they were in a freaking tree.*

She skidded to a stop. Beri seized her arm and hauled her back, while Raven kept going. He cast a wide-eyed look over his shoulder as his wings carried him up. Catching sight of her below him, his features relaxed and settled into smug lines. The tree swayed, and she crouched to keep her balance.

"It's affected her thinking," called Raven. "Stay while I fetch Willow." And he flew off.

"Dammit." Fern straightened...and gasped. A muddy glow was creeping out from inside her right shoe.

5

The Truth

The muck is still on me. Fern swallowed, shivers racking her cold body and the finger-tingling spreading up her arms. She wrapped them around her middle and backed from the edge, unable to look away from the sick glow circling the cuff of her footie sock. What was it?

Something bad, because Raven had insisted on getting help.

A wave of nausea hit her. Was it from the muck? Her imagination? Or that she'd nearly fallen from the tree hollow, *stories* high in the air. She lowered to the floor, where the wood crumbles cushioned her ungraceful landing. Was the slime poisonous? Her foot had been numb before. It wasn't now. The muck didn't *seem* to be moving, but her sock logo was half covered. With a trembling hand, she reached for the laces.

"Do'na touch it!" Beri said.

Her head whipped up, and she planted her hands to shove to her feet.

Spreading his wings, he eyed her, knees bent, arms loose—good form. "I am nae keen on fighting."

Neither was she. "No," she mumbled numbly, sinking down again. "You surprised me...I forgot you were here." She wiped damp hair from her brow and took a breath she hoped wasn't too obvious. *They really do want to help me.* Their methods seemed odd because they were completely different from her. *I have to trust him.* "Wh-what is it?" She gestured to the muck on her sock. "And what happened back"— she pointed randomly—"there, with the changing portals?" She crossed her arms over her wet clothes and pretended she wasn't dying to lie down.

Beneath his reddish curls, Beri's eyes narrowed. "You haven't heard?" He shrugged one shoulder to a freckled cheek. "Energy issues. The isle is short of energy, and that has thrown the land out of balance. Our shielding won't hold in place, and the stretching has caused energy rips along many habitat boundaries. Rips dump you outside, as nearly happened."

"Into the sea?"

He nodded. "Or to other habitats. The elders monitor the spots, spelling the land to hold and, where they canna, warding the worst ones so no one walks across them. That rip is nae as bad as others and 'tis rather isolated, so folks avoid it. Lady Lark didna show you where it was?"

She shook her head.

"Do'na worry, the watchers have a way of telling if anyone gets sucked outside, plus make sure no one enters the enclave. After this weekend's inspections, they should have more energy to begin repairs."

He'd answered—unlike some grandmothers she knew— but knowing she'd almost gotten sucked outside hiked up her nerves again. "And this muck?"

"Energy," Beri said again.

Magic, she translated. It couldn't be anything else.

"The mixing by the shifting shield makes it rather sticky.

Raven tried, but controlling sticky rip energy takes someone experienced, which is why we need Willow. Rest yourself until she arrives." He crossed the room, took a green blanket from the cot and offered it to her.

"Thanks." She swung it around her shoulders and huddled into its warmth and nice spicy scent. "This is your place?"

"Aye. It's not much, but it's all mine."

"The entire tree?" It made sense he'd live here, since he had wings—which also explained why Gran hadn't introduced her to the neighbors.

He leaned one shoulder against the wall, hands in his pockets, huge feathered limbs taller than he was folded behind him. "This Scots pine grove is mine to manage as a trial until I come of age at my eighteenth year and can be manager of my own habitat."

"What exactly is there to manage in a tree like this?" *Rot?* She couldn't ask that.

"Salamanders. Lichen."

Beri's earnest eyes held hers, their green so much prettier than her dark brown ones. He was not only chattier, but less grumpy than Raven. But her mind was crap after nearly dying. Nothing had gone right this entire day, and now she just wanted to do her work and go to bed.

"Perhaps nae the most interesting of my trial areas."

It was, and she wanted to ask more, but what came out was, "Why are you apprenticing to Lady Lark?"

"Usually, the lessons pass down within the family, but they made an exception for me because my parents have died."

Oh. That bit of honesty did her in. Having no father stank, and it was worse living with the possibility of being one accident away from being orphaned. Fern hugged the blanket around her, and the silence grew between them to the point of being uncomfortable. For something to do, she picked up a handful of the wood chunks and dropped them piece by piece. A glance at the ceiling confirmed the reddish chunks came from the tree's rotting heartwood, probably left from carving out this room.

"What happened to your parents?" Her question came out in a whisper.

He shrugged one shoulder again, apparently a habit. "One of the rare times me mum left our settlement, she died in what's called a car accident. Then when Da became ill, he brought me here, where he grew up. He died of cancer when I was in my eighth year."

"You've no family left at all, then?" she asked gently.

"Exactly. With no family, I must make my own way."

As terrible as she'd always imagined it might be, Beri spoke evenly about his losses and had his act together. If he was apprenticing to be a habitat manager, then Gran was a great teacher, even if they hadn't figured out that last plant on their list, the ratna. "Are you trying to get a job here?"

"Correct. 'Tis an excellent place to live, wild and beautiful. Most of my mentors have no direct descendants. It's been proposed I take one of their habitats to contribute to the support of the Isle of Giuthas." He pronounced it as Gran did, the G as a K, *Kyuh-hash*, but in his deep voice, the accent sounded rich.

Gran had told her the name was Gaelic for the Isle of Pines and that the isle was magically hidden to protect one of the few remaining ancient groves in the British Isles. "These are the Scots pine trees the isle is named for," she said to herself and yawned.

Beri shoved from the wall and came to sit near her, the wings shrinking at his back. "Aye, and the Windborne prize them." He smiled broadly.

"Who?"

"Not just those from the isle, you ken? But settlements on both sides of the Irish Sea."

Her tired mind struggled with the details. "Who are the Windborne?"

His smile faded. "Do you not call the People of the Wind by that name...or...Fern, she told you our name, didn't she?"

She who? Gran? Wait a sec— "How do you know my name?"

"Lady Lark, of course. She told you we were coming today to—"

"To help."

"Right. But you weren't there, so we got started on what we could do."

That explained the cut saplings and why these winged guys were around when she fell.

Beri's eyes were wide in a way that put Fern on guard. "She needed family help," he muttered, not exactly to her, yet he didn't hide the words either. "She told us her cousin's granddaughter—you—only partially knew why, but I would have thought... No, obviously, she didn't explain."

Cousin? Is that what Gran had told them? *Darn it all, Gran!* Fern leaned forward and tugged his forearm. "What don't I know?"

He drew in a breath. "The Isle of Giuthas is a Windborne enclave, hidden from the outside world to protect the trees, but"—he frowned at her—"also us. Winged wizards, the People of the Wind."

She stared. Would Gran have told her these things if she hadn't been late today? "Are you telling me everyone on the island has wings?"

"Aye."

Does that mean Gran does, too? Her head seriously buzzing, Fern released his arm and slumped back on her rear. *Hidden. Winged. People. An island of them.*

Gran had covered this up—secrets, barriers, whatever—until now. The inspection. The trial. *Her* trial. And this weekend Gran was taking her to the Council Gathering. She'd talked excitedly about introducing Fern to her friends. *Of course, Gran had to tell me all her secrets. I just wish she wasn't making me keep some of them.*

Fern swallowed. "Lady Lark is Windborne?"

"Aye." Beri looked at her in a funny way.

Gran had never answered how they were to travel there. *Duh.* Isolation wasn't a problem—these people *flew*. And—Fern touched the pouch—she traveled halfway around the world in an equally strange way.

Gran should have known that learning about wings wouldn't freak her out. *So if Gran is Windborne, is Mom, too? Am I?*

6

Time is Running Out

Being winged wizards explained why Fern's mom and Gran hid their relatives. But...*I have no wings.* Fern pushed unsteadily to her feet and, with Beri shadowing her, walked to the front of the tree room. Bracing herself against the wall, she pulled her phone from her pocket, automatically unlocked the screen and dialed Mom's number after the international codes she'd looked up ages ago. The call would be expensive, and it was the middle of the night in Colorado, but after she told Mom where she really was, Fern would finally get answers.

Beep, beep, beep.

The call failed.

Biting back a whimper, she put the phone away and leaned on the wall, too tired to move. She shouldn't be this tired. Besides packing Mom's SUV, she'd hardly done anything physical today. She turned back toward Beri. "How bad is it that this rip energy has stuck to me?"

"Not stuck—" His gaze flicked away. "Bad. Wherever it touches the land or soil, it'll open another rip." He gestured to the floor. "It won't affect heartwood."

Then, if she'd gone to Hillux... "Oh—uh, thank you for not exposing the Meadows."

"You should thank Raven. He suggested we come here,

and in the rush to get you out of there, I merely agreed. He knew we'd have no way to land there that didn't involve you touching the ground." Beri gestured outside to two birds winging their way across a sky now filled with thick clouds.

Except they weren't birds. Raven was returning with a woman. The graceful beats of their wings would have been something to watch if they hadn't mimicked the swaying of the tree.

"Hopefully, Willow can dispel it," Beri said, "and you'll be right again."

"Hopefully?"

"It, uh, *should* be the same process even if you are nae Windborne."

Fern twisted her fingers together. This wasn't good magic, and likely *dispel it* wasn't the same as *wash it off*. The closer they got, the younger the woman appeared. "How old is Willow?"

"Seventeenth year, but Willow is learning the ways of the Forest from her mother, who is the Witch of the Forest. She has caught on fast to her mother's lessons. Here, step back so they may land."

Beri tugged her to the side while Raven and Willow glided into the tree and alighted on the wood-covered floor. Both drew in their wings, or whatever they did with them, and Raven unclipped a harness to remove a leather bag hanging over his chest. He scowled at her.

Fern's fingers curled around the blanket edges. *Face blank, competition look.* "I'm sorry," she said, not quite loud enough. "Thank you for helping me," she managed louder.

He snorted.

Her body stiffened, and Fern made herself turn to the

other girl.

Willow was the kind of girl her name suggested: fair, slender and placid-looking. Her yellow blouse and long tan skirt made Fern's wet gardening clothes look even grubbier. Willow seemed not to notice. She smiled sweetly and held out a hand. Fern grasped its warmth with her cold one, and Willow flinched.

"Flights, you're freezing." She rounded on Raven. "You didn't dry her off?"

"She should have done that for herself," he muttered.

"Not everyone has the same skills. Which I believe you are well aware of." She shot him an exasperated look—clearly, this girl didn't have nasty in her attitude stock—and waved a hand over Fern. A yellow light shimmered from her fingers.

Fern startled back, but the light coursed over her, blowing her hair and clothes like a warm Chinook wind coming off the mountains at the end of winter. The heat settled onto her clothing and sank through, toasting her as if she'd been in a dryer. It felt wonderful. If only she could crawl onto that cot and close her eyes. "Thank you," she whispered.

Willow flashed her a smile, then her gaze dropped to Fern's foot. "Sit." She pointed to the cot, very businesslike, and said to Raven, "The washbasin."

Fern obeyed, but her steps faltered. Beri took her elbow and guided her, then helped her lift her leg so Raven could slide a deep enamel basin beneath. They set her foot into it, shoe and all. Beri perched on the end of the cot, and Raven stepped back into a crouch while Willow knelt beside her.

"You will need to stay still." She flicked her amber eyes up to meet Fern's gaze.

That sounded easy enough. Fern nodded.

Willow held her cupped hands to either side of Fern's foot, and the yellow glow flowed from her fingers again. The bubble of light swarmed around her foot, heating it, and Willow made a rubbing motion that didn't seem to do anything.

Just when Fern was about to ask, "Is that it?" the warmth shifted to pins and needles, like when her foot fell asleep, and...were pieces of her skin peeling off? She wanted to stomp, but instead pinched her eyes shut to hold herself still.

"It's started," Willow murmured.

Fern blinked her eyes open. Tiny sprouts of the mucky magic had emerged—at her ankle, along the sock's edge, between the laces, near her heel, her arch. They twined like dirty roots through the yellow bubble. A new one sprang from her big toe, and she swore her toe was being pulled off.

Her leg jerked, and just as fast, Beri pressed a large hand onto her knee.

"Hold steady," Willow said kindly.

"How?" she whined, not meaning to. When was the last time she had to sit by, unable to do anything to help herself? Like, never. She leaned forward, reaching down. "Has it done something to me?"

Raven sprang forward, hand out, but Beri pulled her upright again by her shoulder.

"Besides sneak along your channels? No," huffed Raven.

Willow shot a glare at Raven. "It hasn't, bless the Golden Orb, though I have no idea why."

Why had she done that? She'd been told not to touch it. Inside the bubble, the roots of muck were unfurling into different-colored strands that swirled like ribbons through the bubble.

Watching them, Raven frowned. "Still, the lass is—"

"Oh, for Pete's sake, I'm right here. And my name is Fern."

"So be it." Raven tucked his hands into his armpits. "Fern, you're contaminated."

What? Her gaze darted from Raven's frown, to Willow's returning glare, to Beri waving his hand in a placating way at Raven.

"The rip energy is *inside* you," Raven plowed on. "And spreading it to the Meadows is the last thing Lady Lark needs on top of the inspection."

Oh, gross. This was...disgusting. Fern pressed her fingers to her temples to try to stop the runaway thoughts. Beri had conveniently skipped telling her that, and she should be mad, but she wasn't. This was too sickening. Or she was too tired. She was...something more was wrong.

"Dispelling is nae something to hurry." Beri shrugged one shoulder. "She has to get it all, you ken?"

"You weren't in it long," Willow said. "I'll know after I remove the first layer."

A fresh wave of nausea coursed through Fern. "And if you can't?"

"Well, no one has died of it...yet," Raven said, and Willow and Beri both glared at him.

"I could die?" Fern gasped. It was getting hard to catch her breath.

Beri frowned at Raven. "Willow won't let that happen, will you?"

"I'll do my best. Now be brave and hold very still, Fern. This will hurt more the longer I go." Willow bent her blond head to the bubble.

That was true. Barbs jabbed inside her foot. Fern gritted her teeth and crossed her arms. Weird images and random thoughts slipped in and out of her mind, until the only thing keeping her steady was Beri's hand on her knee. *This is helping me. She is helping me.*

"Is this magic, um, energy why I'm"—Fern didn't want to say *feeling drugged*—"tired?"

"I promise you are having a typical reaction," Willow said. "Pain, exhaustion as it robs your energy, some"—she glanced away—"difficulty thinking clearly."

"How about something to eat?" Beri asked, and Raven spilled out a handful of cloth-wrapped bundles from the messenger bag he'd had when he and Willow arrived.

Fern sighed out loud, which she didn't ever do, not even when telling regular people she was vegetarian. What was wrong with her? She bit her lower lip, fending off horrible thoughts of them unwrapping a carcass. But Beri only offered her a grainy, moist-looking muffin, just the kind Mom would approve of—not a chicken leg or freaky-colored yogurt—but Fern shook her head. A clawing at her ankle cut to an end, and Willow poked a wad of shiny red magic out of her bubble. Raven tilted a small bowl up to catch it, and the red clump slid to the bottom. Fern swallowed and looked away.

She tried to ignore the next stabs and pulls by closing her eyes and thinking of what she'd do early tomorrow, the ditch, then...the pond plants. Or she'd plant first...

"Late," Raven muttered, "but it'll finish before we do."

Fern startled, and her eyes flashed open. Outside, it was raining. Which meant she couldn't do something. But what? Was it important? She hurt, hurt, hurt, in a way that dulled thought and had her holding her stomach. The steady rain hissed down, and the tree swayed.

"This will take a bit," Willow said. "Why don't you lie back?"

Fern blinked at the assortment of enamel bowls sitting around her foot basin, red magic in one, orange in another, blue in a third. Willow was working brown ribbons on two fingers while Raven held another empty bowl. She was dying to do as Willow suggested, lie down and escape into sleep— but wasn't she supposed to be doing something?

Oh, yeah. "How much longer? I have work to do."

"Don't we all," Raven deadpanned, and she caught the start of an eye roll, but Willow had also looked his direction, and Fern was sure something passed between them, for Raven frowned harder at Fern. "Welcome to what the rest of the wizards on the Isle of Giuthas deal with every day— faulty energy."

"Nae every day," Beri countered.

"Every week, then."

Fern waited, but Beri didn't contradict that. *So, Gran, did you think if you presented the icky side of Giuthas life, I'd leave?*

"Can't this be done...like tonight?" No one answered. "You—" She pointed at Beri. "You're her apprentice. You understand. I can't be contaminated. I have to help Gr—Lady Lark," she corrected. Oh crap, what would happen to Gran if she couldn't finish? "I have to finish...projects by..." *When was it?*

Shifting, the three shot side-glances at each other. What was wrong? Pressing her fingers to her head again, Fern struggled to collect her thoughts.

The only sound was the rain pattering on the branches. Had Beri no sense of loyalty? Maybe he'd just better move on and let her be the only one to work with Gran. Unless Beri was behind this? He'd admitted he was in the market for a habitat. Was he trying to sabotage Lady Lark's plans to get the Meadows for himself?

She'd opened her mouth to ask just that when Beri spoke. "Aw, lass, we understand this all too well. Trust me, we'll do all we can to help Lady Lark and you, her cousin. You'll be safe with us, safer than in your world."

"Lie down," Willow said softly. "This will go smoother if you aren't tense and worried."

"Then..." They were saying the right things, but she wasn't. She couldn't keep her plans straight, how long until her deadline, or even what Gran said to keep secret. Helplessly, she looked around the darkening tree hollow, the most unexpected place she could have imagined being today. She drew a breath. "Then all I can do is sit here and wait?"

"At last you understand." Raven grinned in a clearly fake way. "I'm starting not to dislike you so much."

Fern flopped back onto the cot so she wouldn't have to look at him.

7

Beri

Pressure below her gut woke Fern—she had to pee. But she snuggled under the covers, swinging in her hammock. The blanket smelled different. Spicy. And...like pine?

It wasn't her hammock.

She bolted up, heart racing. She'd nearly fallen into a rip and had contaminated her foot. Winged guys had taken her... Damp air brushed her cheek. Eerie light filled the tree hollow through a light fog entwining the tops of Scots pines outside.

Fern threw back the blanket and stared at her feet. Her *foot*. No glow. She peeled off her right shoe and her footie. To her nonmagical view, her foot looked fine. She flexed her toes, turned her foot this way and that. No numbness, no glow, no stabbing or peeling.

Willow had fixed it, and Fern had slept the whole night.

And I feel good. Her confused thoughts had vanished. *Geez, please don't let me have said some of those things aloud.* She peered around the dim tree hollow. She was alone.

She swung her legs over the side of the cot, memories of the night before becoming clearer. They'd told her some new things, but others went unspoken, in the way of tight friends. A way that said it'd be harder to get to know them than kids at high school or their mountain town.

Mom! She slapped a hand to her belly. Her pouch was still

there, teardrop safely inside. So was her phone. And the lump that was her Snickers bar. Stomach growling, she peeled open the wrapper and ate-licked the entire mess, ignoring the food set out on the messenger bag. She found the bandanna that had fallen from her hair onto the bed, stuffed it into one cargo pocket and rose. She tested her foot. Walking was no problem, so she searched for a bathroom.

Which didn't appear to exist in the hollowed-out tree Beri called home. Figured. Would they return for her after dawn, which wasn't too far off?

But I have to pee!

She trod to the opening. Even in the dim light, it didn't look the same as before, and as Fern got closer, she saw why. Something spread across it like green plastic wrap. She poked it. The thin membrane lit at her touch, and when nothing else happened, she pushed. The entire thing lit up, but it held.

"Beri?" she called, whispering first, then louder. "Beri? Raven? Willow?"

"Wha'? Lass—Fern? Are you all right?" The deep voice came from above her.

Beri—it had to be him. She tried to pinpoint where he was. "No, I need help."

"A second and I'll be there."

The branches above shook, their needle clusters too thick to see through. A pair of feet kicked through an opening, followed by long legs, then Beri's torso and head. His arms extended up—he was hanging from a branch. He started swinging, and when his feet hit the barricade, it vanished.

"Stand back," he called.

Ah! Fern plastered herself against the wall, and he landed lightly, knees bent, the heartwood cushioning him.

He straightened and turned to her, eyes half closed. "What's the matter?"

"Is my foot okay—that rip magic gone?"

He yawned. "Aye. Willow did a right job of it."

"Good." The word whooshed out with relief. "I need to get down. I need to go—"

"It'll be easier with the others."

"To the *bathroom*!"

"Oh, right." He scrunched up his face. "I do'na suppose you can perch over the edge?"

"I beg your pardon?" Boys! Beri might have wings, but like every other boy she'd ever met, he didn't get it. "No. Take me to the ground." Then, realizing she was at his mercy, she added, "Er, please."

"Hmm. I'll try to." He roved his eyes from her head to her toes as if measuring her for a uniform.

"What? Can't you just fly me down?"

"It's nae so simple. After yesterday, we learned you canna adjust your body like we can."

She pressed her hands to her head. That's why she'd taken Raven down, because of insults about her weight—which was totally reasonable for anyone six feet tall. "I can't take a magical science lesson in losing weight right now."

"Nae lose it," he muttered. "Make the air give you buoyancy. But, no matter. If I hold on to the branches, I should be able to support us both. C'mere."

Beri led the way to the edge, unfurling his wings. The huge feathered limbs came through slits in his woven shirt, projecting from his shoulder blades. He flapped them a few times.

Their breeze fluttered strands of hair into her face. Ugh,

most of her ponytail had come loose. She must look a sight. A shower would be nice. Anything resembling a bathroom would be nice at this point.

"I need my hands free," he said. "Think you can hold on to me for the ride down?"

"Piggyback?"

Beri laughed. "That truly was the first time you'd seen anyone fly, wasn't it?" He took her hands and placed her arms around his neck. "With wings, the only side to carry someone is the front, and the only place to hold is around my neck. You ken?"

Fern swallowed. At least it was dark enough he couldn't see what a mess she was. Both outside and inside. He was willing to fly her out of here, so she had to do it before she chickened out. "Let's do this," she said with her best bravado, and wrapped her arms tighter.

"Tuck your legs around my waist," he murmured, his breath warm on her neck.

Before she could even process how close that put them, his wings arched and Beri stepped off the edge. They swung and dropped, jerking with each branch he grabbed and picking up speed. Beri uttered what had to be a curse. Fern cringed. The time between jerks came faster and faster. Rough bark loomed close. Needles swiped her arms. They were practically falling.

Fern clung to Beri, her face pressed into his neck. Damn, this was going to—

"*Owww.*"

They landed with a jolt. Her legs crumpled, and Beri came down with her, his chest crushing her into a cushion of pine needles and ferns.

"Ah, sorry." He scrambled off her and stood, brushing his shirt and hair. "Seemed to me we'd stay on our feet, but we overbalanced before I magicked away my wings... Say, are you all right?"

Heart pounding, she lay staring up at the now wingless boy.

"Fern? You can breathe, can you nae?"

Breathe? After a free fall like that he asked if she could breathe? "No."

"Aye, you can." He grasped her hand and pulled her up to a sitting position. "Nothing broke, I suppose. We didna take a hard fall, the forest floor being like it is in the grove. You'll be right in a moment."

Gulping air helped dispel the lingering rush.

Beri patted her shoulder. "Do'na tell me I scared you?"

"Ohmigod," she muttered.

"Pardon?"

Fern wrapped her arms around her knees and bent her head while her heart settled. "Yeah, that was scary."

"To you, Lark's brave cousin coming from afar to this isle?"

She lifted her head. "Believe me, getting here is a piece of cake compared to that. Look, I gotta go. Make yourself scarce." She stood and cast around for a likely spot. Ferns and other herbaceous plants carpeted the ground but nothing bushy. Behind a tree trunk would have to do.

"Er, you do'na want to do this proper?"

Proper? Before she could figure out that one, he grabbed her hand. "C'mere. 'Tis nae far."

He pulled her through the ancient trees. They wove around ferns and the huge trunks, the ground springing with every trotting step. Centuries of shed needles lay here. Ahead, the trees were smaller and clustered closer, normal oaks and birches, as along the edge of the Meadows.

A few yards into these woods, Beri pushed his way between bushes, and a tiny cabin stood before them. He released her hand and waved to it. "Now I'll make myself scarce." Then he strode off through the trees.

She squeezed the old-fashioned door latch and peeked inside. A compact kitchen lay to one side, a sitting area with a neat desk to the other, and over the rear half was a loft bed with tumbled quilts. A door ajar in the corner revealed a *real* bathroom, and she hurried to it. The toilet flushed with water, and the sink water heated by the same type of solar power Gran had. Fern grabbed up a bar of tan soap dotted with flecks—ah, that's where Beri got the spicy smell. She took another sniff, but the herbs smelled better on his skin.

Using the mirror, Fern finger-brushed her hair and tied the bandanna over the mess. Watching her reflection, she stroked the spot on her forehead that Mom had traced her last design on. Did it tickle now? Fern studied her fingers, rubbing across them with her thumb. No, not her forehead. Her hand tingled.

She looked away. It'd quit if she stopped thinking about it. Time enough for worrying when she was face-to-face with Mom again, asking questions and having to explain why she even knew what questions to ask. Thanks to these guys, she hadn't spread the bad magic elsewhere. She could hike back to Gran's and do the pond-planting and ditch-digging.

Fern's shoulders sagged. She and Gran's progress stood at the same spot as yesterday: a day's worth of work to do. And now, only hours to do it. The inspection would begin at noon today.

She opened the cabin door and emerged. The sun had risen, casting layers of color on the sky beyond the trees, pale below and a dark orange above. Beri was nowhere in sight, but birds scattered before her, leaving blackish berries bobbing on the branches. Blueberries? These forest plants were new to her. She hadn't known the Meadows' ones either at first, but gardening with Gran meant Fern now recognized every plant in their habitat.

Huh-uarrp!

Her breath caught. A wild animal? Fern whirled, but couldn't see beyond the closest bushes. A *crunch, crunch, crunch* turned into a rapid trampling. She raced to an oak with low branches, jumped and pulled herself up. Below, the noise got closer.

On the other side of her tree, Beri marched into the clearing, carrying an armload of branches and followed by a small, darting figure. A fawn. With its eyes on Beri—or, more correctly, on the brush he held—the young roe deer leaped again and again, nipping at the leaves. More deer trailed them, bigger ones.

Fern released her breath and slumped against the rough bark. Deer, that was all. Seven of the native orangey-red-furred deer surrounded Beri. He dumped the branches, which made a huge pile, more than she could have carried. The fawn rushed in to eat, even though the leaves looked wilted. Beri stepped back, and she had her first good look of the day at her tall, freckled rescuer. His angular jaw sported a night's sparse growth of beard...and a streak of mud. Another brown smear crossed the front of his shirt, and the rump of his trousers seemed to be his preferred towel. What had he been doing?

He pulled up the hem of his shirt and wiped his brow. She glimpsed his belly—flat, muscular—and disappointment hit her as it got covered again.

Aw, come on now. Fern thudded her forehead. Okay, he was in shape, and she enjoyed the look of muscles on a boy, but not the macho attitude that seemed to go with them.

Then Beri waved encouragingly to the other deer, and something inside Fern melted. Here in his element, Beri radiated a gentleness that touched her. As if to confirm it, a deer stopped and nuzzled his forearm.

Grinning, he scratched the animal behind an ear. "Now do'na think this is going to become a regular thing."

He talked to the wild animal like it was a pet. Fern grinned to herself, half embarrassed at witnessing such an intimate moment.

The deer gazed into his eyes before joining the others to eat, but another raised its head and stepped up to Beri. He petted this deer as well. "And now I'm your best friend, because of this sweet sapling treat?"

Fern's gaze shot to the branches—yes, saplings. *Oak* saplings. Beri had said he'd done some work, that she'd been late. The council rules permitted only Gran's family members to work on their meadow plants. Removal of invasive plants could be done by anyone. Tree saplings in their field could be considered invasive to a meadow, right?

Fern huffed an exasperated sigh, and Beri looked up. Every deer did, too.

Looking curious, he walked over, and the deer went back to eating.

She climbed down. Geez, she hated to admit she'd run

from deer—and tiny ones, at that. "I heard something coming and didn't know it was deer," she whispered. "Are they part of your trial to manage this habitat?"

"They don't need me to supply their food, as they have plenty on the land"—he gestured to the woods—"but I'd rather carry the cuttings here than across to the brush pickup, and this lot has kept away from some other plantings we do'na want disturbed, so it's a fair trade."

Like Gran, Beri believed he'd made a bargain with a deer herd, like *really* believed it. "Is talking to animals some sort of special power that comes with having wings?"

"Nae. Most People of the Wind canna hear them. Only a few Windborne settlements keep to the old ways and nurture the energy to communicate with wildlife. That's why me da wanted me to return to the isle."

Fern massaged her temples. Gran had wanted the same for her, and now that Gran had revealed her secrets, Fern had so many more questions.

"Are you feeling all right, Fern?" he asked, his voice laced with concern.

She lowered her hands. "Uh, yeah. Do you think I could pet one?"

"Aye. Here, stay beside me."

Her stomach did a little flip being close enough to see each freckle spattered across his high cheekbones and narrow nose. When he cupped his hand—solidly freckled—over hers and guided it to stroke a deer's back, her insides fluttered worse than before a wrestling match.

Oh geez, what is going on with me? I can't be attracted to a guy I've only just met.

A gentle glance from the deer saved her. She ran her hand

over it again. Coarser hairs lay above finer reddish ones, making a thick, protective coat. The fur wasn't soft like a cat's, but it was much prettier than the brown mule deer around her house.

Another edged closer, and at Beri's nod, she reached out by herself and patted its neck, then worked up to the spot between its ears. The deer butted its head into her hand.

"He likes it," she whispered.

"*She* likes it." Beri's eyes lit up, their green brighter. "But 'tis time to go. The others want to get down to some serious eating, and you're a stranger."

True, three of the closer animals had stopped to watch her.

She glanced at Beri as they fell into step. Why, why, why had she gotten off to a bad start by attacking his friend? Would Beri hold it against her? Her gaze locked on his crown of red curls—she had to look up. That rarely happened. "How tall are you?"

"One hundred and ninety-five."

Huh? Did he measure his height in centimeters?

He grinned. "Taller than Raven's father Merlin, and he's the tallest adult in the settlement."

Merlin again. She had to ask. "Is he the wizard Merlin from King Arthur's time?"

Beri burst out laughing. "Merlin is only in his fortieth year, and he was my da's boyhood friend, so I know he was young nae so long ago. So, Merlin is nae that Merlin."

Great, he probably thought she was an idiot. "Well, Merlin was imprisoned by the Lady of the Lake, so he could have been." She wasn't up for a confrontation with him. Raven, yeah, but not Beri. If he ditched her now, she wouldn't blame him. It'd be a faster trip back if he led the way, but she hated to ask.

Out of sight of the deer, she stopped to get her bearings. With the cabin and the ancient pines to her right, the Meadows lay straight ahead, beyond a ridge of rock. Anyway, she hoped that's where it was.

Beri halted, head tilted in question.

Steeling herself for his refusal, Fern stepped toward the Meadows. "I've got to get back so I can finish by noon."

He gestured in the direction of the ancient trees. "No need to hurry. Willow and Raven will be along shortly, and we can walk together."

There were many things she could say, reasons and deadlines and what was left to do. But she just said, "You may not think it's urgent, but I do," and began walking.

Beri caught up and when she side-glanced at him, he was watching her. She looked away quickly.

"I'll show you the easiest way," he said. "If you like?"

"Yes, thank you."

He wasn't holding it against her.

8

Back to Work

They hiked, not over the ridge as Fern had expected, but along a mountain stream. It was more bushwhacking than hiking. No trails.

"That's a nice little cabin," she said to make polite conversation. "Yours, too?"

Beri nodded.

"Why couldn't I have stayed there while Willow removed the rip magic?"

He tripped. "Spells, no," he choked out in a deep voice. "You can use the loo, but I'd be in a heap of trouble if a lass stayed there."

At his obvious horror, Fern couldn't stop a particular grin from stretching over her face, the one Mom called her obstinate look. "I thought you lived on your own. Are you telling me you'd get grounded for having a girl in your house?"

He looked skyward and shook his head. "Where you live must be verra lenient. No tracing or quashing?"

She didn't know those terms, but they sounded like grounding. Lots of kids were regularly threatened with it. Her mom hadn't grounded her in years. "How would they know? There's no one out here."

He rolled his eyes. "Magic."

Magic. He said it matter-of-factly, but Fern stopped to see if he was serious. He was. She'd never considered magic would be used for something so mundane. But yeah, spying on your kids, who wouldn't? She giggled at the idea, making Beri frown. She rapped his arm with her knuckles. "It can't be that bad if they catch you. Sure you're not scamming me?"

"I don't ken this scamming, but a spell lies on us until the eighteenth year. You don't have the air of it about you, but if the elders discover I've broken the rules, there'd be trouble."

"The air of *it*? Of magic?" She skirted a couple of trees on the opposite side than Beri, mind racing. *Why did Gran say not to tell?* She didn't want to lie either. When they came together again, she gave a faint shrug. It worked for him.

"You must have some," he persisted in an exasperated voice. "Where you're from, can Windborne hide it?"

True, the glass teardrop was *some* magic. It held a spell she'd accidently worked the first time, and Gran had taught her how to use it again. These kids must not know how she got here—another of Gran's secrets. But she was curious: Was his magic like Willow's yellow glow? "Can I see your magic?"

His face flushed red, but Beri shrugged and smiled sheepishly. "Sure." He stopped and brought up his hand, his *empty* hand, and a ball of rich emerald-green magic appeared. Not plain like Willow's or murky like the rip's. It swirled in clouds of mist, slightly thicker here, slightly lighter in color there, dancing in a mesmerizing play within his long fingers. It was different from her teardrop, but the glow was every bit as appealing.

Above it, Beri watched her.

Her stomach gave another flip. She averted her gaze to the ball of magic. It reminded her of glassworking, when she held the glass over the flame and was bending and shaping it, and the colors moved in ways you didn't expect, or could exactly control. "It's, er, very lively, your...ma—energy. Nice."

"Thanks." He pressed on the top of the glow with his other hand and melted it into his skin. Well, obviously, *he* could control it. Beri cocked his head.

"Mine isn't—" Oops, now she'd blown it. "I can't do that." She turned and walked toward Gran's. There wasn't anything else she could think to say.

By scrambling over boulders, they got around the end of the ridge and headed into the isle's central valley. Beyond the treetops, the two mountains rose in a familiar view. The Meadows wasn't far, the forest bordering it easy walking.

They came to the edge of the woods, and the familiar, sweet scent of the flowers flooded Fern with relief. The morning sun spilled over the treetops to light the grassy land, busy with insects and birds catching their morning meals. Hillux wasn't far now. She turned to say goodbye.

"If 'tis nae too forward of me," Beri said in a rush, "would I be able to see your magic sometime?" He looked down at her—which so few boys could—waiting for her answer.

So he had heard her slip. "Uh, sure." Not that she'd ever be able to do that, but if she could, she certainly wouldn't mind showing Beri. "Thanks for walking me back."

"I—uh, also have a favor to ask of you, Fern."

He was nice and all, but she had projects to do, and now less time than before to complete them. "Could it be later? Tomorrow?" she asked. "I have to work on the pond, our last project."

His lips turned up slightly at the corners, but it wasn't a

mean smile. She knew those. Beri looked like he had a secret.

"You're hiding something from me." She drew herself up to full height and crossed her arms. Usually, this tall stance and her broad shoulders made kids back down. He chuckled and copied her. When Beri drew himself up, *she* had to look up. This was so unfair. She'd always wanted to meet a taller boy, and now that she had everything seemed so complicated.

Beri took her by the elbow and marched her through the grasses.

"Hey. Where are we going?" she demanded.

"To this pond. Anything to settle you."

"I don't need settling." She tried to say it without snapping at him. "The pond is dry. We dug out the muck and fixed the dam, but I still have to clear the ditch and put in the plants..." Fern stumbled to a stop at the top of the hill where she'd been about to point out the repaired basin that lay below.

Instead of dirt, a patch of *water* shimmered in the sunlight, fed by a silvery stream diverted from the nearby creek.

"Your pond seems to be there," Beri said with a sigh.

"H-how?"

Now Beri's muddy clothing made sense—but did this break the rules? Thinking furiously, she took off down the hill. Sir Humus' rules stipulated that only she and Gran could do the planting. Eighty percent of new plants in any season had to be cultivated by them. The council forbade altering the landscape without prior approval. So what exactly had Beri—and Raven?—done?

Set out around the pond, *just as she and Gran planned*, were the wetland plants she'd grown and the few Gran had acquired elsewhere on the island. Drawing closer, she saw they weren't planted—*oh, thank goodness.* Under each pot, the holes were dug, compost mixed in and extra heaped to the side of—she did a quick count—sixteen of them. An additional eight were lined up along the water's edge to be planted in the pond.

Fern stopped between them, her heartbeats racing. The plants *hadn't* been planted. The ditch was in the same place, but cleared. She rubbed a fist to her forehead. *As long as they didn't dig any new connections to the creek in the woods, we should be fine.* She eyed Beri coming down the hill more slowly. He must know these rules, too, since he was apprenticed to Gran and Sir Humus. Preparing to plant didn't count, did it?

Should she ask? Thank him? Or be blissfully ignorant?

Oh...*to hell with it.*

She strode to three bur marigolds, dropped to her knees and grabbed one. Beri came up behind her, but she didn't look at him as she loosened the root ball, set the plant in the hole and scooped the loose soil around it with her bare hands. When she finished the three, he plopped down a bucket of water beside her. She watered them and began planting marsh St. John's worts.

Her pulse returned to normal. Beri had clearly been worried about how she'd react to his work—and it hadn't been great. But neither had it been terrible. She felt like an idiot. He had promised he'd help Gran, and had. *After they spent hours helping me.*

Fern pressed her knuckles into the dirt. Gran had said it was time for her to take charge, but really Gran had consulted with her from the start. This winter, Fern had taken over the seedling growing and planting. She knew in her gut when to water, when to fertilize, when to pinch back. Growing plants had always been easy for her, starting with the bean-seed experiment in first grade that produced a crop lasting all summer long. Honestly, she'd been in charge for months. To have other people doing stuff in the Meadows without her knowing was...weird. She felt a kind of ownership—well, not a kind of. *Absolute* ownership. But having everything laid out for her helped *so much*.

She got to her feet and wiped her hands on her pants while she walked to where Beri sat on a nearby rise, staring off down the valley. He turned as she stopped beside him.

"Thank you," she said, loud enough this time. "For rescuing me, fixing my foot and for spending your night mucking out a ditch and setting this up for me. I've been a complete jerk thinking that you guys were getting in my way, when really it's been the other way around." She put out her hand.

With a grin, Beri shook it. "Maybe not a *complete* jerk. You have the real makings of holding your own among us. I hope you still want to."

"I do." She sat, keeping her gaze on a butterfly checking out several of the new marigolds' yellow flowers. This was moving toward friendlier ground. Wait. She wanted to be on friendlier ground with Beri? Sheesh, she did. But what would he think when he discovered she was just a human? "You had a favor to ask me?"

"Aye. 'Twould be most helpful if you do'na mention we spent the evening removing rip energy from you."

"Why not? Raven said everyone has to deal with faulty energy. Weekly, you said."

"We were supposed to be doing something else. I canna

say more about it, but you could return our help if you said naught of tripping into the rip and everything that came after."

"I can keep a secret," she said. Very well. "Those rips are some nasty magic. Can they be fixed?"

"We hope to start once these inspections are completed. The energy the new Windborne would bring has everyone excited and on edge. Six months of applications and then a year of trials, you ken, since our elders put out the call to test if others can work Giuthas' land."

A year and a half ago. When the portal had first opened for her. It couldn't be coincidence.

"Like me." She blew out a breath. "Why are they making it so hard? If the isle is in a crisis, you'd think they'd just open the doors."

Beri shrugged a shoulder to his freckled cheek. "Merlin says the old ways are hard to break. He and others argue to relax certain rules, while some fight to keep them. 'We've always done it this way' is their mantra. 'Tis improving. The process was shortened for the new wizards."

Gran had implied they didn't have to be wizards—*'Tis clear you've inherited the touch, and tha' is enough*—just people working on the land.

"I'm missing a connection here, that maybe Lady Lark forgot to tell me," she said, not even trying to cover her ignorance. "We—or I, since it's my trial—needed to replant to pass inspection to keep the Meadows. My wildflowers have flourished, but where does the energy come from?"

Beri side-glanced at her, and Fern knew Gran's omission was huge. "Maybe 'tis nae the same where you come from, but working with the plants and wildlife on *this* land *creates* magic. Plants supply the most, being directly in the soil. The energy can be drawn off for personal use, but a portion stays with the land, used by the enclave for our protection."

Yeah, huge. Fern hugged her knees and made herself ask, "Is anyone else conducting a trial in the Meadows?"

"Several of us."

"But—" *This land is Gran's!* She nearly blurted it. Anything she said now wouldn't come out right. She rose and turned away when she couldn't keep her eyes from welling up. If Beri and other *wizards* passed their trials in the Meadows, then they might be given charge of their family land, the land Fern often now considered hers. The thought was like a thorn stabbing her heart.

She liked it better when she didn't know everything about this island.

9

Awful Reality

You have to understand," Beri said, rising, "that every one of us is doing all we can to ensure that Giuthas and the pine groves thrive. The decisions will be hard, but they will work out for the best."

Fern dashed her fingertips across her eyes. Her hands tingled. And he was watching. Would nothing go right this weekend? "I get it." Gran. She had to talk to Gran. No, she had to finish their projects. It was up to her to *put things very right*, as Gran had said.

She strode to the pond and picked up a sedge plant. She planted it and the next, while Beri hauled water and collected pots. A half hour later, despite the chill in the morning air, she stripped off her shoes and socks, rolled up her cargo pants and waded into the clear, cold water. Silt swirled up and clouded her view as she dug holes for the species that had to have their roots submerged.

Afterward, she sat wiping mud from her white feet with her socks and surveying the pond. The sparse plantings were a start, and they'd fill in. But was it enough? Strangers were doing trials that would or would not be approved this weekend. Beri was doing a trial. She should ask him about it.

No, this wasn't a competition. *And he's helped me.*

She put on her socks.

"'Tis on its way to returning to a proper pond." Beri squatted beside her.

"How did you know which species went in the water and which to plant along the edge?"

"Well, there was a drawing..."

Yes, she knew that—*her* drawing, the one she'd left in Hillux. But the sketch showed only their rough locations.

"I also apprentice to the Ponds," Beri said. "Old Snap, the Ponds manager, taught me to recognize these plants when we worked on a pond restoration on the mainland. He does a bit of consulting work over there, because they have many more problems with invasion from non-native plants."

Beri knew as much as she did—more, likely, because of the other habitats. He was the first boy she'd ever met who was as interested in gardening and nature as she was. She peeked at him with new appreciation...and caught him staring back. Her throat went dry.

"Soon," he said, "we'll see if your work gains back what Lady Lark needs for her part in helping the isle."

The meaning hit her. The Meadows' list *was completed*, at least the projects they could do. One missing plant—the ratna—couldn't count for that much. Over a year of planning and work, done. She'd always imagined celebrating with Gran by clinking glasses of lemon thyme kombucha—at least, she'd hoped Gran would approve of her having a drink of her homemade alcohol.

However, finishing hadn't delivered the rush she'd imagined. Flying people and trials on their land upstaged everything else. *And I don't have magic.* Despite what Gran had told her, that's what the Meadows needed.

He pointed northward. "I'd like to show you something."

Curious, she nodded. She stashed the bucket to use again, Beri carried the pots, and they walked together, easily matching strides. Past Hillux, past Gran's onion-scented gardens where Beri dropped off the pots, past the beehives and then uphill past their burn and compost piles, toward a ridge she'd never crossed. Gran had gotten permission to postpone work in this part of Upper Meadows until next year. Maybe it was the low morning light, but the valley had a hazy cast to it and seemed to extend farther. This...wasn't the usual view.

Fern shaded her eyes, hesitating. "A barrier is gone here, too, isn't it?"

"Not quite *gone*, but now you can see the entire Meadows habitat."

Any more secrets to divulge, Gran? Hiking on, she tried to take in the change. The new land doubled their habitat...doubled her work, because these hazy hills were still spotted with invasive bracken ferns.

The haze snapped into a shimmering wall of green before her.

Fern flinched from it, stopping dead. "Whoa."

"This barrier still separates a portion of the habitat," Beri said. "Inside is my trial area."

Not *her* work—his. Great, just...great. Nice-guy Beri was her rival. She couldn't make herself look at him. Or away from the land behind the magical plastic wrap. The grass seed heads swayed in a breeze going the opposite direction from the gusts she felt. The area lacked the variety of wildflowers she'd planted, and with the bracken, she was ahead of him for providing the diversity the council required.

He crouched and slid his hand into the magic and lifted. An opening formed, like parting a stream of water. "I've been looking forward to showing it to you. With both sections done, they may be reopened to each other. Please come in." Beri waved her through, she stepped past the film, and he pushed the sides back together. Tiny hooks on each side melded to each other.

"Like Velcro," she said.

"I suppose? They are patterned after seeds that stick to your socks. Try it." He pinched a piece of the wrap. It peeled like birch bark, and he offered it to her.

The magic slipped through her fingers like nothing was there. It soaked into the ground.

Beri looked stunned. "Barrier magic is linked to us and to the land. It should be linked to you, too. Why can't you hold it?"

Fern turned from Beri's scrutiny and walked into his trial area. *Without magic, I won't be able to help Gran more than I have.* But Beri hadn't eliminated the tall bracken ferns...oh. These weren't clumps of bracken. "Willow shrubs," she murmured. "And..."

"Gorse."

Waist-high. They'd been here awhile. "How long has it been your trial area?"

"Six years."

"You started this at...eleven?" A year's work versus a six-year-old project. She felt like she was down for the count. Beri wasn't a bad guy. If he took over... She swallowed the lump in her throat.

"Aye. Not the whole area, a smaller plot, with Raven at first. A few willows and a dozen pheasant. I quickly learned I needed more cover or fewer birds. I chose to expand, and they have helped control the insects and voles so other plants flourish. Look there." He pointed to the waving grass.

Between the stalks, brown shapes moved, a large flock.

"'Tis been successful," he said. "The numbers we harvest meet the community's needs. It will be easy for you to maintain the population."

He said this like she'd be approved, not him—oh no. *Harvest*. He meant—

"I'm vegetarian."

"Vegetarian?" Beri asked. "What is this type of person?"

"I don't eat meat. I don't believe killing animals is right."

Beri peered at her intently. "Many folks on the isle believe the same. I do. Others..." He shifted and looked away. "'Tis expected for this habitat to rear the birds."

She'd known that, academically, when she and Gran had started raising their partridge. She'd hoped to persuade Gran not to allow them to be hunted. *Harvesting* was a too-nice spin for killing the birds—but it looked like he'd be the one dealing with it, not her.

One bird neared them and cocked its head, looking warily—

Kok, kok, kok, came a call, and the flock burst from the grass and flew off up the valley.

When they disappeared, Fern turned to Beri. "It looks amazing. You *are* done, right? And it adds into the magic the isle needs?" Gran would still be living on the isle, even if she didn't have the Meadows.

He laughed. "There is always more to do. But I have finished this trial."

"I think you'll do well."

"I did." He shot her a confused look. "I mean, 'tis approved. Three years ago. Did you think—nae, I've moved on.

They're inspecting my Scots pine grove this weekend. I have no inspection here."

"Then you're not trying to get approved to manage the Meadows?"

He shook his head. "I... Actually, I'm not sure what habitat I want to make my life's work. The grove trial is my fifth. I have no pressure to decide, as long as I continue to contribute, and I do. I have to trust what happens will be right."

Geez, he was so nonchalant. But he had nothing to lose. "Sounds like you need a gap year."

He looked even more confused. "I need something, or so people say. If you're ready to go, I'll let us out." He did, without any further comments on using magic. When Hillux came into view, he asked, "Will you stay at Lady Lark's cottage until I tell Raven you've agreed to keep last evening's activities secret and can return?"

She raised a brow. "Do you make any decisions without Raven?"

"Not here." Beri dismissed her question with a wave.

The favor and Raven were connected. Raven must still have a trial in the Meadows. If he'd been working as long as Beri—*crap*—she was out. Fern's wrestling training kept her face blank, her voice even. "So, Raven's trial—"

"I canna answer for him. Ask him about his work."

Great. Why did Beri pick now to stand up for himself? He'd asked that she stay at Hillux. "I promise to wait for you," she said, thinking how to word this, "before I set foot outside Hillux."

"Thanks. Unlike Raven, I trust you." His wry grin morphed into a yawn. "But don't mention that to him, you ken?"

Well, she didn't trust Raven either, yet she had to learn

what his trial was. "I won't." Beri looked tired and must want to sleep after a night of ditch-digging—and in his own bed this time. That thought led to another—would he sleep in the same bed she'd slept in last night? The tingle coursed her hands again. *Not going there.* "You can go if you like," she said. "Will you fly home?"

"Aye. Say, 'tis too bad you can't fly. Lady Lark told us."

"Uh, yeah. At least not like you do."

"You come from a verra different enclave, she said. You must find us strange."

Well, Beri was different from anyone at school, but much friendlier than some guys she'd known for years. Never once had he put down her differences, and he was quite cute, with his freckles, unruly hair and those green eyes peering down at her.

Oh geez. I'm falling for a winged wizard.

Giving a shrug, he took a step back, and his wings appeared, the feathers reflecting reddish highlights in the morning sun. He stretched them wide, gave a hop and two strong downward flaps that stirred up a breeze.

Loose hair flipped across her face. Darn it, she'd gone too long without answering, and now he was leaving. "Wait! Beri!"

Wings arcing, he hovered above her. "Aye?"

Suck it up, Fern, this might be your only chance. "I didn't realize until yesterday how very different life is here, but I don't find you strange. I've never met anyone with wings, or who could do the"—she cupped her hand as he had—"magic thing the way you did. Or was nice enough to explain all this to me."

Beri gave her a lopsided grin. "Thanks, Fern. I think

you're nice, too. And verra pretty."

Oh. My. God. He thought she was pretty? "Thanks!" she blurted before turning and running for her grandmother's house.

She ran her hands down her warm cheeks. Damn her traitorous body. That'd been as close as she'd ever come to gushing while talking to a boy. Any more and she'd have sounded like an idiot and never been able to speak to him again.

But he'd returned the compliments—and even said she was pretty. She spotted Beri's winged figure flying south over the woods and flushed again.

She walked toward the largest hill in the Meadows, the one encompassing Gran's house. Fern wasn't sure if the stone cottage had been built into the hill, or if the hill had been built around the house, but Hillux was the most enchanting house she'd seen outside of movies or fantasy stories, and she dreamed of living there someday. From beneath a sloping carpet of green that met the surrounding land, a porch and deep-set windows peeked through overhanging mosses and clumps of flowers. Even with rectangular windows and solar panels sprouting on top, Hillux looked like a hobbit house, and Fern loved how it disappeared into nature.

Now it looked like this dream would stay a dream.

Inside Hillux, she crouched to scratch Hilda behind the ears. The guinea pig's little pink nose rose from the towel-lined basket, and she *churred*.

Fern sighed. "We both miss Gran." Reviewing their plans and everything Gran had taught her didn't help. She didn't have magic, nor could she create it like these people did. She couldn't get council approval for Gran, however much she wanted to and had worked for it. Gran wouldn't intentionally set her up to fail, but her grandmother was stubborn about having things her way. Could she have overlooked that this was impossible?

Hilda quit her little purrs of pleasure and began nudging her food dish.

"All right," Fern said sadly. "I know where your priorities lie." She washed her hands. It'd take more scrubbing before her fingernails came clean, but she got Hilda lettuce greens, rinsed them and put them in her bowl.

Fern pulled out her phone to check the time. It was dead. "Must have been searching for a signal all this time," she muttered. Her battery was crap. It'd take only a few minutes to slip home, plug in the charger and get clean clothes. Giving Hilda a last petting, she headed for the bathroom.

When she took out her teardrop, a twinge of guilt ran through her, sending that annoying tingling into her fingers. She'd promised Beri that she wouldn't *set foot outside* of Hillux. She wouldn't, just like she'd promised Mom that she'd stay safe at their cabin. "The sooner I can drop Gran's secrets, the better."

Holding out the teardrop, she said, "I wish to go home." The rabbit hole opened. Its colors shone pure and bright, so different from the muddled rip energy. A wave of longing hit her. *If only I had a way to get this for the Meadows.* Beri was very knowledgeable and had been helpful—*and he thinks I'm pretty.* Maybe she could ask him for ideas.

Dipping her head, she stepped into the portal—and something moved behind her. *Gran?* Fern checked midstride, and a person stumbled against her, pitching both of them through the rabbit hole and into her bathroom in Colorado.

10

Real World Magic

Fern whirled—and found herself nose to nose with Beri. He gaped, his eyes darting wide and frantic around the moonlit bathroom. She tried to move away, but he clutched her shoulders. Tingling washed her arms.

"Where are we?" he whispered, his breath warm on her cheek.

"What are you doing here?" she demanded.

His hands tightened. "I saw you use magic—*major* magic." He didn't sound happy, and his grip—ouch.

She tensed to throw him down, but he released her at the same time, seeming surprised he'd been holding her. *He's frightened, worse than me.* Fern backed to the sink. "How could you? You flew away—hey, were you spying on me?"

"I wasn't," he said hotly. "I came back to tell—never mind. You said you wouldn't leave Lady Lark's cottage."

"I didn't leave," she hissed. "I walked into another room." Okay, that sounded lame even to her, but she didn't take it back.

He jerked his thumb toward the window. Shadowy spruce trees loomed all around, outlined against a starry sky. "It's night. And that is *not* the Meadows. You canna deny we're someplace else."

"Yeah, I suppose. Colorado." She pushed by him and

flipped on the light—and saw herself in the mirror, hair and clothes messed up from her mishap and spending the night in them. *Ohmigod, he's seeing me like this.*

"In the United States?" He clasped her upper arm again. "You canna leave before your inspection. Lady Lark asked me to keep an eye on you."

Crossing her arms, even though he still held on to one of them, she fixed him with a look she hoped would gain her the upper hand. "By following me into the bathroom?"

He glared back. "The magic showed me that you weren't using it."

"I got news for you, buddy. In my world, boys get into trouble for stalking girls and peeping at them, or coming into bathrooms after them! It's illegal. It violates privacy. It's..." She searched for a way to put it in the terms they used on the island. "It's breaking the rules."

Beri pursed his lips. "You don't have to tell me it was wrong. That, I ken. I didn't mean to. I was only"—he clenched his jaw—"trying to stop you."

The spot where his hand held her grew warm, then prickled. When Fern glanced down, he snatched it away, but not before she saw a flash of green.

What the heck?

Her gaze flicked to his face, the anger now gone. He turned to the window and leaned against its frame, staring out into the night. His forehead furrowed, and finally he raked his fingers through his hair, tousling it further.

"I believe you didn't mean to spy," she said in the calmest voice she could manage, "but why did you return?"

He blew out a breath. "I ran into an elder and confirmed the inspection schedule—yours is indeed at noon. I thought you'd like to know, but when I walked into Hillux, thinking of you, the image of you working magic came into my head. I saw you were leaving, and I didn't want you to."

Thinking of her allowed him to see her? And what had that green flash been? She couldn't say she'd also been thinking of him...nor did she want to ask more about spying. Her arms prickled fiercely. "Right. So, thanks for letting me know about the inspection." Though she'd told him she had to be done by noon, so what was up with the excuse? She took a breath. "I'm a mess to meet people. I wanted to clean up and change into nicer clothes that I have here."

He shook his head. "Don't leave when you're supposed to be on Giuthas." He wiped a hand over his face. "Where you belong."

"No, it's not like that." She held herself tightly against the increasing numbness in her arms. "The Isle of Giuthas is a dream life. It always has been. I live here. My mom's a single parent, and I'm her only child. I take care of the cooking and house stuff, so my mom can flamework glass and run her business. I'm a senior in high school, and in another year, I'll be going to CU in Boulder."

Beri's eyes bored into her. "I ken what you're saying, but for these few days, it would be best if you stayed at the Meadows. For your trial. For Lady Lark."

Crap, why hadn't Gran revealed her secrets and plans earlier?

With no islanders visiting, it'd been easy to agree to Gran's eccentric secrets, like pretending she was Gran's cousin's kid. Heather Fields deserved privacy, Gran insisted. But now a very nice and honest and good-looking guy wanted to help her, and her stomach wanted to move this out of lie territory. Perhaps if she could get him back to his world, she could return to hers. "All right," she muttered, and thrust out the glass piece still wrapped in her sweaty palm. "I wish to go to the Isle of Giuthas."

Nothing happened. She tried again, several different ways. "I wish to see Lady Lark," and "I wish to go to the Isle of Pines," and "I wish to go to Hillux." She couldn't say her usual "I wish to see Gran," and the longer it didn't work, the more her hand shook. *How will I get back for the inspection?*

Fern bit her lip and closed her fingers. "I don't know what's wrong."

"What usually happens when you use the peregrinator?"

"The what?"

"The peregrinator. That's what we call a device used for magic travel. What does your family call it?"

She couldn't look Beri in the eye. "My mom hasn't told me what she calls it."

"Where is she now?" Beri asked. "Maybe she could get it to work for us."

No way was that happening. "She's at an art show." Fern had never mentioned the glass teardrop to Mom, and Mom thought Fern's pouch held a carved-stone Zuni fetish, a turquoise bear. Lots of Western artists carried the good-luck or healing talismans, thank goodness, because Fern made sure the teardrop, more precious than anything she owned, never left her side.

"I've never needed help before," she told Beri. "I just say I want to go and it glows, opens the rabbit hole and takes me."

Beri burst out laughing. "Rabbit hole? But of course, you're a Meadows. You *would* call it a rabbit hole."

She rolled her eyes at his totally missing the *Alice in*

Wonderland reference and waited for his chuckles to die.

"Fern, you don't really want to go, so 'tis nae working. That's the problem."

Wait. I control the teardrop?

She pivoted and left the bathroom. Pausing in the hall while her heart pounded in her ears and her fingertips tingled worse than ever, she tried to look normal. It shouldn't be this hard. Everything in their cabin was just as she'd left it. Her trip through the bathroom yesterday should have been like the hundreds of others she'd made. Only, she'd had a crazy adventure with winged people, one of whom decided to follow her home into her nice, normal life.

Aargh. The finger-tingling was driving her nuts. She clenched them, and it stopped. Great. Now, to get away from this bathroom and Beri, and chill enough to think.

But the creak of floorboards signaled he'd followed her.

Think. "I guess I don't want to go back. Not right now, at least."

"I give in, Fern." Beri shrugged one shoulder. "I have no choice, as I don't have my own device. What do you wish to do here before you are willing to return?"

This was too simple—she could do what she wanted and use a magical device as an excuse? Fine. "Take a shower—in private, mind you. No thinking of me," she said with a pointed glare. "And eat."

"Well, go ahead."

She should be thankful the easygoing boy had followed her, rather than the grumpy one. "Thanks," she said and started up the stairs where their bedrooms and a full bath with a shower were.

But he followed. Three steps up, she turned and put her

palms to his chest. It was firm, muscular and far too close. Fern hastily dropped her hands.

"Just me, buddy. If you think you're going to get in a heap of trouble for having a girl in your house, you have no idea the trouble I'd be in if Mom caught you upstairs. I get the 'wait to be involved with boys' lecture about once a month. My mom has only me, and she's overprotective."

He backed down the stairs, and his eyes darted around in a comical copy of the roe deer he'd tended. "Then what should I do?"

"Uh, watch TV?" He looked at her blankly. Oh, yeah, Gran had few modern conveniences. Beri probably didn't have them either. "Hey, TV is great. Come see this."

When he hesitated, she waved him along their short hall, turning on lights. In the cabin's front room, she skirted Mom's desk covered in business files and had to rummage around the couch and chair to find the remote.

"Sit here." She pointed to an easy chair in front of the bookcase, then pressed the power button. The small screen on a side table flared to life.

Beri's eyes widened. "Flights," he whispered. "What is this magic?"

"Special." She had to bite her lip to keep from grinning. "I give you control of it with this device." She demonstrated the "magic" of how to change channels and gave him the remote. "Stay here until I come back." She ran upstairs, plugged in her phone and locked the bathroom door.

Mom better not come home early—Fern wasn't supposed to have boys in the house while she was away. And *this* introduction would betray Fern's secret trips before she could delicately ask for the blessing Gran wanted her to get.

Twenty minutes later, wearing nice jeans and a hand-dyed purple top and having left a message with her mom to check in, Fern found Beri standing across the room from the TV, arms crossed. The remote lay on the back of the couch, pointed at the screen.

"Didn't you like it?"

He startled, then relaxed. "Ah, you're back." Using his thumb and a finger, he gingerly handed her the remote, then backed away. "I am returning your magic. I'm afraid it's beyond my control."

Huh? "What did you watch?"

"'Twas odd. One picture showed a place where people played jokes, another loud machines moving quickly, and then whole rooms of people watching others saying things best kept in their own houses. I'm nae sure those people will be safe. Do you think we should do something for them?"

She laughed. "It's pretend. Those people are all acting, er, putting on a performance." The last one might have been a talk show. "Well, most of them are. Don't worry, though." She clicked off the TV. "Are you hungry?"

"Aye, I have nae eaten yet today. Do you keep your stores here?"

"Aye, er, yes," she said, shaking her head. "In the kitchen." She led him to the back of the house and flung open the refrigerator. Her colas were in the back, and now she was dying for one. "Here." She handed Beri a can. "I like to keep my food simple, even though Mom hates it." She popped the top on hers and slung back a long drink.

Beri copied her.

Seconds later, his eyes bugged. Frantically, he looked around, yanked open the back door and bolted outside.

Dammit, I've given him something poisonous to them. Fern ran after him and pounded his back as Beri doubled over spitting, coughing and gasping for air.

"What's wrong? Are you allergic? Do I need to get a doctor? A—" She cast about for the words Gran would use. "Are you ill? Do you need a healer?"

"Nae," he choked out. "Water."

"Oh, right." She dashed inside and sloshed water into a glass and ran out again.

He gulped a mouthful, swished it about and spit it to the side. Then he downed the rest. "What," he finally said, "was that foul liquid?"

"Pop." Was that the problem? He'd never had one?

"You like this pop, I ken."

"Yeah. I have one every morning." And every afternoon.

"How do you take to its acrid flavor? And the"—he fluttered his fingers on each side of his face—"the fizz up your nose?"

She stifled a laugh. "Oops. It's not supposed to go up your nose. Sorry. I bet you were surprised and inhaled it. Maybe if you drink it slower next..." He raised a brow at her suggestion. "We have other food." Inside, she surveyed the refrigerator's contents with Beri looking over her shoulder.

"Hey, how about some orange juice? It's the fresh-squeezed kind, high in fiber, good for you." She turned with the jug, and he narrowed his eyes. "My mom always says that," she explained while pouring him juice.

This time, Beri sipped. "Much better."

"How about some cereal?" She grabbed bowls and set a few boxes on the counter. Mom complained Fern's cereal was like eating dessert for breakfast, so Fern bought them with her own money.

Under Beri's watchful eye, Fern poured a bowl of fruit loops, said, "Help yourself," and went to get the milk.

When she returned with it and two spoons, he had one loop of every color lined up on the counter and was inspecting a pinkish one pinched between his thumb and forefinger. "'Tis a grain, right? What makes it this color?"

"Red dye No. 40," she mumbled.

"Dye, like you color cloth? From berries?"

I'm sooo not impressing him right now. Hold it—she wanted to impress him? She slapped her forehead. He was the first guy she'd ever served a meal, and yeah, impressing him mattered.

"Something wrong, Fern?"

"No, no, not at all. But you know what?" She pulled the cereal across the bar and set everything aside. "I think we have time for a decent breakfast, as my mom always says." She turned the oven dial to three-fifty and retrieved a bag from the freezer. "How many pancakes do you think you can eat?"

Mom's homemade buckwheat pancakes and pure maple syrup should satisfy a guy with too-wholesome eating habits. Beri requested four, and Fern arranged them on a baking sheet with three for herself.

"What does your mother do?" Beri asked.

"She makes glass figurines by a method called flameworking."

"I always wondered what it was about art that humans find interesting. Windborne don't get much into crafts that do'na have a use on the isle, you ken."

Yeah, she'd figured out from both Gran's and Mom's

comments that art had little value there. Although Mom's family had expected Mom to settle into their farming business, by twenty-two she'd left to raise her daughter on her own. Whether this was because of a family fight or to pursue art, Fern didn't know. Money was always tight, but they had each other and worked hard running the growing business.

"And your father?" Beri asked. "What does he do?"

Darn, everyone she met asked that. You'd think by now she'd be used to answering it. "My father isn't part of our lives," she said, her standard answer.

"So where does he live?"

"I don't know."

"You don't?" Beri shook his head in disbelief. "My parents have died, and yet I know what they did, where we came from. Doesn't your father's absence bother you?"

She stared at him across the bar, and his gaze held hers. He was the first person, teen or adult, to ever ask. To *care* to ask.

She took a breath. "Yes. It bothers me a lot. I wish I knew my dad. Or even something about him. But my mom won't talk about him."

"And Lady Lark? Have you asked her?"

Had she said *Gran* by mistake? No, she was sure she hadn't. Had Beri assumed *Lady Lark* would know about her father because of the cousin lie? Fern watched him closely for a reaction. "She says it's my mother's story to tell."

"I wonder why."

He didn't press more, and Fern relaxed her guard and half-smiled. "I used to wonder, too."

The oven beeped, signaling it was hot enough, so she put in the pancakes. Gran had glossed over lots by saying, *Humor your old gran*, but Fern would have her answers after she passed the inspection—she just had to hope she knew enough to bluff her way through any parts Gran had skipped. Being surrounded by nature, seeing their plans come alive, knowing Gran...this land and life had become a part of her. How could she give it up? Stubbornness welled up inside her.

She wouldn't.

Casting about for a distraction to get off this topic, she caught sight of a glass star she'd made, dangling at the kitchen window. "I'll show you Mom's art while we wait for the pancakes."

He rose immediately. "Making art gets you trade credit here?"

He must mean money. "Yeah. Mom's good. She apprenticed or something—I never got the story straight—to a glassworker who went to fairs and sold her stuff, too. So she's been at it more than twenty years and has built a fair business."

Mom had a personal display in their sunroom just off the kitchen, making it a quicker visit than the studio. Fern opened the door and turned on the lights. These weren't for sale, nor, Mom told friends, would she copy them, but Beri wouldn't be here long enough to ask about that.

She ushered him past the ficus trees, ferns and her herb collection surrounding their cozy sitting area. "My mom flameworks glass, but doesn't create the usual dragons or little netted baskets. She takes her inspiration from nature, like chipmunks peering from beneath fern fronds or a wren perched on a twig. Her favorite subject is—"

"Spells upon us!"

Beri's words weren't loud, but forceful, like a curse. What

was wrong? In two strides, he reached the chest-high display table Mom had bartered for from another artisan. On its walnut top, she'd arranged her most precious glasswork, fit together to make a scene that people usually squealed over with delight.

What was freaking him out? Fern shifted her gaze from Beri's odd stance of leaning over the table with his hands tucked behind him, to the glasswork.

Every piece, from the large gnarled oak with a falcon perched in its branches, to the shimmering green pond, to the shrubs laden with berries, to the little hidden animals, was perfectly and accurately crafted. The best by far were the hummocks of wildflowers flowing between the other pieces, tying together the entire display.

Flowers—Mom's specialty. The delicate petals of color always seemed to glow with life. Fern expected them to sway in the breeze, especially the sage-green mound of lavender-flowered heather Beri seemed to be peering at. Mom had made her namesake piece out of a type of glass that had a kind of inner light.

He turned to her. "'Tis magic."

"I know. It's beautiful."

"Nae. *It is magic.*"

Magic...like *his* magic? "My mom made it out of glass."

"Your mother's name is...?"

To heck with Gran's secrets, she had to tell him. This felt too important. "Heather. Heather Fields."

"Aye, Lady Heather," he said with a nod. "The Witch of the Meadows. And the light inside this"—he pointed to the glass flowers—"is the magic missing from the Isle of Giuthas for years."

11

Magic or Not

"Bbeing any other wizard?" Fern sat at the bar in her
kitchen, enveloped in a state of disbelief, her hands numb to
the point of cold.

"*Something* of your family should have been explained to
you." Beri fixed her with a grim expression, pausing with a
piece of pancake on his fork. "The Windborne's creation of
magic with the land forms a bond. 'Tis stronger among family
lines with repeated bonding to the same habitat. Typically,
one person holds the bond, the Witch—or Wizard or Warlock, if the person prefers another title—of a habitat, the
formal Windborne name for the habitat manager."

But Mom had taken the Meadows family magic and left.

Beri washed the dishes while answering her questions. He
didn't know why Fern's mother had left, because no one
would talk about it. What he did know, he'd put together
from comments while working with various elders. The
Meadows had been so healthy from Lady Heather's magical
influence that her bond with the land hadn't died until a few
years after she left. Then, the Meadows declined and the little problems increased, until one day the isle's shielding
wouldn't hold and the rips formed.

Fern stared at her hands. "I never thought to ask *why* the

shield had lost energy," she said in a small voice.

He slid onto the barstool next to her. "I was washing up in Hillux's bathroom when several elders arrived to confront Lady Lark about chunks of Giuthas falling into ether rifts. An elder spat it out before I could leave through the back door."

Fern shook herself to attention. "Wait a sec. Chunks *of land* falling off? You never mentioned that."

"Sorry, I was nae clear. If rip energy pools, it creates a hole, a rift. The best the elders can do now is rig a bypass so no more land falls in. The spots require constant attention."

"I saw one. A piece of ground fell into a rift."

Beri started to shake his head.

"Into an ocean portal. Like a calving glacier, it just collapsed."

"You didn't say that before." He pressed the heels of his hands over his eyes.

"I didn't know. I mean, it was all new and bizarre to me." A bad feeling came over her. "Where did you say the land goes?"

A moment passed before Beri looked at her, his brows low, gaze intense. "The ether, some call it. Others say the void. The space between. When you use your peregrinator, 'tis the space you travel. It does nae matter so much *where*, as that the isle is losing land that can't be replaced and...is breaking apart."

"Damn," she whispered.

"Aye."

Of course, the solution to preventing the loss of more of the island was to bring in more wizards with more magic to bond to the land. She looked at her hands again, like she could will them to glow. Fat chance.

Mom had magic. But Mom would never return to work their family land, as Fern had told Gran countless times. Gran must have believed her, because she'd set up the trial for Fern. *But I can't use magic.* Which was why Gran said not to tell anyone that. Darn it, if Giuthas was missing magic and Mom was a witch who could stop an entire magical island from dropping into the ether, those things *should have come up before now.*

"Fern?" At Beri's quiet call, she looked up. "If you have nothing left you wish to do, I should like to return. Also, it must be an hour until noon back home."

Her gaze flicked to the stove clock. Forty-five minutes.

She rose and led the way to the bathroom, taking out her teardrop. With Beri at her back, she aimed the teardrop toward the wood-paneled wall. *Please work.* "I wish to go to the Isle of Giuthas." The glass warmed as it always had, and the bright green changed to the other colors—including the sage color that matched the magic in the glass heather mound.

Mom's magic.

The various colors whooshed into their circular rabbit hole, and Fern stepped through it with Beri. Once in Gran's bathroom, he opened the door and left, but she turned to watch the portal shrink and disappear, the green glow in the teardrop dim.

Hilda's welcoming *wheeks* echoed down Gran's hall, and Beri returned, holding the quieted guinea pig. "Fern? Are you coming? Hilda says no one has been by—what's wrong?"

He cradled Hilda just like she did. And right now, she wanted someone to hold her and stop her world from crumbling. "Why don't *I* have magic? And wings? Why can't I talk to animals? Why is this"—she held out the teardrop—"the only thing I can do?"

"That is a question," he mumbled to the floor. Hilda chirped a few sounds, and he glanced from her to Fern. "Not every Windborne is gifted with wild animals. Your gift is with plants, and it appears to be strong. But..." He sighed. "To inherit a place managing a habitat, you must be able to magically bond to it. Otherwise, the isle falls apart. So if what you say is true—"

"Ohmigod." She pressed her fingers to her temples. "Forget I said that. I wasn't supposed to tell anyone I don't have magic. Or about my mom. Not until after my trial. More of Lady Lark's secrets."

"Flights." Beri rolled his head back and stared at the ceiling. "Fine, I trust Lady Lark. Forgotten." He shifted the guinea pig into the crook of one elbow so he could pat Fern's shoulder. "I'll find Raven, and we'll check how badly the Meadows' rip energy is pooling before the elders arrive for your inspection." He smiled kindly before heading for the front door.

She followed, her stomach churning. Ugh, Raven. The guy who didn't listen. Told her what to do. Insulted her weight. "I suppose it's too dangerous for you to check by yourself, but I wish you wouldn't ask Raven. He doesn't like me. I can tell."

"You're nae wrong," Beri said. "Smooth over the rough patches. Let him get to know you, so he can tell you what's bothering him."

"Beri." She exhaled his name sharply enough that he stopped. "That makes no sense whatsoever. It's like he's judged me before we even met and decided I wasn't good enough for the Meadows."

At her words, Hilda squealed. Fern took her from Beri.

"It's okay, sweet piggy." She ran her fingers through Hilda's long fur, but the guinea pig's shrill cries continued. "Lady Lark will be back soon," Fern cooed.

Hilda switched to unhappy teeth-chattering. Beri stroked the back of a finger over the animal's forehead, settling her. "'Tis nae your gran she's worried about. Your negative talk about Raven upsets her. Try meeting him again. Things will work out to be right, if you trust them to."

She liked Beri, but he was too nice. Too willing to let others take advantage. Fern rubbed her nose. Yet, things at the Meadows *had* worked out for her. Quite well, in fact. Still... "Why Raven? If the Meadows is losing land, it's serious. *Lady Lark* needs to know."

"Fern!" Beri sounded as frustrated as she was. "Lady Lark is in a delicate position with regard to the council. Raven has worked this land, too, and his ties are important to helping you and your gran."

Suddenly, his words registered. *Your gran.* "But Lady Lark is..." Oh hell. She'd given it away revealing Mom's name, because Beri was too damned nice.

"I might have still thought you were a cousin if I had nae heard Lady Heather's name before." His mouth curled into a wry grin as he took Hilda and lifted her level with Fern's face. "But neither does this one keep a secret as well as the rest of your family." He placed her on the floor, and Hilda scampered under the counter and buried herself in her hide.

"Busted by a guinea pig," Fern muttered. She pulled a blue-tie-dyed bandanna from her pocket and tied it over her hair. "Who else knows?"

"No one. Until you or Lady Lark tell them. Or your mother returns."

Fern sighed. "She is invested in her work. I asked, and Mom says she'll never go back to where she grew up."

"But she kept the magic safe." Beri shrugged one shoulder. "Having it within reach again seriously changes things. If she won't return... You *are* her natural-born child, correct?"

"Well, I haven't had a DNA test, but yeah, she's mentioned giving birth to me, and her worst lecture ever was 'Don't get pregnant.' She had me at twenty-two"—*which was way too young*—"and they fought"—*over me*—"and split up. Having me changed her life." Fern had pieced half of this together.

Beri leaned in. "She's changed life on the Isle of Giuthas for many people. She took you and the magic and walked away from here, from her family, from her responsibilities."

"She gutted her youth working on this isolated land. Never went to college or dated other guys and was being forced into work she didn't want to do. Finally, she did something for herself and chose a career she loves."

"I'm nearly in my eighteenth year, younger than she was," Beri said. "Growing up in my world, in our settlement, you learn your place early on. You work to your potential. You do what is expected of you to help the community."

"Or you leave," Fern whispered. "You leave it all behind and move on to run your own life. The life you truly want to live."

"Her one decision does nae mean she has to stay away." He blew out his breath. "At this point, the people of Giuthas will forgive a lot to regain that magic. Especially if she were to restore the land bond and shielding."

"Will it stay in place if she doesn't maintain the land?"

"Nae. I think that's up to you. Something Lady Lark has

set up despite your lack of..."

"Gran can't have some impossible plan for doing this without magic?" Fern shook her head.

"You want to help Lady Lark? Sort this out. I'll help if I can." Beri smiled hesitantly.

He still offered his friendship, knowing she was the daughter of the witch who'd abandoned the island and left it to fall apart? Or what if the only reason he wanted her to stick around was to get Mom's magic?

Geez, this was a mess. Fern raised her gaze to Beri's. Gorgeous green eyes. Honest eyes. Forthcoming. Nice. *Really* nice. She wanted to believe this was about being friends, so for now, she would. She would also stick to the plan she and Gran had made—that she would become the Meadows' manager, magic or not.

"Thanks," she said and smiled back.

"Ho," came a shout from outside, and they both lurched to the screen door.

Across the field, winged people flew low over the grass, skimming the wildflower blossoms, like a flock of Gran's birds. They called to each other as they pointed at different plants. Some hovered, while others landed in the tall grass.

Beri pushed open the door, and they stumbled outside. "It canna be—"

"It's not—" she started.

"Noon," they said in unison.

A Windborne elder spotted them and waved. Sir Humus.

Unfurling his wings, Beri raised a hand in greeting, then nodded to her. "Good luck, Fern. Your inspection has started."

12

The Inspection

It was finally here. Their—her inspection. A nervous buzzing settled in Fern's stomach, and all her brain could stupidly think was, *They're early!*

Beri slipped away in the confusion of the wizards arriving. The elders converged on Sir Humus, swallowing the white-haired man in a crowd. Ten people, maybe? *Do I have to talk to all of them?* Most were adults. Some, like Gran, were elderly, but others were close to Fern's age.

Sir Humus broke from the group and walked toward Fern. Behind him, the wizards scattered over the Meadows. Every one of them glanced at her.

Fern swallowed and jerked her gaze to Sir Humus. The head of the council had been aloof while delivering their Meadows notification and was again dressed in an old-fashioned tweed suit. The formality made her nervous.

"Happy to see you are ready," he said in a deep voice. "Your inspection should run two to three hours. Be available to everyone, and good luck." He hailed another man, and they strode northward.

That's not where most of our planting is, she wanted to call after them, but a woman in a loose-flowing dress was approaching, so Fern made herself smile. "Uh, hello...?"

"Lady Pina." The woman gave a little laugh. "Lady Pina of

the Pines, a poor joke my father bestowed on me, but never mind, with the inspection schedule we're on, I haven't a moment to spare..."

Geez. Did this woman ever take a breath? Fern froze her face into polite attention, waiting as the lady chattered about her interest in seeing what her friend Lark had been up to in the Meadows.

Though she stood tall and strong, nearly Fern's height and build, she was old. Older than Gran. Her gray hair lay neatly braided in a thick plait, and her evergreen dress was like Gran's linen dresses and neatly ironed, making Fern self-conscious of her jeans. At least her fingernails resembled Fern's, short and edged with persistent soil from gardening.

"...ought to see wild carrot, teasel and devil's bit, if you have them."

"I do." Fern thought fast. She couldn't run all over and still be available to the other inspectors. "I can point them out from the top of Hillux." Mouth dry, Fern led the way around the side of Gran's house and up the stone steps in the earthworks. But at the top, Lady Pina wasn't behind her. Fern retraced her steps to where the older woman lingered, bent double, in a patch of pale blue harebells.

Moving as carefully as a butterfly, Lady Pina fingered a few spots left from leaf miners, swiped a stem covered in a hatch of aphids the ladybugs had yet to find and poked her finger into the soil of the newest plantings that barely showed wilt. She took a notepad and pencil from her pocket.

What was she writing?

When Lady Pina glanced up, her smile went into her eyes. "Incredible, do you have this variety of colors and textures planted throughout the Meadows?"

No one had ever paid such attention to her flowers at home, and a pleased rush came over Fern, along with a finger tingle from nerves. "Yes, and each species planted here, too," she explained like she would to a science fair judge. "As a study garden, to keep track of plant stages elsewhere in the Meadows—"

"Hallo." A thin, faded man in wire spectacles flew into their path and landed. "How have you prepared the ground for seeding?"

Lady Pina sniffed. "Chinook, I am not finished gathering my infor—"

"Let the lass answer, Pina."

Fern glanced between them and managed to explain Gran's method.

"Chemical herbicides certainly make the job easier." His husky voice was quiet but hard.

"No, sir. There was nothing easy about it. I can show you," she said, carefully polite. She apologized to Lady Pina and promised to return. Then she led him out to a recently cleared plot and the burn pile full of drying plants.

Fern excused herself to return to lady Pina, but she'd walked only a few minutes before she ran into a short, barrel-shaped man, jingling because of the loops of wire strung with various-sized rings hanging from his sportsman's vest—and from bundles of net and aluminum framing dangling from one hand.

Bird traps.

Fern blurted, "I thought the partridge wouldn't be hunted until next year."

The man blinked rapidly and shot a guilty look at the traps. "I only *monitor* the birds on the isle." He stuck out his hand. "Mr. Grouse. I'm here to ring your partridge." He dipped his head of thinning brown hair several times and jiggled the metal rings with his free hand.

She tried not to stare at Mr. Grouse's odd behavior. Unlike the other islanders, he was dressed in modern outdoor clothes and hiking boots. Stuffed in his fishing vest's pockets were tools, a ruler, pens and a notepad like Lady Pina's.

"Is *ring the birds* like birdbanding?"

"Indeed, what you call it in the United States. I'll be ringing any other bird life I catch as well. I'm curious how many partridge survived from the four-dozen birds Lark told me you released in the spring." He rubbed his scalp. "Where do you suppose they're feeding?"

"In the knapweed along the oaks at the eastern edge of the Meadows." Thank goodness she knew this answer.

Mr. Grouse peered at her. "A bush?" When she opened her mouth to correct him, he said, "No, the wildflower, of course. New patch this year?"

"Yes." Shouldn't he know the local plants the birds fed on? The plants that were on their list *because* of wildlife? Strange, but maybe this was his idea of an inspection for the trial?

He turned, jingling. "Point the direction and I can make my way. Perhaps you could find me later?"

"Of course." Fern dashed back to Hillux, where Lady Pina waved her over to a new patch of wildflowers on the rooftop. Over a hillock in the distance, Fern spotted two people walking toward the cottage.

"Hurry, we have several minutes," Lady Pina said.

Fern identified ten more wildflowers before the newcomers climbed to the rooftop. While Lady Pina made additional notes, Fern peeked to make sure the witch and wizard didn't mind waiting. The woman looked just like Willow. Her amber eyes shone and a pleasant smile softened her pointed face. She had to be Willow's mother.

At last, Lady Pina sighed. "I have enough to start on and will return."

Fern followed her toward the other council members. The man held out his hand, but Willow's mother joined Lady Pina, their heads tucked together over Lady Pina's notepad as they descended the stone steps, a blond braid swinging alongside the gray one.

Fern shook hands with the Sir Dolph of the Seas, a wizard with graying hair, and deeply tanned, weathered skin. He wanted to view Gran's vegetable gardens.

Not the required plantings? Gran had grown the vegetable gardens for decades. The conversation turned to other aspects of raising food, such as Gran's beehives—which Fern had not touched—and the game birds.

Hunting. She hated this and had to be honest with him. "I understand the birds are intended to be food for the isle. I'll do my part for their shelter and food, but harvesting them is not something I'm going to be able to do. I'm sorry."

Sir Dolph studied her with his piercing blue eyes, then gave a slow nod. "Thank you for your candor. Good day." His wings unfurled, and he flew off.

Damn.

A grizzled old man intercepted her on the way back to Hillux. He was wiry and bent, with a beard trailing over his chest. He had a bucket in his hand, three-quarters full of murky water.

"Glad to run into ye," he said in a gravelly voice. "I don't have time to haul myself all over this field lookin'. Spent half my night fightin' to keep a damned slab o' land from droppin' away. Where did ye put 'em?"

He was able to stop the land from falling into the ether? She didn't dare ask, as angry as this man was. "Uh, put what?"

"The plants. Are they doing right by ye?"

The bits of information clicked into place. "The wetland plants. You must be Sir Snap."

"Aye. Sir Snap of the Ponds."

It was clear why Beri called his mentor Old Snap, although she didn't dare to. His craggy looks, tattered clothing and gruff manner reminded her of an ancient snapping turtle she'd seen on a school field trip to a lake.

She took him to the pond, where he cast a critical eye about. None of the plants had wilted, thank goodness, but Sir Snap didn't like the placement of one species. She committed to moving them onto drier land and promised him root cuttings of another he didn't have. Finally, Sir Snap hefted the bucket he'd abandoned when they'd arrived. "This here's to prime yer new water."

Fern peered into it. What she'd thought was mud moved. She grinned at him. "Pond insects. Thank you so much."

The wizard's face crinkled with a proud smile. "Strained 'em with a plankton net, I did. Wanted to bring ye the critters, but not haul buckets of water. 'Twas Beri's idea back when we worked on a pond on the mainland."

They poured in the insect-rich water and watched the cloud disperse, while Sir Snap listed dragonflies and mayflies and other bugs she didn't know. It was very companionable. Then he said, "Seen all I need to."

Fern glanced at the elderly man. "Do you have questions

for me?"

He grunted. "No time. Rifts aside, they run us elders ragged on these inspections." Lips pursed, he cast another look over the pond and picked up his bucket. "Less about knowing facts and more about how you approach your work. You'll see." He shuttled off.

Fern had to go past the knapweed plantings, so she checked in with Mr. Grouse. She found him extracting a bird with pretty rust-colored feathers from a fine net suspended between poles.

"Ho there," he called. "We've caught a chaffinch, male. Quite common here. Don't suppose you have them in the States?" He blinked at her in question.

"I have no idea," she said.

"Would you hold him?" He transferred the warm body to her closed palm and strode to his equipment.

She could hardly breathe. The chaffinch's heart raced, a tiny pulse against her fingers, reminding her of Mr. Grouse's blinking. Each delicate feather lay in a perfect gray cap over his head like a hood around staring beady, black eyes.

"Now, I can take him." Mr. Grouse blinked enthusiastically.

He popped the chaffinch into a small can, placed it on a scale and wrote the number in a logbook. Another notebook lay open. Her gaze caught a familiar word: knapweed. Other plants were listed before it, with page numbers and short notations off to the side, just like her school papers. The page was labeled "M."

Was Mr. Grouse studying?

It didn't take him long to record the bird's measurements and use a special type of pliers to fit a small metal band on his leg. When he was finished, the ring had disappeared.

"Where did it go?"

Mr. Grouse sighed heavily. "It's invisible. Unfortunately, using hidden rings is the only way I can conduct scientific research in Windborne enclaves, because I can't disclose our locations. I can't even submit these records to the European Union for Bird Ringing with my other research in the UK." He blinked. "Time to turn this little fellow loose. Do you wish to do the honors?"

He transferred the bird to her, and Fern opened her hand. The chaffinch perched on her palm for a second, then flew to a nearby bush to preen.

"This island is a sanctuary for them," he said quietly, still watching the chaffinch. "It's been difficult to watch its resources unravel. Your plantings are a step toward reclaiming the Meadows' energy. What next?"

Her throat tightened. *No need to mention magic*, she told herself. She listed any connection to birds—the plants Gran's birds fed on and those in the pond restoration. "The cover we'll create around the water will be a huge draw to birds." And, ill as the topic made her, she couldn't skip the game birds. "We'll continue to raise partridge until their populations do as well as the pheasant..."

Mr. Grouse had stopped moving. Could he be vegetarian also? *I may have just shot myself down—again.* She took a breath. "But I don't agree with killing them. I'd prefer they remain as part of the habitat."

For a moment, neither of them said anything.

Then Mr. Grouse adjusted his equipment. "The lack of energy is the main issue in the Meadows," he said without looking at her. "Some say it will be years before the bonds are restored. This island doesn't have years. Lark has kept your skills quiet, so we've only seen the results, not your magic. How long will it take you to return the Meadows to full strength?"

A direct magic question. Fern swallowed, her palms tingling *and* sweaty. She drew a breath to settle herself like Mom always said to do. "That's hard to say, since it can take seasons for plants to establish themselves, and for insects and wildlife to find them and keep returning. After working here, I have ties to this land and its plants. Any person would. For each of us, the connection is a very individual thing, but that's something the council would expect, right? I mean, it's not like they're expecting an instant energy reboot—er, a complete revival. Not like if Lady Heather's energy returned?"

Mr. Grouse jerked his gaze to hers, his eyes rapid-fire blinking. "No, not like that. You are not Lady Heather." He shook his head sadly.

"Neither is anyone else," she said with false bravado. "So I'm as good a candidate as the next person."

When Mr. Grouse didn't ask more questions, Fern excused herself. Maybe she could use the magic in Mom's glass mound back home like she did the teardrop. Then, wouldn't Fern be the natural choice to manage the Meadows, just like Willow working with her own mother?

She snatched off her bandanna and her ponytail elastic and scraped her fingers through her hair, thinking how best to approach Mom, to ask. Because she could always ask.

That makes two inspectors unhappy, Mr. Chinook and Sir Dolph, and one happy, Sir Snap. Mr. Grouse wasn't pleased, but I answered the best I could. She'd better find Lady Pina, or another elder, and continue. She scanned the fields, but saw only someone flying in the distance.

A new woman stood on Hillux's porch, lowering binoculars from narrowed eyes. Her mousy hair was pulled into a bun, and she didn't smile when introducing herself as Lady Roda.

"I want the animal lists you have compiled for the Meadows," she said curtly, her attitude as stiff as her pressed trousers and tucked shirt.

After Sir Snap's warning, Fern didn't bother with small talk. She pulled Gran's observation notebook from the kitchen cupboard and started copying, but she could feel Lady Roda's impatience. If only she had her computer.

Fern glanced toward the bathroom. "Excuse me," she murmured. In three minutes, she was back with the pages copied on Mom's printer, right as Lady Pina walked in.

Neither woman acknowledged the other, which seemed odd. Fern handed over the pages.

"This isn't many. I'll have to do my own survey," Lady Roda snipped and left.

Instantly, Lady Pina began asking wildflower questions. Fern tried to stop reviewing her own shortcomings, so it helped that Lady Pina did most of the talking.

She thought she'd identified every species when Lady Pina put up a finger. "This is a fine collection, but where is your ratna?"

The one question Fern couldn't answer. The ratna was the only plant on the list for which Gran hadn't known the scientific name, and no amount of searching on the Web had located the species. "We can't find a source for it," Fern admitted.

The lady looked her up and down, her gaze lingering on Fern's hands, clasped together to keep from shaking. Then Lady Pina shook her head.

Fern's stomach clenched. *Damn. This is the one person who genuinely likes my work.* "Ma'am? If you know where we can get some, I'll start it in my sunroom and have mature plants ready for fall planting. Or spring, if that's better."

Lady Pina sighed. "If it were up to me, this would be acceptable, but it is not." She pushed through the screen door.

Fern trotted after her. "Not up to you? Or not acceptable?"

"Not up to me."

Apparently, they hadn't *failed.* Had they? "So will you support our approval?"

Lady Pina turned to her and nodded. "I will, you have reason to be proud of yourself, young lady," she said. "The ratna would be yours if Heather would come around, but now I canna delay another moment. Goodbye." Lady Pina strode away through the tall grass.

Mom wouldn't help here, not with a plant.

Fern pounded a fist into one hand and spun toward the cottage. "No, we won't have our work dismissed because of one plant." Gran would...

Not we. Gran wasn't allowed to help with her inspections. Fern blew out her breath.

Was it over? No one seemed to remain in the Meadows that she could see. That meant her tally was three unhappy inspectors—Mr. Chinook, Sir Dolph and Lady Roda—two happy—Sir Snap and Lady Pina—and she still wasn't sure about Mr. Grouse. What happened to Willow's mother? *I never got to talk to her.*

Inside Hillux again, Fern crashed on the couch with a chattering Hilda. "Geez, it's the third degree, guilty until proven innocent." While she ran her fingers through the guinea pig's hair, a knock sounded on the screen door.

Rising to her feet and placing Hilda on the floor, Fern caught sight of Sir Humus and pasted on a cautious smile.

"More excitement today than you're used to?" Once inside, he shook her hand and gestured to a girl accompanying him. "My niece, Duffy, visiting from the mainland."

Fern shook hands with Duffy, too. Like Mr. Grouse, who spent time off the island, her clothes were khakis and a green blouse in a current style. Her highlighted brown hair was cut in an asymmetrical bob, layered longer in the front and on the left side. Gold hoop earrings dangled against her neck.

"Duffy attends Bonterra Academy, in their botany program. She and her brother have apprenticed for me as part of their studies. Soils aren't exactly her main interest"—he smiled at his niece, who flashed a wry grin back—"but we manage to include a lot of plants. You girls probably have a lot in common."

Adults always said things like that when they wanted kids to talk to each other. It was never easy. They exchanged looks, and Fern searched for something intelligent-sounding to say.

But Sir Humus got to the point. "I'm checking to ensure you have met all the inspectors we scheduled."

Present and accounted for...but instead, she listed her visitors. "I know more people were here." Such as Willow's mother.

"Apprentices. Your other inspectors..." He consulted a notebook. "Satisfied. Your initial inspections are complete."

He handed her a paper. "Here are the items you may correct."

Fern glanced at the list.

Lack of Meadows ratna.

Questionable bond to land.

"If you correct them before your interview tomorrow evening, contact me."

Fern nodded, but inside she was shaking. A nonexistent plant and an impossible magical bond, and she had only one day to correct them?

Outside, running feet pounded up to Hillux.

"Fern," Beri called. "I—oh, sorry. Sir Humus, I hope I'm not interrupting. Hi, Duffy."

He threw her a casual glance, but Fern caught the smile Duffy gave Beri in return.

Did Duffy like him, too? Damn. Would nothing go right today?

13

A New List to Deal With

Like looking toward screeching tires, Fern was curious to see Beri and Duffy together, but Sir Humus strode to the door and waved Beri outside.

"You're one person I'm looking for," he said. "Have a minute?"

When they left, Duffy went to the refrigerator, got a carrot and sat on the floor to hold it for Hilda, as if she'd been to Hillux many times.

She probably had. Fern's spirits fell further.

"The Meadows was one of my first study areas two years ago," Duffy said while the guinea pig bit into her treat. "Flying over your land, I see a lot of changes."

This wasn't *quite* a compliment, probably because Duffy managed to sound superior. Mom's perennial advice echoed through her: *Take a breath and settle yourself.* Duffy wasn't even looking at her, so it was easy to not answer.

"The native species you've grown seem to be thriving," Duffy continued. "You certainly have this gift with plants that Lady Lark brags about."

Okaaay, that was a compliment. "Thanks."

"Strange."

Why did Fern feel like she'd just gotten hooked into something? She wanted to shake it, but her defensive feeling about this older girl wouldn't go away.

Duffy paused to adjust the remaining hunk of carrot so as not to get bitten. "Every Windborne story I've heard says habitat success depends on having your specific ratna."

"There's a particular one?" The words were out before Fern could check herself. Dammit.

A smug smile crossed Duffy's face. "You haven't gotten it? Then it's true you haven't inherited the family energy. Too bad you won't be able to return the bond that died out when the last Witch of the Meadows ran off."

Great. Duffy's jabs were as good as any Boulder High student's. Fern bit back any response—wait, wait. *The bond that died out.* Did the ratna create the bond? If she could grow it, then did it matter if she had no magic? What else from Duffy's mesh of honeyed comments might help her? Plants. This girl studied them... "Do you know where I can get seeds for the ratna?" *Since you're supposed to know so much about plants.*

"Of course I do, that's why I asked. I wondered if you'd given it a try and failed."

Footsteps crossed the porch, and they both turned. Sir Humus filled the doorway. "Duffy? Beri will also check that stream question. Do you want to come with us?"

"I'll meet you there."

He moved off, saying something to Beri, who replied, "I'll be right behind you," and opened the screen door. He darted a glance at Duffy before staring at Fern. "Can I have a word?"

Oh yeah. She went outside and joined Beri a short distance away, shaking the tension from her shoulders.

"I couldn't talk to Raven," Beri said. "He's busy and should be tied up until I can get back, but if he stops by, please tell him to wait to talk to me."

Fern nodded, but now thoughts of Raven and the rip energy weren't bugging her. "Beri, do you know what ratna is?"

"Lady Lark didn't tell you—no, of course not, because the ratna is a magical plant. Hundreds of years ago, the Windborne cultivated it for different habitats. The plants are imbued with the energy of the wizard family and the land, and they help the vegetation on it to prosper. Some consider its presence critical to the health of the habitat, but others do'na put too much stock in it. That's pretty much the dividing line between the plant people and the wildlife people."

No wonder Gran had had her search repeatedly. This could split the elders in their decision. "Why didn't Lady Lark keep the ratna she had alive?"

Beri grimaced. "From what I've heard, ratna are a particular wizard's plants and only respond to that person." He looked northward, distracted. "I should go. They only need me for a few minutes."

She caught his arm. "But ratna bond the wizard to the land?"

"Exactly."

He flew off, and Fern walked back into Hillux. Duffy was still petting Hilda. Odd that she'd stayed, but Fern pounced on the opportunity. "You mentioned you know where to get ratna seeds."

"I do. My community doesn't use the old-time magical plant, so I'm not sure how much power is needed to activate its magic. But you could give it a try."

Huh? Why did Duffy now sound so helpful? Had she read her wrong, and the girl's intention never was to snub her? Of course, she did get her chance to shine in knowing where to find the seeds.

"Excuse me!" came a sharp call. A scowling Lady Roda stood outside, the animal lists lifted in one hand.

Fern straightened and went to open the door, saying, "Come in," while Duffy scrambled to her feet.

"You have a severe overpopulation of rabbits in Upper Meadow," the lady snapped. "Few plants are left to support them or the other small mammals."

What was she supposed to say? "The focus of our work this last year was Lower Meadow. As soon as the inspections are completed, we'll be introducing predators"—which they had discussed, but then Fern added something she'd never thought she'd say—"and if that doesn't work, we'll trap the surplus animals. For...food. Don't people here eat rabbit?"

Lady Roda's glare lasted what seemed like forever, and Fern's palms began to get sweaty, but finally she said, "Very well. See that you do. Before the summer's end."

Fern released her breath. "We will, ma'am."

Lady Roda strode off, and when Fern turned, Duffy was staring openmouthed.

She shook her head. "You didn't just say that to the Wizard of Wildlife, did you?"

Oh. *Lady* Roda.

"I can't believe you'd suggest that to someone who values every vole on the island."

What had she started? Now she had to stick to this plan until she talked to Gran, in case Duffy reported back to her uncle or anyone else. "With no food, the rabbits would die. Wouldn't it be better for them to benefit someone rather than face slow starvation?"

"You're tougher than I thought."

"I've worked hard to bring back these plants."

Duffy cocked her head, her hair swinging perfectly. "How far are you willing to go to get the ratna?"

Was the wording of that really the dare it sounded like? Fern's eyes narrowed, while Duffy gazed back in wide-eyed innocence. She needed that plant, so chose to take the meaning literally. "Where do I have to go?"

"Not too far. My great-grandmother grows the plant, but she's something of an eccentric." Duffy grinned. "Plants are Lady Soila's life's work, and the ratnas her most prized possessions. Uncle Humus has finally convinced her to share her collection at this Council Gathering, but she's still grumbling. I can get you to her land, but you'll have to have a good trade to tempt her. Any ideas?"

Fern listed several possibilities. Duffy dismissed each until Fern named the wetland species Sir Snap was interested in.

"I've never heard of it, so that's the one," she said with assurance. "You tell her Sir Snap wants that plant, and Great-Gran will prize it, too, especially if you bring it to her first."

Rats. Losing her plants better be worth it for ratna seeds that wouldn't grow into much yet this year. She'd dig hers and take root cuttings to grow more. But this girl's change seemed suspicious. Was Duffy jealous that Beri had asked to speak to her alone? Fern tried for that wide-eyed innocent look Duffy had given. "I appreciate the help, but it'll take you away from your work."

"After today, I have the weekend off."

"Your free time then." She wanted a reason why. "I don't want to impose."

"My Great-Gran has the plants, you need a hand here,

and...and seriously, she will like that I helped you with a plant. I'll get brownie points with my relatives."

Seemed reasonable, and Duffy had looked her in the eyes while saying it. They arranged a time to meet in the morning, and Duffy left to rejoin her uncle.

I so need a pop right now. She might have one left in Gran's refrigerator, so she started searching.

"Still here?" asked a deep voice behind her.

"Whatthehell!" Fern whirled, slamming her elbow on the door and nearly tripping before spotting Raven, perched cross-legged on the counter. "You can't sneak in here!"

A snarky quirk crossed his lips. "'Tis my grandmother's home. I have the right to be here."

"To hell with your rights." His grandmother's... Fern fought to keep her face blank with her competition look. If Gran was his gran also, then Raven had to be her cousin. How? Could Merlin be Mom's brother? Or was his wife Mom's sister?

Family. What she'd wanted her whole life.

Fern fisted her hands, which, of course, chose this moment to start up their inconvenient tingling. If Raven's dad was anything like him, no wonder Mom left.

Crap and double crap. Raven had a trial in the Meadows that Beri wouldn't discuss. Raven was family. Raven was her competition.

He leaped in a way not humanly possible and landed a foot from her. He swelled his chest into a threatening stance. "*You* should leave," he snarled, his pale cheeks flushed.

Uh, no. His posture was intimidating, but only one notch more than a wrestling opponent. "Listen, buster, I'm not going anywhere."

The screen door slammed at the same time Beri shoved his way between them. "Back down," he growled at Raven.

Raven glared over Beri's shoulder, and she glared back, her chest pressing against Beri's shoulder. That touch registered. *This is pure crazy.* And even if she didn't say the words aloud, they helped her keep her head together. She shifted her weight back from Beri.

He inched in, jostling Raven away. "She knows something of interest to you," Beri hissed. "Not to mention, we don't beat up girls."

"I can't imagine what that would be," Raven said pompously. "Something to make up for the hours I lost removing rip energy—" He pressed his mouth closed.

Damn, it was *his* project they should have been doing. That made her indebted to *him*.

The foot between them looked smaller now, even with Beri filling it. No way was she chastising him for spying on her this time. She'd do her part to break out of the argument, but she was doing it for Beri's sake. She stepped back. "I have nothing to say to him."

Beri backed up a step, too.

Raven held his ground. "As I have said all along, a loner has nothing to offer us. My grandmother was dreaming when she brought you here."

What was he talking about? She'd given Gran lots of help. Damn, she wanted another reason to put this antagonistic boy on the ground. She affected a sweet smile. "I've changed my mind. I do wish to say something. Because of *my* research and *my* seed purchases and *my* devotion to Lady Lark's plan, my trial in the Meadows looks pretty damn good."

"Aye, you have done these things *alone*," Raven said.

"Alone and your way, in your...*your place*. People who work alone are not interested in cooperating with others. But this is our place, and our way is to work with the community. You would argue to continue in your way. I find it easiest to get you out of the way."

No matter that she had just learned about their community *yesterday*. She jabbed him with her fingers. "I can say the same of you, mister, since your trial area is hidden from me."

His nostrils flared, and suddenly, she was nose to nose with Raven.

Heat radiated off his body, and Fern swore the orange had taken over most of his irises. In fact, a glow illuminated his skin.

Magic.

I shouldn't have touched him. That irritating tingle in her fingertips rushed over her arms, then surged down her back and legs. Her toes went numb, like they were squished in too-tight running shoes.

Just like with the rip energy.

She stumbled back, scanned her body for it, for any sign of a glow. There wasn't any. Confused, she caught Beri's gaze. He jerked his head for her to move aside, and she did, shaking out her arms.

Raven started to follow, but Beri grabbed him by the shoulder. "Airing your grievances is all fine and good, but not if you can't avoid magic." He pushed Raven to the door and outside, and though the dark-haired boy was resisting, that didn't stop Beri.

She went to the screen door to track their progress up a nearby hillock, while rubbing her arms and fingers into more of a normal feeling. *It's not rip energy, just stress.* Too much was at stake.

The boys stood apart, Beri's words low and cajoling, not at all like hers had been. Damn, she didn't like Raven. He was too much like...her. Wanting to do things her way, standing up for herself, no fear of physical confrontations.

Humph, it seemed they had more similarities than hair color. Fern ran her hands over her hair, removing the band and fixing the loose strands back into a ponytail. She almost had it pulled through the band a last time when she looked back at the boys.

Raven was also sweeping back his long black hair. Their gazes met. His narrowed, and she looked away, then back. Raven had crossed his arms as Beri knocked his shoulder and pointed across the Meadows. Touching and compromise would have never worked between Raven and her. In fact, she was lucky he hadn't poked her. She would have socked him one. He'd glowed at her. What could that have been leading up to?

Just as a tingling rose in her fingertips, the two boys broke apart. Raven paced a circle—just as she did when excited—and Beri walked back into Hillux.

"Will you wait here?" He tilted his head toward Raven. "We're going to check the rip energy for a rift."

Without her. Probably a good plan. Fern rolled her eyes. "I won't go home, if that's what you mean. Now that the inspections are over, I should be able to talk to Lady Lark."

"She certainly will want a report. If you need me, come to the porch and shout. I ken you have no other way to call, so...it'll have to do." He gave her a little smile.

What other way would there be to call someone except to shout? He didn't have a cell phone. It didn't matter. She was tired. "Sure. Go ahead." She flopped onto the couch, pulled Gran's afghan over her and shoved Raven from her mind.

Sometime later, a squeak jerked Fern from a half slumber.

"You're awake," a girl said in a high voice, and Fern scrambled to sit up.

Willow sat in the opposite chair, holding Hilda on her lap. She looked very proper in a long tan skirt and a golden blouse similar to what she wore yesterday.

"Where's Beri?" Fern asked.

She pointed to the door. "Talking to Raven about something to do with a change in the Meadows rip energy. That's all they say I should know about it. Or my mother will learn, you ken."

She didn't *ken*, but likely Beri was hiding the ocean rift. Fern closed her eyes briefly, seeing the clump of grass splash into the waves again. "The rips change?"

"Aye, and this isn't the best time to present habitat problems to the council. Monday would be soon enough, if you understand my meaning."

She did—anything wrong in their habitat would be a black mark against them in the inspection. "I'll let Beri and Raven decide, then."

Willow smiled. "Beri said your inspections are done for the day and you wish to talk to Lady Lark. My mother can send a message faster. Also, he thought you might be hungry. Are you?"

He was concerned about her? That was so nice—on top of him inspecting the rift. Fern's stomach growled. "I am."

"Come, I'll take you to my house." Willow said goodbye to Hilda, placed her on the floor and stood up.

But... Willow's easy manner with Raven last night had

made Fern think they were a couple. "Raven is mad at me. Sure you want to catch the backlash from that?"

Willow waved dismissively. "Honestly, Raven jumps into things before thinking, and I wish it wasn't up to me or Beri to smooth them over."

"Thanks, then." She swung her feet to the floor and gestured to her right foot. "And thanks for this, too. I won't tell anyone, but I'm grateful it's gone. Let me know if I can return the favor."

"I'm sure you will someday."

When Willow reached out a hand to help her up, Fern hated to refuse, noticing only once she stood that Willow held something in her other hand—a glass bubble attached to a fine chain around her neck. Something fluttered between their fingers, followed by warmth and a glow like when Willow had dried her off.

Willow closed her eyes.

Fern's stayed wide open, and seconds later she wished they hadn't.

14

Willow

A globe surrounded Fern and Willow, like one of those little snow globes, but with no snow. Instead, the world outside the glass whirled, zooming past, colors blurred with everything moving at super speed like the mixer ride at the fair.

Fern's stomach heaved. She doubled over, managing to stop herself from vomiting...but just.

The spinning stopped, and the globe disappeared. Willow held her steady, asking, "Are you all right?" alternating with cries of, "Mam!" and "I'm so sorry!"

Someone else grasped her firmly under the arm. "Take deep breaths, my dear," a woman crooned. "Deep, even breaths."

A bucket appeared on the floor, and a cool cloth pressed against the back of Fern's neck.

After a minute of quiet, the queasiness left her. Her breathing quit coming in gasps, and she could straighten. They stood on a porch surrounded by trees.

Willow's mother was the woman from the inspection. They led Fern inside to a huge couch across from a wood-stove and settled her into it with a fuzzy throw about her shoulders and a mug of warm tea in her hands. "Ginger and chamomile. It will settle your stomach," Willow's strong-looking mother said before hurrying from the room.

Willow perched anxiously beside her, fending off the three little boys who darted among the furniture carrying toys they left on the braided rug at her feet. The boys looked alike, tanned with sun-bleached blond hair, but theirs fell straight into pageboy cuts at their ears. They wore matching golden pullover shirts and twig-brown shorts.

"Does she not look like Raven, Willow?" asked one of the boys.

"Aye, she has hair like him, long and black. Hush now, Kory, so she can rest. No, Maple Sugar, Fern canna look at your toys right now. She's ill. Please, baby, just cuddle up with me."

Funny this little kid would notice only their hair, not that Raven had white skin and hers was a warm beige. That was nice.

The littlest climbed up on the couch and settled back with Willow, clutching a teddy bear. Something stroked her knee. Fern looked, expecting a cat, but the next youngest was lightly petting her jeans, almost in awe. When he noticed her looking at him, he snatched his hand back and quickly buried both in his pockets.

He looked so frightened, Fern whispered, "It's okay. I don't mind."

The middle boy gazed at the material. "It is as blue as the sky."

"Bluer," said his brother, who'd come to stand beside the arm of the couch. "Where do you get such a color to your trousers? And to your shirt?"

It was just a cotton V-neck, hand-dyed in a bright swirling purple pattern. "I traded a glass moon I made for the shirt," she said, which was the truth. "I don't know how the artist got this color. But it's pretty, isn't it?"

All three boys nodded.

"So what's your name?" she asked the oldest.

"Haw. Er, Hawthorn."

"Me! I's Maple Sugar!" cried the littlest, scrambling across the couch to her.

"You are Maple." Willow laughed and caught him up again. "We just call you Maple Sugar. Stay with me, baby, so you don't spill Fern's tea."

"I's not a baby. I's almost three."

"But you are still two," Willow said quickly.

"Two is such a big boy," said Fern. Maple smiled at her and snuggled back into Willow's lap, very pleased. Fern turned to the middle boy, still standing at her knee. "And you are?"

"Hickory," he said solemnly. "Everyone calls me Kory. You can, too, if you like."

"I'd like that, Kory. Thank you." She smiled at him over her mug, feeling a welling up inside her. They were all so sweet. Willow smiled back over Maple's head. "You're so lucky having three brothers."

"Four," said a deep-voiced boy who'd entered, an older version of the three little boys.

"This is Chestnut," Willow said, "who we call Ches. He's taller than I am, but three years younger."

"Aye, she never fails to point that out." He handed Fern a hunk of bread on a napkin. "Mam said start with bread to see if your stomach has settled. Do you always get ill when you pereport?"

"Ches! Hold your tongue," Willow admonished. "Please

ignore him, Fern. He has a tendency to say whatever comes into his brain, without thought to politeness."

"I want to know if I'll be needin' to grab the bucket again, you ken?" he said to Willow, then leaned toward Fern and added, "It's all that learnin', gone to her head. She thinks she knows what's right and wrong for the lot of us." Ches pulled up another stool and scooped Kory onto his lap.

"Ah," Willow cried. "It's not always a blessing to have four brothers. Mam says since I'm the only girl and the oldest, I should rise above their attitudes."

Fern stared at them, not sure what to make of this. Sibling arguments were foreign to her. What she wanted was to get back to his question about pereports. She took a bite of the brown bread, which was tasty, grainy and similar to what her mother made when she had time. She hadn't in months.

"What of your family, Fern?" Ches asked. "Are you the oldest and that's why you've been allowed to come here to the isle?"

"No, no sisters or brothers. I'm an only child."

"The only child?" Maple's eyes were wide. "Who do you play with?"

"My friends," she said. "Sometimes there's no one, so I do stuff with my mom or by myself."

"What kinds of things do you like to do, Fern?" asked Willow. "In your settlement, there must be as many different things to do as the different clothes you wear."

Beri had been horrified by the TV shows. She'd skip anything that would make her seem strange to them, just as Beri had feared they appeared to her. She looked around the room for ideas and noted overloaded bookshelves and walls covered with artwork.

"I suppose there are, but I like to read. I make some glass art pieces in my mother's studio to earn, er, trade for things. I like school." At their frowns, she corrected, "My studies. And I tutor younger children who need help."

Haw wrinkled his nose. "You like doing these things? The reading and the studies?"

She laughed at his obvious disgust. "I can't fool you, but reading exciting adventure stories"— romances, really, but she didn't need to tell a young boy that—"is fun. I'm good at my studies, and I'm fond of the kids I help. I like to play card games, but my favorite thing to do is to grow plants."

"Oh!" Kory's eyes shone. "That's what I like to do."

"You do?"

"Aye, we grow the herbs, Willow an' I, but I almost do it by myself now. Maple helps me sometimes. Ches and Haw tend the kitchen garden with Poppa, though he spends most of his time on the crops. Mam runs the Forest, and she's teaching Willow and sometimes Raven."

"That's when I'm not running the house and a family of seven." Their mother entered, carrying a bowl. Willow's mother *was* an older version of Willow, whereas Fern and her petite, delicate-boned mom looked completely different, from height, body shape and facial features, to hair and skin.

"Hello, my dear. I'm Mimosa," she said.

Lady Mimosa, Fern mentally corrected, because this modest woman was the Witch of the Forest.

"You're looking much better than when you first arrived. Have you eaten some bread?"

At Fern's nod and a chorus of yeses from everyone else, Lady Mimosa took her mug and handed her a bowl of chunky vegetable soup seasoned with the familiar scent of thyme. It smelled wonderful. Fern thanked her.

"Willow tells me you wish to speak to Lady Lark," Lady Mimosa said. "I reached her for a quick minute. She's been told you have items to correct"—she looked at Fern for confirmation—"so she can't advise you until you submit those items. She says for you to do what you feel is best."

Gran always said that, darn it. *And it's like an exam.* Well, she had her appointment with Duffy to get the ratna seeds tomorrow. That was a start on the new list. Fern nodded.

"Take a break before you continue. Have dinner with us. Then I can pereport you back, or you're welcome to sleep here tonight. Willow has an extra bed in her room."

"My room is nice!" Maple said. "She can have my bed."

Everyone laughed. "Your bed is way too short for this leggy girl," said Ches. "Mine is the right—"

"Ches. Time to bring in the wood," Lady Mimosa said firmly. "Scoot, all of you, outside and help your brother. Not you, Willow," she added as all her children rose at once.

With a smile, Willow sank back onto the couch, this time closer to Fern. While their mother escorted the boys into the kitchen, she leaned over to whisper, "Ches has been so on about girls since I've prebonded with Raven. Though he's still years from it, he tries many things before his age allows."

So she'd been right—Willow and Raven were together. Fern stirred her soup. "Like what?"

"Casting spells, trying his hand at growing things magically, pereporting when he can sneak Mam's device."

"A peregrinator? That's what you used to bring me here?"

Willow nodded.

"Why did I get sick if I've done it before?"

"Is that how you come to the isle? Your mother has gifted

you with a distance peregrinator?"

"I guess?" Fern set aside the bowl. Might as well show her since Beri already knew and would certainly tell Raven, which would get back to Willow. When she pulled out the teardrop, Willow squealed.

"Yes, it's rod-shaped for distance, but the roundness at one end means the destination is set. You can only travel between two places, according to the magic she put into your device."

"Home and Hillux."

"Still, that is far! Generally, distance peregrinators are stronger than enclave peregrinators, like our family's." She took the small clear globe from her blouse and compared it to the multicolored teardrop, her lip caught between her teeth. "Did it feel different to you?"

"A lot. How do you stand that..." Fern waved her hands about. "It was like the mixer ride at the fair, making me sick seeing everything go by so quickly."

"When you *see* it? Fern! You are *not* supposed to be watching." She sat back with a satisfied nod. "When a wizard releases this device's magic to teleport, he or she needs to visualize the new place, the path to it. You do so with your eyes closed, concentrating, you ken, to get yourself there. If not..." She grimaced. "Ew, you could have an accident."

"Well, that's easy enough. I'll try that the next time."

"I've earned my approval to teleport my younger brothers on the isle, but sorry I didn't warn you. Do you usually have trouble?"

"No. Mine opens a portal and I step directly through."

"Oh." Willow looked impressed, even though this had to be idiot-proof compared to what she did. "Are you saying"—

she dropped her voice—"that it looks like the energy rips in the shielding?" She spun a finger in a doughnut shape.

"Except the colors are these, and they stay separated." Fern stroked the teardrop. "Is that bad? Oh, wait. Lady Lark has seen it. If something were wrong, she'd have stopped me."

Willow released a breath. "Oh, good." She side-eyed Fern. "That was your first time seeing a rip, Beri said. Everyone is on edge trying to keep the isle safe."

"I expect so when out-of-control magic causes your land to drop into the ether."

Willow raised her hands in a helpless gesture. "Anything could have caused it. The activities of the animals, harvesting a crop, the amount of magic a wizard ties up with projects versus what's available for shielding. So many details Mam and the other wizards must balance to prevent more rips. Some she won't tell me. It's so frustrating. I am her heir, but she holds back the parts for which she feels I am too young, saying when she passes management of the valley forest on to me, I will know."

"You want them now," Lady Mimosa said as she walked in, "but I daresay you'll feel you've grown into them far too quickly."

The two jumped upright, exchanging startled looks.

But Lady Mimosa simply lowered herself onto the stool before Fern, studying her with golden eyes. "How are you feeling?"

"Much better. The bread and soup were wonderful, thank you."

"Oh, Mam, we figured out why Fern got ill. She didn't close her eyes as I pereported her. The sight made her dizzy."

Lady Mimosa chuckled. "But now you've been here. Next time, visualize the porch. It'll make your travel easier and be a lesson for you."

Fern nodded.

"Now then, Willow can take you to Hillux, but Lady Lark will be staying overnight with friends up north." Lady Mimosa smiled. "Is your mother expecting you tonight?"

Fern tweaked the throw around her shoulders before she murmured, "No." Darn it, Gran really was being kept from her. Fine, she'd trade for those ratna seeds, start them growing, then get help with the magical part. Family help, according to the rules—Mom, if she had to. Her gaze caught Willow's hopeful look. It would be fun, plus she'd learn more being among wizards. "I would like to stay here, if that's all right," Fern said, "and return to Hillux tomorrow to work." She turned to Willow. "Would you be able to take me back in the morning?"

"Of course."

Lady Mimosa nodded. "It sounds like a good plan, one Lady Lark would be pleased by. When does your mother expect you to return?"

"She'll be back Sunday." Despite her best intention to keep her eyes on Lady Mimosa's, Fern looked down. Shoot, secret-keeping was getting so hard.

"Fern?" Fingers gently tilted her chin up. "Does your mother know you are here?"

She stared into Lady Mimosa's golden eyes and found herself whispering, "No." She closed her eyes and tried to stop them from filling. It didn't work.

Willow scooted closer and put an arm around her shoulders.

"Fern, you have made good choices all along. I am sure of it after visiting your habitat." Lady Mimosa handed her a cloth napkin, and Fern used it to wipe her eyes. "This is naught but the stress of preparing for inspections, something we all feel. I want you to be able to set aside your worries. Will you allow me a check to see if all is as it should be?" Lady Mimosa cupped her cheeks.

Fern gave a little sniff and nodded. Here it all came. Lady Mimosa would call her mother and tell her. Mom would be furious that Fern had left the house—though, technically, she hadn't—and take back the peregrinator and never allow her to come again. But she was tired of the sneaking around, and things might be better this way than if Mom found out from Fern.

But Lady Mimosa didn't leave. She continued to lightly hold Fern's cheeks, and a flutter of warmth tickled her skin. Oh no. Lady Mimosa had said *a check* not *call*. Were they going to see her mother? Fern closed her eyes to prepare for leaving, but nothing happened.

Seconds later, Lady Mimosa dropped her hands to clasp Fern's again and began to laugh.

"Mam, what is it? What do you see?"

15

Trust in...Friends?

The polite thing to do, what Fern *had* to do, was wait until Lady Mimosa finished laughing.

Finally, Willow's mother covered her mouth. "This is one of the craftiest charms I have seen, and it is very definitely Heather's work. My dear, your mother knows exactly what you are doing. And where." Lady Mimosa touched her forehead, where Mom usually kissed her goodbye.

Fern clapped her hand to the spot. "Do you mean those little patterns Mom traces are—really? Those are like magical spyware?"

"Spyware? It's not bad, you ken?" Willow patted her arm. "Retrieval charms collect information so she can confirm you are safe."

So much for being sneaky. But—*wow, Mom didn't stop me.* She hadn't said a word. And considering Fern was old enough to work and drive and almost vote and be legally responsible for anything she did, she wasn't sure whether to feel loved or outraged. Oh, mothers made no sense at all. Fern rubbed her throbbing temples.

Lady Mimosa pulled Fern's hands down and held them in hers again. "This is naught to worry over."

No, probably Mom didn't love her less for lying, not if she'd kept quiet and continued to put charms on her. What would happen when they actually talked about it?

Lady Mimosa bent close. "You've come to help Lady Lark, and you have."

"But what I thought we were doing...isn't quite it."

"Do you need to understand her plans to continue your work?"

"I-I don't know. I still have things to finish, and with her gone, I'm on my own. Some of the inspectors don't like what I've done, or..." *Me*, she wanted to say, but that would just make her sound like a whiner.

"Fern, do you know your own mind? What the Meadows should be?"

A year ago, her dream had been to see only wildflowers out every one of Hillux's windows. Somewhere along the way, that vision had changed to a valley of plants feeding all sorts of insects, birds and wild animals. It wasn't just about the plants anymore, but making a place for them to continue—both Gran and the wildlife. Blinking away a stray tear, she nodded.

Lady Mimosa smiled. "Good. Hold on to that image, because the Meadows *will* be that way, given time." She rose. "Would you girls help me get dinner on?"

Later that night, Fern and Willow retreated to Willow's room, where she made up a bed for Fern on a cushioned window seat, lent Fern some pajamas and got her a toothbrush.

Willow was settled upon her bed when Fern closed the door and got into her own bed.

Am I wasting my time when I have no magic? Will they even accept me when they find out? Maybe she should be researching colleges and scholarships this summer, like Mom kept suggesting. Thinking over her coming plans had made her darned fingers tingle again, so she laced them together around her pulled-up knees.

"So," Fern started, her throat dry, "a person *must* be magical to oversee an island habitat?"

"Aye, to even live here."

Oh. This was worse than she'd realized. Struggling with her fears alone was too freaking much. Willow knew so much about this community that Fern felt compelled to confide in her. "I...can't take over the Meadows, not the same way you're an heir for your mother. I-I'm not as good at magic as you are. Is there a certain level required?"

Willow frowned. "You must have enough. The council approved you to conduct a trial."

Fern picked at the edge of a quilt. The peregrinator responded to *something* inside her, but nothing that would ball up in her hands. Was "the touch" enough, like Gran had claimed? Maybe that magic Mom had stashed in the glass mound would jump-start the ratna—if Mom agreed. She'd ask, easier to do that now that she knew that Mom wasn't in the dark. But what then?

Didn't matter. She couldn't let Gran lose her home.

Fern lifted her head. "I'll push through the inspection. They'll either accept what I've done or not."

Willow grinned. "I won't say anything, because you'll do fine."

Throwing her a halfhearted grin, Fern shook out her hands and shifted her thoughts to one of the more interesting things she'd learned about today. "What's this prebonding arrangement you have with Raven?"

"It's a trial before a bonding application can be made.

We're allowed to hold hands, hug, kiss, to sit next to one another. Er, naught more physical."

Uh oh. She and Beri had kind of held each other when
they'd fallen through her rabbit hole. Not in a romantic way,
of course, but...was that against the rules? As casually as she
could, Fern asked, "Just hugging and kissing, huh?"

"How else would you know you even want to enter the
application? Waiting until sixteenth year was very difficult."

"That's strict." Fern shook her head. "Where I live, at sixteen everyone can legally marry, or bond, whatever you all
call it." Their prebonding sounded like a permit for going out,
something everyone she knew fell in and out of casually. Except her. After she'd grown taller than all the boys in seventh
grade, they'd never been interested in dating her.

"It's worth the wait," Willow said. "In prebonding, you
can test sharing energy. It takes a long time to learn to exchange power, and knowing if you can helps decide if you
want to go on to a bonding application, you ken." At Fern's
confused look, she said, "You have to get along magically
with someone, too. It's very important that your energies
work together well, just as your personalities get along. Raven will manage the Forest with me. He's already moved his
energy here to conduct projects and train."

But Fern didn't have magic like they did. "I guess I'll never know about that."

Willow looked surprised. "You will. If you haven't met
someone in your own settlement, perhaps in this one. Or ask
your mother to take you visiting to another. Don't be dis-
couraged. It takes time to meet the right person."

Ha, she knew that. And then other stuff, such as height,
and now magic, got in your way.

"Some adults feel we should wait until older. Raven's father is one of them," Willow said quietly. "Merlin felt he would not have lost his young woman if they'd waited and had time to settle. A few years ago, he and others asked to raise the bonding age to twenty-third year. They also proposed that after habitat trials and approval, the young people should take time off, to travel and view other settlements or attend academy. Apparently, a people named the Amish offer this break, called *rumspringa*. The council voted to allow this break and added prebonding, but still allow bonding at the eighteenth year if anyone wants it."

Willow slipped lower on her pillow and adjusted her quilt over her shoulders. "Raven and I do. We're very lucky to have found each other." Her smile turned into a yawn. "My days have been very long. I have to rest, or I will miss the fun of the Gathering festival. No one really sleeps during it. What do you say we bid each other good night?"

"See you in the morning." Fern snuggled into the window-seat bed that was quite comfortable, even for her long legs, and turned to find the moon shining through the paned windows. The white orb was so nearly full that only the faintest bit of a rough edge showed on the lower left. It would smooth out in two nights on Sunday, July thirty-first, the night of the second full moon in the month—a "blue moon"—and the Council Gathering would start.

Willow's breathing soon deepened, but Fern watched the moon rise and mulled over her new discoveries.

The next morning, Fern stopped Willow when she put out her hand to pereport them to Hillux. "How exactly should I visualize where we're going?"

"Can you picture Hillux's front porch?" At Fern's nod,

Willow clarified a few details. "Close your eyes and imagine we'll be standing before the door on the slates. Take my hand and let's go."

As the warmth enveloped her, Fern dismissed every other thought but of Gran's porch. No rushing sensation overtook her, so when would they go? A cool breeze replaced the coziness, and Willow released her hand.

"Fern? You can open your eyes."

They stood sheltered under the porch while a light rain fell on the fields.

"Wow," she breathed. "I did it! And I'm not sick." Fern snapped her fingers and wiggled in a happy dance. "Thank you so much."

Willow laughed. "You're catching on to Giuthas life quickly. I'm so glad Lady Lark has finally allowed us to talk to you." She clasped Fern's hand. "The boys—Raven and Beri—didn't especially mind, because they have each other. And even though I have Raven, it's different. Boys, boys, boys! That's all there are on this part of the island." One corner of her mouth lifted hesitantly. "When I heard her new apprentice was a girl my age, I so hoped we might become friends."

Fern's chest ached with the thought, and in a spurt of happiness, she hugged Willow. "I'd like that."

Lady Mimosa wanted Willow back as soon as she'd delivered Fern, so she left, which was just as well. Once Fern had the seeds, she wanted to be alone to plant them how Lady Soila had directed.

Wearing one of Gran's waterproof wool capes and carrying a shovel and an oiled canvas bag, Fern ran through the rain. At the pond, she dug two plants and took root cuttings that she carefully stored in a wet rag. She left a fair amount of wet dirt clinging to their roots when she placed the plants in the bag, which weighed more than she liked, but ensured the plants would stay healthy. She had to show Duffy's great-grandmother, Lady Soila, she knew what she was doing.

Back at Hillux, Fern put the cuttings in dirt trays, washed up and changed into spare clothes she kept at Gran's—jeans and a nicer shirt, one a subdued yellow that fit with the natural colors the islanders wore. She'd braided her hair at Willow's house so it'd stay neat for her meeting.

Duffy arrived at the door right when they'd agreed.

Sheesh. Good thing Fern'd spent some time on her appearance. Duffy wasn't wearing work clothes. Under her rain jacket, she had on a fuchsia skirt and a brightly patterned top over a camisole. She wore nice sport sandals, the hoop earrings and makeup, including pink lipstick that coordinated with the shirt. Her hair looked perfect, of course. Compared to yesterday, the older girl looked like she was going on a date and sounded just as excited when she greeted Fern.

Was her great-grandmother the formal sort? "Nice skirt. Intense pink."

"You like it?" Duffy ran her hand over it. "Madder. Took forever to get the color this deep, but I've got the dye mix right and did an entire bolt. I'm checking the colorfastness now."

Fern vaguely remembered the plant. "You do your own dying?"

"With plants I'm raising. Part of a practical botany course I picked up this summer."

Fern's gaze traveled down the cape she wore to her own jean-clad knees and second-best running shoes. "Maybe I should have dressed up more."

"You look fine." Duffy zipped her jacket. "I have somewhere to go afterward and didn't want to go back to Uncle Humus' in between. Are those your plants on the porch?" At Fern's nod, she breezed out the door. "Let's get going. We can't get to Great-Gran's by any magical way, so I've arranged a human transport. I've heard you can't fly, and I couldn't borrow Uncle Humus' peregrinator, so we'll walk the first part." She jerked her head and headed south into Lower Meadows.

Fern closed the door and looped the bag handles over her shoulder. In no time, she'd caught up with the shorter girl and slowed her strides. She'd ask about the plan later, because Duffy's mention of flying reminded her of something. "What was your Meadows project?"

"Soil nutrient differences between overlying bedrock less than five meters deep and stream deposits of a half meter or more. I've repeated it across the isle for my trial."

Sounded like a research paper, not a trial for habitat management. "And?"

"Stream deposits are richer, but, sorry, that's a tiny portion of your habitat. Seventy-five percent of the Meadows overlies bedrock." She gestured to the mountains on either side. "You do have some ancient deposits that could be put to better use. See that cove between the ridges? Follow it down to where it ends in the grass. Notice how the ground is lower? The swale?"

Fern squinted at the wide depression. She and Beri had emerged there yesterday, after following a stream.

Duffy pointed out other streams from coves that did the same. "Over the centuries, the old streams dumped enough sediments to increase the organics. Meaning it's richer and holds water better."

"Thanks for the lesson," Fern said, "but why hasn't anyone else pointed this out?"

"My paper is just completed," she said. "The council is inspecting my project this weekend, along with everyone else's."

Another trial in the Meadows to rival hers—a very scientific one. Fern couldn't say anything, not when Duffy was doing her this favor, so she wished her luck.

Duffy brushed it off. "Appreciate it, but we're running late."

They reached the woods and took a deer trail that quickly turned into a series of ledges to scramble down under pine trees, relatively small ones. The wind picked up, underlain by a rhythmic rushing, and then the trees abruptly ended.

In the open, the wind whipped at Fern's cape, raindrops pelted her blinking eyes, and a briny smell filled her nose as she gasped for breath. Up and down the coast, the land fell off abruptly, not leaving much room for the waves crashing on a pebbly beach below the pine forest.

This must be the Irish Sea, the first time Fern had seen it.

Wow, this is within walking distance? She'd become used to the faint trace of salt in the air, but now she could come here to watch sunsets over the water. *Thanks, Gran, for hiding that for nearly two years.*

"What're you waiting for?" Duffy called through the wind. She'd walked down a rickety set of wooden steps to an equally weathered gray dock, where a motorboat bobbed on the waves.

Fern yanked the cape's hood over her soaking hair and tightened her hand on the bag. After climbing into the rocking boat, Duffy put on a life jacket, handed her one and turned to untie the rope to the dock.

Automatically, Fern slipped on the puffy vest on under her cape and zipped it. *Heck, what am I doing?* Motoring out on the ocean with a girl she didn't know? Ratna or no ratna, this was getting in over her head. She blocked Duffy, holding on to a dock post so they wouldn't float away. "Where is your great-grandmother's land? Ireland?"

Laughing, Duffy pointed. "Far closer, a little island less than two kilometers west. Don't worry, I drive our boat—just like this one—along the coast, but I'm not about to attempt farther over the open sea."

Fern peered in the direction she pointed, seeing only dark waves. Two kilometers was about a mile, and the horizon was clear despite the storm clouds blowing overhead. "Shouldn't I be able to see this island?"

"Even I can't see it." Duffy snorted. "Great-Gran keeps her land shielded even from Windborne. You have to know where to fly or, in this case, point the boat, until you bump into her protected space. Here, I'll show you how we do it."

Duffy threw the rope into the boat and darted to the small covered area over two seats. On a dashboard that was less complicated than a car's, she tapped a dial. "From this dock, I keep the compass needle pointed at two hundred and seventy-five degrees, nearly straight west. It's simple." She took a key from her pocket and held it up. "All right? You don't seem so sure you want to do this."

You're not kidding. And here she was being offered an out. *But I have to. I need those seeds.* "I'm going. I'm doing this." Fern let go of the post.

Duffy flashed another of her excited grins and slid the key

into the ignition.

The descriptor *manic* came to mind, but Fern immediately squashed the thought. She was just comparing Duffy to Willow, with whom she'd spent more time and felt more comfortable around because...why? Both girls had helped her. Just, Duffy didn't seem as sincere, like some people at school who looked out for their own interests first—which Duffy had even admitted.

The engine roared to life. "Store your plants between the seats so they don't spill," Duffy shouted. Fern did and sat in the seat next to Duffy as she skillfully steered them across the incoming waves. With frequent glances to the compass, she set their course. Ahead lay brighter water, lit by rays of sunlight streaming from the far side of the bank of clouds.

Duffy looked so confident, Fern couldn't help saying, "You like boating, don't you?"

"Yep. Maybe another time I can borrow the Seas' boat again and tour you around the isle. An overall look will give you a better feel for the island, since you can't fly."

Okaaay, nice offer, and Duffy had remembered to protect her bagged plants. When they'd ridden out of the rain and her flapping cape dried in the breeze, Fern relaxed. "Sir Humus mentioned you and your brother visit Giuthas. Where do you live?"

"Bonterra in England, where I attend academy. I expect you wouldn't find it too different than a smaller human city, except there are hardly any cars, and everything is fueled with wind and solar power."

That explained why she didn't use old-time phrases.

"My family is from an enclave as backwards as the Isle of Giuthas when it comes to ridiculously outdated policies,"

Duffy went on, "but it's not nearly as interesting botanically." That excited look came into her eyes again. "My plan now is to combine a strong, rugged portion with my education that will eventually give me modern comforts."

Huh? A strong, rugged portion of what? Fern had to be missing something in this conversation, but felt just awkward enough compared to this older, sleeker and more magically knowledgeable girl that she didn't want to ask.

Duffy slowed the boat. "It's another half kilometer, but I'll play it safe."

Fern peered ahead, looking for any sign of land. "How do humans randomly traveling this area avoid hitting the island?"

"Actually, it's an *islet* it's so small. At only a quarter mile across, it'd be hard to hit, plus Great-Gran has a disorienting charm on it. It's mild, since humans are innocent of trying to find it. But if a wizard tries to pereport there, they get blasted. Same with flying, swimming or boating without the charm passwords. It left a couple of teen pranksters powerless for a week."

Duffy didn't smile at this, which made Fern swallow.

"I should probably start chanting the passwords to get us through." Duffy mouthed something over and over, slowing the boat more and more. Nothing, then... The islet popped into view, a tiny hunk of land compared to the surrounding ocean. In spite of how cool it must be to live there, wasn't it dangerous when storms came? Duh, the *witch* probably just flew herself somewhere safer or cast a protective spell.

At least the land was high above the sea; it looked like a top hat that had been set afloat. A narrow brim of sand and chunky black rocks surrounded the base of the cliff. A waterfall broke the expanse of dark rock with a narrow stream, a whitish sheet flowing from the top to a pool below. A lone bird circled above it.

"How are we going to get up that?" Fern asked.

"We can't even dock there. Around the point, it's better."

But not much. A floating dock bobbed below brush-covered rocks. Halfway up, a gentler, grassy incline looked easier to climb—if they managed the first part. She wouldn't complain. Duffy must know what she was doing.

The older girl pulled alongside the empty dock, threw a rope loop around a post and cut the engine. The cries of gulls and other shorebirds added a higher chorus to the waves beating the rocks. With the boat secure, they left the life jackets, Fern got her bag and they walked to the end of the dock.

Duffy pointed to a narrow dirt trail. "Go ahead. Great-Gran becomes cross when the perimeter has been breached. That's a hermit for you. I'll warn her and meet you up there."

Fern had taken several steps toward the bush-lined path before the words registered. "What?" She looked around, but Duffy was gone. Furious squawking from the birds made her glance up.

High overhead, Duffy soared on brown wings, spread and tilting to and fro with the current.

"Wait," Fern shouted, but the wind sucked away her cry and lifted Duffy out of sight.

16

The Guard

Ohmigod, she left. I don't believe it. Of all the..." Fern's rant trailed off. What did she expect? To be coddled? Kids here did stuff on their own, as Beri had reminded her yesterday.

Yeah, independent and strong. She cradled the bag that held her plants in her cape-covered arms. Not as strong as Beri, whose chest and shoulders were taut with muscles, probably warm if he wrapped his arms—she shook away the daydream of having his help. The trail would be no worse than the switchbacks in the Colorado Rockies.

The path immediately climbed between the blocklike rocks, and when it narrowed, the wet shrubs on either side brushed against her cape. Within a hundred feet, the damp and cold sank into her jeans. Mud sucked at the soles of her shoes. Crossing ledges of rock along the cliff face, she could gauge her slow progress upward, but she frequently lost the trail in the bushes. Pushing through another narrow opening, she slipped and fell.

"Dammit!" Her knees smarted. Pinching back tears, Fern scrambled to a level section, skidding with each step. She hadn't fallen on the bag of plants, but... "Crap. I'm filthy."

Nothing she could do about her muddy knees. Nor should she complain about anything to Lady Soila. Was this Duffy's idea of a joke? Or a test? She'd said, *How far are you willing to go?*

Well, Fern would show her.

She stopped to catch her breath at the next ledge. Lowering the bag to rest her arms, she slumped against a boulder, her breathing leveling out as she listened to the waves crashing a hundred feet below. "A real Colorado hike up a fourteen-thousand-foot mountain would have been easier than this winding mess. And drier."

To stop herself from cursing Duffy, she dug out the Snickers bar she'd brought from her stash at Gran's. Her teeth ground the nuts and caramel, and Fern savored the chocolate with closed eyes. Damn—that made her feel better—this was good.

Raising the bar to take another bite, she hesitated. She'd brought this for an emergency snack, since she didn't know how long they'd be out. Now, she really didn't know what to expect.

With a sigh, Fern folded the wrapper closed, dropped the bar into the cape's front pocket and snapped the flap. The wind had blown off the clouds, and the sun felt good. She pulled off her cape and wrapped it around the wet bag. She should have brought water, but she'd get a drink at the top. She picked up her plants and started hiking again. If she ever did get magic, her first spell was going to be cursing Duffy so that girl had to walk, too.

In a few steps, Fern screwed up her face. This wasn't like her. She hadn't even had thoughts like this about Raven, and his attitude begged for cursing. Well, she'd certainly never go anywhere alone with this girl again.

Around the next corner, she broke out of the shrubs. A

field of wildflowers spread across a gentle slope, the path rising in zigzagging switchbacks, dry and firm. Fern hiked along quickly, trying to make up lost time. Seeing the familiar plants calmed her. She knew them all—buttercup, harebell, devil's bit and knapweed, among others—so she'd have lots to talk about with Lady Soila. They'd trade plants, and Duffy would take her home.

Fern turned another switchback corner and spied a different plant. She bent to inspect the dark, five-lobed leaves and cluster of small, creamy-white flowers growing a little taller than her knees. It reminded her of spiraea.

Grrrr.

The growl rumbled, close.

Fern's gaze shot toward the sound. Not five feet away, squarely in the middle of the path, stood a badger, lips curled back in a snarl.

She straightened and inched back, the edge of the cape swinging between them, a flimsy barrier.

The badger stepped forward. His black-and-white-patterned face rose, his nose sniffing.

Oh no. She froze. What had Gran said about the UK's wild animals? With the badger staring back, Fern couldn't think, and when he took another step toward her, she backed up too fast, stumbled over her feet and fell on her rear, dropping everything.

Another snarl broke from the badger as he leaped—backward.

"*Ahhh!*" She snatched at the bag, dragging her plants as she scrambled away. "Nice badger. There we go. You're over there, I'm over here, and we both have plenty of room to get away from each other. You take the path, and I'll cut across the grass."

The badger growled again, sharp teeth bared.

Oh, damn, damn, damn. Her hands were shaking, and worse, tingling was spreading up her arms. She clenched the bag tighter. "Or not. I'm not going to hurt you. I just need to see Lady Soila about some plants."

The badger unwrinkled his snout and plopped into a sit.

What the heck? Fern bit her lip.

The badger sniffed again, raising his pointed black nose as far forward as it would go and poked at the cape between them.

"Uh, you can have the cape. It'll make a nice bed, I'm sure." Fern got her feet under her and crouched.

The badger cocked his head, looking from her to the wool fabric.

"Take it. Really. I only need the bag of plants to trade." He seemed to be listening to her. Maybe. At least he'd stopped growling and moving forward. Was he afraid to cross the unfamiliar material? She straightened slowly and, when that went well, sidled back a few steps. The badger sniffed at the cape again, then settled back on his haunches, back flattening into a broad platter of gray fur with its solitary white strip cleanly splitting it.

I won't run or turn my back on him. Better to step to the side, off the path, and angle her way uphill with the badger in sight. "You're a beautiful animal," she crooned. Hilda always liked hearing that. "Yes, I've never seen such a beautiful coat." The badger cocked his head. He was listening—and he liked the compliment, too. *Probably a stress-induced fantasy, Fern.* Her whole body was zinging with nerves. *Just make the first step and go.*

Ever so slowly, she lifted a foot and put it on the grass. She shifted her weight to take the next step.

The badger's head flipped around, his lips pulled back, and he rose, snarling. She froze. He looked pointedly at her feet. In a klutzy shuffle, she landed both on the path again. The badger lowered to a sit and sniffed at the cape again before looking her placidly in the eye.

This was crazy. Clearly, the badger didn't want her cutting across the meadow. If he didn't leap at her after that wild dance, he probably wasn't going to. "Well, how am I supposed to get up there, then?" She jerked a thumb toward the top. "I've gotta trade these plants for one of Lady Soila's. What'll it take to get you off the path?"

In answer, the badger pawed the cape pocket and then backed off the path between two bunches of grass and stared up at her.

"Duh. I get it. You don't want the cape. Not with your fur coat. You smell my Snickers. Food, right? You want food?"

The badger laid his head on his front paws, looked up with a most mournful expression and whimpered.

Oh. My. God. She, Fern Fields, was having a conversation with a badger. Wait until she told Beri about this. With a grin, she set aside her bag, jerked the cape to her and got out the candy. The badger didn't take his eyes off of her while she unwrapped it and placed the chocolate bar on the path between them.

"It's yours."

Daintily, he walked forward and picked up the candy. Then the badger turned his back on her and disappeared into the tall grass.

With trembling hands, she picked up her bag and stepped

carefully past the spot he'd been. Among thoughts of magic and how this might mean she really had some, the most bizarrely practical consideration cropped up: She shouldn't be giving wild animals people food. But, shoot. Just how much junk food was this badger likely to eat in his lifetime? Not as much as the ground squirrels at Rocky Mountain National Park.

Minutes later, she topped the rise. Across the shallow basin of open meadowland was a nice little pond about the size of hers, vegetation crowding the perimeter. At the far end of this islet, a grove of trees grew on a higher rocky outcrop. They looked like the oak and birch mix from the Isle of Giuthas. Lady Soila's property was nice, but deserted. Not even a sign of a house. So where was Duffy?

She'd taken a few more steps along the path, debating whether to shout, when movement above the trees caught her eye. A figure in black was flying off. Not Duffy, but—

"Hey!" She began running. *No, not after that ordeal.* "Wait!"

"Fern! Over here." Duffy trotted to meet her. "Everything's set. You took so long, and Great-Gran had to leave. But she said the trade would suit her. She left this." Duffy shoved a piece of paper at her. The words *Filipendula ulmaria* were scrawled across it.

"This is it? The ratna?"

"Yep. I told you whatever Sir Snap wanted, she wanted." She rolled her eyes. "Old people are so competitive. Come on, she said you'd find it in her seed storage room." Duffy gave a winning smile, pivoted and walked back the direction she'd come.

Fern stared after her. She'd never met anyone so on and

off, so helpful one minute, so disappointing the next. But she followed. Her elusive ratna was within reach.

Duffy led the way to the towering rocks. Tucked right up against them was a little cottage made of the same dark stone. No wonder Fern hadn't seen it. The front patio was warm in the morning sun, the front door propped open and inviting.

"She asked you to put the plants in here so they wouldn't dry out." Duffy motioned Fern around the side of the cottage and opened the lid of a wood box. Inside was a trough with water in the bottom.

Good, it was cool, exactly how the plants should be stored. "Lady Soila thought of everything. I wish I could have met her." Fern lowered the bag, and Duffy closed the lid.

"Maybe another day," she said vaguely and headed around front. Sunlight reached through the windows over the sink in the main room to the fireplace and rockers, looking restful after Fern's hike, but Duffy didn't stop. She breezed down a short hall, opened a wooden door and flicked on the light. Shelves lined the small walk-in closet, their surfaces filled with labeled jars of seeds.

"Great-Gran didn't have time to find the jar, so she said for you to help yourself. You can take all of them, because she'll be harvesting more from the plants going to seed. She invited you to collect some, but I told her you don't know what it is."

Fern looked at the paper again and scanned the jars. Faded, spidery handwriting on their labels matched the note. Luckily, the letters were neatly formed. "They don't seem to be in alphabetical order. Sorry, but it might take a while."

"That's all right. You getting seeds doesn't bother me."

Fern decided to ignore the odd comment. Selecting the

shelf level with her nose, she started checking labels. "Thanks. Do you think I could have a glass of water?"

"Sure, I'll get it." Duffy returned in a half minute and set the glass on a shelf. "Think I'll get one, too."

"All right." Fern had this figured out. The plants were grouped by family. She wished she had her field guide to look up the name Lady Soila had left and was about to ask Duffy if her great-grandmother had one when she heard a faint metal click.

The door had shut. Fern grabbed the latch to open it. A jolt of electricity zapped her.

"Yee-ouch!" She snatched her hand back. The shock had been more intense than Colorado's winter static. Thank goodness both of them weren't inside. "Hey, Duffy! Something's wrong with the door." There was no answer, so she called again. "Duffy? Can you hear me?"

A faint thud sounded outside the door, then silence.

17

Trapped

Duffy! You there?" Fern pounded on the wooden door. Surely the noise would rouse Duffy from a faint? Or had she left? Fern heard nothing from outside the seed room.

Alternating between shouts and pounding, she tested the old-fashioned metal latch and received a second jolt. The closet contained only the jars, a stack of blank labels and a tattered book. She used it, a jar and then her shoe to press the latch, but each transmitted the shock just as strongly.

"It's got to be magicked," she muttered. "Because this certainly isn't natural."

One throw of her shoulder against the wood confirmed it was solid, and the pain of the impact was her undoing.

Heart hammering, she sank to the floor, face hot, throat raw, hands and shoulder aching. Duffy had deliberately locked her in, betrayed her.

Ohmigod, what was wrong with her? Fern slid her hand to her pocket—no phone. Damn. She'd left it at home, forgetting since she never used it at Gran's. Probably wouldn't work out here anyway.

She sat for a long time with her head propped against a shelf, staring at the rows of jars, their contents brown and dry behind the paper labels glued on the outside.

Trapped. Like a seed, alive inside a plain wrapper. If she

were like a seed and had a magical energy inside her, she could wish herself out of here.

Fern's hand found her pouch and fingered the teardrop beneath the soft leather. But Willow had said the destinations were set. Even if they weren't, would she be able to control the magic for pereporting? She could definitely imagine getting back to Hillux. Finally, Fern dropped her hand.

She hadn't found the ratna, the *Filipendula ulmaria* on the paper. First, she'd focus on that, then she'd deal with breaking out of this trap Duffy had set. A wave of dread rolled through her, like heading off to finals. She made herself stand and picked up the book she'd tried on the latch—Lady Soila's wildflower field guide. The well-used book had lost its cover, and the edges were soiled, making it blend with beige-papered jars of seed. She'd found it by pure dumb luck.

Fern flipped through the index at the back, located *Filipendula ulmaria* and turned to the proper page. She found the right entry. "*What?* No way, Mom."

Filipendula ulmaria—the ratna—was meadowsweet. *Meadowsweet.* Mom's pet name for her echoed from every conversation she and Mom had had: *Don't feel guilty, my meadowsweet... You keep doing what you love, meadowsweet, get into a good college and have the life of your dreams... You're growing up so much, my meadowsweet.*

Of *course* it was a real plant. Mom had said it was a plant from home, from Ireland. Fern's tired laugh caught in her throat. Everything from this weekend—from the weeks working and months of planning—came barreling down on her. They'd worked so hard, and she'd come so close. Gran would be devastated. A sob ripped through Fern, and she collapsed to the floor.

Curled on the hard stone, she clutched her pouch and cried. If only she were curled up with Mom, but she wasn't, and wishing that might not get her home in one piece. Lying there seemed to be all her aching body could do. And cry.

At last, she couldn't even do that. She wiped her face, hauled herself up, found the glass of water Duffy had brought her and drank it all before opening the field guide again.

Meadowsweet was a member of the rose family, widespread throughout Europe and once classified in the genus *Spiraea.*

Spiraea? She'd seen this plant with the white flowers just before she'd encountered the badger. The leaves were similarly divided ones. *Yes.*

Fern marked the place in the book with a blank label. It sucked that Duffy might make her miss the deadline to show the council she'd planted her ratna seeds, but eventually someone would let her out. They'd have to see reason that the delay wasn't her fault, and if Fern had the seeds... She restarted her hunt for the seeds again, in case Lady Soila had labeled the jar with the common name meadowsweet, not the scientific name. Even though Mom's nickname for her would have stood out, now, with her heart racing, she didn't know if she'd seen that particular name on her first check and wanted to make sure.

I've got to slow down, look at every jar. Still, she was trapped in the small closet. "I wish someone would hear me and let me out," she shouted.

She'd shout again each time she turned a shelf corner, and often in between, just in case *someone* was nearby, but her throat was getting sore. Without a watch and no windows to judge the time, she didn't know how long she worked. But it was long. Six shelves ranged from eye level down to her knees. She checked those before starting on the two higher ones. There was no stool in the closet. Lady Soila must bring in a chair when she needed to, for Duffy's great-grandmother couldn't be taller than she was. Fern had to reach up and lower each jar to read its label. It took twice as long.

On the tenth jar of the highest shelf, *Filipendula ulmaria* was written on the top line and *Meadowsweet Ratna* on the second.

Hands shaking, she tilted the jar—it was empty.

Fern slammed her fist against the door. "Ohhh," she moaned and cradled her aching hand. Her knuckles were red, some split. Staring at the jar, Fern sagged against the door, her fit of anger throbbing through her arms and shoulders. "Tomorrow I'll be black and blue, and I don't even have the seeds to show for it."

Her sour feeling had just as much to do with being thirsty as her emotions. Trying not to think about water, she replaced the empty jar and glared at the next one on the shelf. Should she continue to look?

Well, she still didn't have any ratna seeds, but she knew its name, what it looked like and where to get it. If only the plant she'd found earlier in bloom had been further along. She snorted. "There haven't been any other duplicates, but I seem to have plenty of time to search."

A faint yip sounded outside the door.

Had someone come with a dog? "Hello? I'm stuck in the closet," she yelled despite her sore throat.

A scuffling answered, followed by a thump and a familiar whimper.

"Badger?" Her hopes of escape sank.

18

Comeback

The badger yipped again and scratched at the door, the sounds higher than he ought to be able to reach, even standing on his hind legs. In fact, as high as the—

"Don't touch the latch!" Fern shouted. "It'll electrocute you."

Hold it. She was talking to an animal. Well, he'd seemed to understand her earlier, so like Beri had said, she did have magic, even if she didn't understand back. Fern squared her shoulders. "Careful, the black metal stings."

He let out another series of yips, no different than the first ones—not cries of pain.

"Good boy. The latch opens the door, but we can't touch it. We have to figure out some other way to open the door." Not that the badger would be able to help her there, but at least she wasn't alone anymore.

A thump sounded, followed by scuffling that grew fainter. He was leaving. So much for company. "Come back soon," she whispered.

A long time passed. Fern reread the field guide's description of meadowsweet until she'd memorized everything. Its other common names included pride of the meadow and lady of the meadow. No wonder the first Wizard of the Meadow had chosen it to infuse with magic.

The plant grew in damp areas and bloomed from June to early September. She'd seen one in flower, so maybe she could find another that had finished and set seeds already. It was worth a try...if she ever got out of here.

She'd moved on to reading about other British Isles plants when something scraped beyond the door, faintly, but her prison had been so quiet, she would've heard anything.

"Badger?"

Clunk. A yip. The scraping started up again.

"Oh, I'm so glad you came back. Did you see anyone else around?"

Clunk. His answer was a whimper.

No. Well, she hadn't really expected he would. "That's okay. It's good you're here."

After louder—and closer—scraping, a thud hit the door. A dull grating drew across it, over and over, with lots of grunting. In Fern's hurry to find the ratna, she hadn't paid much attention to what the hall leading to this room looked like, so she couldn't imagine what the badger was doing.

Then the latch began to rattle. It wavered up and down, then dropped fully down. Fern scrambled to her feet, her hopes rising, and then so did the latch, snapping with sparks.

Darn, the pain he must be feeling. That gave her courage to reach for the metal. It fell, but then immediately jiggled again.

The latch flicked down and stayed. Fern shoved the door. It banged into something solid, but it'd moved an inch, and she wasn't about to let it close again. She pushed with muscles built by digging and hauling, and the thing behind the door gave way.

It crashed, and she cringed until an excited yip followed.

Ducking her head through the foot-wide crack, she peered around. A sturdy wooden bench lay on its side, and beside it was a branch, freshly gnawed at both ends. Beyond, stood the badger. Their gazes met, and he shook all over like a dog after a bath, his lips pulled back into what looked like a grin.

Pushing the door wider, Fern squatted. "Oh, thank you, badger!" He leaped into her arms, licking her face with a long pink tongue. Together, they started to fall into the closet, but Fern scrambled for balance and lunged forward.

"Oh no. I'm not going back in there again." Cuddling the hefty badger to her, Fern scooted completely into the hall and leaned against the wall. "Thank you," she murmured through her sore throat. "Thank you so much." Her gaze fell on the branch again. Even wood would've transmitted the shock, so how had he stood it?

Then she spotted the nail lying nearby. Fresh cuts scored it in two places, like it'd been pinched between metal. The latch—yep, the latch had metal bits with holes to put a lock through.

She could have opened it after the badger had pushed out the nail. "I'm sorry you hurt yourself," she whispered to him, "but I really appreciate you freeing me."

In answer, the badger shook his head and gave her a last lick on the cheek before hopping off her lap. She righted the bench, moved it to prop open the door and—while still standing outside the closet—reached in and grabbed the field guide. Then she hustled down the hall and out the front door after the badger.

The sun hung halfway to the horizon, marking the time as late afternoon. Butterflies flitted over the flowers in the meadow, the gulls cried from the trees and, not too high up, an osprey carried a fish across the island before diving out of sight over the rocky edge.

Fern shook her head. She'd been trapped for hours. Duffy had probably left the island right after locking the door. "I've been had," she told the badger and lowered to sit with him on the warm patio slates. "I can't figure out why, or exactly how. Duffy brought me here to get the ratna and gave me the name of it. I bet she sent Lady Soila away. They may or may not have known that jar was empty, but it made a good ruse to get me into a locked closet. But why?

"Of course, she had no idea I'd have an ally on the island." Fern smiled and stroked the badger's long flat back. "You're a very smart and brave animal to release me."

The badger grunted and closed his eyes. She laughed. He was enjoying his praise and petting. Now that they'd become friends, the forty-plus-pound animal with sharp canines seemed no different than two-pound Hilda. Not that she'd put them in the same room.

Fern ran her hand over the badger's stiff guard hairs a last time and opened the field guide to the meadowsweet entry. "So, I just have to find another plant with a dried flower head containing mature seeds. I collect them and... Damn!"

She'd been so focused on escaping the closet, she'd forgotten she was still trapped—on the island.

Duffy had fixed her good. She'd likely taken the boat, since Fern recalled she'd pocketed the key. No one knew Fern was here. When Gran and Beri and Willow couldn't find her on the Isle of Giuthas, they'd assume she'd gone home to Colorado, where no one could easily reach her. Worst of all, Beri would think she'd broken her promise not to leave.

She should have told him or Willow her plans. A sob caught in her throat. But what good would crying do now? Fern wiped her eyes and went into the cottage in search of a tissue. She used the bathroom, washed her face and got herself and the badger some water. She helped herself to an apple from the bowl on the counter, and when the badger prodded persistently at a metal canister, she gave him a piece of meat jerky from it.

"Duffy hasn't beaten me yet," she whispered. Maybe, like Raven, she had some bizarre reason for wanting Fern to abandon Gran and the Meadows, but it wouldn't work. "I'm here to stay."

She thumbed open the field guide again to the meadow-sweet entry and held it up for the badger. "Remember this plant? The one I was looking at when you first saw me? Are there any others in Lady Soila's meadows?"

He cocked his head, his ears perked up, and he snapped out three short barks.

Fern laughed. "Right, there are. But listen, I have to find just the right one. The flowers have to be all dried up." She pointed to the flower in the picture. It was a long shot that he understood all of this, but he was looking, and he might be able to help her shorten her hunt so she could focus on getting off the island.

The badger trotted out the door, looked over his shoulder and yipped.

"I'm coming."

He marched along the path she'd taken to reach the stone cottage, then veered the opposite direction from where she'd climbed up, turning toward the pond on the far side of the top of the island.

Oh, yeah, ratna, aka meadowsweet, liked *wet* meadow-land. Lady Soila's pond was located at the lowest point of the islet, collecting rainwater before the water cascaded over the rocky edge. The vegetation surrounding it was varied and lush, and Fern slowed to search, her hopes rising. A hundred feet from the open water, she spotted a meadowsweet plant. Every blossom was full and fresh, and so were the ones on the next she found.

The badger barked, cutting through the roar of the water-fall.

"Impatient, are you? You know where more grow?"

The narrow path skirting the pond took them onto mushy ground, some parts open and grassy between shrubs and stands of reeds and rushes and even some water iris. She'd just planted many of these species at her and Gran's restored pond.

One of Fern's shoes sank. She hopped aside, landing on a clump of grass, and used more clumps like stepping stones. It wasn't like she was clean, but wet shoes would feel nasty. The badger just plowed through the water up to his short armpits. Fern giggled. Her new friend looked so serious and intent on the mission. Maybe she'd have her ratna seeds in hand soon, but for now, finding the next footstep took all her concentration.

Then the badger stopped. He bit out a string of excited yips and bowed to the ground, like a dog teasing to play. Fern tiptoed along on the higher hummocks to his side and looked at the plant.

Several of the meadowsweet flower clusters still had pet-als clinging like small tan peelings, but the central one had no petals left. Its dry pods were still closed, so the seeds must be intact. "Is it dry enough?"

Fern tested the brittle stalk. It snapped off cleanly.

"Yes!" She held it close. "Badger, you've done it. Thank—"

A shrill call cut the air, and a sharp object whacked Fern on the head.

"Ahh!" She stumbled, ducking and trying to see what had hit her. She fell, the badger's growls mixed with the shrieks of a bird. The large thing flew at her again, beak open wide and eyes blazing as it swung its legs and spread its talons.

An osprey.

Fern rolled away, and the ground beneath her disappeared.

In surreal slow motion, two ospreys dove after her. The rock of the cliff blurred, and the water cascading over looked motionless as she plummeted alongside the silvery threads. The narrow strip of beach rushed closer, the black rocks filling her view.

Her free fall bloomed into terror. "Stop, stop, STOP!"

The dark ground raced into a green flash of light.

19

A Change or Two

She'd hit the ground and died. Fern knew this for sure. The green color only meant she'd gone to her own personal heaven. The mist wrapped her like soft petals and held her warm and safe in its hazy chlorophyll folds. The fresh fragrance of spring filled her nostrils, and a steady thrumming comforted her like the purr of a cat, or the life flow of the plant she'd gone to live in.

And that was okay. Living—or dying?—in a plant would be peaceful.

"Fern!"

The distant call of her name woke her with the dreamlike sensation of falling. She landed with a small thud, cold rocks pressing against her arms and cheeks. Goose bumps rose across her skin. Her hands hurt, so she kept them balled into fists. Crashing waves lulled her toward sleep again, but the deep, garbled shouting continued over a motor puttering in the distance. She lifted her head and looked around the shadowy beach. When chilled droplets whipped her face, she closed her eyes again.

The motor cut off. The voices sounded clearer now. They called her name.

What was going on? With a groan, she stretched an arm and rolled over. In the shadow of the looming cliff, a pinpoint of light shone, and three angels descended on her.

If she was dead, why did she hurt?

"Fern! She's moving. She's alive!"

Oh. That was why.

The beam of a flashlight darted over her, forcing her eyes closed. Three voices talked at once, Beri's strong among them. "Don't move her until we're sure nothing is broken. Mr. Grouse, you'd best check."

Hands ran over her limbs while Beri spoke soothing words and stroked her hair. A shiver ran through her, and she blinked her eyes open. How badly was she hurt? Her head pounded, but beyond that, only her shoulders and hands ached.

"No cuts or blood seeping." Mr. Grouse bobbed his head furiously. "Here now, can you move your feet?"

She flexed her ankles and then bent her knees.

"Good, no damage there, and we've seen your arms working. You look like you took a muddy slide after a disappearing heron. Caught in a rip, were you?" Mr. Grouse moved his fingers delicately over her scalp, and she flinched when they hit a tender spot. "Ho, what's this?" The light played over the top of her head. "Bit of blood and a goose egg?"

"Dangerous swelling?" Beri asked.

"Nothing to worry about. It's not even goose egg-sized. That's just a phrase. Fern's lump is more of a half robin's egg. Ready to sit up?"

Beri lifted her by the shoulders, but the world was woozy, and she slumped into him.

"A mite of a pick-me-up, that's what this lass needs." Sir Snap held a flask to her lips. "Drink," he ordered.

The liquid burned her throat, tasting worse than Mom's

Irish Cold Cure. She coughed and sputtered a spray onto Sir Snap's legs, but enough of the whiskey made it down to send a charge through her body.

Sir Snap had skipped the lemon, cloves and honey. And water.

"Tha's it," he said. "Another shot, lass, and ye will feel right."

She shook her head and lifted her arm to block him. Pain flashed through her. "Ahh," she whimpered.

"What happened here?" Beri gently cupped her swollen fist in his warm hand. "Did you take a fall on your hands?"

"No," she mumbled hoarsely, her throat cutting with every syllable. "I hurt them banging on the door."

Sir Snap chuckled. "Ye knocked this door down with yer bare hands?"

"No, the badger let me out."

"Tha's a tale worth the tellin'," Sir Snap said with approval and waved the flask in a toast.

"Can you open your hands?" asked Mr. Grouse.

Fern did and found a crushed stalk, the ratna seed head. Her body sagged at the sight of it. Amazing, after this whole mess was over, she'd come away with what she'd set out for. She closed her hand and drew it in protectively. Unsure what to say, she looked at Beri.

"You need to keep those safe?" he asked.

She nodded. An instant later, Beri wrapped a blanket around her, crossing it in front almost papooselike, with her hands safely covered.

"You're a jump ahead, lad," said Mr. Grouse. "Good to keep her warm. Those hands can wait until we're back. Fern, we'll get some bruise balm on you, and the swelling will dis-

appear like magic. Ho-ho. Don't you worry, you'll be gardening again tomorrow."

Beri laughed, too, the first happy sound she'd heard from
him since they'd appeared on the beach. "Aye, lads. Let's get
her to the boat and back to the isle."

Boat? So that was how they'd gotten here, but how had
they even known where she was?

Mr. Grouse said he'd check the rip, and Sir Snap flew off
to a boat sitting offshore in the sunlit part of the ocean.
Numbly, she watched, still leaning into Beri—an experience
that would've been head-muddling all by itself. Nothing
would be better than snuggling her face into his neck, but she
stopped herself and settled for breathing in his spicy scent.

She hadn't died. Above the cliff, the sky was growing into
a bloom of pink. This beach area sat in shadow because the
sun had dropped behind Lady Soila's islet. Hours must have
passed since she'd fallen from the cliff like the waterfall Mr.
Grouse was studying.

What had happened in between? Why wasn't she hurt
worse? She was going to walk away from what should have
been her death or, at the very least, an emergency run to the
hospital. The rest of her day seemed long ago and practically
a tale, as Sir Snap had said.

Beri dipped his face to hers, his gaze suddenly fierce. "Did
Duffy fight with you? Hit you?"

He knew. Somehow, he'd found out and come to get her.
Happiness flooded her, but the horror of it pulled her emotions into knots. Fern bit her lip to hold back her tears, but
one trailed down her cheek. She shook her head and looked
away, trying not to embarrass herself.

Mr. Grouse interrupted further discussion. "Snap is steadying the boat, so let's go." He pulled a chain from one of his vest pockets and held out a slender tan rod to Beri—a distance peregrinator.

Beri breathed a low curse and then said louder, "You better take her, Mr. Grouse. I'm not practiced on an average day, so I dare not chance it now."

The stocky man tucked a hand under Fern's elbow. "Nerves a little shot, lad?" he asked Beri with a smile accompanied by much blinking.

Abruptly, the sound of the surf was fainter and a boat deck rolled beneath her feet. Fern stumbled. Sir Snap helped lower her to the bench seat on the same boat she and Duffy had taken that morning. Beri landed on the deck and wrapped another blanket around her legs before sitting down with one arm firmly around her. It felt nice to be so protected, and by someone who looked like a winged Greek god, no less.

"All set, then?" asked Sir Snap.

Fern closed her hand until the rough stem poked her bruised palm. She nodded.

Sir Snap steered the boat in a wide arc to turn away from Lady Soila's islet. Bright pinks, blues and oranges silhouetted the dark top-hat shape. The boat sped up, and she leaned into Beri, whose gaze never seemed to leave her.

"I did it," she whispered. "I got the ratna seeds. The badger found one plant that—oh no."

"What's wrong?" he asked with concern.

"The badger. He won't know what happened to me. He saw me fall."

"Sir Snap? Hold the boat."

They slowed to a stop and rocked with the waves, both

men in front turning to look at her along with Beri.

Shoot, this would sound kind of stupid, but... "A badger befriended me. When I got locked in Lady Soila's seed closet, he rescued me. I know this sounds silly, but he seemed to understand what I was saying, so..." They were all grinning at her. *Geez, they must think I landed on my head.*

Beri gave her a gentle squeeze. "Go on, Fern. You know I talk to animals. Of *course* they understand."

"No one here thinks it's silly," said Mr. Grouse.

Sir Snap gave a hearty chuckle. "Jus' don't try tellin' this story to the humans where ye come from, lass."

She heaved a sigh and smiled back. "I won't. Anyway, I told the badger I needed to find a ratna plant that had gone to seed and showed him the picture. He led me to one and I picked it, but the osprey whacked me, with his beak, I guess, and I rolled off the cliff. I'm sure the badger wonders what happened."

Now they were just staring. Had she gone too far with what she believed the badger might be thinking? "Fine, maybe he's not wondering what happened to me, but it would make me feel better if he knew I'm all right." No one moved. "Or, we could just see if he's still up there?"

Blinking, Beri shook his head. "Er, aye. I'll do it. Where was this?"

"Near where the waterfall comes over the cliff, there's a pond. We must have been closer to the edge than I realized."

"The *top* of the cliff," Mr. Grouse said flatly, and for once, he didn't blink.

Oh. Fern looked back at the waterfall.

"You fell from the top of the cliff?" Beri asked.

Fern closed her eyes. "I-I thought I did, but I didn't die. I don't remember hitting the ground."

After a pause, Sir Snap said, "Perhaps ye didn't. Stranger things have happened to Windborne. More important is dealin' with those crazed birds. Wha' got inter that osprey, attackin' someone like that?"

"Nesting. They have two half-grown chicks right at that waterfall." Mr. Grouse's head dipped multiple times. "You got too close, and they were protecting their young. It wasn't malicious."

"I don't suppose," she said. "But you'll be careful, won't you, Beri?"

"I'll be larger with my wings," he said, "so it won't be an issue." But he was frowning. "Could you wait until I return to tell the rest of your story?"

There wasn't anything else to it. She'd fallen and woken up when they came. Yet right now, she'd do anything for Beri, so Fern nodded.

He flashed her a brilliant smile and did the winged Greek god thing again. When he became a dot above the cliff, she closed her eyes. She'd almost dozed off in her corner when a low comment from Mr. Grouse pulled her back.

"Incredible change has come over that lad."

"Aye, I couldna agree more," said Sir Snap. "He's been on three of my projects, absorbs a hell of a lot of information and regurgitates ideas when ye ask, but he never was one to lead."

Listening in wasn't usually Fern's thing, but right now, she couldn't exactly leave.

"That's what's different," Mr. Grouse said. "When he marched into the meeting and practically dragged us out, I lost every doubt I had about Beri's ability to take his place.

Not that I haven't always liked the lad, but he's been a fol-
lower. Tonight, he had sound reasons for needing our help
and had the trip exactly plotted."

"And was willing—even eager—to go himself. Canna tell
ye the trouble I had gettin' the lad off the isle for that work
we did on the mainland."

"At least you succeeded." Mr. Grouse gave another of his
low chuckles, and she could imagine his blinking eyes. "I still
can't get him off the isle with me, nor can anyone else. Maybe the motivation has come in the form of this pretty
stranger? She's been good for Lark, and I think she's been
working the same magic on our lad."

"Aye, he's keepin' a close eye on her. Don't suppose we'll
ever know how she got herself into this."

"I assumed it was the rip I helped repair at the base of the
falls, but the seal looks solid."

"Ach. I'll be hard-pressed not to question Soila, but ye are
right. The lad deserves to handle it. How do ye think she
survived the fall?"

Fern held her breath, straining to hear Mr. Grouse's low
response.

"Whoever got her onto the islet must have saved her,
even if he brought her here for some wicked purpose."

Then Duffy had caught her? Magically?

His voice turned speculative. "Do you know any others
with the password to enter these waters? It's fortunate Beri
remembered I come out here to assess her birds every season. Here he comes now."

She shouldn't be hearing this stuff about Beri, but why
was he afraid to go off the island?

The boat tilted when Beri landed. "Asleep?" he asked.

"As soon as ye left, lad. Get a hold on her again so she doesn't end up sprawled in the bottom of the cabin, and I'll take us home."

"Was the animal there?" asked Mr. Grouse.

"Aye. He'd worn a track pacing the edge he was so beside himself. He's formed a strong attachment to Fern over a gift she gave him called Snickers, a food he'd never tasted before."

"I wonder what tha' could be?" asked Sir Snap speculatively, while Mr. Grouse laughed.

20

Reasons and Ratna

Fern woke on Gran's couch to Hilda's shrieks, while Beri tried to hush the guinea pig. Outside it was dark, so she hadn't slept long.

"Hey," he said when he noticed her movement. He carried Hilda over and sat on the floor near her head. "I told Hilda you're fine, but she says you smell wrong." He released the guinea pig onto the couch. She sniffed and sneezed before licking Fern's cheek.

"Another animal—the badger, of course." Beri patted Hilda's head. "He won't be coming here."

"Sweet piggy," she croaked. "I'm okay."

"Spells! You can barely talk. Willow will know what to do for your throat. She and Raven are collecting supplies to fix dinner here. But I'm glad you're awake, Fern. There's something I want to discuss before they arrive."

Hopefully the same thing she wanted to discuss. "Duffy?"

"Aye."

"Did she tell you where to find me? Or did you see me again with your magic?"

He scowled and picked up Hilda. "Duffy dogged me for hours today, hanging around dressed like she was headed to a festival and talking while I worked. I couldn't believe she didn't have any of her own work to do, and several times I asked her why, hoping she would leave." For a moment, he concentrated on scratching Hilda's chin, before he set her loose on the floor.

"Duffy finally said spending time with me was the most important thing in her life. I've been over this many times with her, and I thought last winter she understood. I don't romantically like her, and I can tell she doesn't feel that way about me either. Prebonding with an islander seems to be a passing fancy she returns to when the mood strikes her. Anyway, I told her again, very thoroughly, and she left in a fit of anger."

Yes. Fern's heart was taking a flying leap just as Beri darted a look at her, so she forced her face into a more serious expression. This was serious, actually. Duffy locked her up *and* nearly got her killed because... "She wants to live on the island?"

He nodded, not meeting her gaze. "Here, can we treat your hands while we talk? I'm afraid to have Willow see the state they're in." He helped Fern sit up, then unwrapped the blankets from her.

The crock of healing balm Gran kept, along with other supplies, sat on the coffee table. Beri probably suggested working on her hands so neither of them had to look each other in the eye. He knelt in front of her and arranged a towel and a bowl on her lap. "Put your ratna seeds in this first."

She lowered one swollen hand to the bowl. Taking her hand in his, Beri eased up her thumb. A stab of pins attacked her purple fingers, and Fern bit down to keep from crying.

"How did you find out where I was?" she whispered.

"I finished my work and came to look for you. I couldn't find you. I worried you'd gone home." One by one, he straightened her fingers, and broken tan bits of the plant rained from within. He dusted her palm and each finger to shed every piece. "The more I thought about you, the clearer the image came. As you guessed," he said quietly. "Sorry for spying again. It's only happening if I really focus on you. I can stop it, and I have been."

Darn it, he was so nice, it was impossible to be mad at the guy. But Fern kept her eyes on her hands when she cleared her throat the best she could. "I'm not upset about you watching me this time," she said hoarsely. "I made a mistake in not telling anyone where I was going."

When he spoke, Beri's voice held a frustrated edge. "You should be able to trust a Windborne in your community, but—although it doesn't really excuse her behavior—Duffy is a visitor to the isle. I suppose you can tell we vary like humans do." He shrugged. "After all, we are still people."

Your community? Except for Gran, she hadn't thought of Giuthas as her community. Before. Now, she'd like to know these people better, especially—her gaze darted to Beri's face, then away as she flushed.

Don't go there. Not yet.

Would he—the islanders accept her if she had no magic? "I'm also a visitor. Duffy has no allegiance to me."

Beri shook his head. "That's not the way of it. You are kin to Lady Lark, though Duffy doesn't know exactly how."

"Raven doesn't see it that way."

Beri clenched his teeth. "He will. But I have a more important matter to discuss before Raven arrives." He lifted the bowl and tilted it so she could see the seeds.

Fern smiled. "Not many, but I've got ratna."

"They're damp. You do plan to plant them soon, right?"

"Tonight."

"Good." He traded the seed bowl for the crock. "Next, the balm." He slathered the greenish cream over her hands and on the welt on her head.

The healing heat of the cream eased her pain, enough that she was able to spread her fingers and rest them on her towel-covered lap. If only she had the nerve to ask him to put Gran's ointment on her shoulders, but that would be too personal. She'd do it after the shower she desperately needed. Thank goodness the washable blanket lay between her muddy jeans and Gran's couch.

Beri set aside the crock and sat back on his heels. "Back to the story. I saw you in a pantry taking jars off a shelf and thought you were at your Colorado home. I was upset you'd left and couldna help myself. I looked again. That time, you were crying, and I knew something was wrong. I kept watching. You started reading about flowers. I knew the only flower you were still looking for was the ratna, which you'd asked me about yesterday when Duffy was here. I put that together with how she'd flirted this morning and went to find her. It took some doing, but I could tell she was behind what happened by the way she refused to answer questions about you. When I recalled she'd mentioned talking to her great-grandmother today, she finally owned up to her stunt."

"Why didn't she come back out to Lady Soila's to undo what she'd done?" Fern wished her raw throat didn't make her voice so harsh. "Was she afraid of facing me?"

"I think it's me she's afraid of at this point. I was furious to learn Duffy stranded you when—" Beri looked everywhere but at her.

When what?

Before Fern could ask, Beri raised an index finger. "Let me finish. Duffy also made sure Lady Soila left before seeing you, so her great-grandmother wouldna know you were on the islet and you'd be trapped there until after she returned from the Gathering. Lady Lark would be expecting you for the final interview with the council and nae know where you were. Her work, your work, all her plans would go awry and possibly shift the approval to another person. That would truly crush your grandmother. Things Duffy never considered, because the girl too frequently plunges into ideas on mere whims."

"What did she plan to tell Lady Soila when the woman found me? I sure would have told her what Duffy did."

Beri shook his head helplessly. "I asked her the same. Said she hadna thought that far ahead. Unbelievable. Again, nae an excuse, but if you have nae noticed yet, Duffy is nae the best at analyzing situations."

"Not even thinking about the shape I'd be in after a weekend locked in a closet?" she croaked.

"The door was spelled to open at sunset so you'd have access to Lady Soila's house." Beri leaned forward, his gaze fixed and compelling, and Sir Snap and Mr. Grouse's talk about him becoming a leader flashed into her head. "'Tis nae my place to tell you what you can and canna say about what happened and where you found your ratna, but can I make a recommendation?"

Fern wrinkled her nose. "Like when you asked me not to mention falling into the rip energy, does this suggestion mean forgetting Duffy was involved?"

"It does. Right now, only you and I and Duffy know the truth. If she had pushed you off the cliff, of course everyone would need to know. Windborne have laws about attempted murder, too. But that was an accident. Her reason for trapping you there, if it became known, would only add fuel to what is already a bad situation for me."

"You're in a situation with Duffy that's worse than her pulling this scam?"

"By scam, you mean trick, right?" Beri smiled a little. "Since there are no other lasses my age here, the isle elders have been...*encouraging* me to give prebonding with Duffy a try. She wants to do it, but I do'na."

Now Duffy's cryptic remark about a strong, rugged element made sense. That was Beri.

"You are nae familiar with our ways," he said softly. "Sometimes, all it takes is one youth to say they're interested and the elders insist on a year's trial. Though her plant trial a year ago didna succeed, she meets the energy requirements." He tapped his chest. "My energy is already bonded to the land. 'Tis well known I do'na intend to leave. They believe she would settle here with me. If we bonded, they would find land for us."

Damn. Duffy might still have to deal with the enclave's "outdated" requirements, but she'd have more interesting plants on Giuthas.

"But I do'na think she will. She likes a busier lifestyle. And I...do'na."

That fit with what Duffy had said about liking modern comforts, but why was it Beri wouldn't leave the island? Better stick to the topic. "If she meets the energy requirements and wants to live here, can't they just let her?"

"In her prior trial, her energy didna bond to the plants," he explained patiently. "It has to bond to our plants, animals or some part of our natural cycling to be available to the isle and be used by the community."

"Her soils project—would that make a bond?"

"If she engaged magically with her sample plots." He sighed. "I hope she has. She's flighty, but nae a bad sort."

"But if she fails, there's nothing you can do to stop her from attempting to prebond?"

He drew a breath. "If Lady Lark finds out what Duffy did to you, she could make significant trouble for Duffy. The deal I'll propose to Duffy is for her to tell the elders she's nae longer interested in me. In exchange, you and I won't tell what happened, and Duffy won't be banned from the Isle of Giuthas."

"You mean because my mom is the Witch of the Meadows, I'm special?"

"Exactly, and since you fell off a cliff and didna die, you must accept that you have magic."

Oh. If Duffy had been with Beri, she hadn't been on the islet. *I must have saved myself.* Fern fell back against the couch, pressing her hands to her forehead. *Ohmigod. I. Have. Magic.*

And ratna seeds. She just might be able to pull off this trial.

"Raven and Willow will walk through that door any minute. Will you do it, Fern?"

She looked up, and again, his compelling look sought her agreement. "What do I tell people about how I found the seeds?"

He leaned close, his voice intense. "All the more reason to keep quiet. Wait and see what happens with your seeds. If they grow, smile and say your magic led you to them. I've heard lots of Windborne use that line."

Fern stared at her hands. They looked much better. She clenched them experimentally. They felt better, too. So, she knew everything except... "I still don't understand why Duffy wanted to jeopardize my work with Lady Lark on the Meadows, or why she'd agree to your deal."

Beri seemed to be gauging what to say, frowning in a way that looked a little like pain. "She'll agree. She did it—" His gaze flicked away. "She did it because she's jealous. She saw that I like you."

Fern caught her breath. Beri liked her—*liked* her. She ought to say something back, but her brain had checked out.

"I ken 'tis a lot to ask—to hide her trickery, I mean. I'll be forever in your debt. I'll do your bracken removal and soil improvement for your planting. Whatever you want."

Say something, Fern! "I'd rather have you as a friend." As soon as she said it, she knew that wasn't what she really wanted.

Beri didn't meet her gaze. "Friends, then."

He didn't want that either. "Wait," she croaked. Her tongue darted out to wet her dry lips. Insistent throbbing in her ears almost drowned her thoughts—thoughts that she'd been lucky today. Lucky to find the seeds. Lucky to be alive. Why not press her luck? "How about more than friends?"

Rich green light flashed over him and disappeared. Beri stared at her, the only motion in his body the rising and falling of his broad chest. "That's okay, too," he said, his voice hoarse.

Okay? *Beri never said okay*, some stupid, practical part of her brain said, while the rest of her took a dive into la-la land, leaving her hot and jittery inside. And from the glow in his eyes, Beri looked like he'd just won the lottery. Compared to

Duffy stalking him, maybe he had. Maybe Fern had, too.

"Beri?" came a call from outside. Raven.

Bummer. She leaned close to Beri. "Don't tell Willow and Raven?"

"Nae," he whispered back. "What one knows, the other knows, and then Lady Mimosa knows. Then all of the other elders will know."

Giving a nod, she reached out and squeezed his hand. "Thanks for rescuing me." The screen door creaked open, and they dropped hands.

"Hello—ah, Fern," cried Willow. "What has happened? You've got blood in your hair." She rounded the couch, got a full view of Fern's dirty clothes and balm-smeared hands and recoiled. "Upon the Golden Orb! Beri. You didn't say she was hurt. I'll take her home so Mam can heal her."

"Nay," Beri said firmly. "Lady Mimosa is nae going to find out about this. Neither is anyone else. I do'na want Lady Lark having a heart attack."

"Neither do I," said Fern. "I'm going to be fine." Though her raspy voice didn't sound fine at all.

Willow's mouth opened and closed as her wide eyes flashed yellow. Then, with her lips pressed tightly together, she turned from Fern and glared at Beri.

He rose to tower above her. "Do'na cross me on this, Willow. 'Tis important, or I wouldna ask." Without waiting for her answer, he strode to the kitchen, where he and Raven banged about and started chopping vegetables.

Hands on her hips, Willow continued to glare after him. An onion scent had wafted over when she finally turned.

Fern beckoned to her. "Can you put this balm on my upper arms and shoulders? I didn't want to ask Beri, and I can't do it myself."

Willow gave her the same exasperated look she'd bestowed on her brother Ches. But she knelt on the couch and rubbed balm where Fern indicated. Then, in a calm voice, she asked, "What happened to you, Fern? Where did you go?"

"To get the ratna for the Meadows. It was difficult, but I was successful."

"The Meadows ratna." Raven came up behind them. "Are you sure?"

Fern narrowed her eyes. She hadn't seen him since they'd nearly fought again yesterday. So much had happened since then. She was in a good place now—she was friends with Willow, she had the ratna, she knew for sure Beri was on her side, and she'd gotten a sign that she did have magic. She could afford to put aside her animosity toward the guy who was likely her cousin. Besides, Fern didn't want to answer Willow's question.

"Yes. Very sure. *Filipendula ulmaria*." She pointed to the bowl.

Raven leaned over to peer into it, then with a sideways glance, he asked, "May I?"

"May you what?"

Raven straightened. He shifted his weight from foot to foot and stared at a spot over her head. Beri came to sit on the couch arm beside her, and when Fern cast a glance up, he was nodding encouragingly at Raven.

Raven said, "I am a Meadows. May I check a seed?"

Really? The guy had done a one-eighty. Given his politeness, she was dying to ask how exactly they were related. But she'd promised Gran secrecy, and talking about how they were related might flip Raven into rude again. This Raven was much easier to handle. "Yeah. Go ahead."

With a nod that seemed almost gracious, coming from him, Raven sat beside the coffee table and took the bowl in his lap. He selected a single seed and held it pinched between his thumb and index finger, then closed his eyes.

An orange-brown energy ball grew around the seed, and Fern sucked in a breath. The haze pulsed and swirled in much the same way as Beri's had done, but it matched the coloring of Raven's eyes.

Sparkles of light began to twinkle at the core of the ball.

Beri cheered, and Willow squealed and hugged Fern, the embrace a little painful considering her sore shoulders.

The glistening dots roved the ball. Fern had been focusing on the magic phenomena so intently she hadn't noticed the change in Raven's features until his shoulders sagged with a sigh.

His gaze met hers, and she was surprised to see a slight smile on his lips.

"Aye. It is the Meadows ratna."

21

Closer

After Raven verified the plant's magic, the evening became a celebration. Beri raided Gran's stash of kombucha and split a bottle so everyone could toast her, much to Fern's embarrassment. Then Fern drank herbal tea liberally laced with honey to soothe her throat and devoured Raven's vegetarian stir-fry. The onions, garlic, peppers and carrots were the only vegetables she recognized, but the other island crops were good. Especially the pine nuts from the Scots pinecones.

Mom would love these. Geez, she probably *had* loved them, growing up here...likely why Mom was vegetarian. The others confirmed that nearly all their food came from Giuthas, as Gran had told her. No one traveled to the mainland to shop. The Seas family—of which Sir Dolph was a member—transported the isle products to the closest Windborne settlement on the coast of Scotland. From there, they brought back staples, such as flour, baking soda and cornmeal, things that weren't practical or environmentally sound to grow and still maintain the isle's resources. Other things, islanders just did without.

How would she live without chocolate, pop and her favorite cereals? The significance of this thought caught Fern by surprise. With her rabbit hole, she could always get some...but that would be cheating on living like them. She and Mom had always planned on her going to college. She still wanted to, but now the idea to move here after graduation was growing stronger.

After another round of soothing tea, Fern knew this wasn't a decision for tonight. First, she and Mom had to clear the air about their secrets, and Gran's.

"Fern, will you sleep at Lady Lark's tonight, or do you wish to return to my house?" Willow asked. "Or, um, go home?"

Not home. It'd be too lonesome after all this excitement. "I'd rather hang out with you, but I should shower first. Avoid some questions, if you know what I mean."

Willow smiled. "Brilliant idea. Go ahead while we do the dishes."

Fern headed down the hall, but seconds later, Beri caught her arm. She turned, and her hand ended up in his.

Beri flushed red and dropped his gaze to their hands. "Hey, the swelling is down." He flipped hers over. "Your bruising has faded as well. You can do your planting tonight since they're back to normal." He let her go.

Not *quite* normal—not after he'd touched her. Tingling buzzed up her arm, and Fern edged away. "Yeah, thanks for reminding me. Will you tell Willow I still have to plant the seeds?"

"Fern? You're nae going...er, will you be long, uh, so I can tell Willow how much longer, you ken?"

It wasn't hard to guess what he'd wanted to ask. *You're not going home?* She smiled up at him. "Would you do me a favor?" Pulling her pouch from beneath her T-shirt, she unlooped the cord from her neck and wrapped it around the suede. "Will you hold this for me?" She held it out.

He didn't move, just stared with his mouth hanging open, so she put the pouch into his hands. "I have another set of clothes here to change into. Tell Willow fifteen minutes."

Beri's green eyes flashed, and he was transformed, looking as happy as he'd been when she'd asked about being more than friends. He raked his fingers through his unruly hair and gave her the lopsided grin she loved.

She wanted to kiss him. Her hands now vibrated so strongly, she was surprised the buzzing wasn't audible. Ignoring the sensation was next to impossible, so she crossed her arms and tried to get it under control before touching him again. How did you kiss a boy you'd met only days ago? One you hadn't even hugged? His arm around her earlier didn't count. That'd been injury support, and she hadn't put her arm around him.

Then Raven called, "Beri? Your turn to do the dishes." And it was almost—but not quite—a relief to break away.

She scooted into Gran's spare bedroom. Thank goodness she hadn't embarrassed herself by kissing him in front of Raven.

Fifteen minutes later, clean and wearing fresh jeans and a shirt batiked with fern imprints, she made a beeline for the bay window in the living room. She and Gran had converted it into a greenhouse by partitioning off the sunny tiled surface with heavy plastic sheeting and installing cross-spectrum lights.

Ducking around the edge of the plastic curtain, Fern flipped on the lights and opened a bag of potting soil she'd brought from Colorado. The plastic behind her lifted, and Raven joined her in the small space. Whatever he wanted, she was determined to be polite.

"Hi," she said. "Thanks again for dinner. It was great after such a long day." Oops. She hoped that didn't sound like an invitation to talk about how she'd gotten the ratna. Fern started dipping cupfuls of the black soil mixture into a seed tray.

"What is that?" Raven asked, his question more of a challenge.

"Potting soil," she answered warily.

"You can't grow ratna in that barren matter."

Her hackles rose. What he said was true—this seed-starting mix had been sterilized—but damn, she'd always used it. "I think I know what I'm doing."

Raven didn't back down. "I believe I know more about *magical* plants than you do." His words were biting, but somehow, his tone remained even. "A ratna bonds with the wizard and the land. You must...I'm asking you"—his voice dropped to a cajoling cadence—"not to take these amazing energy capsules you've managed to find for the Meadows and subject them to that lifeless substance." His gaze drilled into her. "Please allow me to fetch you soil, real soil, containing the life of our land."

Oh. This sourpuss who had opposed her very presence here nearly had her in tears with his perfectly eloquent and tender view of her precious seeds.

"Fine," she grumbled to hide her wavering voice. "I accept your offer." While waiting for Raven to bring the soil, she poked parsley seeds into the cells of the filled tray to start another batch for Hilda. Then she plucked a ratna seed and held it before her. How had Raven done what he'd done earlier?

Show your magic.

Fill with magic?

Nothing happened before Raven returned with a bucket of the Meadows soil. Its earthy smell filled the enclosed window. She kneaded her fingers into it and drew another deep breath. He was right. This rich, dark soil was what the ratna needed.

He watched while she filled a new tray. Raven had said he was a Meadows. Maybe he should... She shoved the bowl of seeds toward him. "You have magic. Use it to do whatever you all do for planting."

"I can't." Raven stepped back, tucking his hands up into his armpits and shaking his head. "That's against the rules. I can perform some of the physical labor, but growing seeds and plants has to be done by you. It's your trial."

She eyed Raven. "Tonight you're acting like you want me to succeed. Why were you so rude to me when we met?"

He narrowed his eyes in return. "Because you were late arriving. We'd waited hours, and I didna want to deal with an outsider on my family property." He looked at his feet. "Also, I was running late with my projects."

Annoyed about other stuff, and she had been in the way. *Sounds like something I would do.* Fern turned back to the seeds. In her hands, they still looked like plain brown husks.

If only I could do what Raven can.

Some bond it'd be with her minimal magic, but she planted one seed in each section of the tray, silently chanting, *Grow quickly.* When she finished, she filled their watering trays and slid them under the lights. At last, she turned to Raven with a little shrug. "All done."

He nodded thoughtfully, and the calm, slight smile from

earlier passed over his face. "Good job."

Fern returned from washing her hands and discovered Hillux was dark except for her plant lights. Out on the porch, Beri leaned against one of the posts, staring into the night.

"It'll be a minute before Willow returns," he said. "They're saying goodbye."

Oh. *Kissing* goodbye. Her gaze darted over the shadowy fields, but the two lovers weren't in sight. Geez, that left Beri and her free to—

He was holding out a hand to her.

Her stomach flipped pancakes, and she wanted to take his hand, but didn't. Somehow, she'd make a fool of herself, she just knew it, especially if he wanted to kiss. She wasn't ready for that. She'd never...

Something was in his hand. Her pouch. Right. She reached out to take it and stumbled.

He caught her. "Ach, watch yourself, Fern. You don't need another fall today."

"I don't," she mumbled, staring up, then looking down, anywhere, but...oh, shoot. She shouldn't *avoid* him, because as soon as the magic charm on her forehead told Mom all about her fabulous, nearly lethal adventure today, Mom was going to kill her.

Beri's hand on her forearm loosened to a gentle clasp, and he nudged her pouch into her palm. "I know how precious such a device is, especially for you, coming so far from your home."

Both of his hands were around hers, warm and caressing her fingers ever so slightly. She made herself not stare, to look up again, and managed to say, "Thanks for keeping it safe."

From his extra inches of height, Beri looked down solemnly. "Does nae having any other way to return to your mother make you nervous? I mean, no easy way. I'm sure there are human ways to get to where you live."

"It used to, but not so much anymore. I'm having fun here."

"Fun? With Duffy?" Beri laughed. "That's verra sporting of you, Fern."

Her lips curled into her obstinate look. "Yeah, well, how I feel is going to be no secret from Duffy, so maybe it will be sporting."

Beri grinned and shook his head. "I like your spunk. Just be sure one of us is there to keep her from blasting you with her energy."

That reminder sobered her. She'd *never* have the upper hand among these Windborne kids. "I forgot. A confrontation with Duffy won't be a wrestling match."

"Nae," said Raven, making her jump. He and Willow walked up from around the corner. "And that brother of hers isn't going to say, 'Fight fair,' like some lads we know."

"Eh, admit it. You were lucky I stopped you from zapping this lass." Beri dropped Fern's hand and snapped his wrist, fingers extended, as if throwing a ball. A stream of green magic shot across the porch.

She flinched back.

Raven fended off the energy blast with an orangey flash from his open palm and pointed his fingers, but Willow grabbed them.

"You two are scaring her." She elbowed Raven. "And you know how Mam feels about us putting down the newly allowed visitors, so don't get me in trouble by telling tales.

Come on, Fern. Let's go home and leave these boys to their games."

So she left without finding out what it would be like to kiss Beri—or even hug him good night.

Later that night, with her knees curled to her belly on Willow's window-seat bed, Fern listened to her friend's steady breathing. She couldn't fall asleep so easily and, ironically, not because of her incredible day, or even the amazing magic Raven had shown with the seeds. Unable to stop herself, Fern brought her pouch to her nose and again sniffed the wonderful spicy scent clinging to it.

Beri had to have worn it against his bare skin. The thought sent flutters through her chest and heat over her face. Grinning, Fern tucked the leather sack beside her nose on the pillow and snuggled into dreams of one particular winged Greek god.

22

Sparks Fly

A dull thud woke Fern. She lay still, listening, her eyes adjusting to the dark and moonlit areas of Willow's bedroom. A rustling of cloth rose and fell so softly she nearly missed it. Then Willow straightened and crossed the patch of light before the window.

She was fully dressed.

"Hey," Fern whispered, rising up on one elbow.

Willow froze and then turned to her. "You should go back to sleep."

"Are you going out, alone, at night?

"Don't worry, I've done it before. I won't be alone once I get there."

Sweet, rule-following Willow also has secrets? "Are you meeting Raven?"

"Aye, him and Beri, too."

Beri, too? Then this wasn't a date, but still... "Can't your mother tell you've been sneaking out at night?"

Now Willow really sighed and sank to the floor at her side. "I feel so bad. I-I'm hiding it from her...and some of what we've been doing."

"My foot?"

Willow nodded, her features crumpled in misery. "I'm not blaming you, but you recall that night we cleared your ditch? Raven was supposed to have completed this project for his trial. He didn't, but he told the elders he did."

"He lied to them?" Not that she hadn't done that herself, but in this small community? "That's bad." Fern patted Willow's hand. "Well, you are good at magic if you can hide it."

She wrinkled her nose. "Aye, but now he has to finish it, and the boys don't understand why it bothers me to lie to Mam. They are not heirs to a witch and therefore have no one holding them accountable. But they need me and my magic for this," she said, rising.

"For what?"

"A wildlife project. I'll be fine. You go back to sleep."

Fern threw back the covers. She wanted to see Beri again, but also if this was going to be magic with animals, she wanted to see it. "Wait, I'm coming with you." Oops, that would happen only if Willow agreed. "Please, will you take me?"

They faced each other in the moonlight, Willow studying her while rubbing one eye. *She doesn't trust me yet?* Fern took Willow's hands in hers and brought them up to her temples.

"Do it. Read me. I want you to know I'll help."

Willow pulled her hands free. "*I* believe you. It's Raven who can't let go of his worries. I'll take you, but prepare for him to grouse. He won't take chances, because this means so much to...well, it means a lot to all of us." She shrugged. "Sorry I'm not telling you anything, but I can't."

It didn't matter. This girl trusted her, and as strange and foreign as it was that Fern had come into their community, they were friends. Even if things didn't work out with Beri, they always would with Willow, and being friends with her would make it so much more fun to visit Giuthas.

"Great." Fern quickly changed, and together, they

sneaked downstairs.

Outside on the porch, Willow took out the glass globe. "We come and go from here since my mother does not approve of magic use in the house. But also, she won't detect me leaving." She gave a sheepish grin.

"I won't say a word, I promise." Smiling, Fern reached out a hand, then snatched it back. "Tell me about this place so I can visualize it?"

"It's Hillux."

Oh...*Raven's* wildlife project was in the Meadows? Why, when he had a place with Willow? Seconds later, the moonlit fields spread before them, stars dusting the night sky above the dark mountains. It was stunning.

Willow looked around and listened. "The boys aren't here yet."

Having followed Willow's glances, Fern spotted the plant lights in the bay window. It was stupid, really, but she wanted to make sure the soil Raven had brought didn't need more water. "I'm going to check my seeds."

Willow nodded, and Fern ducked into the house alone. Behind the plastic sheeting, the trays looked the same as when she'd left them. Well, it had been only a few hours. Fern returned to the porch. Willow was nowhere in sight, but she heard faraway voices. She strode toward them. "Willow?"

"Quiet," a deep voice snapped. "Down!"

Fern crouched in the tall grass. When Willow appeared a few yards off, Fern darted forward, careful to stay bent.

Eyes wide, Willow motioned for her to stop.

"What's—" she whispered, just as Willow put her finger to her lips and disappeared.

Someone tackled her. Falling, Fern twisted, trying to keep the upper position. They landed with a flare of green light. A sizzling sting ripped over her.

"Owww," Fern cried. Scalp prickling and goose bumps rising, she rolled, scrambling to escape, but her legs wobbled. She darted a look in case she had to fight...

The other person lay still. Slowly, he raised his head and shook it.

Raven.

Feeling like jelly, she slumped into the grass.

Willow reappeared close by. "I forgot the elders might be in the Meadows tonight. Two are left, and they're arguing," she whispered. "I'm sure they didn't see or hear us."

Raven sat up, holding his head. "Why did you bring this shouting fool?"

Fern rounded on him, as well as she could on all fours. "Did you have to smack me with magic?"

"I pushed you, no magic," he shot back. "That *zap* was your doing." For someone who wanted quiet, Raven was sure eager to argue.

"What are you two talking about?" whispered Willow.

Beri scuttled through the grass, calling, "The last of them have gone."

"I'm *not* the one with wings!" Fern said to Raven. "If something magic happened, it was your fault."

Rising on his knees, Raven jabbed a finger at her. "Well, I have news for you, lassie. I've never had *green* magic in my life. That flash was *you*."

"True." Beri squatted beside them. "I've lived with Raven and his dad for nine years, and I've seen naught green from the pair of them. You must carry green magic."

"*Me?* I ..." Fern pressed her fingertips to her temples. She'd seen a green haze during—after?—her fall from the cliff. *That stopped my fall.* Had she dreamed a seed surrounded her, or not? Its warmth, the floating sensation, the security, it had seemed very real at the time. It must have been. Because she distinctly remembered *wanting* to stop falling.

Wishing it.

"It saved me," she whispered. "I saved myself." Fern lowered her hands. They didn't look any different. And they felt like crap, numb from the tingling that ran through her torso to her toes.

Only Willow was smiling. Beri was frowning. Raven stood, fists balled at his sides.

"I have been keeping my energy reined in, but I see 'twas unnecessary." His voice was low and edgy. "Why have you deceived us? And tried to get me in trouble—ow!"

"You grump. *She didn't know.*" Willow smacked him on the shoulder again, and Raven flinched away.

Despite being unsteady, Fern scrambled to her feet. Another wave of buzzy feelings ran over her, worsening when Raven caught her gaze. He brushed past Willow, heading for Fern, but Beri stepped forward to block him, and Willow yanked Raven by the arm and hauled him around to face *her.*

She poked his chest. "We all forgot, admit it. We come casually flitting over here any night we please and forgot that, with the council in session, the elders would make rounds whenever it suits them."

Raven darted out of range. "I didna bring someone to this project who is not supposed to be here."

A yellow light burst from Willow and raced at Raven. An ocher shield flashed around him like a glowing bubble. Fern was already staggering back, her legs threatening to give out at any moment. If this was what magic did to her, so much for thinking she could handle herself.

Raven glared at Willow through his orange-brown dome.

She circled him. "We don't know that. You won't talk to her, and I don't blame Beri for not telling you what he's learned. You're so out of sorts, all we do is argue."

"Sorry," he muttered, throwing a glare to Fern.

With his attention diverted, Willow shoved her yellow-lit hands through Raven's magic. Sparks shot everywhere.

Fern ducked, stumbled and fell. Before her, green light flared. Beri stood between her and Raven and Willow's crazy fight, his arms flung wide in a protective curtain of magic.

"'Tis not just me you should be apologizing to," Willow snapped. "I know you. You didn't simply push her down to hide her. You're still upset Lady Lark has chosen her. Well, *I* have chosen *you*, and your path lies in a different direction. Unless you'd like to renegotiate that."

Sheesh, Willow had guts, despite looking so girlie. Fern got her feet under her and staggered toward Gran's house, intending to escape.

Beri clasped her elbow. "C'mere. We'll wait around the other side of Hillux for this to be resolved."

They left Raven and Willow yelling and hustled off, the green magic like a cloak at their backs. Out of sight of the others, Beri dropped his hand and reached back. The green shield disappeared. Fern stumbled, and he caught her arm again.

"Uh, thanks. I'm a little shaky."

"You have nae seen them go at it. It can be intense. Willow grew up in a family of boys, and she is nae afraid to swing magical punches." Near Hillux's back door, Beri helped her lower to the grass, then also sat.

Fern abandoned keeping a strong front and sank her head onto her knees. Her heart wasn't pounding, nor was she breathing hard, but she didn't feel normal enough to go home alone. Her whole body buzzed, as if a fire barreled through her veins. Then the worst tingling she'd ever had ran over her arms. "Oh, c-crap—"

Crack!

Fern jumped up at the thunderous sound, her first thought to get away. Her scalp prickled, and a burnt, electrical smell hung around her—

Magic. *Ohmigod, that was me.*

On his feet, Beri waved his hands. "Whatever it is, I'm sorry. I'll leave you be."

"Wait!" She grabbed his arm. "Beri, please!" Green sparks shot from her fingertips. She snatched back her hands, and the glow faded. "How do I stop it?" she pleaded.

His brow furrowed. "None of this is on purpose?"

"Of course not!" A tremor ran through her, the buzz building again.

"Aw, do'na fret yourself into another flash." He took her hands into his, grimacing when more sparks flew. He moved his hands to her forearms. "Close off your finger channels."

"I-I..." *Can't.* Her trembling lips wouldn't form the word.

"Magic is loose in you, newly so, I suppose," he said in a low, soothing tone. "If you canna see it the way we do, I can only suggest to think your way through to taking charge of it."

She closed her eyes to focus on Beri's solid hold and his deep voice, a lulling comfort in this scariness. By blocking everything else, she felt the strange feeling of something racing slow. She concentrated on just that. An image of spring green rivulets came into her mind, a fine network of glowing channels running throughout her body.

This was magic? *Her* magic? How exciting—

Like a dam breaking, the small streams flooded into a raging river. Fern opened her eyes in time to see green burst from her fingers like water from fire hoses.

Beri ducked away. "Spells, I thought you had it." He clasped her shoulders from behind. "Try again."

Take a breath and settle yourself. Fern calmed her body until the buzziness left her skin and only dribbled from her fingertips. She had to close them.

She visualized sealing over each tip, but just as one was blocked, another began leaking. Sparks escaped, once a burst of them. Beri jerked each time. He didn't drop his hold— thank goodness, because she still shook like her teeth would rattle loose.

Just when she thought she'd gotten them all, another flash shocked out.

"Spells," Beri muttered. "How can you be packing waves of energy and not know? I thought lasses were supposed to be all into noticing—"

"I notice plenty of things. Like how several times today flashes escaped you."

That shut him up, and it stiffened her resolve. *I mastered wrestling, the peregrinator and keeping a huge secret from Mom. I didn't buckle when Duffy tricked me. I can do this, too, just like I'll grow the ratna and keep the Meadows for Gran...*

"The ratna." Her hands glowed up again, but this time, it sent a thrill through her. "Shouldn't I put this on my seeds?"

Beri clapped a hand to his forehead, then opened the door for her. At the window, he swept back the plastic and stepped aside.

"What am I supposed to do?"

"Whatever feels right to your magic," he said quietly.

Fern held her glowing hands over the ratna tray. If only she could plant them again, but finding each seed would be a pain. The magic didn't sprinkle off when she shook her hand, so she stirred a finger in each cell and *thought* about the magic flowing to find the seeds.

No way to tell if it did, but that was what she had. She brushed off the dirt, along with a few sparks, and backed from the window.

Beri dropped the plastic into place.

Now, to stop this energy leak. Proving to Beri that she could would be nice, but heck, she wanted to prove it to herself and, even more, to Mom. Coming home with magic under control would make her argument much stronger. Fern squared her shoulders and imagined her fingertips, all of them at once, closed off, watertight. It took several tries, but she sealed them. She held still, like she did when pinning an opponent to determine whether she really had.

No green. Not even a tingling. A huge grin spread over her face.

Beri raised a brow in question.

"I've done it," she said. "I've sealed the channels."

He tapped experimentally at her fingertips. Nothing happened. "Aye, you have. I'm quite happy for you, Fern." He grinned and, unexpectedly, hugged her.

It felt incredible. She wound her arms around him, snuggled her face into his neck and hugged him back. He smelled so good, felt so warm, stood so tall.

Bolts of green energy gushed through her channels. Magic broke from her, not a tingling, but a warm flush across her skin. Even being a newbie, this felt *quite* different from the buzzing. *Let it be blushing, just simple human blushing.* She peeked.

Light—spring green—flowed over her arms and chest...and coated Beri's torso.

Oh. My. God.

Fern eased away from him. "Sorry, I..."

He also glowed, and emerald magic crept over to her and across her hands, still resting on him. Her fingers marked the difference in his magic versus hers, like petting two cats at the same time but not being able to describe how the textures of their fur were different, just that they were. You still liked both and kept petting both.

Willow had mentioned an energy exchange—she'd said that helped decide about bonding applications.

Her mouth formed into a little O, and her gaze met Beri's.

His mouth curled in a wry smile. "Ah, I showed you my magic, and now you've shown me yours. So what do you say, Fern?"

Her gaze dropped to his chest. In something that looked like half-set gelatin, clouds of green swirled together, wound around her stroking fingers in misty tendrils and surged back and forth like miniature waves. Fern was so dizzy from it all, she could hardly think straight. What did she have to say about this Scottish guy's magic?

"I like it," she whispered. And a smile crept onto her face.

Beri broke into a wide grin. "Aye, I do, too."

23

Raven

A squeal broke the quiet of the cottage. Fern and Beri jumped apart, snapping away the magical glow.

"Beri!" Raven snarled. "Where are your brains?" He yanked Beri to the door and marched him outside.

"You canna," Willow cried, pushing her nose to Fern's. "They'll quash you—unless you're in prebonding. Not without the approval from the office of... Fern, are you listening?"

Some office, somewhere. Whatever.

Willow lit into her like she had Raven—without the shoving—while Fern fought to gather her magic back under control. Beri liked her. More than liked her, so now she could go there. Mom would—ugh. *But Beri.* The thought of him sighed through her. Never had she been so open or honest to a boy.

This darned magic didn't hide stuff, at least not with her inexperience.

"Do you realize the trouble you can get into?" Willow paced around the living room, spewing words as fast as she walked. She woke Hilda. Giving a concerned squeak, the guinea pig scuttled to them.

Fern picked up the little animal and sat on the couch, stroking her soft fur, but Willow's tirade continued. "Look, Willow," she cut in. "I know you're trying to help me, but I don't even know what half these words mean. I get that we broke the rules. I won't hug Beri again until I, until…"

Willow stopped in front of her. "Until you make a pre-bonding application. In Magemoor."

Like her mother would go for that. Maybe she could be talked into it—it sounded like a basic dating agreement. "Right," Fern agreed. "I promise to do what you tell me. Would you please sit down?"

Heaving a put-upon sigh, Willow climbed onto the couch beside her and curled her feet under her, still perched to spring into action. "'Tis just I know how strict they can be. You've never seen this youth panel over in Magemoor. That's our closest Windborne city in Ireland."

"An entire city?"

"Shielded, of course. The humans see naught but a wind-blown blanket bog." She threw her hands up. "Well, it is naught but a windblown blanket bog. The isle is much nicer. The application is quick—as long as you have no marks against you—and then you can be hugging him all you wish."

"Yeah." Fern knew her grin was the obstinate one. Good thing Willow didn't know about that. "So that glowing thingy we did *was* sharing energy?"

"That *thingy!*" Willow leaned over and shook Fern's shoulders in a joking way. "Aye, you neonate witch! Raven and I are just getting the hang of it after a year of trying. You have magic for minutes and do it *before* you are even in pre-bonding. I can't believe it."

"Neither can I," Fern said dreamily. "It felt wonderful. Does it always feel so warm and…nice?"

"Aye." Sounding wistful, Willow slid down until they leaned against each other. "It's a good thing I like you—and Beri, too—so much, or I'd be really jealous of you matching energies so well."

They were still sitting shoulder to shoulder when the boys tromped in a few minutes later, and Fern was too tired to straighten or care what they thought. Surveying them, Raven took a stance before the couch with his arms crossed and a stern look on his face. Geez, here came more of his flak.

"It has finally happened, Beri," he said.

Beri came around to the front of the couch, too. "What's that?"

"Willow finally has someone to go all gushy with over love," he replied in a syrupy tone, cutting a grin to Fern. "Thank the Golden Orb. I canna stand it when she gets like this on meeeee!" Raven leaped and swatted at his rear like he had ants in his pants. "Stop it, Willow. I'm just jesting with you."

Looking very satisfied, Willow rose and stood before Raven as he squirmed. "Apologize," she said sweetly.

Laughing, Beri plopped next to Fern.

"What's happening?" she asked in a hushed voice.

"Ah, she is doing something twitchy to him. Something I prefer not to ask about, you ken." Beri petted Hilda, and she churred for him. He leaned in closer, putting his arm on the couch behind Fern.

Aw, just being beside him was nice. If they got Mom to agree to this prebonding, it would be like having a boyfriend. Wait a sec. Not *like* having a boyfriend, it would *be* having a boyfriend. Her first boyfriend. Without *quite* meaning to, she leaned into Beri, and his arm slipped onto her shoulders. He'd be nearby when she came to Gran's...or would he? His apprenticeships and trials might take him elsewhere—

"Don't you dare," gasped Raven, glaring over Willow's

head. "Willow, mind Beri."

"What?" Willow whirled to *them*, and abruptly Raven stopped his gyrations. "Holding hands *only!*" She punctuated the order with a poke to Beri's chest.

He shifted a few inches away and eased his arm down to his side. "Curses, I didna figure my friends for chaperones."

Raven's steely gaze skimmed over her—a relief—and settled on Beri. "We wouldn't need to be chaperones if you didn't need them."

"Beri." Willow tapped him again. "Remember, if you break the rules while we're present, we also will be punished."

"Right," said Raven. "I don't wish my power quashed at seventeenth year."

Willow met Fern's gaze and mouthed, "Locked up."

"I ken," Beri grumbled. "Did you nae find these feelings irresistible in the beginning?"

Willow and Raven looked at each other and burst out laughing.

Beri shook his head and looked at Fern. "Can I hold your hand? No magic or anything else?"

She slid it over. "Yeah, we can try that. But I'm warning you, I don't have much more control than I did fifteen minutes ago."

"That's what I'm hoping," he said with a grin.

———

Willow and Raven gave them a few minutes alone—hardly enough as Fern struggled to keep her magic closed off—then Raven stepped back inside the cottage.

"The elders are done with their inspection," he said. "Let's head out."

What? Fern cringed. "That was part of a Meadows inspection?"

With an eye roll, Raven left. Well, he hadn't glowered. Willow must have promised him something as irresistible as sitting with Beri had been.

"The council meets until they have a decision for each habitat," Beri explained. "Sometimes even after the opening celebration. Someone must have had another question, or discovered something they wanted to check at night."

Raven's fury made sense now—inspection time was not the time to get caught doing whatever they were going to do. As they left Hillux, Beri asked Raven to explain his wildlife project, the last on Raven's list.

"It crossed both Meadows and Forest habitats, so apprentices from both may help. We need to move a mated two-year-old red fox pair," he said, "and their den."

Fern's mind could grasp handling animals, but a den?

"This pair settled too close to the family of the female, and with the additional hunters in that area, the rabbit population has dropped."

"Mam has had the reverse problem at a Forest edge miles away," Willow said. "A lone elderly fox died over the winter, allowing rabbit and field mice populations to explode. They've decimated the woods' ground cover and have moved on to the adjacent herbaceous plants in Upper Meadow."

"Wait a second." Fern stopped in her tracks. "In Upper Meadow? Lady Roda reamed me out about their overpopulation yesterday. But you, Lady Mimosa...and Lady Lark? You all knew this?"

They looked at each other. "We do," Raven answered. "Dad, also."

"So…" *Phrase this nicely*, she reminded herself. "Why did Lady Lark tell me not to worry about that area yet, instead of explaining the problem?"

"I believe I know why now." Willow wrapped an arm around her waist. "It involved too many of us, and Lady Lark didn't want you scared off by our magical methods."

"Do'na worry," Beri said, "you won't be left out again."

Raven peered at her in the soft moonlight. "What exactly did you tell Lady Roda?" He seemed to choose his words carefully.

"That we'd be introducing a predator."

"Well done," said Beri.

Raven grudgingly added, "Good."

She hated to blow this, but she'd had some time to think about Duffy's reaction to what she'd told Lady Roda. It might be better for Raven to hear it from her, and while she had Beri and Willow at her back. "A second option I gave her was to trap and eat them."

"You didn't," Willow shrieked.

Raven's eyes widened, and his mouth flew open—into a howl of laughter. Beri joined him.

Willow swatted at Raven, but kept her gaze on Fern. "That might have been a mistake. Lady Roda takes population balance very personally. What did she say?"

"To go ahead, to have it done before the end of the summer. If she's taken offense, maybe I should tell Lady Lark so she can smooth things over—"

"I'm sure Lady Roda has already told her." Willow took her arm and started walking, while the boys punched each other in a giddy play fight. "Raven? I thought you didn't want the foxes waking."

Dropping their voices but talking excitedly, Raven and Beri followed while Willow led them south of the new pond, then into the Forest. From the things Raven was saying, he and Merlin had way more responsibility for the animal management than Fern did.

Duh! Raven. Merlin. They had animal names. Lady Mimosa, Willow and their whole family had plant names, as did Fern and her mom. But then it got confusing. Gran had an animal name, but had been showing Fern the plants. Was it because they were shorthanded in the Meadows? And what was the significance of Beri's name?

Fern didn't get a chance to ask, because they'd gotten within view of a fallen tree. Raven went alone to feed an herbal sedative to the foxes he'd barricaded inside the den below it.

"They burrowed among those upturned roots," Willow said. "Raven chose a spot similar for them, another root mass from a windblown tree."

Raven returned quickly enough, but couldn't stand still and wanted to go over their magical techniques to move the den. What they tried to explain to Fern seemed impossible. Willow and Beri planned to use their energy to surround the den, carry it between them in Willow's pereport to the far end of the Upper Meadow and insert it underground. Simple, right?

Fern put up her hand. "Does anyone mind if I water the pond plants while you do what you need to do?"

"That suits me," Raven said, "but I could use your help to watch over the foxes while I inspect the new den."

He was asking her to help. *Don't point that out.* "Sure, I'll help." The sedation would take twenty minutes more, so Fern arranged a meeting spot and left.

Thank goodness for the moonlight! She found her way and the bucket with no problem. Now she wouldn't need to water tomorrow and could focus on seeing her mother. Mom was due to return midmorning—Colorado time. It would be afternoon here. Walking back to meet Raven, Fern debated leaving her mom a note early enough to cut out again before Mom could stop her.

Raven was watching for her. Alone with him for the first time since their fight, Fern steeled herself for more of his sharpness.

"Our timing is perfect. I think the kits will be born within the day." This was delivered in his usual brusque manner, but then Raven waved for her to follow him. A few yards away, towels cuddled the sleeping fox pair. "Look at this belly."

Kicks within the vixen's belly made her gasp. "Awww, so many little paws," she whispered. Cool, but Raven's return to how he'd acted with her seeds piqued her interest just as much. Somehow, his attitude had softened. Maybe. And maybe there was something to why Beri and Willow liked him.

If only he would stay that way. Coming to the isle would be so much more fun if they *all* accepted her.

"I don't know a lot about wildlife," she said, "but isn't July late for them to be having kits?"

Raven nodded and, wonder of wonders, gave her an appreciative look. "Normally, the birth would be about March. But with the decreasing small mammal population, Dad recommended I intervene."

Fern frowned. "What'd you do, put them on birth control?"

"Aye." Raven flashed her a grin. "I slipped the vixen an herb the healer recommended."

"An herb did it?"

"Aye, in a treat every day since September, before the rut season. I quit before March, but nothing seemed to happen, so then I had to"—he gave a fake cough, the ham!— "encourage them a tad."

No, she would not ask what that had entailed. Raven sounded proud. He cared for these animals as much as Beri did. All that snarling and flashing anger had to be his toughboy cover. This complex move might not succeed, but Raven was committed to it. She liked him for that.

"How will they make it through the winter?" she asked.

"I will continue to help them along. 'Tis a trial for me as well, so they must survive."

Not just a project, his *trial*. Carefully, she asked, "Is this fox trial with the Meadows or the Forest?"

"Both. This species ranges over both habitats and affects both, so both managers frequently cooperate with Dad on the broader wildlife issues."

"Your *only* trial in the Meadows?"

He frowned. "'Tis enough to manage the eleven individual foxes in the two habitats and ensure the balance of their prey stabilizes. Those rabbits and rodents threaten your plants' health and energy production."

That didn't answer her question, but she quickly agreed, "Yeah, it is a lot of work. I hope the council passes you."

Still watching the vixen, Raven shrugged. "Oh, it isn't so bad." A hint of a smile crossed his face before he stiffened and turned to her. "I want to apologize for pushing you over earlier tonight. I-I'm sorry to have treated you harshly."

"Um, it's okay. Apology accepted."

His brow smoothed out, and his overture made a good lead-in to having everything in the open. She still wasn't sure if they were rivals or not. "I heard Willow say you were upset Lady Lark has chosen me. Were you hoping to take over the Meadows, but I bumped you?"

Raven averted his gaze. "I *was* learning the plants from her, along with Beri, but Willow is right, it is not the spot for me."

His voice was calm and even, and Fern relaxed a bit.

"I relate to the beasties much better than green things. I only did it because..." He finally looked at her directly. "I wanted to help my grandmother on our land, but I couldn't tell her I preferred wildlife, not when she needed to boost her land energy."

Seemed like they all agreed on that. "When did you tell her—or have you?"

"Before Willow and I applied for prebonding, but Gran knew already." He gave a crooked smile.

That was at sixteen, so a year or so ago? Again, close to the time the peregrinator opened the portal for her. "What if Willow had ended up with a bonding partner who didn't want to work with animals, or didn't have the skill for it?"

"He would learn. That is the way of it. We're lucky in that regard, that Willow loves plants and I love wildlife. We are a perfect match for a habitat's management and are in love."

Wow. He'd tell a near stranger this? Maybe Beri's honesty on the couch meant he'd be just as open. Fern hoped so. She liked knowing where she stood.

"And you, lass?" Raven asked. "Are you in love?"

Eek, maybe open wasn't such a good thing. "That's between me and Beri."

"So you can't take advice?" he asked, once more in that exasperated tone. "Because I warn you, you abide by the isle's rules, or they *will* send you home." Raven crossed his arms. "I won't see Beri hurt, not by rule-breaking or you."

She wasn't letting this guy tell her she was in love. "I don't plan to hurt him," Fern ground out.

"Things are different in a small community where everyone knows everyone else," Raven huffed back. "That's why we have rules to abide by and look out for each other. Not just for prebonding and exchanging resources, but for maintaining the land and our shield, our protection. Do you ken?"

"Geez, that's some lecture coming from a guy sneaking around to complete his project." He frowned, so she rushed on, "But, yeah, I ken. Don't worry, I won't ditch Beri without giving prebonding a chance." *If I can talk Mom into that.* She needed to lower her guard like he had. "I just need time to sort out what this all means. Love and magic are both new to me, and I'm a bit confused."

Raven nodded. "Aye, that's a fair assessment. For all we complain, the trial of prebonding is a good test. A year is a long time to get to know one another."

"I thought we just had to wait until eighteen?"

"Or a minimum of a year if you are under twentieth year."

A whole year? "Ugh."

"You aren't eighteenth year yet, are you?"

Fern shook her head. "Not until next April."

"April? My birthday is in April, the twenty-seventh. When's yours?"

"Hey, isn't that odd? Mine's the twenty-seventh as well."

"You are pulling my leg," he said with a smile. "I'll be eighteenth year, too. But I was born here on the isle, and you were born in the United States."

"Uh, no. I have an Irish birth certificate. We applied for US citizenship when I was eight, both my mother and I together."

"Your father?"

"She never talks about him. Um, I suppose your mother died?"

"Not that I ever heard. Dad never talks about her." Raven's gaze bore into her with an intensity Fern felt, too—right to the pit of her stomach. "Say, Lady Lark is your...?"

Fern took a breath to settle the pounding of her heart. This was just too bizarre. Gran might not like her revealing the secret, but right now, being honest with Raven was more important. "She's my mother's mother. But my mother never talks about her. Just this farm in Ireland that she hated and how she couldn't go on farming when what she truly wanted was—"

"To be an artist," Raven said, the gruff edge returning to his voice.

"Yeah. Beri told you."

"No." Raven swallowed, and he looked like he wasn't going to say more. "My dad told me that's why my mother left. Lady Lark is *my* mother's mother, too."

24

Growing Ratna

Fern heard the words, but it seemed like forever before her brain caught up. *Twins?* She and... For a moment, they locked gazes.

Raven pivoted away first. While he bent over the foxes, she crossed her arms over her jumpy stomach. How had Mom pulled off this *Parent Trap* thing? Why had her husband—partner—let her?

Ohmigod. Merlin. He wasn't Mom's brother. *He's my father.* Her gaze darted to Raven. *Their father.*

Should she be excited-happy, excited-nervous or mad at being deceived?

Raven—*her brother*—finished placing a cage over the wrapped foxes and straightened, his dark wings appearing. "Time for me to check the den. Will you watch them, please?"

"Hold on a second," she hissed. "You can't—*we* can't not talk about this."

"*We* have *work* to do," Raven muttered.

Boys. So practiced at ignoring their feelings—and yours. But focusing on work to ignore other stuff wasn't only a male trait. "I should have seen it, because in some ways, you are just like Mom."

Raven's mouth fell open for a second before he managed

to compose himself. But he cared, Fern could tell. She sank to the ground beside the animals while Raven unfurled his wings and shuffled around.

"Let me tell Willow and Beri," he finally said. "Please?" Then he flapped his way skyward without waiting for an answer.

Fine, his departure gave her space to think about why, if they were twins, his magic gave him wings and hers didn't. Would it eventually or did she have too little for something like that? Fifteen minutes later, Willow called to her before Fern made out two shadowy figures nearby.

Raven removed the cage and held out one bundle to Fern. She took the warm weight of the fox, searching Raven's face, but he wouldn't meet her gaze. Willow simply waited with her glass globe. Clearly, Raven hadn't mentioned their conversation.

When he had the second fox in his arms—and his lips pressed tight—Willow linked their arms and teleported them to the edge of another wood. There, Beri waited by a hole in a mound, gripping dirt that had been rolled like a glowing blanket between tree roots.

Supporting the vixen in one arm, Raven folded onto his belly and squirmed forward, scooting the animal into the opening on the towel. He disappeared to his hips before he wiggled out again.

He gestured to Fern. "The other?"

Bending carefully, she handed him the fox. Their gazes met.

Raven's mouth crooked in a quick smile. Then he was all business again, moving the second fox inside. He backed out more slowly, dragging an orange-brown glow and rising beside Beri. Together, they wove their hands back and forth, releasing the dirt layered between glowing magic that re-shaped itself...

Fern had to rub her eyes. This looked so wrong.

Yawning, Willow tugged at her arm. "While Raven gets the entrance and scent right, want to come with me to use the bathroom at Hillux?"

The pereport was quick. Inside, Fern raised the plastic to recheck the ratna seeds—

"Ahh!"

Newly sprouted two-leaf seedlings filled the tray. She brushed her fingertips over the inch-tall sprouts, so sturdy looking, so *green*. Did *imbued with magic* also mean *grows like magic*?

I have my ratna.

When Willow joined her, she was just as surprised. "Oh, Fern, how exciting!"

"Does having the plants mean I've corrected this?" She pulled Sir Humus' list from her pocket and showed it to Willow.

She shook her head. "Perhaps they will be big enough to put in the ground tomorrow."

Fern's heart sank. "Transplants need to be six inches tall to make it."

"Aye, which you well know, Willow," said Raven, the screen door banging behind him and Beri.

Fern showed the boys the list, and they debated transplant survival, but the sprouts were only sprouts. Yeah, that was a lot to ask, even from magical plants. "Bummer," Fern yawned in complaint.

Beri reached to pat her shoulder, but Willow intercepted

his hand.

Raven shook his head kindly. "This shows promise, but your magic is new. The ratna is a tricky species."

Still, for the leaves to be this sturdy, the seeds had to have put out good roots. Fern pushed the bottom of one planting cell and eased up a slender stem. The soil slid out in a neat clump laced with fine white roots.

"Aha." Willow poked Raven. "You cannot deny that is a well-developed root mass."

"Too well-developed," Fern said. "They need to be repotted."

Rolling his eyes at Willow, Raven grabbed a bucket and headed outside.

———

"I'm telllling!" The high-pitched squeal broke through the lulling rustle of leaves coming from the open window.

When a crash—evidently caused by Willow's brothers—made it clear Fern wouldn't be able to sleep more, she rubbed her face and squinted at the sun high in the sky. She dressed and headed downstairs, only to run into Ches carrying an armload of blankets.

"I'm in charge of bedding and these two." He nodded to Kory and Maple, blocking the kitchen doorway with a pile of pillows and stuffed animals between them. "Everyone else is moving our weekend supplies for the Gathering to the northern end of the island. Get going," he said to his little brothers.

With much grunting and swinging of arms, they shoved their load onto the porch, and Ches kicked anything they dropped back into the pile. "Mam said your breakfast is in the basket," he called over his shoulder.

Fern ate hard-boiled eggs and apple bran muffins while the boys traipsed upstairs and down. After a second trip, Kory, the middle boy, drifted into the kitchen and leaned against the bench she sat on.

"Hi," she said.

"Hi," he said back. He glanced toward the other room where Ches was telling Maple to choose *only* three books, then asked, "Do they give you the blue trousers to wear?"

Poor kid, having to wear what everyone else did. "I get to pick what I want to wear. You will, too, when you're older."

He nodded, still solemn. "I like green better."

"Green is my favorite color."

"And you like growing plants like I do."

Fern had taken another bite of muffin, but smiled.

"I heard Mam say you didn't have magic when you were little either, like me."

Oh God. She put down the rest of her muffin. "I didn't."

"Did you miss it?"

Please let me say the right thing. "I didn't know any different. No one where I live has magic." He bit his lip, and her heart wrenched. "How old are you?"

"Kory?" yelled Ches from upstairs. "Where are you?"

He started for the door, then turned back and answered, "Fifth year."

Fern had lost her appetite. By the time she'd cleaned up, Willow, Beri and Raven walked in. She met Beri's gaze, but Willow reached her first and hugged her. As they released, Fern gripped Willow's elbow. "Kory was just in here and told me he has no magic."

Her gaze flicked to Raven. "We're not—"

Footsteps sounded behind them, and Ches marched in, his brothers trailing him.

"Oh, right." Ches flicked a guilty glance toward Fern before he scrambled for the door. "I forgot that Willow said you should be ready to go to Hillux."

"Thanks for delivering the message," Raven called after him.

Willow pulled Fern down to whisper, "We're not supposed to talk about it. It worries Kory, but some kids start at different times."

She was clearly ending the conversation, but Fern couldn't. *That little boy is me. I had*—thought *I had no magic.* "And if he doesn't?"

"The council decision has been postponed, thanks to Lady Lark's intervention. They will make another review at sixth year. What happens then is one of the things Mam won't discuss."

"No one will," Raven added, leaning closer.

Beyond them, Beri shook his head—*oh geez, I told him I had no magic*—and reached over Willow to pat her shoulder. Fern flashed green.

Raven scowled and punched him in the arm. "You two are asking for trouble." He pointed at her. "You have plants to get into the ground."

"What? No way."

Raven measured eight inches between his spread palms, and Beri's hands echoed the same.

She headed for the door. "Let's go."

When they arrived at Hillux, Fern saw that the slender stems now boasted two more sets of leaves, both spreading toothed, crinkly looking leaves made up of five leaflets.

Gathering three of the pots, she marched to the top of Hillux and chose the wettest spot in her study garden, a ditch that drained water from Gran's roof. The damp soil relieved her worries about their survival, but she still watered them extra well.

She stood and pivoted in a full circle, scanning the Meadows. Her gaze landed on Raven watching her as he leaned on his shovel. He'd dug the holes, and except for asking politely if the depth was adequate, he'd been quiet while Beri and Willow chatted. He hadn't told them they were brother and sister. Willow would have said something the moment she'd seen her. Despite Fern's growing friendship with both of them, she couldn't cross Raven. But darn it, how long would it take him to do it?

Fern sighed to herself. She also had to respect his needs in this.

"Besides the pond," she said to him, "where do you suggest I plant them? Most of our habitat is too dry for this species."

He gave a wry grin. "Thought you'd never ask. Despite that, a ratna must be spread throughout the habitat to allow its magic to penetrate the land. They'll need extra care."

Willow put up a finger. "Choose carefully. Once planted, the ratna takes on a wizard's energy and is no longer just a plant."

"If nurtured magically, it becomes that bond you are missing," Beri said.

Fern scanned the Meadows again. These planting spots would be more important than any others she'd chosen. *Wet areas, wet...* She snapped her fingers. "Low areas. Swales. What about planting them in the old stream deposits?" Raven and Willow looked confused. "Duffy's soil trial?" Fern explained Duffy's research and pointed out the spots. "She didn't lie to me, did she?"

"Nae," Beri said. "She's told us the same thing whenever we work with Sir Humus."

"I haven't heard about better soil," Raven said, "but those low places collect water in the spring, so that makes them your better choice."

"Will you all help me water the far-off ones today?" asked Fern.

"Beri?" Raven said. "You know the Land wizards better."

Beri inclined his head. "While you start, I'll go explain to Mr. Chinook the nature of the species you're putting in and ask if he can arrange an earlier and lengthy shower for the Meadows this afternoon."

"That sneaky little man who accused me of putting poison on the bracken ferns can make it rain?" Fern said.

Raven snorted. "He's been making it rain nearly every evening since you began planting. Or had you nae noticed?"

She shrugged. "It's the UK. I heard it rains all the time here."

Beri smiled. "Likely his questioning was testing your commitment to what humans call 'green living.' Mr. Chinook's specialty is the water cycle. He can form up clouds anywhere he pleases and saves us a lot of work."

Beri left. Willow and Raven pereported to the pond with armloads of pots, leaving Fern to walk to plant a ratna in a closer low spot she recalled.

It was strangely quiet after being with the others, but peaceful, like the months she'd worked here alone, ignorant of what she was doing. The sun beat on her back as she knelt in the grass. Churning the soil and compost reminded her of stirring soil in the seed tray. Should she be putting magic into the plants again? Gran always said, *Whatever you feel is best, dear*, and Beri had left it up to her, too. Apparently, no directions existed for working your magic with the land.

Fern stripped off her gloves, removed the ratna from its pot and held it. Thinking of opening her magic channels again was a snap—a little too easy, in fact. In the sunlight, the glow was faint, but her hands tingled around the roots.

Not too much. She didn't even know how fast magic recharged. Every ratna ought to have a little, so she closed her channels and set the plant in the hole. She filled in around the root ball with loose soil, thinking of this richer soil nourishing the roots before they worked their way into the rest of the Meadows.

Done, she rose and headed toward Hillux to meet Willow—

Someone was going through the back door. And by the pink swinging skirt disappearing inside, it wasn't Beri.

25

Tricks and Favors

Fern slowed before crossing the front porch so she wouldn't make any noise, but it didn't matter. Inside Hillux, Hilda was shrieking—and not for food. Fern flipped open the screen door, her gaze shooting to the guinea pig *wheeking* outside the plastic sheeting over the bay window. Inside was someone in pink.

What the hell was Duffy doing?

Trotting forward on tiptoes, Fern reached—

Her hand was green. Both were, glowing with magic. *Damn these channels!* An obstinate wave overcame Fern. She wanted to keep her magic—and lack of control—secret from Duffy. Tucking one hand behind her, Fern concealed her other within the plastic and lifted it. "What's up?"

Duffy whirled from the tray of parsley seeds and almost tripped. She sucked in a breath, her wide eyes darting around before she sagged against the counter. "Damn, you scared me."

Good. "Then you know how I felt when you trapped me in the seed closet. *For hours.*"

Duffy plastered on a fake smile. "I heard you got back. Sorry I had to take off."

Yeah, right. Did Duffy think Beri hadn't told her what really happened? "Why?"

"Is that really a topic you want to discuss when we're both waiting for trial decisions? You got your seeds." She waved to the tray.

She was refusing to answer? Seriously? Fern's hands tingled fiercely. She clenched the curtain harder and balled the other hand at her back. She had to be careful. Maybe Duffy had a point—neither of them had passed their trials. A confrontation could come later. For now, she'd keep her real plants safe.

The parsley tray didn't look any different—nothing glowed anyway—so Fern nodded.

"Since you don't have your family's energy, I brought a fertilizer for you, to make up for ditching you out there." Duffy offered Fern a brown dropper bottle with no label.

"Uh, thanks." No way was it fertilizer. Duffy must think non-Windborne were idiots—or at least her. Fern's anger rose, and so did her magic's buzzing. Sparks would fly if she took that bottle. "My hands are too dirty. Just leave it, and I'll apply it later."

Duffy looked at her, hesitating a moment too long. "Can't. I have to return it to Great-Gran. And besides"—she dropped her voice—"you don't really want anyone else to know."

Crap, she'd been right. Thank goodness this wasn't the ratna seed, so Fern could just toss the lot. "Then can you do it for me?"

Giving a big grin, Duffy unscrewed the cap and squeezed up a dropperful. She dripped several drops of a yellow liquid in the center of the first cell and moved quickly to the next, like she'd done it many times. Perhaps she had.

"This will make them grow like magic," Duffy murmured as she finished. "And I won't say a word." She screwed the cap back on and tucked the bottle in her skirt pocket. "Is all forgiven?" Duffy stared, her chin lifted in challenge.

Was this girl for real? Fern stared back. "I'll think about it. In the meantime, you should go." She pulled the plastic aside and gave Duffy room to get past.

Eyes narrowing, Duffy didn't move. "Let me give you some advice. Lady Lark might be desperate enough to dig you up from her cousin's kids and let you try for this, but you aren't going to make it with so little magic unless you form alliances with people who can help you."

The cottage was dead silent. Slowly, Fern released the plastic, feeling the warmth of her magic but refusing to look at it as she straightened to her full height, her hands hanging where Duffy could see them. "I'm doing fine, thanks," she said as evenly as she could.

Duffy gaped at Fern's hands. "Have you been lying about your magic to trick the council into special accommodations?"

Fern's skin itched in the most awful way, and it took everything in her control not to squirm and set off anything. But the fighter in her couldn't resist. She raised a brow. "Why would you think *I've* tricked anyone?"

Duffy's fingers twitched, then flicked to a glow.

Their bright red made Fern's breath catch. Panic sparked her magic—literally sparked it. Duffy flung up her arm. Fern did the same. Red light flashed, a crack like thunder sounded, and a blast threw Fern back. She slammed into something solid. Hands caught her, stopping her fall and pulling her upright. The smell of burning filled her nostrils, and her leg stung with pain.

"Spells." Raven cast a frantic look downward. He swept

his hand—and water drenched her leg, followed by sizzling. He glared at Duffy. "What the hell were you thinking?"

Choking and waving off the smoke, Fern realized that a pocket was gone, burned up, from her soggy cargo pants.

Duffy was laughing. "That's the funny part. I didn't do anything. She did it to herself."

"Just—" Fern coughed. "Just wait until I can control it."

"Be happy to," Duffy said.

Another coughing fit stopped her from answering, likely good timing. Raven held her shoulder and thumped her on the back. When she straightened, Duffy was watching them.

"What's going on here?" she asked.

"I might ask you the same thing," Raven said edgily. "You no longer have a project on the Meadows."

"And you do?"

"What I'm doing here is none of your business."

So Raven didn't reserve his nastiness for only her. That made Fern feel better. Then he put his arm around her shoulders, surprising her more.

"She told you to leave, so go."

How much had Raven heard? Obviously, Duffy was thinking the same thing. Her gaze flitted between the two of them, her eyes narrowing like they had before, but this time, Fern held her hands stiffly at her sides.

"I see how this is," Duffy said. "The outsider has moved on to someone else. No deal, then."

Raven's grip tightened. "What are you talking about?"

The deal with Beri for Duffy to tell the elders she wasn't interested in him in exchange for Beri and Fern not telling what Duffy did to Fern on the islet.

"This doesn't concern you, birdbrain, just her." Her gaze

pierced Fern. "I told my uncle I'd changed my mind, but I know he hasn't told anyone else, and since you obviously don't appreciate Beri as much as I do, I'm keeping my name in the ring." She marched toward the front door.

Raven sucked in a sharp breath. He'd put it together. But worse, Duffy was going out the front door—she'd see the ratna plants on the porch.

Fern pulled away from Raven and—stupidly—caught Duffy's arm. "Faster to go out the back, don't you think?"

Duffy's eyes flashed red, but her glare was directed at Raven. "I don't need to use either door." She shoved her hand into her pocket, the air shimmered and she was gone.

Fern looked around. "Has she really left?"

He flung out his hand, and a flash of his magic spread across the room. "Unless you'd like me to check the bedrooms. I put Hilda in one, so I know that's empty."

"I didn't want her seeing my plants on the front porch." Fern shuddered, the close call sinking in.

"She didn't." Raven's mouth quirked in a smug smile. "Willow came to fetch more and overheard you talking. When she saw it was Duffy, she got me and said she'd move the rest as fast as she could. Her mother would learn about any confrontation, and she couldn't risk that."

Fern brushed her burnt pants. "I guess we did fight."

He snorted. "I didn't get a good look at who did what, but she's experienced. You are not. I canna believe she would blast you one, but the evidence is right there." With a sigh, he flicked his hand and dried her pants. "No matter how awful you think I am, I have scruples. I would never take advantage of the inexperienced."

One corner of Fern's mouth curled. "Thanks. You're not

so bad. In fact, you were so nice to me, Duffy thinks we're an item now." At his confused look, she added, "Interested in prebonding. You put your arm around me."

"To shield you if necessary."

"Doesn't she know you and Willow are together?"

He eyed her. "Gran gave me her blessing to prebond with Willow, but when I moved my energy to the Forest habitat, the rips worsened. My land bonds aren't growing well, and some rips are losing land to the ether, so people blame me."

Oh. No wonder Raven was angry most of the time.

"They got so hostile, the council had to step in. In deference to Dad and Willow's parents' wishes, people do not speak of our prebonding."

Fern wrapped her arms around her middle. "Just like they never talked about Mom. Or me."

———

At the pond, they found Willow guarding the ratna plants. Fern had to count them, then told Willow what Duffy had done.

Willow bit her lip. "You should report it. *I* should report it." She cast a worried look at Raven, who rolled his eyes.

"It'll do no good," he said. "It might be enough to ban her, but what if the fertilizer is what she said? Fern's not allowed that help, but worse, we'd look mean-spirited to nonislanders. We have to accept them and their energy."

With the retelling, Fern's hands had begun tingling again, so she tucked them into her armpits. "I'm not a tattletale." *That* would only come back to bite her. "But I need to learn how to use my magic as fast as I can."

"Mam can help," Willow said at the same time Raven said,

"Merlin will teach you."

Oh crap. *My dad.* She'd be meeting him soon. *What I've always wanted.* But now that it would happen, she was nervous.

"Teach her what?" Beri called from above them.

In answer, she held out her glowing palms. "Duffy snuck into Hillux and may have poisoned a tray of seeds she believed were my ratna."

Beri landed and reached for her hands, then drew back and curled his fingers. "That girl. I canna believe—" He pounded his fist. "*Ach.* Yes, I can believe Duffy would do anything to get what she wants."

His gaze met Fern's, and at the same time, they nodded, then told Willow and Raven everything that had happened on Lady Soila's islet.

Willow hugged Fern so hard she couldn't breathe. "She didn't intend to kill you, but her trickery is no little thing. We have to report it."

"I can't," Fern said. "Gran is so worried about this inspection. We have to get past that first."

"After, then," demanded Raven. "I won't have my sister threatened and an outsider getting away with it."

"Your sister?" Willow and Beri said in unison.

Raven's lips quirked into a smile. "Turns out my mother didn't leave alone."

Both Willow and Beri smacked him before hugging Fern and asking a ton of questions about how they'd figured it out. It was a relief to tell them, and the smile on Raven's face made it evident that he felt the same.

All the while, Fern clenched her fingers in fists, but finally the buzzing was too much. Sparks shot in all directions. Instead of trying to stop the magic, Fern snatched up a potted ratna and pulled the root ball free. "I'm putting this to work."

Fern planted at the pond and the ditch, while Raven scouted the low areas. Two hours later, she'd planted ratna in every old streambed swale across the Meadows, the dirt and grass adding mottled green stains to her charred cargo pants. She and Beri were carrying the shovels back to Hillux when they passed the gully where the saplings had been cut.

Fern found the loppers and pop can she'd dropped. "This is where I slipped and slid into the rip. Is there any way to tell it's there before you're caught?"

"First, they are always on a habitat edge: meadow to woods, pond to stream, streambank to trees, stream to marsh. Some boundaries are nae so obvious and vary with the terrain, like the sea with its wide tidal zone."

"This one is obvious. Grasses meeting trees," she said. "But that doesn't explain the non-native flowerbed I landed in. It's not a natural habitat."

He shrugged one shoulder. "Someone has their forbidden garden near their boundary, and a rip has encroached into it. Rips also sparkle, the energy shorting out." He flicked sparks in demonstration. "And the land no longer fits together right."

Yeah, she'd seen all those things, just hadn't recognized them for what they were. "And a rift—how's that different?"

Beri frowned. "The only outward sign would be the rip edge retreating over your land as the land falls in. You'd see the loss, but Raven and I didna find a rift here."

The falling grass clumps had been real. "I saw what I saw." Fern crossed her arms. "I know it's dangerous, but would you check again?"

He put out his hand. "Together, then. So you can show me what you saw."

"My original questions were so I *didn't* cross one." The entire idea felt terrible. Well...not *all* of it. Willow and Raven had gone ahead...and they *were* allowed to hold hands. She tightened up her channels before placing her fingers in his. A little magic leaked out, and Beri grinned.

"You save that," she admonished him. "Put it on a plant for me."

"I will." He pointed toward the edge of Forest shrubbery. "Look for a difference."

It took a minute. "Before, I only noticed the trees slanting and the ground lying in puzzle pieces that didn't match up. Now, I see a line like someone dug a narrow ditch with a skinny shovel, chopped the dirt into square pieces and then dumped it back. The ditch is refilled, but not exactly as it was."

One foot at a time, they stepped forward. Prickles of light flickered over the grass and shrubbery.

"Rip energy," Beri said. "We should see a gap."

Finally, a slender, muddy glow appeared between two unmatched edges of ground.

"'Tis nae as manly, but it's safer if you poke your way in like I did. You have about a meter of ground to work along before touching the actual rip." He released her hand and dropped to his knees.

Fern groaned, but copied him. Her nerves raced as Beri pulled the gap wider, like he had when he'd opened the barrier to show her his trial area, and leaned into it. Next to him, she eased her head inside.

Close enough to spit on, a line of energy cut through the

land like a small stream. But instead of tumbling along, the murky magic twisted in an ever-spinning rope. Beyond it, both far and near as the image distorted, lay the forest with rays of sunlight piercing the shade between tree trunks. To her left grew the non-native plants in their tended plots, the yellow faces of the sunflowers towering above the other plants—

Holy crap. That bedstraw-looking one was madder, the plant Duffy said she got her pink dye from. These were Duffy's plants. The sneak had planted stuff on the Meadows' land.

Fern had to push her anger aside. The real issue here was the hole. Salty waves splashed from the four-foot-wide opening, their rumbles muffling the quiet woodland sounds.

"Same as before," Beri said. "No ether rift."

"What? It's right there." She pointed to the right.

Beri peered at the spot, then at her. He reached over and took her hand. "Oh." Eyes wide, he stilled for a minute, then he sat back on his heels, pulling her with him. "That rift was hidden until I used your energy to view it."

"Meaning?"

"It's linked to you. To the Meadows."

26

Testing Magic

Fern waited while Beri fetched Raven—Willow should not know, they decided. They checked the rip, each holding her hand, then sat back into the safety of the Meadows.

"It's small and does nae appear to be pulling energy." Beri wiped his face. "Who could we ask and still..."

Raven shook his hair from his ponytail, raked his fingers through and fixed it again. Both boys stared off, but Fern didn't think they were excluding her this time. Just thinking.

"You haven't told anyone?" Raven asked.

"I didn't know there was anything to tell."

Raven drew in a breath. "Tonight is soon enough to tell Gran. After the ceremony. Something like a rift will skew the entire inspection's focus." He looked at Fern again. "After you've beaten out Mr. Grouse."

Her heart stopped. "He's in contention for the Meadows?"

Beri smacked Raven's shoulder with the back of his hand. "You are nae supposed to divulge—"

"Meh," snapped Raven. "She needs to try her hardest."

Fern caught her breath. "But he inspected, asked me questions—"

"Snooping." Raven nodded.

"What is his trial?" she asked, but Beri was already shaking his head.

Raven said, "Someone in our family has to keep the Meadows. You. To do that, we canna introduce anything that will fail us. You grew your list plants. The ratna is planted. It will grow a bond at some point. There is naught they can poke at on your trial list."

But an experienced, adult wizard must have those bonds already. Fern pressed her fingertips to her temples. *Don't go there.* The Meadows. Gran. Keeping the rift secret was irresponsible...but crap, Fern had already decided to trust Beri and Raven.

"You'll give it everything you've got?" Raven asked.

"And more," she said.

Once back at Hillux, she slipped through her rabbit hole to home, changed into jeans and collected a few overnight things and something else she'd thought of. When she came out of the bathroom at Gran's, Willow was holding another potted ratna.

"You'll need it for tonight," she said, "for show and tell. Mam can help you practice sending your magic within it."

"That's likely to be a disaster," Fern said. "I'll probably burn it or something. How about I just talk about the plant's habitat and growth, stuff I learned from Lady Soila's field guide?"

Beri shook his head. "They'll expect to see something, if you want approval."

Fern sighed. "Thanks. I'd never have gotten all this together myself." A wave of gratitude swept over her. "Thank you all, for everything, both last night and today. I can't wait to tell Gran we have our ratna. I just hope"—her voice faltered—"we pass." Fern wiped her eyes.

Beri caught her hand and squeezed it. "Fern, you canna worry. You've done what you can."

At Willow's house, they fixed lunch and finished eating just as the Forest family returned. The kitchen became chaos with everyone clambering for the plate of sandwiches, so Raven and Beri left to pack for the Gathering.

Lady Mimosa took her food and gestured the girls into the living room with her. "The three of us will shower first and fix our hair."

Willow clasped her arm. "Mam, we hoped you'd have time to help Fern."

"Of course." Lady Mimosa looked at her questioningly, then laughed. "New magic?"

Fern rolled her eyes. "Some secret."

"'Twas until you allowed me to check within you for Heather's knowledge of your visits. I ignored what I wasn't supposed to see." Mimosa smiled. "Now it's quite present in you."

Fern opened one of Gran's bags and picked up her potted plant. "Maybe because I'm so excited about my new ratna."

Lady Mimosa exclaimed, and so did a younger voice behind her.

Kory looked up at Fern in awe. "You're a real wizard to grow a ratna. It's a very fancy plant," he said with a solemn nod and handed his mother a glass of water.

"Thanks." Fern took out two small books that she'd brought from home and squatted beside Kory. "These were my favorites when I was your age. They're stories with gardens." She handed him the books.

"And rabbits?" He pointed to the drawing on one cover.

Willow looked over his shoulder. "*The Tale of Peter Rab-*

bit."

"Yep," Fern said. "The other is *The Tale of Beatrix Potter*, about the lady who drew Peter and wrote his story. She also loved things that grow, especially mushrooms. I'd like you to have them."

Kory broke into a smile and hugged the books to his chest. "I'm gonna like these. Thank you."

Lady Mimosa kissed his forehead. "Go find your brothers and have Haw read these to you." She smiled at Fern. "This is very kind of you." She admired the meadowsweet, saying all the things another plant lover would.

But Fern was still thinking of Kory and how this must look like a promise that one day he could be able to do this...and that made her miserable for the poor kid. How could it be helping him not to talk about it?

Or her? The magical bond was out of her control, so she might as well admit it so she could talk to Gran. "Lady Mimosa? Could you send a message to Sir Humus that I've completed his correction list? I want to surprise Lady Lark with my plant."

Willow's mother agreed to, left for a moment and returned. "Give your plant just a touch of energy."

Easy for her to say. Fern tensed, but extended her hand. Her skin tingled—and her fingertips zapped green sparks.

Lady Mimosa flinched back, and Willow covered her mouth.

"Sorry," Fern mumbled. "Any thought of magic and it shoots out."

"I'll shower first," Willow volunteered and left.

"I'm sure your plants benefited," Lady Mimosa said, "but magical accidents won't do around people. Here, sit and let's try a few things." They settled on the couch, the plant on the coffee table before them, and Lady Mimosa examined Fern's hands.

They glowed.

"At this point," Lady Mimosa said, "you must think through each step of moving your magic. With more experience, the movements will come naturally. Start with putting the magic away." She gestured to Fern's middle. "The abdomen is the easiest to use of a Windborne's energy cores, or storage areas, and farthest from your hands, giving you more time to move magic with purpose. Try to push your magic to your belly."

Fern concentrated. She visualized the bright green rivulets. *Now move.* It did. The glow disappeared, but the tingle remained, flowing up her arms.

"Where is it?" Lady Mimosa asked.

Fern jabbed her knuckles to the buzzes at the crook of each elbow.

"Push."

It moved. Fern felt it swirling in her sternum. Then, like something she swallowed, it sank to her belly and swirled again. *Yes!*

Lady Mimosa laughed. "It's there, isn't it? I can tell from your pleased face."

"Pleased? I'm thrilled, Lady Mimosa. Thank you so much for helping me."

"An excellent start. Now, let it out, move it to your fingers and move it back again."

What if I can't put it back again? But under Lady Mimosa's instruction, Fern repeated the exercise. She'd done one good, controlled move when Willow appeared, hesitating a few feet back, her hair wet and a brush in hand.

"Enough for now," Lady Mimosa said and sent Fern to shower.

When she returned, Lady Mimosa was gone and Willow's long blond hair was plaited into about twenty tiny braids.

"I'll braid yours, if you like," Willow offered. "'Tis the fashion for special ceremonies."

"Gran skipped mentioning a ceremony, but sure, I'll prepare in any way you think is best." She sat, and Willow separated three strands for the first braid.

"Practice your magic more, Mam said."

As soon as Fern focused on the twitching in her core, her energy jumped and churned. She caught her breath. "Does magic always come alert when you think about using it?"

"Aye, and that is a good thing. There will be times you need an immediate response."

"Like when Duffy challenged me today?" She eased open her core. A trickle, not a rush, of the tingling filled her arms. Her fingertips sparkled.

"Oh, careful there," Willow said. "Situations like with Duffy need a delicate hand, as Mam says. I was thinking of the fall you and Beri described."

When my green cocoon exploded out. With that memory— and Beri holding her afterward—the sparks flashed into flames.

"Ahh," Willow squealed. "Put it back!"

Fern sucked at the energy. The flames disappeared, and the tingling ran in reverse up her arms. She grabbed her middle as the magic converged there and held tight.

"Fern?" Willow waved a hand in Fern's face. "It does not take holding your breath!"

Fern sagged on the stool, air whooshing from her. "Crap, I could've set fire to your house."

Willow giggled. "Wouldn't be the first time someone did that. Better for you to practice here where we can stop it. Try again."

By the time Lady Mimosa returned, Fern couldn't keep from smiling at her amazing fingers. Willow braided her mother's hair while Lady Mimosa directed Fern in flowing straw-thin streams of magic onto and into her ratna. It was there, she said, though Fern couldn't see it.

"Well, that ought to keep you safe through the evening. Think 'contained,' and you'll be fine. Just don't spend much time touching Beri."

"Mam! Fern, I didn't tell her."

"You didn't have to. I see it in her." Lady Mimosa leaned over and patted Fern's heating cheek. "You are a mindful lass, don't worry. Now go with Willow to the Gathering Place. Your Gran is waiting to talk with you."

27

Gran's Plan

The tang of the sea filled Fern's nostrils before she even opened her eyes, but grass surrounded the spot Willow had landed them. Her gaze skimmed the people scurrying over the mowed center and found the ocean. She turned, taking in the sparkling water on three sides, the woods making up the fourth, with the isle's mountains rising behind them.

The Gathering Place was situated on a bluff, with the water far below, and as Gran had promised, they would be able to see both the rising and setting sun—and the rising moon, the blue moon Gran called a *fourth* moon.

"It's beautiful." She squeezed Willow's hand. "You are so lucky getting to camp here overnight. I hope—"

"Don't worry. Your mother has to say yes!" Willow tugged her toward the people carrying chairs, crates and plants to roped-off areas around a large fire ring.

It was far—the bluff spread as wide as several football fields—and Fern's mind spun with Willow's descriptions of the food, music and fun of the celebration, and then what might happen when she did go home to tell her mother...everything.

A dark-haired figure broke from the crowd, and Raven strode toward them. "Good," he called. "You've finally brought her."

Willow clasped his elbow. "My father is expecting me at our display. Will you help Fern find Lady Lark?" At Raven's nod, she said, "See you," and took off.

"I would like to introduce you to my—*our* father," he said.

His gaze didn't leave her face. Was he nervous? Scared? She still couldn't read him, but they'd learn to know each other eventually. So...her dad. She clenched the handles of the tote bag holding her ratna. "Which one is he?"

"The warlock on the far side, with the long black hair. Like mine. Like yours."

Yeah, it didn't get any more obvious than that. Few others had hair like theirs, and none as straight or long—falling to their waists—as their black strands. Fern's was now done up in more than a dozen braids, and Raven had pulled his into one ponytail. Merlin's blew free in an undulating plume, giving him a rather wild look.

She studied Merlin, not willing to think of how utterly scared she was to even attempt this. Because if he said, *No, I don't want to know you*, it'd be over. For years, she'd been hoping and wishing for this moment, fighting Mom for even a word of what he was like, dreaming about a person who made her who she was.

Even at this distance, she could tell Raven's—their—dad was tall. The heads of those nearby came to his chin. Merlin turned briefly, his profile revealing olive skin, the same nose as Raven's and hers, and a full beard, black like his hair, covering his upper chest. Although Beri had laughed at her earlier question, Merlin did look like actors who played the magician, though definitely younger and without the flowing robe. Like most of the men, he wore a linen colonial-style shirt with rusty-brown leather pants, a matching waistcoat and knee-high boots. He looked like he would be interesting to know.

"Does he know who I am?" Fern asked.

Raven shrugged. "Ready?"

What would she say to him, the father she'd waited her life to meet? A dozen things rushed through her mind. *Did your bones hurt, too, when you grew so tall? Will you come to my graduation? Did you love my mom? Can we please try to be father and daughter?*

The possibility he would turn away from her left her heart racing. "No, not yet. Besides, Gran sent word she needs to talk to me. I better see her first."

With an eye roll, Raven pointed her in the right direction, and they set off around the outside of the large roped circle. The interior was divided into pie-shaped sections, and people in each were setting out plants, rocks and...water? Gran had said there would be displays, but Fern hadn't realized it'd be like a garden show by the island habitats.

A flock of songbirds circled one section like a school of fish, swirling and twittering happily, making it easy for Fern to spot her grandmother. Gran, wearing a lemon-yellow blouse with a green and yellow floral-patterned skirt, was speaking with Beri. By the time Fern and Raven wound around to the inner circle—a lawn surrounding the fire pit— and found the entrance to the Meadows' display area, Beri had left. Well, that would make it easier. Telling Gran about Beri was going to be only slightly less painful than telling Mom.

Gran was bent over, her hair swung forward and hiding what she was working on. She straightened, pointing one

finger at a badger. "You be good and sleep until I come back."
Obediently, the animal—with a much grayer muzzle than
Fern's badger—nestled into three spadefuls of grass that ap-
peared to be growing together and closed its eyes.

Days ago, Fern would have freaked that Gran had a loose,
wild animal. Now, she understood—and wanted to introduce
herself to Lady Soila tonight and ask permission to visit her
badger.

Cages containing birds, insects and small mammals sat
among loose clumps of grasses and overflowing pots of their
wildflowers, what looked like every one of their species. A
few shrubs dotted the display edges, already obscuring the
view and framing in their habitat. Why hadn't Gran asked
her to help with gathering any of this?

"Gran?"

"Ah, Fern dear." Gran turned. Her smile immediately
broadened into absolute delight. "You have come into your
magic, lass! I hoped you would if you spent enough time on
the isle. Raven dear, has nae it been wonderful to have her
working with you?"

"Yes, ma'am," he said with a furtive look to Fern.

"The fox pair settled in?" Gran asked.

Raven nodded.

"Good, good," Gran said. "The balancing o' the predators
and returning the old water source should tip the scales in
our favor. Along with the plantings and this year's increase in
game birds, I don't see how they can say the habitat is nae
producing."

"Yes, ma'am, it is my hope, too."

"I can always count on you to help." Gran reached up and
patted him on the cheek.

As Gran lowered her arm, Raven clasped it. "We have more news." He nodded at Fern. "Fern has a new plant to tell you about."

Well, darn, she'd wanted to surprise Gran herself...and yet Raven hadn't *quite* told. Gran looked at her expectantly, and the words bubbled out. "I have the ratna, and it's growing."

Gran's eyes widened, and she stumbled forward to hug Fern.

"Easy," Raven murmured, steadying the tiny woman, and his gaze met Fern's, an entirely new look overtaking his face. Could it be pride?

Fern beamed back.

"Oh, my dear. You have done it! They canna refuse us now." Gran hugged her a moment more, then half turned to Raven. "You have seen the plant?" she asked fiercely. "A proper Meadows ratna?"

He smiled, and Fern was shocked at how friendly, and familiar, he now looked. His hazel eyes—Mom's eyes—sparkled, but his nose and cheeks caught her attention for the first time. How had she missed the resemblance to hers?

Raven waggled glowing fingers at Gran. "Indeed it is, ma'am. Beyond a doubt."

"See for yourself, Gran." Fern opened the bag she carried and lifted the pot, the plant now bearing another compound leaf near the top of its rising stem.

Gran drew a breath and didn't seem to stop. Luckily, Raven's hand still hovered at her elbow. She ran a crooked finger over one crinkly leaf. "It's...stunning. I canna tell you how pleased I am." She closed her eyes for a moment. "So much has happened."

"I'll say." Fern told her about the correction list, which the ratna partially satisfied.

"Bonding to the land will take longer," Gran said. "But they will see your plants are in the ground. The magic will connect."

That reminded Fern of Kory. She turned to Raven. "Can I talk to Gran alone, please?"

He had barely stepped away when Gran caught her arm. "Did you like having the help and getting to know them? I figured you should, since my duties would take me away."

"I did," she murmured. "But, Gran—"

"What did your mother say about the change in you?" asked Gran. "Is she pleased to hear the news of the ratna?"

As always, Gran was running full speed ahead, with work plans, directives, making it easy to answer only one of her questions. "I haven't seen her. She wasn't due home until today."

Gran frowned. "You must see her. Your final interview with the council is last, but that's still only four hours from now."

Great, now she had an interview? "Yes, she'll be home soon, but it's going to be harder to tell her about me working here when now I'm doing"—helplessly, Fern lifted her glowing palms—"this."

"I knew you would be green." Her grandmother sighed with a satisfied smile. "And a beautiful color it is indeed, like the unfurling of the first buttercup leaves." Gran set the ratna pot back in the tote bag and stored the bag in a cluster of gorse, sending three pheasant hens running. She wrapped her thin hands around Fern's larger ones. "Precisely the reason you must see her. Your mother must give you her blessing and all that comes with it." She gave a knowing nod. "Remind Heather I bestowed mine. She canna refuse to give you hers." Gran began to steer her to the display exit, the flock of birds fluttering around them. "Get yourself home and back here, dressed proper for me to present."

"Gran?" Fern planted her feet. "I had no magic."

"And you've done brilliantly."

"And if no magic had come?"

"Pfft." Gran waved a hand. "Your talent for the flora *is* an energy, one you've put to use for over a year. The council canna ignore that."

Gran sounded much more confident than after Sir Humus' visit. Which meant she was still hiding something. Fern leaned her face to Gran's. "I know it's bigger than just the Meadows. Giuthas goes down if we do, and they won't let that happen."

Now Gran frowned, and several birds landed on her shoulders. "That's the problem of turning you loose among the others. You've discovered all the stakes and let them intimidate you. Beri told me you have seen Heather's magic and learned she is the Witch of the Meadows."

"I don't understand that," Fern said. "She left. You're here. Why is it Mom and not you? Is it because you got"—she hated to ask this, but had to—"too old to do it?"

Her snort sent the birds into the air again. "Age has nothing to do with wielding energy. I passed the responsibility to your mother years before she left. So the last word lies in her hands. The ancestral family magic lies in her hands." Gran took a breath. "Heather will understand what the blessing means, but I suppose I should have told you. The council considers both the habitat and how the wizard has bonded to it, as well as the energy a wizard brings to that habitat. Your work with the habitat is beyond question. However, you have no accumulation of magic. They might approve you, but with Giuthas' lack of energy—"

"Caused by Mom."

Gran sighed. "I will never hear the end of this. Aye. We have a stronger case for the land staying within our family if Heather acknowledges you as her heir and returns the magic she removed. Some might still harbor a grudge against your mother, but the others are not fools. They should snatch it like a child grabs candy. Only a family member can work it, but if you canna, I will ask her to restore it to me, and we will manage things together. Then, in a few years, perhaps a child of Raven's can apprentice and share with you. Or take over if you do not wish to continue."

"That's a long shot, Gran. As risky as my magic appearing."

Gran shrugged. "'Twas all I had."

Fern flipped up her hands, fingers spread. "I'm lucky my magic has emerged so I have even a hope of doing this. But what about..." Geez, Willow said they didn't talk about Kory. Should she even bring up his name to Gran? "What about kids who don't have magic?"

Gran's eyes narrowed. "This is about a little boy, is it?" Fern nodded, and Gran closed her eyes for a moment. "I became a council member to help, and I have, as much as anyone can wrangle changes in a centuries-old society. I have a plan, but it relies on Heather. Will you speak with her first about her energy?"

"Okay," she said. "But I don't want this shoved into a corner and forgotten. I'm getting the bad feeling people here only consider talents worthwhile if they're magical."

"Oh, believe me, we won't forget about it." Tears welled in Gran's eyes, and she patted Fern's cheek. "I am so proud you see beyond a special gift. Don't have doubts, lass. I don't. Managing the Meadows is a job you can do. With or without magical talent."

Fern pinched the bridge of her nose. This discrimination was troubling. Duffy had complained about ridiculously outdated policies, and people treated Raven terribly when he moved his magic because he was in love. What else were these old traditions controlling?

When she lowered her hand, Gran, a little woman shorter than even her mother, had crossed her arms and raised a single eyebrow. Gran had never before given her this don't-mess-with-me look. Mom, on the other hand, used it frequently.

"Young lady, you canna weasel out of this now. I set this plan in motion years ago when the last Grain Moon was followed by an extra and I had no one to present as heir to the Meadows. I could tell Raven knew his heart by that season, even though he refused to admit it, even to himself. Unless I present you, the family line will fold and our ability to work the Meadows will cease. If the habitat leaves the family, its future would be put to a vote of the Windborne of the Isle of Giuthas, and anything could happen." She gestured to the plants and animals surrounding them, and for the first time, worry creased her brow.

Then everything would change—from what was planted, to who lived in Gran's cottage.

Fern looked at the clustered pots of familiar flowers, yet in them saw acres of wild meadowland. Plants she'd grown.

Plants she loved. Land she loved.

Gran leaned close and whispered, "We lose our land, but worse, we lose our ability to influence the direction the Giuthas Windborne take on issues like what happens to our community members with no magic."

That magic might be her undoing, but Fern nodded. "I'll do it." Somehow.

28

Dad

In the circle of displays, Fern spotted Willow working among roe deer beneath tall trees...really tall trees, maybe two stories high. And it wasn't only the Forest habitat flourishing, growing lush over hours instead of years. In the stream next door, water appeared and disappeared at the edges of the ice-blue energy, running continuously through it, tumbling over rocks, while trout jumped at flies.

Raven intercepted Fern. "Now can I introduce you to our father?"

She bit her lip. "I was about to ask Willow to take me to Hillux. I have to see Mom before this evening."

"Ach, not before meeting our father." He took her elbow and led her out of the displays and across the field. Merlin was unloading a cart at the tent area, his figure unmistakable. Arguing seemed pointless, and at least she'd get to meet her dad away from other people.

Halfway there, a *snap* sounded.

Fern flinched back, though she instantly recognized Duffy and her pink attire.

"What the hell are you doing?" Raven choked out, strands of his ponytail flying with electricity. "Surprising people is not allowed."

"Meh, no one enforces it." Duffy waved him off, a brown

glass globe in her hand. "And you're not in charge of the Gathering."

"Neither are you," snapped Raven, adding something else Fern didn't catch under his breath.

"Scram, birdbrain." Duffy crossed her arms. "I have business alone with Lady Lark's pet protégé."

He cut his gaze to her, and Fern pressed her shoulder to his and crossed her arms. Raven's grouchy attitude felt just fine for facing Duffy. "First off, his name is Raven. And whatever you have to say to me, he can hear."

If possible, Duffy's gaze narrowed even further. Her arms dropped, fingers spread.

Raven's hand dropped as well, and Duffy shifted to the balls of her feet...like a wrestler would. *Damn*—she better pay attention when *wizards* uncrossed their arms. Fern dropped her arms, copied Duffy and, though it might be a mistake, opened her core.

"Fine," Duffy said. "I saw you with him"—she jerked her chin toward Raven—"*again* and decided enough with you toying with Giuthas' available warlocks. My uncle has presented my appeal to the council to work a year on the isle combined with a prebonding trial with Beri." A smirk settled on her perfect, glossy pink lips.

"He'll never agree," said Raven. "You're wasting everyone's time."

"Am I?" Duffy tilted her head. "None of the isle's wizards know soil chemistry like I do. They've approved my soils trial and want to implement my research, so I'm sure they'll approve the rest tonight."

Duffy might have studied to get those skills, but Fern had no tolerance for her entitled attitude. Whether she and Beri tried prebonding, he shouldn't be forced to date Duffy, especially after keeping her trick a secret. But Fern might also be accused of trickery if she didn't clear up this misunderstanding. "Before the council considers it, you should take a good look at the two of us."

Duffy sneered. "Why? So I know what a two-timer looks like?"

"So you know what twins look like."

The smug smile faded from Duffy's face, replaced by disbelief and then anger as she flitted looks between them.

Raven gave a satisfied grunt and muttered, "Won't help." Pulling at Fern's arm, he turned. "She's not teachable."

Fern held her ground. Wrestling had taught her never to look away from an opponent. Duffy's hand swung up, and her fingers flew out. So did Fern's. Her green magic moved sluggishly, while Duffy's hand flickered red.

"Raven! Help!"

Duffy flinched and looked around. Fern did, too. Willow's brother Kory ran across the lawn with Haw chasing close behind. He didn't appear to be in danger, but the shout drew the attention of many others—all who would see any magic Fern let spurt out. She folded in her fingers.

Duffy's eyes narrowed, returning to Fern, and she let her hand fall. "Even Lady Lark being your grandmother won't stop me." She stalked off.

"Heard that before," muttered Raven. "She believes she deserves special treatment." He dropped Fern's arm in time to catch Kory and swing him behind them before Haw caught up.

"I was hiding, and he cast a spell to find me," whined Kory.

Aw, heck. Though she knew from babysitting that siblings picked on each other in the most creative ways, this magical unfairness crushed her heart.

"Hide-and-seek?" Raven asked. "Haw, you've got to play fair."

"He's got to hide better, like Maple does. I didn't spell to find him."

"Then I did hide better," Kory said proudly. "Tell him he can't, Raven."

"You can't," Raven said solemnly. "Find Maple and play another round with no magic."

Kory ran off, and Haw scowled, but followed.

"Red energies tend to be hotheaded." Raven nodded toward Haw. "He's one, like Duffy, though she's got years on him for learning that calculated control."

"She's not that in control," Fern muttered. "If you ever see her headed my way, come over and pick up the pieces. There's only so much I'm gonna take before I knock her flat, and I bet I'll end up a crispy critter in the process."

Raven cleared his throat. "Nothing would make me happier than to help my sister. Perhaps she will forget to mention to anyone that I made a mistake and excluded her from decisions on her trial project."

Ha, he was finally admitting his mistake in not listening to her. This was their chance to really start fresh as siblings. Still, Fern took a minute to think it over. "Deal, and I need help with something. How many kids here are like Kory, with no magic?"

Raven shook his head, staring off. "No one says. It's...invisible."

"Is that how it always is for him, like with Haw just now?

He's picked on?"

"Yes," he said quietly.

"Then it's not invisible. And it can't be. People have to acknowledge that these kids are different and help them."

Now Raven met her gaze. "It won't be easy."

"Doing the right thing usually isn't. Gran has a plan that I want to work."

He smiled, all teeth and glinting eyes. "I'm in."

Together, they approached Merlin, who was now putting together a cot.

"Dad?" Raven said when he didn't immediately notice them.

Merlin straightened. "Raven, my lad, just in time to—" He caught sight of Fern. "And who..." His wide eyes searched hers, their dark brown matching hers. His forehead creased in confusion before he swallowed. "Fern," he whispered.

Mouth too dry to speak, she nodded.

"You can be no one but Fern. You are all grown up. A young lady. You must be—"

"Seventeenth year, Dad." Raven rolled his eyes.

"Aye, of course, seventeenth." Merlin threw a glance at Raven and winced. "Ach, I understand now. Fern is the supposed cousin Lark made the arrangement for."

"When were you going to tell me I had a sister, Dad?" Raven said. "Or that my mother was reachable?"

Merlin kept his gaze fixed on Fern. He reached out a hand and gently stroked her cheek. "You were such a tiny mite, and now look at you. Every bit as tall as Raven." Merlin shook himself a little and, with a wink, added, "But much more beautiful, my lass."

A wink. He winked at her.

"May I hug my daughter?"

Fern burst into tears, but made herself nod, and the tall wizard swept her up into the bear hug she'd always dreamed about.

"Why are you blubbering?" Raven asked in an annoyed tone. "I thought you wanted to meet him."

Merlin—*her dad*—continued to hold her tight and rub her back. Why hadn't it always been like this? Everything she'd always wanted was coming true. She should be happy—oh no! She squeezed as tight as she could, but the familiar tingle raced her arms and out—

"Why are you—wait, you have magic?" Wincing, Merlin eased her away.

"She's just come into it," Raven said, "and has no control whatsoever. You must train her up."

"Me?" He studied Fern at arm's length. "What was Heather thinking sending you here without a magical education?"

Fern licked her lips. "She doesn't know I came. Or I *thought* she didn't know. Neither she nor Gran told me I should have magic."

Raven snorted. "Gran left out a few details in my history, too. So did you," he added with a glare at his father. "I want to meet my mother."

Merlin froze. "Is she here as well?"

"No." Fern started to explain, but Merlin was staring at the sea, a faraway look on his face.

"Dad?" Raven leaned close. "Are you still in love with her?"

Merlin wiped a hand down his face and stroked his beard. "I never stopped being in love with Heather. The circumstances were not ours to control, but that's a story to sit down to tell, with Heather, of course. Meanwhile, I am scared to see her again, truth be told."

Scared? Of her itty-bitty mom? This towering man? A giggle burst from Fern.

Raven glared at her. "What do you find laughable about this? We have grown up apart, without a complete family. To love someone so much that you are willing to live without the person is a rare gift. You better hope you find—"

"Right." Fern's heart leaped to her throat. Raven couldn't blab about Beri. "When you see Mom, you'll understand why I'm laughing about anyone being scared of her. And...I'm just really excited about everything."

Merlin slid an arm around Fern and reached out to lightly pat Raven's cheek, before also pulling him into a hug. "This is one of the happiest days of my life. I'm sure getting to know Fern will bring many more. We will talk after Raven has the opportunity to meet his mother." He hugged her again. "I never stopped loving you either, lass. I regret missing the last fourteen years when I look upon you."

He released her with a sad smile, and she wanted to ask—so badly—then why? *Why haven't we always been together?* But the moment was so perfect, and she chickened out.

"I would like to be the one to announce you to our community, but I suspect your grandmother has a plan for that."

"Does she ever," Fern said. "One I hope Mom will agree to. I'm headed home now to ask her."

Their father cocked his head, as if he was about to ask a question, but instead he nodded and squeezed her shoulder. "You'll be seeing her to Hillux?" he asked Raven.

"Willow will," Raven said. "She is coming."

"Good." Merlin clapped him on the back. "See you both later." He strode toward the displays, passing Beri, who just might have been waiting for their meeting to be over.

He grinned at her, but a wave of empathy and guilt flooded Fern. "Oh, Beri. I'm sorry about your parents. This must bite to see me find mine."

"Bite?" Beri shook his head. "You have the most interesting way of saying things. Don't fret about it. My memories of my parents are good ones, and I have family. Merlin has been a splendid second dad to me. Lady Mimosa has mothered both Raven and me. Although, I'm curious to meet your mother. I feel I must if we might prebond."

Of course Mom needed to meet Beri if they were going to—oh geez.

Willow walked up in time to hear what he'd said. "We can all go, can't we?"

Raven nodded. "I wish to meet our mother, as you have met our father."

Fern pressed her fingertips to her temple. "Sure, why not?" What would happen when she turned up with these three to introduce to Mom, one who was her son and another Fern's new boyfriend?

29

Mom

Having warned the others to let her talk to her mom first, Fern hustled them through her rabbit hole, then quickly closed the bathroom door to a crack and listened with her ear to it.

No sounds came from their cabin. After a warning finger to her lips, she eased into the hallway and tiptoed to the base of the stairs. "Mom?"

No answer. No luggage sat inside the front door, and no SUV was parked in the drive. Still, Fern searched the house before checking the answering machine.

"You're not answering your cell," Mom's recording said, "but I suppose you forgot your charger. I'm having breakfast with some people from the show and will be home about eleven. See you soon, meadowsweet!"

"Another hour." Fern reset the answering machine. "What do you want to do while we wait?"

"Teevee!" Beri rubbed his hands together. "May I show them this unique magic?'

She'd thought he didn't like the TV, but with that gleam in his eye, this had to be about showing off for Raven. "Sure."

"Perhaps we should change clothes to be ready for the Gathering?" Willow asked.

Raven frowned at her. "You sound like your mother." She

whacked him in the stomach, but he caught her hand. "Our clothes are back—oh."

The small bag Willow carried was expanding. She undid a tie and opened it. Beri reached in and plucked out a pressed shirt, vest and leather pants on a hanger.

"Fine," grumbled Raven, and he took out another set of men's clothes, leaving a dress on a hanger. "But I wish to have time for Beri's teevee."

"Then hurry," said Willow. "Where's your room, Fern?"

Upstairs, Fern pulled the outfit Gran had made for her from the back of her closet. It seemed so long ago that they'd planned for Fern to attend the Gathering. Her excitement hadn't diminished in the months between, just projects had filled her thoughts. On winter days, however, they couldn't work outdoors, so Gran had sewn her green linen dress. She'd taught Fern how to embroider the simple twining stitches of vines and leaves along the hem, while she decorated the neckline and skirt with elaborate flowers and ferns.

It wasn't the sort of dress a typical high school girl would wear, but the style matched the eclectic ones worn by their artist friends and cosplayers at the fairs. Fern's dress flowed around her legs as she spun, the flowers sparkled, and the leaves shimmered, fancier than most of what Mom owned. Putting it on made her feel special.

Willow cooed over it. "It's beautifully done, more intricate than mine."

"Thanks," Fern said. "I love yours, too."

Willow smoothed the dark gold dress embroidered with russet, orange and gold falling leaves before turning to Fern's closet. "Most of my clothes are this hue. You have so much variety." She fingered a bright magenta shirt. "Including more of those trousers."

"Jeans, we call them." Fern could hear the longing she sometimes felt herself on seeing other girls' closets. "Hey, want to try on some? My clothes should fit you."

Willow didn't hesitate. She tried on several things, rolling the too-long legs into cuffs and loving them all—the brighter the better—until time ran out, and she had to dress. They undid their braids and brushed out each other's hair. Willow deftly twirled strands back from her face and then did Fern's, securing them with clips she'd brought.

They came downstairs to find Beri showing Raven the contents of the refrigerator.

Beri glanced up. "Could we...oh!" His wide-eyed look sent Willow, then Raven, into gales of laughter. He ignored them and took Fern's hand. "You are beautiful. I canna tell you how well you clean up."

"Stop at 'you are beautiful' next time." Willow separated their glowing hands.

"Verra. You, too, Willow, of course."

"Exactly my thought," Raven said, so absently it bordered on rude to Willow. "How much longer before our mother comes?"

That explained his distraction—nerves. Yikes, her brother was in for more. Mom's manner was nowhere near as easy-going as Merlin's appeared. "Should be anytime."

"Could we have some of that squeezed orange?" Beri asked.

"No pop this time?"

"Nae, thank you. 'Tis so bad I won't even taunt Raven into trying it."

So, of course, Raven had to try it.

While Beri served himself and Willow orange juice, Fern opened two colas, poured each in a glass and passed Raven one. She tipped hers back and took a long drink. He copied her, so she did it again. He mimicked her, but his cheeks sucked in, and his eyes watered.

The other two laughed. Willow poked his arm. "Raven, do you not think that is enough of a, uh, different drink?"

Aw, she shouldn't be this obstinate. But this was just too good. Fern drained her glass.

Raven couldn't. He really tried. He didn't spit it out, but his face soured with each additional swallow, until finally he said, "I canna do it."

Beri howled, and Willow covered her face. Fern took Raven's glass, thought about drinking it, too, but poured the pop in the sink. She'd rinsed the cans and dropped them in the recycling bin when she heard the key in the front door lock.

She waved everyone quiet and hissed, "*Shh!* Mom."

"Fern? I'm home."

Fern scooted out of the kitchen. "Mom, hi. I, uh, have some friends I'd like you to meet." Shoot, already this was on rocky ground, since she was allowed to have only friends her mom already knew over when Mom wasn't home.

In the front hall, Heather Fields was closing the door, her curly hair swinging around the folds of her long skirt. In a green empire dress and a coordinating band in her hair, she looked especially nice this morning. Except for the frown.

Fern darted forward, hugged her mother and whispered, "I know, but this is different." She waved to the others to join them. "Mom, this is—"

"Mimosa?" gasped her mother.

"It's Willow, Mom. Lady Mimosa's daughter."

"Ahh, you are the fair image of her and—" Mom stopped when she came to Fern's brother, and she squeezed Fern's hand so hard she yelped. "It canna be...Raven?"

He lifted his hands, then dropped them. "It's me."

A tear slid down Mom's cheek, then another. "I don't know what to say." Her voice caught on a sob as she glanced from him to Fern. "You have met and have questions, I am sure. 'Twas so difficult..." She drew a deep breath and resolutely wiped her face, but the tears kept coming. "'Twas hardly a choice. Certainly not ours." Mom covered her face.

Raven shot Fern a wide-eyed look. Fern shook her head helplessly. She'd never seen such an emotional outpouring from her mother. *This*—whatever it was—had to be the heartache Mom really meant, not that story about hating farming and wanting to do art. At the same time, each of them raised a hand toward Mom, saw the other and stopped. Then Mom drew a shuddering breath. Awkwardly, Fern hugged her, while Mom wiped her face another time.

"I never wanted our family to split. Merlin loved you two as fiercely as I did, and though I couldna see you, I never had a lack o' love for you, Raven. I think about you every day, and now to see you here, in our world..." She shook her head. "I'm sorry."

There was *the* accent. When upset, Mom dropped deeper into her Irish inflections.

"Then...why?" Face naked with emotion, Raven stepped forward. "If you...love me, then why did you leave?"

This. *This* was what Fern hadn't had the guts to ask Merlin. She'd asked Mom plenty of times, but had never gotten an answer. Her stomach twisted while she waited as Mom drew another shuddering breath. Would she finally answer?

"Oh," Mom whispered, "do not ever think that I didn't want you, too. It was what had to be done, with each of you so different and needing different things. Besides, if I had returned, they would have known where to follow and come after Fern."

"Me?" Her mom made it sound like Fern had committed a crime—*as a baby*? Fern put a hand on her shoulder. "I think you better sit down. You've had a long weekend."

"No, I think I better ask this son o' mine for forgiveness. It's a story I will tell, but we need to start with this. Will ye forgive me, Raven lad?"

For a moment, he didn't move. Then Raven dipped his head. "I will try to, ma'am."

Fern's breath sighed out, and Mom leaned into her for a second before straightening.

"Thank you," she said, gaze still on him. "Your magic, if I might ask? Is it as strong as you showed as a teeny mite?"

"Yes, ma'am."

Mom tried to smile, but it didn't come out quite right. "You may call me Mom. Or Heather, if ye like. We don't do the 'ma'am' stuff in this house."

Raven's lips twisted into a crooked smile, too, and he shifted, making his body look less hard and distant. "We don't in our house either." He lifted a hand, and a flame in his palm rose to a ball of chestnut-brown magic.

Mom stepped closer, admiring the energy swirls in terms that Fern didn't understand.

Whoa. Mom wasn't just her mom anymore. That was weird, after thinking she was an only child her whole life. This probably wasn't as weird for Raven, since he'd had Beri as a brother for years.

Beri caught her look and edged behind Mom to her side. "That might be because there is no *ma'am* in our house," he whispered in Fern's ear. "No one this short either. I'm glad you got the tall genes."

"Me, too," she whispered back, and for once it was true. How would Beri, already a part of Raven and Merlin's family, fit into their new family? She certainly didn't want him as an adopted *brother*. Fern wrapped her arms around her middle and sighed. Or would they even be a family? Considering the boys had their own places and Raven had Willow, the time might be gone for them to be the family she'd always wished she had.

This was definitely one of Beri's *trust what happens will be right* situations.

Mom squinted at Beri, then raised her brows at Fern.

Quickly, Fern said, "Mom, this is Beri." Geez, she didn't even know his last name, if he had one.

"I'm happy to meet..." She frowned. "Not Marten's son?"

"Aye. Marten and Beryl's son. I am named for my mum. Beri Moors."

"Yes." Her eyes widened. "Beryl of the Moors of East Galloway. She'd come summers. Marten fell in love and moved to the mainland with her. They worked her father's Scottish moorland there."

"Aye, you remember correctly."

"How are your parents? Still on that land?"

"Nae. I'm sorry to bear the news to you that they've passed away."

"No." Mom clasped his arm briefly. "You poor boy. How?"

Beri told her how they'd perished, same as he'd told Fern,

apparently *his* standard answer.

"And Merlin took you in?"

"Aye. Da wanted me to grow up learning the animals, same as he had. Merlin had been like a brother to him and—" Beri shrugged one shoulder and grinned. "Who better to teach me the wild beasts than Merlin?"

"Oh my," Mom said. "This is a lot to absorb. On top of"— she put an arm around Fern and looked up at her—"finally discussing your visits to my childhood home."

"Gran needed me, which you knew."

Mom nodded.

"Why did you pretend not to know all this time? But maybe you don't know everything. Because I didn't." Fern drew a breath. "Tonight's the Council Gathering."

Raven cleared his throat. "It's the Summer Fourth Moon Council Gathering."

"Oh?" Mom seemed surprised. "And my mother wants you to attend?" She looked Fern up and down, worry crossing her features. "I suspect, from the way you're dressed, that's not all she has planned."

"I'm to be presented tonight."

Mom's arm tightened around Fern. "So soon? But..." Her features firmed into a familiar stubborn look that made Fern's stomach clench. "We need to talk. Please, sit while I make tea." She gestured to the living room.

Fern held to her arm. "I'll get it." And decide if she should just leave now.

"Let me." Willow was already turning for the kitchen, Beri on her heels.

Blowing out her breath, Fern crossed her fingers and threw herself into making sure this went well. She tucked her mom under a throw on the couch and pulled up a chair, then shoved aside magazines when Raven decided to plant himself on the coffee table. He darted looks at her and Mom, concerned but clueless. She was, too. A *talk* could be anything...or everything. She didn't have time for either. Beri returned first with a glass of orange juice. After the kettle whistled, Willow came out with a mug of tea.

Sipping the hot chamomile, Mom looked from one to the next of them. "Thank you all. Fern, I've assumed my mother's been behind your travels. You have so much in common, loving plants as you do. And I...glean she has kept you safe and protected on the isle, but this is risky. She canna be thinking o' presenting you with no magic, unless a huge change has—"

"She has magic," chorused the others.

Mom fixed her gaze on Fern, doubt clear.

"I do. Look." She flexed her fingers. *Move.* Nothing happened. Darn it all, how could it be stopped up, especially after sparking all over Dad? Oh no. Had that drained her?

"Go ahead, Fern," Willow said. "Show your mother."

Mom frowned. "Come now, sweet, you've never shown a thing growing up. Mum has probably *loaned* you magic to visit her and has stretched your hopes too far."

Fern continued to *think* about moving the magic, but nothing twitched, except her impatient fingers. *What if my magic disappears as suddenly as it appeared?* "Lady Mimosa and Gran could see it."

"They could, hmm?" Mom smiled sympathetically. "Even with the energy not showing visibly, I should sense magic within you. I never have, and I don't now."

"Perhaps you're too tired," Fern said.

Raven leaned in. "Perhaps you are out of practice."

Mom made a wry face. "Perhaps I've been doing exactly what I tell my daughter not to do—stuff myself with junk food."

Fern stared at her. "Mom. Not the funnel cakes?"

She shrugged. "It was a long show, meadowsweet. You know how it gets, eating on the run." She set down her tea, picked up the juice she'd barely touched and took a long drink.

"But *I* didn't eat show food," Fern said. "I haven't had any junk food in days. Well, some."

"Aye, except for the foul liquid you just guzzled to show me up." Raven grinned.

Fern gaped at him. "No way. Drinking pop shut down my magic? Just like that?"

Mom paused, her glass halfway to her lips. "Where did you get pop?"

"Back of the refrigerator," Fern mumbled. Mom started to laugh, just a bit gleefully, and Fern glared at her. "I know you've asked me not to, but it isn't funny right now."

Mom gestured with her glass, swirling the orange juice. "I suggest some juice."

"Hey, Fern?" Beri nudged her and nodded to his hand.

She blinked. Touching Beri hadn't failed yet. Why not? She slid her hand across and grasped his. The magical feeling tingled faintly down her arm. While not a surging flare like last time, a glow of two distinct greens grew at their clasped hands.

"Fern!"

At her mother's sharp cry, Fern dropped Beri's hand and went warm all over. Oops. Maybe that hadn't been the best way to break the news about them.

Mom fixed her narrowed eyes on Fern. "I'll be needin' to speak to my daughter alone a few minutes, if you all will excuse us?"

"We'll put things away in the kitchen," Willow said with false brightness, pulling Raven up with her and then Beri as she passed him.

Darn. She *so* did not want to have this talk. But before Fern had time to move from the couch's arm, Beri returned from the kitchen. He handed Fern a glass of orange juice and faced her mother.

"Ma'am?" he said roughly, then cleared his throat. "Lady Heather, you should know this has just come about. We met three days ago, and Fern came into her power yesterday. Though I've only known your daughter a few days, I care for her a great deal and am mindful of the isle's youth policies. We'll do naught without your permission."

Then Beri turned on his heel, walked into the kitchen and closed the door behind him.

30

The Meadows' Magic

While her mother stared after Beri, Fern settled onto the couch and doused her dry mouth with orange juice. Mom was still staring when Fern emptied the glass and set it aside. She didn't want to be the one to start, but she had to move things along, or they wouldn't return in time for her interview. "Mom, I know this is sudden for you—"

"You are so grounded," she snapped and crossed her arms without even a glance at Fern.

What? Where had that come from? What if she meant it? Ohmigod. Gran—

"No, Mom, you can't!"

"I-I..." Her face contorted into surprise—at herself?—followed by confusion, and then her jaw firmed, her gaze darting wildly when she finally did look at Fern. "You broke several rules. Getting involved with a boy I'd never *met*. Leaving when you *told* me you'd be here. Going *all the way* to Ireland and *not* telling me—"

"You *knew* I was going. *Be fair.*" Clenching her fists, Fern sucked in her breath and leveled out her tone to one her mother would acknowledge. "And I didn't leave the house. I went straight through the bathroom to Gran's bathroom."

Mom's flustered, irrational sternness dissolving into puzzlement. "The bathroom? What do you mean, the bathroom?"

"The peregrinator opens up the passage in the bathroom. You know."

"No, I don't," she said with consideration. "The one time I chanced going, I worked it from the glen up the hill out back."

Then was Willow wrong about her device containing set magic? "And it took you to Hillux?"

"No, it took me to..." Mom's this-is-the-end-of-this-conversation look started to form.

Fern gave her the look back. "Where, Mom?"

"A special spot o' mine in the Meadows," Mom huffed. "But it wasn't even safe to tread in my own habitat. A security wizard appeared, and I barely escaped. I-I was trying to contact your father."

They must have been furious that Mom took her magic, but right now that wasn't what Fern wanted to talk about. "He asked about you, Merlin did," she said softly.

Mom reached out and swiftly traced a pattern on Fern's brow, her features softening as she brought her hand down. "You've met Merlin."

Fern rubbed her tingly skin and felt an answering buzz in her own channels. Orange juice, huh? She'd have to remember that. "About an hour ago."

Mom looked away, the anger flowing out of her. "How...did he look?"

Fern grinned and leaned forward. "Great. Tall, dark and handsome."

"Still have a beard?"

"Yeah. And did I mention tall? Mom, it's so exciting. I'm not the tallest in the family anymore."

But Mom seemed not to hear. In fact, her eyes looked a little watery. Fern snuggled closer and slid her hand into her mom's. "Mom? Gran's taken good care of me there. Taught me lots of stuff. I'm getting better at growing wild plants."

But her mother stayed preoccupied. Great. Her thinking about Merlin might let Fern off light for the rest. She took a breath and plunged in. "I just met the other kids. I haven't been hiding anything with Beri from you 'cause there wasn't anything to hide. Then...it was just there, Mom. He's been so nice, so friendly, so rule-following."

Mom frowned. "That's what you like about this boy?"

"No, that's what I think you want to hear." Fern giggled. "He makes me feel like I'm special. And he smells great, like the woods." Yikes, this was going too boyfriend-girlfriendish, too soon. What else could she say? "He's tall, taller than me. Shoot. That's rare. I want to know him based just on that."

One side of Mom's mouth quirked up. "Then your energy exchange has no' been strong?"

Darn, they were going there anyway. Plus, Mom had dropped into her thickest accent—she was either really nervous or really mad.

"I canna believe I am askin' my daughter this, but sweet, 'tis so important in the magical world. You need to connect with another wizard in every way, includin' magically. When you feel his energy with yours, does it give you a thrill?"

Whoa, nervous. And this parental inquisition was even worse than the first with Merlin. What would happen when her parents got together? Fern squirmed.

Mom stroked her fluffy hair. "I'm sorry. You don't have to answer me, but you really need to think about it before you take another step with him."

Fern cleared her throat. "I think it does, Mom. For me and for him. I mean, I feel something back from Beri, and it makes my magic jump." Then, before Mom could formulate another question, she put out one of her own. "Is that why you left Merlin? Because his magic didn't connect with yours?"

"It did, lassie, but this talk isn't about me. You must decide, *Is he right for me?* Make sure before it gets more complicated." Her arm tightened around Fern.

"I want to, but I had to tell you first. Raven nearly blabbed it to Merlin, so I'm already getting the worst of having a big brother."

Mom leaned in to whisper, "That would be *little* brother. You were the firstborn twin. But don't be gloating about it, please? We have many other things to resolve."

"Like Beri?"

"Like Beri." Mom sighed. "I can tell he's sincere, honest in everything he feels for you. I haven't totally lost my magic. It only seems that way where you're concerned because I've blocked myself from reading you. In Windborne tradition, the passing of the magical heritage is eased through an open system. If I didn't block it, I'd know everything about you, and that's not fair in this world. Here, you needed privacy so you'd be like the other kids. Forgive me?"

"On one condition. Don't open it again." At her mother's frown, Fern rushed on. "Our relationship is too good, Mom. Let's not spoil it."

"Oh, Fern." Mom hugged her tight. "I don't want to lose you."

"You're not losing me, Mom. We're gaining Raven. And Merlin, if you want him back."

She plucked off her hairband and ran her fingers through her hair. "We'll see."

And like that, Mom was back to being secretive. Every kid from a broken family wished their parents would get back together—*but it's been fourteen years for Mom and Merlin.* "Is he why you never got together with any other men?"

"I suppose. Besides, they're only men." Mom's eyes went all twinkly, and her lips twitched into a smile. "I think you now understand what I mean by that."

Fern couldn't help the grin spreading over her face. "I do." She snuggled closer. "Mom? If I want to go steady with Beri, I have to register for prebonding, like Raven and Willow."

"Raven *and* Willow?" Mom pivoted toward the kitchen. "Raven!"

The door slowly opened. "Uh, yes, ma'am?" he asked.

Mom rose and waved him forward. "Get in here, all o' you." She met Raven halfway, started to put a hand on his arm and then dropped it, her face twisting uncertainly. "I'm sorry, Raven. I've missed a lot with you. I hope we can get the know each other."

Raven turned a bright red. He shuffled his feet and spoke to the floor. "Aye, I would like that." He darted a look at Mom. "If ye don't intend to disappear again. If ye will come to the isle and be a part of restoring our family's magic. If we can put this shame behind us, I can put aside my anger. And disappointment."

Lips pressed into a thin line, Mom looked stony, ready to refuse.

Oh no. Fern held her breath.

"Tall order," Mom said slowly. "I glean that if Fern is undergoing a Meadows trial, then my mum has somehow opened the way for us to return without retribution. I canna promise to return to Giuthas. However, I will help our family. I will do my best not to disappoint you." She offered Raven her hand.

He stared for a second, then shook hands. When they let go, Mom was attempting a smile. "I must sit down with you and Fern and explain what happened." She turned to Willow. "And you, too, Willow. I understand you've chosen each other."

Raven jerked his head around and glared at Fern, but Willow merely smiled in her calm way. "I look forward to it," she said.

"Splendid." Mom smiled. "Well, you young people have a festival to attend."

"Mom, really?" Did she dare ask? "I'm not grounded?"

Mom patted her cheek. "I had to drop that threat the day you took it upon yourself to travel to see my mother."

"I thought you stopped threatening it because I grew taller than you."

Everyone laughed, and Mom rolled her eyes. "If my mother has decided it's time to present you, then I will no' stop her. She didn't stop me when I left—she gave me her blessing and sent me on."

Ah, Mom did remember, as Gran said she would.

She slid a glance to Beri. "My daughter comes from a long line of witches who know their minds and aren't afraid to go after what they want."

Beri darted a look at her over Mom's head. "I think I have learned this already."

"Consider yourself warned, young man."

He broke into the smile Fern was coming to love. "I will. Thank you, Lady Heather."

Mom turned back to Fern, her gaze intense. "Is managing the Meadows truly what you want with all your heart?"

Now she was sure. "I do."

"Then I have something for you." Mom went to the sunroom and returned with her hands cupped together and held them out to Fern.

Automatically, Fern extended her hands, palms up, and Mom covered them. A warmth grew there, and Mom's lips moved in silent speech.

Willow interrupted. "Please, Lady Heather, could you say your spell aloud? Fern doesn't know what they're like. She needs to learn, and this one is special. We'll leave if you'd prefer to cast it in private."

Mom sighed. "I've been away so long I am sorely out of touch with the training of youth. Please stay." And she began to chant:

"In this mix of warming air,
I bequeath a gift to share.
To this hand I bind my power,
From Fern's hand, shall shine a tower
Built of trust and love and light,
Telling all who see the sight
The heir of the Meadows shall be Fern,
When her ancestors renounce their turn.
Magic 'o mine, mind her well,
As I give and set this spell."

At the spell's end, a weight joined the warmth in Fern's palms. Mom drew her cupped hands upward, and between them grew a sage-green beam of light, up and up as far as she could reach. Fern's fingers tingled as her mother—*her mother!*—flourished her hands in a little dance above the light and snapped her fingers. The glowing tower fizzled at the top, shot off a few sparks and promptly sank into Fern's palms. In a flash, the light blinked out.

Wow. Fern stared at the small mound of glass heather flowers resting in her hands. Innocently cool to the touch, the glass glowed with the same slight inner light it always had in Mom's display. So... "Is this *all* of the Meadows energy?"

"Aye," Mom said slowly, "but, Fern, you can't control it yet, so I've tempered what's available. This is enough for proof of my blessing."

Fern glanced at Beri, then Raven—both were frowning—then Willow, who shook her head. "Mom? You probably haven't sensed this problem, because I just learned about it myself. The Isle of Giuthas lacks the energy to maintain its shielding."

Raven shuffled closer to Fern. "When I moved my energy to the Forest habitat, the rips worsened, and the first land was lost to the ether. So folks blame me."

Mom tilted her head, her eyes narrowing.

"'Twas an accumulation of issues," Willow added quickly. "But people blame the incident that pushed it out of control."

"Can Gran help me restore this magic to the Meadows?"

"Not allowed," Raven and Willow said together. "If you want to be the Meadows' manager, then you have to bring the energy to it," Willow added.

Mom checked her watch. "I've meant for this to return to the isle and our people, but perhaps I should speak with Mum to learn exactly what has happened in my absence. Surely, with my blessing to show, tomorrow will be soon enough."

"Yeah, but..." Mom sounded upset—not with her, but maybe with the council? "Could we put in one dose, or whatever you'd call it, before I go to my interview? Like a promise of more to come?"

"That's a good compromise." Mom stared at the glass for a moment. "I-I'll make a call and be ready in a minute."

Something in her voice didn't sound right, and when Mom headed toward the kitchen, the sag of her shoulders confirmed it. Fern trotted after her. "Mom, what is it? Something's wrong."

"Well, not exactly." Mom slid an arm around Fern's waist. "Although, your news has been more exciting than mine. Some people are—were coming this afternoon to see my work."

"Can you reschedule?"

"I hope. Or send photos." She nodded to the sunroom. "They were to see this display, so it's good to have my magic safely away."

This news raced over Fern's growing disappointment. "Mom? You *never* show the sunroom stuff. *Who* are these people?"

"The owners of a jeweler's in New York City. They like my work, and we met over breakfast to discuss something on a larger scale. They have in mind a Winter Wonderland scene to display their Inspired by Nature collection. I invited them here to convince them I could do it. They had other stops, so I should be able to catch them. And likely they'll appreciate not having to drive our canyon."

They shared an understanding look. No one liked driving the winding roads to their mountain town. So, Mom would come. Fern should feel good about this, but she didn't.

Giving her a last squeeze, Mom picked up the phone and began dialing a number on a white business card from her pocket. A rhinestone sparkled in one corner.

Oh geez. This was a fancy store. A New York City store. The deal—if Mom got it—would be huge.

Fern put her hand on the phone. "No, Mom, don't be ridiculous. You have to be here to meet them."

Mom searched her face. "I hate seein' Raven and you caught in the council's sights again."

Again? Fern wanted Mom standing by her and Gran to work out returning the magic with the council, but making a living as an artist was her mom's dream. She would be so happy, and Fern wanted Mom happy. "It's too big of a chance to blow. We have to trust that the council will believe I can do this part, too."

Mom hugged her, and when she let go, the tears at her eyes echoed her wavering smile.

Willow took her arm. "Are you ready to go, Fern?"

Fern pulled out her pouch, loosened the drawstrings, took out the peregrinator and put the glass mound in its place. "Ready."

But Mom grasped her arm. "Sweet, where did you get this device?"

"From your drawer. Uh, sorry."

"Have you ever wondered why I've never missed it?"

This wasn't the chastising she'd always expected. Mom sounded troubled, not upset. "Yeah, but I figured you'd forgotten about it."

Raven snorted.

Mom glanced at him, then frowned at Fern. "One doesn't forget a peregrinator. This one isn't mine."

31

Something Suspicious

Heaviness weighed in Fern's stomach. "Where is *your* peregrinator?" she asked Mom.

"Hidden better than this one was."

"Then whose is—"

Mom raised her hand, Fern assumed to stop her questions, but a glowing ball of energy appeared between Mom's fingertips. She rolled the airy substance into a tight marble and held the magic alongside the peregrinator. Everyone leaned forward. The sage color, the same as the glass mound and the tower Mom created, matched some of the green specks in the teardrop.

"These colors are the energies of different wizards," Mom said, "of which mine is one. I don't recall ever giving energy for the creation of a device and should add that using my energy to create one without my knowledge is forbidden. Peregrinator creation is strictly monitored."

"Then, this one is illegal?"

"Even you being able to return is unsanctioned. Or was." Mom withdrew her energy. "Mum has some explaining to do."

"That's for sure," muttered Fern. She twisted the teardrop this way and that, showing each different color. "Is any of this energy hers? Could she make something like this?"

Mom threw her a questioning look, but pointed. "Mum holds this yellow-green energy."

Raven touched a fingertip to an orange-brown spot. "That matches my energy."

"Others remind me of Merlin's power," Beri added. "And Fern's."

Mom nodded toward the coffee table. "Put down the device, meadowsweet."

Fern did, and the others gathered around. Mom held her flickering palm a foot above the peregrinator and closed her eyes. Her fingers twitched. The teardrop glowed. A wind kicked up, but instead of the whirling glow rushing off to form a doorway, Mom trapped the green vortex beneath her hand. The miniature tornado twisted and turned, but couldn't escape. With what looked like some effort, she pushed down on the swirling energy, and when the others shuffled back, Fern moved with them.

The spin slowed. The energy came to a stop and, ever so slowly, started to reverse.

This was pretty cool, but probably something the others had seen before, so Fern kept her *Go, Mom* to herself. Though, when she looked around, Willow's brow was creased, and Raven was biting his lip.

"Flights," Beri muttered beside her.

Within the slowly revolving vortex, colors separated into bands, threaded by a glinting light. Bright green to sage, yellow green, rusty brown, chestnut brown and back to bright green.

"Mostly the same colors," Fern said, "with that clearish vein weaving through. Nothing unusual, right?"

Mom's eyes flashed open. She darted her gaze to Fern,

then she squatted and watched the glowing light beneath her hand.

Willow slid a hand into the crook of Fern's arm. "What vein?"

The heaviness returned to Fern's stomach. "A line of light that changes color as it weaves among the others." She wove her hand like a swimming fish. "Like, iridescent." The others stared, and it hit her: No one else could see *that*.

Why did I open my big mouth?

In a quick move, Mom squeezed her hand into a fist. The light went out with a *snap*.

She reached for Fern's hand, keeping her gaze on the peregrinator. Mom's hand was warm, much warmer than usual when holding hers. Ah, Mom was searching her, like Lady Mimosa had done.

At last, Mom nodded and gestured to the peregrinator. "You can pick up your device."

Fern reached out, then stopped. Mom hadn't touched her teardrop. "It's safe?"

"Aye, 'tis perfectly safe. The device responds exactly as if cast from a scripted spellbook. The energy is strong, compliant...and tied to you." But she was frowning when she tilted her head back to stare at Fern. "It can't be split to reveal its origin, so the maker is secreted."

"Ohh, Fern. A secret gift." Willow sighed, and Fern couldn't tell if this was a good or a bad thing.

Raven cleared his throat. "I had the idea you don't practice magic in the human world."

Mom gave him a side-glance. "I don't."

"Well." He sent back a shy grin. "That was impressive...Mom."

"Flights," Beri muttered again, and then they were questioning Mom in words Fern didn't understand. Wizard talk.

Mom didn't answer. She pulled Fern alongside her and walked her across the hall to the bathroom. "Come along, everyone."

Okaaay, Mom was good with the trips. With Merlin. With the presentation. With Beri, even. But the peregrinator wasn't Mom's.

Who had given her this? How did the person know she'd have the magic to use it—when she hadn't known herself?

Mom ushered them into the bathroom. "Knowing my mum, you're safe, Fern," she said, "but I should like some assurance of that. I have time enough to speak with her. Open it, please."

Fern opened her portal and led everyone through to Hillux.

Hilda was waiting in Gran's bathroom. The guinea pig let out a shriek, followed by irritated chittering, which brought quick footsteps down the hall. Gran appeared in the open doorway, and behind her, Merlin.

32

Family Secrets

Awkward.

That was the only way to describe this meeting. *In a bathroom.*

Please don't let this be so bad it keeps Mom from returning to the Isle of Giuthas again.

"Good afternoon," Merlin said formally.

"Everyone is dressed for tonight," Gran said. "Good. Heather? Beautiful dress."

"Thank you. Fern chose it for me last Christmas. Er, Winter Solstice." Mom smiled tightly and brushed past Fern to kiss Gran on the cheek. "How are you, Mum?"

"That depends, I suppose, on why you are here."

Together, their delicate pointed faces and slender frames weren't as identical as Fern had imagined, though their voices did sound alike. Mom was making an effort to keep the accent from hers, plus holding herself straighter to make the most of her few additional inches.

Merlin cleared his throat. "We had hoped you might have a few minutes to share our story with our children before tonight."

"We had hoped someone could explain the origin of this device." Mom gestured to the peregrinator in Fern's hand.

Merlin nodded. "Certainly."

"I have less than an hour before an appointment."

"An art appointment?" Gran made a harrumphing noise.

Irritation flicked through Fern. "Gran, not *now*."

Mom lifted her chin and fixed Gran with her don't-mess-with-me look. "As it so happens, yes."

Gran turned. "The water is hot. Willow, would you help me serve tea?"

Willow and Raven both followed her, then Merlin.

Mom glanced at Beri. "You are welcome to stay," she said, then trailed after the others. Despite sounding casual, Mom held her arms stiffly at her sides, her fingers clenched.

Not good.

Beri lightly touched her shoulder. "'Tis nae my place to hear your family stories."

No, maybe not yet. Fern nodded.

He gave her a quick one-armed hug—they both flashed—then left through the back door.

Fern darted forward and wrapped an arm around her petite mother as they walked into the living room together. "I love you, Mom," she whispered.

"Love you, too, my meadowsweet." Mom squeezed her tight. "Beri?" And when Fern explained, she said, "You may share the story with him. If you like."

That was interesting. "Thanks."

Mom went to the couch, opposite the only other armchair, which Merlin occupied, and settled into it as if she sat there every day. Fern sat beside her. The steady patter of rain outside—the watering they'd requested hours ago—filled the silence and made the room more dim and close than usual.

Merlin looked around and stood. "This won't do," he mut-

tered and waved a hand. A love seat popped in from nowhere and swirled into place at a right angle to the couch,
edging out the coffee table, which came so close that Fern
flinched back. It would have missed her knees as it scooted
toward the bay window, but *still*. This was freaky, and just
when she thought he was done, pillows plumped and an afghan straightened in a bizarre mimicry of magic on old tele-
vision shows.

"Er, Dad?" Raven stopped between the couch and love
seat, a cup and saucer in each hand.

"Hmm?"

Raven tilted his head toward Fern, before offering Mom
the teacup.

"Oh, right." He leaned over and patted her knee. "Lass,
sorry. I didn't think."

"Yeah. A little notice next time would be nice."

Willow passed Fern chamomile tea and sat next to Raven
on the love seat. Gran delivered a teacup to Merlin and sat on
the other side of Mom, and then everyone was seated, leaving only enough space in the center for their legs to cross
without their feet hitting. Clinking china echoed through the
now silent cottage, broken by a periodic *whoo* of someone
blowing across the top of their steaming cup.

Then Mom leaned forward, extended her cup and saucer
as if to set it into thin air. A small round table appeared, and
the china landed with a *clink!*

Fern blinked. It wasn't a table she'd seen before.

"So." Mom looked around. "I suppose this story begins
when I was about thirteen. I had a surge of new energy that
year. With puberty."

Sheesh, Mom didn't look at all fazed to be saying *that* in

front of everyone. Merlin and Raven side-eyed each other and put their tea things on the table.

"I, and all my...activities, went from flying under the radar, er"—Mom shot an eye roll to Fern—"from escaping the notice of the islanders, to being under close scrutiny. I didn't like it."

"Of course you didna," Gran said a bit too cheerily. Everyone looked at her, so clearly Fern wasn't the only one to think her attitude was off. But Gran sipped her tea, somewhat smiling as she did, a conspiratorial gleam in her eyes. "She was wild."

Mom sighed. "Aye, to put it bluntly. Thank you, Mum."

Maybe Gran was doing it to make Mom more comfortable, but her comments made Fern even tenser.

"Flights," Raven breathed. "Worse than Dad?"

"No comparison," Gran chirped.

Mom cleared her throat. "Planning to stay, Mum?"

"Now, Heather. 'Twas my fault as well. You were headstrong, but I let you be." Gran took another sip of tea, and Mom sighed again, and Fern got it. This was something they'd been over and over before, an old, rehashed story that'd had no resolution. Even after twenty-some years.

"You must admit," Gran said, "there was a fair amount to *scrutinize*. Dead trees sculpted into rearing bears, the entire Upper Meadow blooming in the pattern of a sunrise over the mountains, the pink bunnies, tropical flowers painted on the backs of sunning turtles."

Merlin spread his hands. "Exotic blooming lily pads erupting over Sir Snap's pond with an arching bridge overhead." The focus of his eyes went distant, and a slight smile played on his lips.

"The water colored azure," Gran said. "Snap feared it would kill the fish."

"Oh, for heaven's sake." Mom scowled at Merlin. "Don't encourage her to remember more." Then her face softened. "I still love Monet."

"Aye, Monet. Molding the winter grass into a dozen of those oddly angled haystacks might have been your undoing." Gran shook her head over her tea.

"Or the spattered cliff face on the north side of Mount Lookout," Merlin said. "Jackson Pollock, right?"

Mom flipped up her hands. "I admit, it got...out of hand. But I did my work"—she looked pointedly at Gran, who nodded demurely—"and directed my energy elsewhere. Away from the isle."

"'Twas a good choice," Gran murmured. "I allowed it as well."

"In a way. You didn't stop me." Mom held Gran's gaze for a long moment, and then her mother's stiff shoulder pressing Fern's arm relaxed, and the hint of a smile curled one corner of her mouth. "To continue with *my* story, I met a witch who needed a helper when she went to Renaissance fairs to sell her love charms. I helped carry her supplies, set up, take down and guarded the booth while she took breaks. Otherwise, I was free to beg the artists to let me try their crafts."

"Oh! Glassworking." This fit the sketchy story Fern had heard before. "That's when you met the glass sculptor."

"Exactly. He and his wife had an old-fashioned lampworking setup for the fairs, but also brought their modern torch for flameworking, and she taught me to use it behind the booth. They let me sell, and as I got better, I reimbursed them for the glass and bought my own materials."

Now the pieces were coming together for Fern. "You'd started your business, way back then."

Mom nodded. "I was clearing a profit, but since I had to hide my travels, I had little I could spend it on except my business. Your father and I bonded. He covered for my absences, too, just as Mum always had. Mum passed me the management of the Meadows because she thought it would settle me on our land. I got pregnant and had the two of you. Then, at the birth presentations, Fern didn't glow."

A week ago, Fern would have laughed at the image of a baby glowing. But now she knew. Or thought she did. "No magic?"

"No magic."

Fern swallowed. "And Raven?"

"Did. Strongly. Twins. They assumed he got all the power, though you were a boy and a girl and obviously not a split egg. Several elders wouldn't listen. This was the way it always was with twins, they said, going back generations. Of course, their decree was to do what had always been done." Mom's face twisted, and tears sprang to her eyes.

Fern's hands shook. She clenched them to stop anything from happening. "Kill me?"

"Oh, no, my meadowsweet!"

Mom's arm swept around Fern's shoulders, and it was like she was nine again, reading her first scary story and wishing she hadn't. The roaring in her ears was so bad, Fern couldn't make out what anyone was saying. She buried her face in Mom's hair. *This is more horrible than I imagined.*

"Fern?" Mom lifted her chin. "That never would have happened," she said fiercely. "Windborne might be old-fashioned, but we would never murder."

"Wh-what would have happened?" she asked. *What's gonna happen to Kory?*

Mom brushed away her tears. "In a small enclave like ours, some people focus unduly on guarding against hard times. The wizards leading the council upheld the policy that Giuthas should only host a population of magical people who would add to its prosperity." Her lips pressed into a thin line, and she looked at Merlin.

"If you showed no magic by your third year, the edict was to seal your cores permanently through an irreversible spell. You would be taken to a human city and left with their enforcement officers for adoption, never to know of or be allowed into the Windborne world."

Oh. My. God. *Totally* cut off from her family, even Mom—*Crack.*

Fern's hands lit up with fire.

"Steady there." In an instant, Merlin knelt beside her, his hands cupped around hers, a red-brown glow suppressing the green flames seeping between her fingers.

"Oh, Fernie." Mom looked as ill as Fern felt. "I never considered it."

"She didn't," Merlin said. "*We* didn't."

"It didn't happen." Raven fell at her knees and awkwardly patted her leg. "Mom and Dad made sure it didn't happen."

"Not as long as I was alive," Gran added. "And Heather made sure they knew how furious their decision made her."

Taking *all* their family magic—yeah, that made a point.

Merlin pressed on her hands. "People now speak of consideration and making allowances for change. After fourteen years, a new system isn't perfectly in place, but council judgments have been more accommodating. They acknowledge that one community member's unhappiness will affect everyone. Lark moved the assessment to sixth year and is pushing to find those children fulfilling roles here, with their families."

"Many of our habitat tasks are nonmagical," Gran said. "My committee presents our proposal at the fall Council Gathering."

A tear rolled down Fern's cheek. She sniffed and tried to stop others.

Teary-eyed herself, Willow leaned over Raven and pressed something into his hand. Seconds later, her brother gently wiped a handkerchief over Fern's face. Their eyes met, dark brown to orange hazel.

"But will they be allowed management positions?" Fern asked. "You told them I had magic, so they'd accept my trial. Is that fair to exclude nonmagical people from having land?"

Gran harrumphed. "'Twas *intended* to include these proposals."

"The isle's current problems have created more dispute," Merlin said.

"Mom did the right thing, *for then*," Raven said. "It's up to us to fix it for the future." Raven gave her a lopsided grin, and Willow wiped her eyes.

"Thanks," Fern whispered. "I want to help. If I ever get a chance." Clearly, she'd never be a good advocate as a late-comer to magic that she couldn't control. She focused on her fingers. *Move.* Her green energy returned to her core, and she closed it. No one had suggested locking her power. "Could you finish telling"—*this nightmare*—"your story?"

Mom squeezed her shoulders. "You were checked month-ly." She shook her head. "Mum and a few others negotiated for a reprieve. Yet, by the time you turned two, it was obvious no one would go against the ones campaigning for the traditional solution."

"We knew we had to make other plans," Merlin said.

Mom drew in a deep breath. "I wanted to disappear into a larger Windborne city. Merlin was willing to go, but four of us would be harder to hide."

"And we would be sought."

"Our elders were very single-minded," said Gran.

"So was Heather," Merlin said. "After a number of go-arounds about what to do, she became set on going into the human world. She knew the ways. She had enough money to buy what we needed and the glass supplies and clients for her work. She was excited. I...I was less sure."

"It's not your fault, Merlin," Mom began, but he waved her off.

"I'd not had the same experiences as your mother. To be a Windborne in another world would be difficult. Particularly to hide Raven as he matured."

"Aye." Mom looked at him through watery eyes, but with a smile. "Those plans fell apart because he did. Much sooner than most babies. Our lad, you glowed whenever you were happy."

"Which was most of the time," Gran said. "And he flashed when he didna get his way."

Shoot. "The flip side of my problem," Fern said. "If baby Raven"—he scowled—"had to live in the human world, he'd have had no life."

"The day it became evident Raven couldna go was the day Heather decided she had to," Merlin said. "Alone."

Mom leaned forward. "I didn't—"

"Ye did," Merlin snapped. "And there was no more talk. No listening."

Mom opened her mouth, closed it and crossed her arms. They glared at each other, and Fern swore the air crackled. She didn't dare move, positioned as she was between them.

Raven nudged Merlin. "You had a fight," he breathed into their tight circle.

Merlin nodded, but kept his gaze on Mom. "The fight to end all fights. I'm surprised half the islanders didn't turn up."

"Too afraid," Gran murmured, and Mom glared at her.

"Heather took our child and left," Merlin said in a rush, "thankfully visiting Mimosa to say goodbye. They could verify I hadn't annihilated her."

"I couldna wait for them to seal my escape," Mom hissed.

Merlin grunted. "I wasna ready to give up on our people." He wiped a hand down his beard and tugged hard. "Perhaps I never would have been."

Mom and Merlin were still staring at each other, but a little less hostilely.

Fern couldn't stand it. "And then?"

"That was it," Merlin said sadly. "Heather was gone. You were gone. No one knew where. The council was vexed, then outraged upon discovering she'd also taken the Meadows' magic. They issued an edict that Heather would be seized and punished. Afterward, no one spoke of her. Of either of you."

"'Twas as if they had never been here," Gran said, equally solemn.

Geez, her guess about the Witness Protection Program hadn't been far off.

"The community—most of them—realized a huge mistake

had been made," Merlin said. "Though, none dared tell the council they were wrong. I tried to find you, but had no success. Years passed. The Meadows maintained awhile on residual strength. People died. Lark was appointed to the council. The edict was lifted."

"Merlin gave up hope of ever seeing them again," Gran said. "But I didna. I managed our system, so when the day came, I could keep both with us. I had more faith in the path he'd laid."

"The peregrinator." Fern took the glass teardrop from her pouch. "Earlier, you knew I needed to travel from Hillux to see Mom."

Mom stiffened beside her. "So it *was* you," she said, her tone abrupt. "Do tell."

Darting an apologetic glance to Mom, Merlin shifted back, stroking his beard. "Before we—you—left, Lark had asked us to keep in contact. You were busy with the babies, so she and I conjured a path back to Hillux into one of your art pieces. As you became more determined, so did I, and because we were fighting, I shifted the spellwork to magically hide the object and cast it to be for Fern alone."

"I couldn't decipher the mix of energy in it," Mom said irritably.

He waved to all of them in the circle. "Yours, mine, Raven's and Lark's. All of the Meadows, so Fern's family magic would remain with her in the human world. I slipped the glass among your things, with a clinging charm and a years-long invisibility incantation. I didn't want you seeing it soon."

Fern rolled the cool glass between her palms. Wow, years? "But I see the green of my magic in here, too."

"That was the tricky part." Merlin grinned. "The device recognized you as a Meadows and added your energy as you touched it. When did you find the gift?"

Holy crap, he could do that? No wonder Raven said Merlin should teach her. "When I was really little, I'd seen it in Mom's things and took it for dress-up. About five years ago, I noticed it glowed."

Merlin's brows shot up. "That's when the first rip appeared at a Forest-Marsh boundary. It couldn't be dispelled, only bypassed."

"What caused it, if it wasn't at the Meadows?" she asked.

Gran and Merlin exchanged glances, and Gran said, "That's another person's story to tell."

Five years. *Kory is five years old.* But could a rip forming at a Forest boundary have anything to do with him? Sheesh, she'd keep quiet for now. "Two winters ago, Mom had the flu. I was in the bathroom, holding the teardrop and happened to say, 'I wish I could go to family for help.' My teardrop opened the portal, and Gran and I found each other. She gave me tea for Mom's fever." She shrugged. "I suppose that's when Raven took his magic to the Forests?"

Gran nodded. "When he left, I used Meadows magic to call to your device. It gave me so much hope when the magic drew you back, but I kept your arrival secret. I'd always wondered if some nonmagicals could eventually open their magic."

"Flights." Merlin pointed at Gran. "You had the whole isle bamboozled."

Mom's lips quirked. "Where do you think I learned it?"

They all laughed.

But not everything seemed settled to Fern. She slipped a

hand through Mom's arm. "You said *some* of the people on the council from back then are gone. Who are the others?"

As she spoke, Mom, Merlin and Gran were already shaking their heads. Raven lifted his eyebrows in a you-got-me look, but Willow was biting her lip.

Her poker face had failed—*and I need that information. But later.* "Are they angry?"

"It doesn't matter," Gran said. "You have magic. You are your mother's heir. You are capable of a portion, perhaps all, of the duties." She faced Mom. "You do not wish to return, Fern says."

With a sad, apologetic look, Mom shook her head.

Gran nodded firmly. "So we shall present Fern, and if they do not see reason, we will appeal. With this magic, the process to repair rips and rifts can begin. No more patching and bypassing to get by. I am not above holding it out like a carrot."

Mom frowned. "I've tempered what she can have, Mum."

With a mirroring frown, Gran asked to see the glass mound. "The isle is failing, Heather. Only Mimosa's steady support has kept the Meadows from crumbling. Instead, other land is breaking apart. Humans linger outside our shield, clearly seeing more than they should. Our people are frightened and angry. We need it all."

Mom took the glass and rubbed it thoughtfully. "Show me our land."

Of course, it was raining—the request Beri had made earlier. Gran pulled out capes and umbrellas, and Fern led the way to the top of Hillux.

Mom looked over the display garden, her smile making Fern's heart swell. Mom hugged her, then held Fern at arm's length as Merlin had done. "I believe you have been here more than I realized, my meadowsweet. Well done."

"Yeah, Mom, about that nickname? Meadowsweet, the ratna? How sneaky-clever can you be?"

"It's not like I forgot this life, Fern." She stroked Fern's cheek. "The ratna, as the Windborne name says, is the most precious thing a wizard has in their habitat. You were the most precious thing I brought with me from my Windborne life. But it would have sounded pretty odd in the human world to be calling you 'my ratna.'"

Fern laughed. "Thanks for sparing me that." She led them to the three ratna plants.

Mom handed Fern the glass mound, squatted with her umbrella and dug her fingers into the soil at the base of one ratna. Merlin did the same to another.

Raindrops beat steadily on the damp ground. Impossible that they thought her plants weren't healthy, but Fern offered, "I can hand-water them again."

Raven nudged her. "Not water. They're checking energy."

"Not bonded," Mom said. "Perfect time to introduce a little of my energy so the plants will accept it."

Merlin swiped dirt from his fingers. "The roots have a good start growing, possibly due to your magic. To move them now would kill the plants. I trust you put them where you wanted them?"

"Fern knows what she's doing." Gran sniffed.

But apparently, only with plants. The small dose she tried to apply to her ratna gushed a bucket's worth, all Mom had allotted, in one dump. "It's stronger than mine. Faster. Like, jumpy and intense...oh. *Mom.*"

Everyone laughed, and Mom lifted her hands. "Can you

understand now why the slow pace of plants doesn't hold my attention?"

"At least it's going to the ratna," Raven muttered, then, catching Fern's glance, added, "Practice will help."

"That's a dose, as you wished." Mom took the glass mound and rubbed it. "Here's a bit more for the council to see. The rest will come once you are accepted."

"Mom." Fern huffed in exasperation. "You can't just hold out on Giuthas and our people!"

"I canna?" Mom offered her the glass, with her don't-mess-with-me look.

When Fern didn't take it, Gran did. "Put it away, dear. This is the carrot. Only if we need it," Gran added quickly. "You have not experienced their mulish attitudes."

She hadn't, but Raven had been treated terribly, so maybe a secret stash would help if they said no because she had no bond.

Back in Hillux, Gran reminded her to be at the Meadows display forty minutes before sunset and left. Fern and Raven walked Mom down the hall.

"I'll try to hurry the jewelers along." Automatically, Mom traced a series of lines on Fern's forehead. She kissed the spot and turned to Raven. "Is it possible I might hug you, too?"

He bent and hugged Mom and whispered something to her.

"Oh." Mom's voice caught, then she sketched a charm on Raven's brow. Her final sealing with a kiss lasted extra long while Mom stroked his hair.

Fern sighed a very happy sigh. Raven was turning out to be not so bad, but better yet, Merlin and Mom hadn't argued for the last fifteen minutes. A bit of hope rose in her chest.

The screen door creaked, and Beri walked in—making her even *more* hopeful. He and Willow came over and said good-bye to Mom.

"I look forward to seeing you all again." Mom's gaze rested on Beri for an extra beat.

He nodded to her solemnly, but when he turned away, his face lit into a broad grin.

33

Is He Right for Me?

Back at the Gathering Place, the lengthening shadows should have signaled the calm and conclusion of the day, but the air rang with excited calls, and people charged back and forth over the grassy peninsula, many carrying animals. Several wagons now sat near the tent area, and a large sailboat had docked at the eastern bluff, with a second one farther out. Families were erecting more tents as the sun made its slow progression toward the sea.

Beri squinted westward. "'Tis over an hour until the sun sets."

It's nearly time. Nervousness hit Fern. "Where will my interview take place?" she asked Willow and Beri.

"The council's grove in the fire circle." Willow waved toward the lush growth of the displays.

Glowing energy domed several now, the closest peach-colored, and behind it a balloon of golden-yellow energy began rising. When Fern exclaimed over it, Willow stopped walking.

"Oh, I should help with that. Do you mind if I run ahead?" Willow gave Beri a pleading look.

"Of course. I'll stay with her."

Beri smiled at Fern, cute with his freckles and reddish curls, but rougher around the edges than some of her fellow high school students. Less put-together, more outdoorsy. *Like me.*

A wave of longing flooded Fern, so she hardly noted Willow wishing her luck and saying goodbye. Mom had okayed Fern's travels to the isle, and by her last look, Mom approved of him. It was up to Fern now. *Is he right for me?*

She ought to practice with the ratna or think about the interview questions, but no way could she get better at either in an hour. Instead, they walked toward the privacy of a deserted cliff. Once school started again, time would be tight. How would Beri fit into her schedule? What was his schedule like?

"Do you often work on the mainland?" she asked.

With a shiver, Beri shook his head. "Not if I can avoid it."

Okaaay, good news, but...she'd overheard Old Snap and Mr. Grouse say something about this when they'd thought she was asleep in the boat. "Why don't you like to leave?"

He stopped at the bluff's edge. The waves crashed on black boulders far below, sending up a constant roar and salting the air. Shoulders hunched, hands in his pockets, Beri spoke to the jutting rocks. "You know the car accident that killed my mum? Some conveniences humans use are an unnecessary risk. Nothing like that would ever happen in a Windborne community."

"But you went to Lady Soila's in a motor boat."

He shifted uneasily. "I had to. To ensure you were safe."

"And?"

"And what?"

Fern wiped her sweaty palms inside the pockets of her dress. "What happens if we prebond? Will you visit me in Colorado? Or will I always have to come here?"

His green eyes narrowed, and his jaw worked. Finally, he pursed his lips. "'Tis not so bad, going off. I suppose my reluctance to travel has changed in the last few days. As much as I love the isle, I've watched Raven. And Merlin. It gets lonely if you don't have someone to share it with."

Did he mean *her*?

"I am willing to go off the isle to be with you. As long as you understand that I intend to live here."

She didn't mind that he wanted to live here—she did, too—but the flush of heat creeping down her neck was making it hard to find something to say.

He heaved a sigh. "Spells. I just like it better here. Pure soil, huge trees. Our wildlife are protected, and the people have room to...*be*. I work outdoors every day, and I find it verra satisfying sharing a beautiful piece of land that's looked like this for hundreds of years and will likely look the same for hundreds more." He darted a glance at her. "My energy and I contribute to the process, not harm it like most of humanity. That might sound preachy to you, but everyone here wants the same, and I don't have to defend my desires to anyone."

Oh. Wow. No one had ever bared their soul to her like this. She touched Beri's arm. "Not preachy at all. I get it. I mean, I feel that way myself when I see development of buildings, parking lots and roads that take down trees. This land is part of my life now and I want to see how it goes with us, but you know I have to go back for school."

"For a year." The hint of a smile returned. "I asked Lady Lark."

"Yeah, for *at least* the next year. Mom's pretty set on me going to college."

"Ah, academy." He gestured that they should continue walking along the bluff. "You could go to a Windborne academy and learn magic as well. Maybe we could go together."

Together. That would be...*ohmigod*. Fern clasped her tingling hands. Seeing him every day. In classes together, studying together. Having a boyfriend to share...everything. "You'd do that? Oh, but what about the Meadows? I wouldn't be able to go off and still watch over the Meadows." Suddenly, her promise to Gran seemed complicated, and her stomach was flipping pancakes again, so she wrapped her arms around herself.

"Fern?" Beri brushed the back of her hand.

Her energy ping-ponged inside her core, and she thought it'd escaped, but it hadn't.

"Don't worry about what will be. Just pass your last interview so you *have* some decisions to make." He blushed a bright red, but still grinned. "Pass or not, I'm hoping Lady Heather will approve a prebonding so we may get to know each other better."

"Me, too." But Mom was leaving it to her. How could she know if he was the one, since she wasn't even supposed to touch him, except for holding hands?

Beri began walking again, and she fell into step. More people were circling the peninsula. Beri introduced her to a few, mentioning where they lived, but she was too nervous to remember much beyond the habitats being ones she hadn't heard of before.

Then a guy approached. A buccaneer? Grinning through a scraggly brown beard, he smoothed his windblown hair and ran his hands down a tunic blousing over belted breeches that ended in black leather boots. Wow. Giuthas probably didn't sanction looting, and this guy didn't have a sword, but a dagger hung in a leather holder at his hip, and he swaggered in a pretty good imitation of a pirate.

He knocked Beri with his elbow, who returned a good-natured cuff to the guy's neck. "Fern, may I present Salmon of the Seas, or Salm as he's known. His family manages the fisheries, a major food source for our people, you ken."

That explained why Sir Dolph hadn't liked her answers about harvesting game birds—he wanted the Meadows to keep up their contribution.

"Pleased to meet you, lass," Salm said. "And I'd be more pleased to get to know you."

Fern kept a smile on her face. No sense in offending anyone, even if this guy was full of himself.

"Coral has been looking for you, Beri. What say I take this lass 'round to show her the schooner while you find her?"

Beri laughed. "After what your sister pulled on me last spring? No."

"That's only because she cares for you and teases—"

"Not interested." Beri urged Fern forward, and Salm fell into step with them.

"Don't seek Coral, then." Salm threw his hands up in exaggeration. "'Tis true. She's on the prowl for a partner, but you're no longer on her list. Beri, my good mate, give a lad a break and let me show this lass around. You know we're rarely ashore. 'Tis a treat to mingle."

Beri raised his brows. "Then why are you interested in taking Fern to your ship?"

"Girls find it irresistible." He grinned even broader. "It helps with the mingling."

With a huff, Beri turned to Fern. "He makes no secret of

his intentions. Do you wish to see his schooner?"

Salm was interested in her without even knowing her? Ha, that kind of guy didn't appeal to her. But she did want to see the boat, and Beri, though clearly annoyed by the request, had just passed one of those tests the magazines said to watch for in a guy: being too possessive and trying to control a girl's activities.

Is he right for me?

"I'd like to see the ship," Fern told Salm, keeping one eye on Beri. "We don't get many chances for that in Colorado."

Beri raised a finger. "Salm, you have fifteen minutes. Can I trust you to return her to the Meadows display by then?"

"Aye, aye, Captain." Salm made a false salute.

Beri's lips pressed into a line. "Laugh if you must, but 'tis Lady Lark who directed me to have her apprentice back before sunset. For her final interview, you ken?"

The smile faded from Salm's face. "Lady Lark's apprentice, I ken." He nodded. "I'll mind the time. Thank you."

Beri was carrying out Gran's instructions, so this wasn't about them. Still, a soft, warm feeling of gratitude spread through her chest.

"Hurry now, lass." Salm grabbed her hand and tugged her across the grass. "Where have you come from?"

She told him the truth—everyone would know soon anyway—and pulled her hand loose. She didn't feel anything from his touch, but if she did spark, she wanted to be out of sight of Beri. He wasn't the only one who would be disappointed if this test showed that her energy sparked with other guys, too. She answered Salm's questions about travel from Colorado, and they arrived at a stone staircase leading down the cliff to a dock. He offered a hand to help her, but she grasped the rail instead.

From behind her, Salm said, "I'll have you wanting to hold my hand again soon enough. How old are you?"

She glanced back. Yep, he was looking her over. "Seventeen. How old are you?"

"Nearing nineteenth year. You are old enough to pre-bond."

Good grief. These wizards were more frank, even if they had additional rules to deal with. *But still,* why would he mention that? Instead of telling him a rude, *Stuff it,* Fern repeated a warning Lady Mimosa had given Ches last night. "You're speaking out of turn."

Salm's laughter rang out, scaring up a flock of gulls perched among the rocks. "True enough. But my family hardly gets ashore. Necessity makes the Seas family members more forward. Or at least those of an age to bond and not having found a partner."

His wave urged her to keep descending. "But I will have me own sailboat when I pass the nineteenth year. There, what do you think?"

They'd reached the planks of the dock, but because she'd been watching her feet, Fern only now noticed how much the ship loomed overhead. She gasped. "Wow. It's huge."

He laughed easily again. "But small when 'tis all the space you have to pace for a week with no females but your sisters in sight."

This guy was *embarrassingly* honest. As they hurried along the dock, he told her about his family on the ship and those living on the Scottish coast. "'Tis boring, except for the lasses. They have a fair many there."

Fern laughed. She'd learned more in minutes about Salm

than some people in three years at Boulder High. He gestured she should climb the boat's ramp. The narrow line of boards swayed with the rolling waves. She waited for the sway to still, but three steps up, another wave hit, and she stumbled.

Salm caught her at the waist, momentarily holding her against his body before taking her hand. "Told you I'd be holding your hand again."

He was arrogant, but she held tight anyway. She inched up the ramp and let Salm lead her over the rocking deck. He named all the parts of the double-masted schooner, the only term she remembered. Fern couldn't stop thinking of his callused palm against hers and the lack of tingling in her magic.

Nothing happened. *Interesting.*

Salm steered her by the arm to the stern to point to the distant cliffs on the Scottish mainland, and nothing happened. Even when he boldly draped his arm about her shoulders, nothing happened.

Geez, a simple brush of Beri's fingers over the back of her hand had... *No, don't think of that now.*

Oh shoot, she'd closed her core. Was she really controlling it that well? *It's now or never.*

Fern took a breath and, out of view of anyone, released her magic.

Energy trickled into her channels. She certainly felt that and the faint, ready whisper of it in her hands, arms and back. When Salm pointed out his sister's approaching schooner, Fern leaned into him to listen to his description. Her magic traveled under her skin's surface, registering on her subconscious as a bright green haze. It was *right there.*

Her energy didn't jump or spark. Fern closed her eyes

and saw Beri smiling encouragingly, slipping his hand into hers and the glow lighting them—right before Mom yelled. Then he'd fixed everything: *We'll do naught without your permission.*

He had to be the one... But was she *sure*?

Sorry, Beri.

Fern pushed her energy to flood her arm against Salm's *and* her shoulder tucked into Salm's chest *and* her back where the weight of Salm's arm rested. It obeyed.

Nothing. This boy's arm about her was warm and pleasant in the wind, but nothing more.

Thank goodness.

"Fern?"

She turned to face him, her lips inches from his, as close as she'd been to Beri when they'd hugged and erupted in glowing, swirling green. Salm acted more like a guy about to kiss her than Beri had.

But when he opened his mouth, it was only to ask, "There's naught for you either? No spark?"

What? She shifted away, and he dropped his arm. "You mean you're checking me out, too?"

"Of course. Don't you always?"

Always? What the heck? This was *not* the guy for her. Yet he'd given her the answer she wanted, and for that she could kiss him. Uh... Fern took a step back. "I'm new at this."

"Your mum's just turned you loose, eh? I ken, don't worry. You'll find someone who sparks you."

Oh geez. Not going there. "Has it ever happened for you?"

Salm flashed a reckless grin. "Aye. But she isn't sure about life aboard a ship, so I keep looking to see if there may be another." He shrugged. "So far, naught. Only her, and she won't come aboard with my family to learn to handle a larger craft with me."

She patted his arm. "I'm sorry, Salm."

"They say 'twill work out eventually." He drew in a breath and unfolded his arms. "I best return you to Lady Lark and scurry back to help my sister dock."

"Right. Thank you."

He narrowed his eyes. "For what, lass?"

"For helping me know my mind."

"You are welcome." Salm leaned in and kissed her.

On the lips.

Not hard or pushy, but on the lips. She froze. He tasted salty.

And that was it.

He tilted back his head and then shook it. "Naught."

While they ascended the stairs, she put away her magic. Beri was waiting a ways off. The boys waved to each other, and Salm disappeared down to the water once more as Fern crossed the grass to meet Beri.

He stopped feet from her, one hand rubbing at the back of his neck. "So what did you think?"

"Their boat is huge. What a way to spend your days."

"Fern." Beri looked exasperated. He rumpled his hair. Lines creased his brow. "What did you think about Salm? About his energy?"

"What? You knew he'd check out my energy?"

"Salm checks out the energy of every lass. Repeatedly."

For real?

"Well, except for Willow after she decked him this spring. She'd had enough since she'd prebonded with Raven. So?"

"Zilch." Telling him was good. Honest and open. She stepped closer, rubbing her hands over her cool arms. "Didn't do a thing."

"Excellent!" Beri raised a clenched fist in the air and hopped a few steps of a jig.

His grin warmed her all over again. "You *were* worried I'd be different. Being new to the isle and new to my magic?" Though, why she'd ever thought anything would happen with Salm was quickly becoming ridiculous—next to Beri, her heart raced like she'd just finished a wrestling match. On top.

"'Twould do no good. If not now, later Salm would find a way. From what I've heard, he's never had success with any lass of the settlement."

Fern wasn't supposed to, but she couldn't help it. She traced a finger along Beri's wrist and up his forearm.

Flames leaped from her touch. She snatched her hand back. *Ohmigod.*

"Spells," Beri yelped, his eyes widening. He lifted his arm, with its line of intermingled bright and dark green flames. His gaze shot from the flickering energy, to her. "Zilch with Salm?"

Fern nodded. The flames died without leaving a mark.

"Did...did you touch him like that?"

She shook her head slowly. "More. He had his arm around me, and I totally released my magic into its channels and pressed into him. Nothing happened."

Beri's breath hitched, and his jaw hardened. "You opened...you tried... *And Salm didna kiss you?*"

"Not then, but he did a minute later." At the narrowing of Beri's eyes, Fern leaned closer and added, "Nothing happened then either."

"Naught. Good." He glanced toward the displays, before looking at her again.

Maybe it was time to go. "We should—"

He bent his head and pressed his lips to hers.

Fern froze. They weren't supposed to be doing this. But she so wanted to! His mouth felt like fire on hers, smooth fire that raced over her face and down her neck before he lifted his head. Shoot, she must be beet red, the heat inside her felt like she'd just run the mile in PE—but much better.

Beri glared at her, breathing like he'd joined her running that mile. "This did not happen when he kissed you?"

Her head swam. How dare he look mad? He'd known what would happen when Salm led her away. He'd needed that to happen. Heck, *she* needed *this* to happen.

"No," she said. "Neither did this." Bunching her hands in Beri's shirt, she kissed him. He tasted spicy, really good, and this time, she moved her mouth like those magazines said to do—slightly forming words—and held to him, more obstinate than she'd ever felt.

His arms came around her, and she wanted to sink to the grass and stay. Finally, she had to take a breath and opened her eyes to see if Beri wanted to keep kissing as much as she did.

Green flames flickered blindingly over them.

She wrenched back, and the magic snapped out.

Beri had a grim smile on his lips. "I'm going to have a word with Salm. You best put your energy away and get over to your Gran." He disappeared down the steps.

Fern brushed her fingers across her lips and flexed them, their hum rising into a glow again. "I had put it all away."

34

Caught

Returning to the display circle, Fern had to veer around a game of tag that included Willow's brothers Kory and Haw. Twice, Kory tripped and been tagged "it."

Hmm. If she hadn't been there during the hide-and-seek complaint, she might not have thought twice, but now she watched closer. Haw wasn't the culprit, and Kory wasn't the only victim. A girl's feet tumbled over a line of blue magic, then seconds later, the same kid sent it to trip Kory.

Anger boiled in Fern. Kory gamely got up and raced to tag. He was quick, quicker than most of the others. He tagged the next kid, and this time, orange magic flew across the ground. Kory nimbly jumped aside and turned, his face twisted in anger. Fern started toward them.

Ches darted into the game first. "Haw. Kory," called their older brother. "Chores."

Both boys ran to him as Ches fixed a steely eye on a girl of about eight. She shrank back.

Fern clenched her humming fingers. The nerve of these kids, bullying nonmagical... *This is what I would have faced. Maybe every day, at every playdate, every event.* Haw ran ahead to the displays. For a second, Kory leaned against his brother. Ches' gaze met hers.

Damn, I want to fix this. She stormed into their display.

Gran sat in her rocker among the wildflowers, the birds on her shoulders clinging to her blouse as she tipped back and forth.

"Gran, I can't stand this."

Her grandmother looked up, her face stony. "When I came to find you, you didna look unhappy to me. Does your mother know about Beri? About..." She flicked her fingers like fireworks. Her birds rose into the air and didn't return.

Fern sank into a cross-legged sit before Gran and wiped her cheeks, now warming for other reasons. "Yes. I told her, and she told me to make sure. I was just making sure."

The rocking picked up.

Fern rose up on her knees, bringing her face level with Gran's. "I had to make sure it worked with Beri after there were no sparks with... Besides, he was mad after I went with—but nothing *happened*. He didn't need to be so mad."

"What I saw wasna nothing. The Beri I saw was not mad."

"He *was* mad when he found out Salm—"

"Ah, Salm," Gran cut in. "There's a lad who's as free with the lasses as a spring breeze. Fresh. I'm having none of Salm of the Seas involved with my granddaughter."

"Don't worry, neither is Beri," she muttered. "Why do I have a protector all of a sudden? And chaperones? And magic? Four days ago, I simply helped you with the Meadows and loved it. Now all these boys are involved."

"*All these boys*?" Gran cocked an eyebrow. "Lass, your mother needs to take you in hand."

No way was that happening. "We'll talk to her later," she said vaguely while drawing out her pouch. She nestled the glass mound on her palm while resting it on Gran's knee. Her skin tingled, and to distract Gran, Fern loosened her energy and tried flowing magic into the glass.

A sage-green glow started in the center.

Gran leaned closer. "A little more, dear."

She urged more of her energy through her palm, and *her* green flooded the glass.

"Ah," Gran breathed. "A fine show of your color. Now see what you can do to control the two powers. Mix them."

Would they stir together like butter and sugar for cookies? Fern flinched as the colors followed her thoughts.

"Excellent. Bring it up, out of the glass."

Like pulling molten glass under the flame? Fern was afraid to move, so instead of waving her fingers as Mom had, she imagined pushing, growing the green energy like a plant emerging from a seed.

It worked, magic swirling in both Mom's sage and her brighter green.

With Gran murmuring encouragement, Fern grew the rising bit of energy into an eight-inch beam of light. Not a tower like Mom's, but she and Gran grinned at each other over it.

"That's it, lass. You shall show your ratna, and Heather left good evidence of her approval and the promise of her energy. Hold it steady, and let's practice your acceptance for the ceremony."

She hadn't passed yet, but went over a few lines until Gran was satisfied and sat back. "Please put it safely away."

Great, she's not thinking about the kissing anymore. But when Fern looked up from replacing her pouch, Gran had on her don't-mess-with-me look again.

"I do not know who else saw, but as soon as you part from me, someone will come telling me the story. People won't believe you are new to our ways when you can flame with

Beri." She tilted her head toward Fern. "Relationships in young'uns are strongly supervised here. Either I or your mother must put a tracing spell on you."

Ugh, no. Even if it was just for magical activities, Fern didn't want it. This Windborne version of parental controls sounded far worse than Internet monitoring.

"Gran, it *just happened* the first time," she whispered in case the display hadn't been as private as it'd appeared. "Then Mom said I better be sure before prebonding. I've never had magic before. I didn't know. Then Salm came along and—you obviously know about Salm's ideas. It was easy for me to touch him and test to see if I'd spark. I didn't. Also, *he* kissed me. Nothing happened. So I was afraid nothing would happen with Beri. But he got mad about Salm kissing me and decided to do his own testing. *Then* it happened."

Fern sat back on her heels and took a deep breath. "So, see? I was just making sure. Not breaking the rules or anything. Just doing a test."

Gran narrowed her eyes and made little *humphing* noises under her breath while contemplating her plants. Finally, she eyed Fern again, her lips pressed into a thin line.

She made herself hold Gran's gaze. Geez, kissing wasn't such a big deal at home. Stuff that came after it was, but not kissing. Considering the way Mom had looked when talking about Merlin, she'd apply the normal, human, rules. Or...

"How about asking my dad?" Merlin seemed more lenient.

Gran's frown had slipped away, replaced by thoughts of who knew what. She glanced off, toward the sun dipping low over the ocean.

No time for a lecture. "The interview? Shouldn't we be going?" She started to rise, but Gran gripped her arm.

"Beri is the only one causing you to spark?" Gran's ocher irises glinted a yellow green for the first time ever. "One boy, that's all? No *all these boys* kind of thing is going on?"

"Just Beri."

"And the sparking is good?"

Impossible, but... Was this going in her favor? Fern hesitated, then nodded.

"I do not have time for this tonight, lassie. But sure as I am sitting here, someone will ask me your intention, so I am asking you: What are you thinking is in your future?"

This was it. Stop or go. "I'm going to make a prebonding application with Beri."

"Before anything else *just happens*?" Another flash erupted from Gran's eyes.

"Yes, ma'am." The only answer possible.

Gran nodded sharply. "Good choice. That should subdue any questions for tonight."

"Will Merlin agree?" Fern asked.

"He'd better. I don't wish that Duffy on Beri, flouting the rules as she does."

Fern squeezed Gran's arm. "Everyone knows about her wanting Beri?"

"Duffy has made sure we know, which says to me she must be up to something." Abruptly, Gran rose from the chair, and her birds gathered above her. "Come along and bring your ratna. Time for your interview." She shooed the flock into a shrub and took off walking with a spring to her step.

Fern scrambled up and grabbed the handles of the tote bag, only to have it swing wildly.

It was empty. Her ratna was gone.

35

The Interview

Who would take her plant? That made no sense. Unless...someone was trying to sabotage her. Duffy?

She didn't know that for sure, so couldn't accuse her. But after Duffy had said she wouldn't be stopped, Fern was damned near positive. She raced to catch Gran, who was headed toward a gathering group across the fire circle.

"I have a problem," she whispered, opening the empty bag. "My ratna is gone. Maybe"—God, she hated to say it—"stolen?"

Gran stared into the bag. "'Twas there when I left with Merlin. I didna look after I returned." She closed her eyes, and a second later, her shoulders sagged. "I can do naught without stirring up problems. Raven," she muttered in a low voice. Gran looked around as if she was calling him.

Fern looked, too. Thick vegetation blocked the view into all the displays, but a dark head that rose above the other people wove through the crowd in the circle.

Gran grasped Raven's wrist when he reached her. "Fern has lost her ratna. I can hold off the interview only a few minutes. Help her find it. Quickly." Gran turned and left.

"Duffy," Fern whispered. "I think she's trying to keep me from earning a place here so she can use prebonding with Beri to stay herself."

"That witch," he spat. "I want her banned for this."

Beri trotted up to them. Then Willow appeared from the direction of the Forest woods, her two youngest brothers running behind her.

"Her ratna is gone. We argued with"—Raven glanced at Kory and Maple—"*someone* who doesn't wish Fern to succeed because of a prior plan." He lifted his chin toward Beri.

Fern cast a look around. "It-it might not even be here any longer. Should I go to the Meadows and get—oh no. They'll die if I dig them up." An obstinate fury heated within her. *I still have ratna plants—and could invite the elders to see those— but I want my plant back, dammit.*

"I don't want Fern to leave." Maple hugged Willow's leg and pleaded, "If she's Raven's sister, they canna make her."

Willow cupped a hand around his head. "Hush, Maple Sugar, so I can help her find her plant. Raven? You touched them with your energy."

"The seeds only. Not enough to find it."

Beri spun to Fern. "You do'na feel it?"

She shook her head. "I'm not sure what that's like."

"I could use my magic to extend yours—"

"That'd upset Gran worse." Fern tucked her hands around her sides. "Can't we physically look? Fast?"

"Not unless you know where to start," Raven said.

"I know." Kory pushed his way between them.

Maple darted from Willow and shoved him. "You're telling. She said if you did, you'd get in trouble."

"I'd rather get in trouble." Kory looked up at Fern. "I was hiding in your display from Maple. I had a good spot in the shrubs and saw someone take your ratna plant out of the bag. That's the plant you're looking for, right?"

Willow crouched beside them. "This is not tattling. It isn't the same when someone steals something."

"She said it was only *borrowing* and not to tell. Maple heard her when he came in to look for me."

Fern squatted down. "Was it the girl in pink?" Kory and Maple both nodded. "Did you see where she took it?"

Kory half turned and pointed with his finger in short jabs along his belly so as not to draw attention. "The one we're not allowed into without a chaperone."

Fog shifted over the display area, leaving only angular rocks visible along the perimeter.

Raven pulled her up by the elbow. "Lady Soila's," he hissed. "Come on. If both of us Meadows send magic through the habitat, we'll find it."

Sir Humus stepped into their path, a frown on his face. "I was about to send Duffy to look for you, Fern," he said. "We should like to start. Please join us in the council's glade."

All Fern could do was nod and follow him to a roped-off area of trees to one side of the fire pit. Once she stepped inside, a grove of Scots pines appeared, the group of wizards standing among the trunks. Sir Humus drew another length of rope across the opening, and the space closed off, dampening all outside sounds. Everyone in the clearing watched them expectantly.

Fern's heart began to pound. *This is it.*

Sir Humus nodded to Gran. "Lady Lark, will you do the honors?"

Gran walked over, her brow creased in question.

Fern bent to her ear. "Raven is looking."

Nodding, Gran took Fern's arm and turned to those gathered. "May I present Fern, Heather's oldest child and direct heir to the Meadows' magic."

Several people spoke at once, the loudest Lady Roda. "But this is the child who has no magic," she said sharply. "You canna."

"I can," Gran said, sounding falsely sweet. "She has completed a trial."

A dispute erupted. Sir Humus put up his hands. "I was informed."

"When?" spat Lady Roda.

"Earlier. She has complied with our policies. Let us continue."

The wizards shuffled uncomfortably, several frowning, but Sir Snap extended his hand to Fern, so she shook it. "Naught has been this interestin' so far," he said. "Go on, then."

Gran dipped her head. "Fern, you have met most everyone, but let me formally introduce the Isle of Giuthas' council."

Following Sir Snap of the Ponds, each of the wizards came forward to shake her hand: Lady Pina of the Pines, Mr. Chinook of the Land, Lady Mimosa of the Forest, Sir Dolph of the Seas, and Mr. Grouse and Lady Roda, both of the Wildlife.

When it came time to shake this witch's hand, Fern steeled herself. "We have introduced a fox pair to the Upper Meadow. The rabbit issue should resolve soon because the vixen is expecting."

To her relief, Lady Roda only sniffed. "A question I had for you. I'm happy to hear you're addressing the problem this way first." She half turned to Sir Humus. "Shall I start?"

"You may, but let me insert for Mistress Fern's benefit

that Lady Lark and Mr. Grouse are excused from questioning and voting because of her legacy and his trial in the Meadows habitat."

That's all they're going to say? Is it fair that he's even here?

Lady Roda said to Fern, "Your new plants have benefited from a no-nibbling charm. That cannot continue beyond the spring equinox, as this must return to a functioning habitat. Once you remove it, one, how will your plants fare? And two, what mammal species and numbers do you believe to be your carrying capacity for that first year, then the next three?"

OMG. The spring equinox is in March, right? Fern quickly added up the remaining weeks of this growing season. "We anticipated the new plants would be favored by the rodents, hare and deer. For the first year, we will ask the wildlife managers of the surrounding habitats to help balance the numbers coming in." She threw out random numbers because she had only the vaguest idea: hundreds of rodents, dozens of rabbits, two dozen roe deer and the two fox families that ate berries as part of their mostly meat diet. "To keep up, I mean, *ahead* of the vegetation consumption, we've collected the seed from every plant and will be sowing half in two weeks. The remainder will be sown at first frost." That was what Gran had told her was usually done.

Lady Roda frowned. "Were no seed heads left for the wild birds to feed upon?"

"Some seeds we missed," she started, feeling like she was backpedaling to cover what this wildlife manager wanted. But it wasn't entirely truthful, darn it. "I doubt that was many. So, no."

Lady Roda gave her a tight smile and stepped aside.

Great. Fail on her first questions.

Lady Mimosa asked about planting techniques, which Fern could answer in her sleep, and Lady Pina tagged into the conversation, affirming her methods were successful based on the healthy plants she'd seen. Sir Snap managed to cut her off and inserted his questions about aquatic plants. Then Lady Roda put up a finger. "Can you tell us which species use which particular plants? In what form—vegetation, blossoms, seeds or berries?"

Fern listed off all the butterflies and the flowers they fed from and most of the mammals' foods, based on things Gran had said, but when Lady Roda pressed her to name bird species, she had no idea, other than the partridge they'd raised and Beri's pheasants, and admitted it.

That was when Lady Roda glanced at Mr. Grouse.

This sounds an awful lot like a question Mr. Grouse would ask. Especially if he was still learning these plants.

He blinked furiously.

So what was his trial?

"The Meadows is an important habitat for maintaining bird populations," Lady Roda said coolly.

Lady Mimosa leaned in before Fern could respond. "Fern couldn't be fully aware of their activity since we magically barricaded the Meadows boundaries for her trial. The barrier did double duty by allowing those plants to establish with less wildlife competition, something we have done for other trials. The question shouldn't be held against her."

Fern gave her a thankful smile. "I look forward to learning more as I work with other habitat managers."

Mr. Chinook queried her about water use during dry spells. Thank goodness her earth science class and Colorado's recent droughts gave her a background in water-rights issues. Sir Dolph asked her to list tasks by season, which she did well enough on. Finally, only Lady Pina was left.

"When last we spoke," she said, "you didn't have your Meadows ratna, but Sir Humus says now you do, so how in a matter of days did you acquire the plants?"

Fern's heart began to race. What was it Beri had said to say? Her magic made it possible? She darted a look at Gran, who smiled proudly. She had to do this for Gran and make it sound like she knew what she was doing.

"I received the seed late, the day after we met. It grew incredibly fast because I had also learned—become *more skilled* in using my magic. I saturated the seedlings with my energy, and they responded well enough that I've planted them."

Brows went up, eyes widened, and all gazes were on her.

"This is nae enough verification." Lady Roda crossed her arms. "Who has checked this?"

"As this was a rather quick turnabout on a significant requirement, I anticipated we should check the habitat energy items together," Sir Humus said.

"Starting with the ratna," Lady Pina said. "You have one at your display?"

"Aye," Gran said and nodded to Fern.

So Fern said, "I'll get it."

36

Retrieval

Fern ran across the fire circle to Lady Soila's foggy display. She'd half expected—half hoped—to find Raven, Beri or Willow, but none of them was in sight.

No time to look for them. She stepped between the boulders marking the entrance.

Sea spray pelted her, cast by a gust of wind that nearly toppled her, and Fern was once again stumbling up the cliff of the islet. Heart racing, she gaped at the dark rock rising around her and branches arching overhead. They dripped, the splats rolling over her face and arms, but not soaking her dress.

It's an illusion. Magic. But the sea wind felt and smelled exactly like it had on that horrid hike, and Fern's body was remembering each and every exhausting step. She steeled herself and marched forward. Within a few steps, the seemingly endless path opened to the knoll where she'd first seen the meadowsweet, and ahead of her grew a ratna plant.

She rushed forward. It was full and bushy—not possibly her small plant, nor in a pot. A touch of the leaves confirmed it wasn't. Fern straightened and looked around. Another grew nearby, and another not too far off... A field of wildflowers lay before her, along with a pond and scraggly conifer trees clinging to the rocks, just like on Lady Soila's islet.

The whole islet can't be here.

But it was. Or appeared to be. *Magic.*

Unlike when Fern had visited the actual islet, other people wandered over the field, stopping to look at the flowers and the birds circling overhead.

Osprey.

Oh, I do not want to find out the cliff is here, too.

Fern forced her gaze down again and caught sight of Beri's reddish hair glinting in the sunlight as he kicked through the grass. Not far from him, Raven waved his hands as he walked, and there was Willow, with Kory and Maple, all of them inspecting the plants.

They hadn't found her ratna. Fern pressed her fingers to her temples. They couldn't find it on a magicked quarter acre. That would take...magic.

Fern looked at her hands.

She had to try. She could cast her magic, like Raven had to check whether Duffy was still in Gran's cottage.

Open, she thought, and the magic jumped. Bright green raced through her channels to her arms and tingled down to her fingers. Fern raised her hand, but now several people were headed toward her.

"I am closing," called the older lady leading the way. The others passed by, but this woman stopped before Fern, waving her hand like she was shooing pesky flies. She was wrinkled and small, wearing an old-fashioned black dress with a high collar, lace and long sleeves. "The ceremony starts soon, ye ken."

"I do," Fern said. "Are you Lady Soila?"

"I am. Ye will be out in five minutes." She gave a firm nod. "I am closing."

Did she mean magicked out? "I-I think something of mine is here. I need to find it."

Lady Soila arched a brow behind her tiny glasses. "I doubt—"

A yip sounded, and the pointed black and white face of Fern's badger poked through the grasses. He stormed up to Fern, wiggled in delight and rubbed against her leg.

"Hi, badger." She scratched his ear. "I'm happy to see you, too."

Lady Soila now looked curious. "Are ye the girl with this Snickers?"

"Yes, that's me."

"And what did ye lose?" she asked, her tone softening.

Fern swallowed. "My Meadows ratna. *Filipendula ulmaria.* One I grew from seeds you gave me in trade for pond plants."

"Remember, Great-Gran?" Duffy's voice was loud and close behind Fern, making her jump. "I told you about her."

Darn her. Either the other girl had just appeared, or had been hiding.

Lady Soila gestured to a nearby meadowsweet. "I have plenty more if ye lost those. Come to see me next week."

"I can bring you out again," Duffy said innocently, taking Fern's arm. "My trial was approved, so I'll be settling here."

Then Duffy tripped. The badger rammed her leg again. "Stop it, you idiotic animal."

He leaped at her, Fern pulled free, and Duffy went down. She scrambled to get up, but the badger was faster. He bounded onto Duffy's chest and let out a string of yips and growls—just like a rant.

She cowered back, raising her hands.

"Here now," said Lady Soila. "We've no time for that."

She shooed the badger off.

Fern looked between the two of them. Neither said anything in answer to the badger's outburst. *They can't understand animals any better than I can.*

But it must have been about her ratna.

Beri had turned their direction. He would know, but Fern wasn't a tattletale, any more than Kory was. Gran wanted them to set things right, not start trouble, and she had only one way to do that.

"Can I look for my own plant? Real quick?"

Lady Soila threw her hands up. "Young'uns these days never listen. Go ahead. In less than..."

Fern flung out her hands. *Go,* she ordered her energy. *Find it.* She spun in a circle as the magic flew from her fingertips. She scanned the fields, trying to see something... Anything. Nothing looked different. Damn, it hadn't—

Lady Soila drew a breath, and a second later, Beri shouted, "You found it!"

"Damn," Duffy muttered.

Lady Soila flicked her a haughty look, then pointed behind Fern. "Is that yer plant?"

A glow shone among the shrubs near the entrance. Fern ran to it and lifted her potted plant. Energy bathed the meadowsweet's stem and leaves, and sparks of green pricked out of the leaf edges and along the stem. The entire plant looked like it was lined with tiny Christmas lights.

"Yes," Fern breathed.

"Please," whispered Duffy, coming up beside her. "Don't take it back to the Meadows."

Really? She dared to ask that? Fern peeked behind them. Lady Soila was bent to the badger, the others a minute away.

Now or never.

In a low voice, Fern said, "I don't know why you have it in for me, pretending to help—and even helping—then going behind my back to sabotage my trial. Locking me in a closet—"

"I said I was sorry."

"—and poisoning my seeds."

"That wasn't poison," she said indignantly. "It really was fertilizer."

"Your help still would have gotten me in trouble. Stealing my ratna is making me look like an idiot. And why have you planted natural dye plants on the Meadows and hidden them?"

Duffy flicked her fingers at her pink skirt. "The rich soils there deepen the colors of my natural dyes, but no one is allowed to grow non-natives here. I never thought you'd get this far in your trial and find them. But..." Duffy's confidence slipped. "It took a lot of energy to hide them. I didn't mean for a rift to happen."

Crap. She hadn't thought things through, like Beri had said. "You upset the energy balance. You *knew* you caused a rift."

Duffy leaned closer, her brow creased in worry. "Those plants started as coursework, but I really love them, and that taught me how to bond to the land. I can do it now, but I'm gonna be in so much trouble."

Fury rose in Fern. "What about me?"

"*Shh!* I-I'll fix it," she said, her voice low and urgent.

"So this isn't about Beri?"

"Of course not. I don't like—I mean, he's not my type."

Something wasn't matching up here. "Then why did you

ask to prebond with him?"

"Listen," she huffed. "He's a friend, that's all. Better than I deserve, actually. I just don't...like boys. Please, don't say anything," Duffy pleaded. "My family doesn't know I'm gay. I tried with Beri to get them off my back. Plus, some others and I have a shot at changing things here."

Well, that explained Duffy's desperate efforts to get a place on the isle. "I get it. I won't say anything."

"I'll drop the prebonding request and apologize. Give me a chance to get rid of my plants and pull all my magic from the Meadows?"

Fern glanced at Beri bearing down on them behind her, and she nodded. "I'm going to finish my interview while you do that—so you better not be lying."

———

In the council's glade, the elders murmured their approval of Fern's energy, while Gran beamed and patted her on the back. "Beautiful, lass."

It was. Incredibly beautiful. Fern could hardly tear her eyes away from her ratna.

Gran turned to the group. "I hope this puts to rest any last criticism of apparently nonmagical persons working on our land. Fern accomplished what she did on her own, opening her magic as she grew her wildflowers. Even if she had not, she has significantly contributed to our community."

"It does nae mean we will allow any nonmagical to live on Giuthas," Lady Roda said stiffly.

Gran leaned forward. "She has magic."

Lady Roda leaned as well. "Enough?"

"Ye would think," said Sir Snap. "She comes from afar."

The line was drawn—no, the line had already been there. Now Fern was aware of it. Several of these people must have been council members when she was a baby. They'd voted back then to have her removed from the island.

And they planned to do it again.

Fern swallowed. "That's not fair." Every elder angled to look at her, but she wasn't stopping. "Some people love plants so much and work hard enough getting their conditions correct that they are just as good at getting them to grow without magic."

To her surprise, Sir Humus nodded. "Exactly what Lark promised you would do. Because of the barrier that kept others out, we know you completed an extraordinary trial without magical help. Congratulations for proving that."

He had ignored her remark with a compliment. "Thank you," she said, but before she could repeat her point, Lady Pina tapped him on the shoulder.

"I still wish to see this plant's bonding, and we have time."

Lady Roda pushed between them. "While Fern has done an adequate job for a *beginner*, that is exactly what she is. Can a beginner address our issues?" She turned to Gran. "You should be mentoring a more experienced wizard to take this position."

"You're referring to Beri." Gran smiled sweetly—a little too sweetly.

Lady Roda darted a look at Sir Humus, who said, "Perhaps this requires a more private conversation."

Gran snorted. "Then you mean Mr. Grouse."

A hush fell over the group.

"Mr. Grouse has magical connections all over this isle through his bird work." Lady Roda gave a sharp nod. "Three decades of birding visits, twenty years as our outside council member."

He'd been on the council when Fern was a baby? Great. Gran had poked another old fight. So nothing she said would hurt. "Look," Fern said. "What is it you feel he can do that I can't?"

Lady Roda fixed her steely-gray eyes on Fern. "Repair the tears in our shielding."

Oh. Her fingers tightened around her ratna pot. Darn it, that was a big piece of magic, something she couldn't... Well, why couldn't she, once she had Mom's magic, the magic that belonged in the Meadows?

"His interest in becoming a permanent resident hasn't been a secret," Mr. Chinook said. "She's done nothing wrong, but I support a more mature wizard to address these difficulties. He understands the ebb and flow of the weather in these parts and how it affects wildlife."

Lady Mimosa raised a finger. "He has no knowledge or experience in growing plants."

"We've been over this," Lady Roda continued. "He's the logical wizard to step in, not a stranger who will spend years becoming bonded to the land."

"I agreed at one time," said Lady Pina. "Until I saw the incredible lush growth this young woman has sprouted, on ground untended by a steady magic for fourteen years, clearly different than Heather and as strong as Heather and just as plainly showing Mistress Fern has been accepted by this land, and as such, the land will work for her, so I say we see its interactions with this plant."

Gran waved to the grove entrance. "To support this, I invite everyone to the Meadows—"

"One moment." Lady Mimosa blocked the way. "I wish to review the requirements for selection of our habitat managers. We have *never* in the past required the wizards applying for this role to dispel rips or repair shielding magic."

That was never a requirement? Fern wanted to slap herself—*or someone*. She and the others had worried for nothing and could have confided in Gran when they'd first discovered the rift.

"These *are* new issues to our enclave," murmured Sir Dolph.

"Thank you," Lady Mimosa said. "Correct me if I am wrong, but the requirement to pass a trial is to show a bond to the land via the interactions of the wizard with the habitat's nature, whether it be plants, animals, or natural components." She met each elder's gaze. No one contradicted her. "Humus?"

"If Fern shows any level of bond to the land, she passes her trial. If Lady Heather desires to pass her magic to her daughter, she may name her as heir or give her position, and we should vote in accordance with those wishes."

Should vote? So they didn't have to?

Lady Mimosa smiled. "Shall we proceed to the Meadows?"

37

Proving Herself

It was still raining at Hillux.

"Bother," Gran grumbled and started inside. "How long is this scheduled for?"

Fern grabbed her arm. "How do I do this bond thing?"

"I tell you, dear, you have the touch." Gran smiled sympathetically and patted her check. "Likely your plants are growing into it. Plant your ratna. Use your magic and ask it to connect you. Do'na have doubts while doing it."

Other wizards began arriving, stuffing their peregrinators away and running for cover under the porch.

After a snapped, "Chinook, can you not make this downpour stop?" Gran plowed into the house.

Fern wished she'd had a few more minutes of privacy to tell Gran about the rift. Was Duffy in the Meadows now removing her plants? Fern pulled a shovel from the tool bin and then put on the cape Gran brought her.

"Where do you wish to plant it?" Gran asked.

Eight people waited for her answer. Fern walked to the edge of the porch and pretended she was looking around, but stared at the beads of light lining the ratna's leaves. She closed her eyes. This one seemed to have more magic than the others had, and—maybe—with the magic from Mom that she'd spilled, it'd bond. "The top of Hillux."

The rain had slowed to a drizzle. She linked arms with Gran and led the way up the steps in the earthworks. At the top, the clouds were blowing off and the sun coming out.

Crack. Thunder boomed with a flash of light, followed in quick succession by three more cracks farther away.

It can't be lightning—the storm has cleared.

Mr. Chinook echoed her thoughts. "Nothing to do with a storm."

Fern searched the horizon with everyone else. Puffs of smoke rose from spots near and far.

"That," said Sir Dolph, "sounded like a rip opening."

"Several," added Sir Humus. "I'll check." He stepped off and began speaking to someone in an otherworldly voice similar to how Gran had called for Raven.

"Gran?" In a whisper, Fern told her everything. Her fall, the non-native garden, landing in the rip between the Meadows and the Forest, and Willow healing Fern's contamination. In a few minutes, Gran knew about Duffy's non-native plants hidden by her applications of red magic and Beri's guess that morning—*only that morning?*—that the ocean ether rift was tied to Fern's energy.

"Between the two of you, 'tis no wonder I canna get it under control," Gran whispered back. "I repair the blessed thing every few days, including the morning I left."

By now they were both looking at the spot where the Meadows rip was. No smoke was rising there, but two figures were flying from that direction toward them.

Sir Humus turned to the waiting elders. "Security is assessing the shield. The flare-ups are indeed rips. They're being caused by removal of magic, but security canna determine whose. Clearly, this has nothing to do with Fern or the Meadows. Security needs our help..." His gaze tracked upward, where others were staring.

Duffy and Lady Soila landed on Hillux. Duffy drew in her wings and walked the few steps to face her uncle. "I need to talk to you."

"It'll have to wait. We've lost energy and have a possible emergency."

Duffy clenched and unclenched her hands, and Fern felt terrible for her. "It's my fault."

Lady Soila put her hand on Duffy's shoulder. "And mine. I made the lass remove her energy, to correct a...situation. I didn't realize exactly how much energy she had bonded to the land across this isle."

Ah, Lady Soila *had* understood what the badger was saying. Duffy's gaze darted to Fern's. But it also sounded like Lady Soila wasn't upset—and maybe even a bit proud of Duffy's accomplishment.

Sir Humus looked from Lady Soila to Duffy, and Duffy quickly confessed about her plants. "I didn't know my magic had gone all over Giuthas through my project."

"Great Orb, lass," Sir Snap said. "Are ye willing to put it back?"'

She blew out a breath. "If I can keep my trial approval and keep coming here."

A flurry of discussion ended with the elders voting, "Aye."

Of *course*. If they wanted Duffy's magic, she had to stay as well.

The elders clustered together and began making rapid-fire plans. Duffy slipped from the group to where Fern stood alone. "Great-Gran was angry until she saw how well my plants were growing. She promised to help me if I came clean about everything. So please don't let all this good-humored cooperation go to waste."

"I hope I don't, but I didn't get a chance to plant my ratna and see if it'll bond."

"Duffy?" Sir Humus called. "We need to go. Reports are coming in of additional rips in our Seas fisheries boundaries. The only way we have now to resolve that is through land stabilization."

Duffy looked at Fern. "I should put some of my energy back where I took it from—the Meadows rip. Fern thinks her ratna will compensate for the loss on the Meadows better if she plants it at the same time. There, at the rip."

Amazing. Duffy had actually thought this one through, better than Fern had.

Several of the wizards unfurled their wings, but Duffy gestured to the stairs and followed Fern down from the top of Hillux. Gran, Lady Mimosa and half the elders walked with them. When they arrived at the rip, the others were waiting.

"Good luck," Duffy whispered. She walked up to the gap Sir Humus and Sir Dolph held open and disappeared.

Trying to appear as confident, Fern followed, clutching her ratna and using the shovel she still carried to balance herself against the erratic tipping of the ground. The twisting coil of murky magic was rope-thin now, and the rift hole was empty—at least as far as Fern could see from here. To her right, Duffy squatted among the sunflowers, red energy flowing like blood from her fingertips to the ground.

Fern didn't wait for a go-ahead. Flipping her long skirt out of the way, she dropped to her knees. She set her plant behind her and pushed her shovel into the wet grass. There was barely room, and the elders all crowded at the gap to watch, but the soil here was rich and crumbly, some of the best she'd dug in the swales. Just, having everyone watching her every move was so not like the hundreds of other times she'd planted wildflowers. Neither was digging a hole in tippy ground while balancing on her knees.

She rolled her shoulders to release the tension. *Take your time*, she knew Gran would say. *Do what you feel is best.*

Getting into the routine helped. She thought of planting the ratnas earlier this afternoon, when they'd decided to request the rain that'd made her curled hair straighten. Of Raven digging the other holes, Willow saying, "Once planted, the ratna takes on a wizard's energy and is no longer just a plant." And Beri adding, "It becomes that bond you are missing."

Fern wished her new friends were here cheering her on, but somewhere on the Isle of Giuthas, she knew they were. In a way, Duffy helping her was nearly as significant.

When the hole was deep enough, she removed the pot from the ratna and sat back on her heels. Holding the root ball, she thought about what she wanted to happen.

Move.

Her hands lit spring green. The light on the leaves sparkled, brighter and brighter until green fuzzed at the root ball's edges.

Fern set the illuminated ratna into the hole and raked the soil around it with her fingers. *Grow and carry magic and connect to the land.* She pressed the soil in place, her eyes closed. *Please.* With a last push of magic and soil, she lifted her hands and opened her eyes.

The meadowsweet trembled, its branches lengthened, and

new leaves unfurled and glowed a brighter green.

Fern's breath caught. *It's growing.*

"I would think this is sign enough," Gran said, her voice rising in excitement.

"We shall test that," snipped Lady Roda.

Way to ruin a moment. Fern straightened and met Duffy's gaze. The other girl rolled her eyes sympathetically.

"We shall give it a minute before checking," Sir Humus said.

At least Gran was satisfied she'd done her best. Standing, Fern backed to her side and tipped her head to her grandmother's. "Thanks." The trial, the inspections and the interview were over. Even revealing everything to Mom was over. And she did feel good about how she'd done...if only her magic would stop its annoying racing. She pushed it back to her core, only to find it already there. So why did she get the feeling it was running everywhere?

"I say!" Sir Snap exclaimed. "Tha' is a pretty sight, do you not think, Roda?"

Fern's ratna shone with the same with beads of magic, so that wasn't—oh.

Magic was spreading to every blade of grass on the Meadows' side of the rip energy. It glowed from the sunflowers, hollyhocks and madder plants. The line of murky magic thinned to a piece of yarn.

Wings out, Lady Mimosa step-fluttered past Fern. She put her hands to either side of the rip magic, as Willow had done with Fern's foot. In seconds, the magic broke into strands within her cloud. The wizards minced forward to collect their various energies. The ground ceased rocking. When the line of energy was completely gone, everyone began speaking—arguing, really—and only then did Fern realize the grassy ground appeared to be wider. The magical rip between the Forest and the Meadows had dissolved.

Gran reached up and clasped Fern's shoulders. "You did it, dear." She hugged her, then said, "Wait here," while she bustled off to join Lady Mimosa and Sir Humus at the rift hole.

With a wave of their arms, magic burst from each wizard—golden, brown and green—and wove together into a glowing blanket that settled over the hole. That seemed pretty amazing to Fern, but no one else was paying attention. They scattered like they had for her inspection and checked the soil at wildflowers across the swale and up the hillsides.

"Fern's magic is here," called Sir Snap.

"And here," Lady Pina echoed before going off on a long-winded description.

Fern could see what she was describing. Magic ran from this ratna to other ratnas across the Meadows, which Fern couldn't possibly see from here—but in her mind, she could. Around each, fine energy lines spread like growing roots. They touched her knapweed, flax and teasel, the coneflowers, bur marigolds, all the flowers she had planted.

This was the magical bond—*her* magical bond. *Ohmigod, I did it!*

Lady Roda and Mr. Chinook complained loudly to Sir Humus that her magic hadn't spread completely across the Meadows, but he ignored them as he did his own poking into the soil and listened to the other elders returning to form a group. Lady Pina pointed and waved, and for a time, she faced off with Lady Roda—and Lady Roda got in her share of the talking.

Grinning, Duffy rapped her arm. "Good job."

Wait. "You didn't help with that, did you?"

She snorted. "They'd be able to tell in a hot second. No, that was all your doing. I just got my energy out of the way. Sorry, I had so much here."

"Perhaps why your plants didn't bond before this," said a quiet voice behind them. Lady Soila.

"Really?" Fern asked.

Lady Soila peered up at her through her spectacles. "Your Meadows has some of the healthiest horticultural specimens I've seen on this island. Maybe you had not pushed to get your bond to take with the new ratna?"

Duffy darted a worried look at Fern.

Hmm, that look said Duffy's magic was likely stopping mine. Fern stretched her fingers and made a quick decision. "I must not have. I-I'm catching on better to working magic. Would it be possible for me to visit you sometime to get more instruction in ratna magic?"

"I shall send directions," Lady Soila said solemnly. "Now, Duffy, let us extract my grandson from these proceedings so we may distribute this energy. I don't wish to miss the ceremony."

"Great-Gran, Uncle Humus *starts* the ceremony, so you won't miss it." Duffy took her arm, and they turned toward the group of elders.

"He does nae control the rising moon, the last I checked," Lady Soila said. "Here he comes."

And Sir Humus *was* coming. Fern must have missed something while they talked, because all the elders were walking their way. Gran was beaming, which could mean only...

Sir Humus stopped before her. "An extraordinary demonstration of your energy's bond with the land. The council has approved Mistress Fern to become heir to the Witch of the Meadows. Congratulations."

38

The Ceremony

Each council member shook Fern's hand—except Lady Mimosa, who kissed her cheek.

Smiling kindly, Lady Pina clasped her hand longer. "I have been told to keep it brief so we may begin the ceremony, but let me say thank you for an incredible ratna display and I look forward to working with you."

"Please go ahead and gather people," Sir Humus said to Lady Pina and then, to Fern and Gran, said, "One last item before you go."

This request didn't give Fern a good feeling. They waited while Sir Humus sent Duffy and Lady Soila to one of Duffy's other trial areas, and the elders left by using their peregrinators. Then at last, it was just the three of them.

"Some question has arisen regarding Fern and Beri," said Sir Humus.

Fern's face heated. Their kiss *had* come up. She had privacy, but geez, telling this to a stranger? "I-I like him." She watched him watching her. "We hit it off immediately. A flying start, you might say."

Still, he said nothing. Duffy was gone. She'd promised to talk to her uncle, so Fern would have to trust her—and maybe remind her.

"We plan to apply for prebonding," Fern blurted.

Sir Humus looked from her to Gran.

"Tomorrow," Gran said. "Don't worry, I have this in hand."

"I shall have a word with...Beri." With a nod, he extracted his peregrinator and left.

Gran huffed. "Don't be telling anyone else anything about Beri without me."

Back at the Gathering Place, most of the habitat displays now sported glowing domes: A rusty-brown magic ballooned over rocks as tall as the Forest's golden-covered trees, icy-blue housed the Streams, and a blue-green dome hid the Ponds.

"Will I have time to see all these later?"

"The entire night. Hurry now."

Fern cleaned up at a wash station, and Gran magicked the mud from her dress. The sun was dipping closer to the horizon, signaling what was supposed to be the start of the ceremony. In the Meadows' display, waist-high wildflowers tilted their pink and purplish blossoms toward an invisible sun that warmed Fern's cheeks. A pair of songbirds exchanged familiar notes in the branches of a shrub, and a butterfly alighted on an embroidered flower on her dress. It was just like an evening at the Meadows—if only her stomach wasn't jumpy with excitement.

Gran strode to the middle of their space and swept her arm in an arc. Waves of yellow-green energy coursed off each fingertip.

Fern ducked. The glowing ribbons fluttered before running together into one film of light. The color was intense, and stable, better than an aurora.

Gran's gaze met Fern's. A smile played across her lips and

lit up her eyes, not with magic, but pure orneriness. "Your old Gran still has a few tricks up her sleeve."

Fern straightened to tower over the small woman. "More than a few *tricks*. No more secrets?"

She laughed and flapped the energy into an upside-down bowl. It drifted downward, reshaping itself to their pie-shaped ground before snapping around the edge of their shrubbery. Show-off.

"Gran? You want me to manage the Meadows, then everything has got to be out in the open. No hiding any plans."

Her grandmother offered up her open palms. "There's naught left to hide, lass."

Fern helped her release the animals. Mice and rabbits, toads and snakes, birds, butterflies and bees scampered, slithered or flew around the grasses and wildflowers, really giving the small space the look, sound and feel of their special Meadows.

As they stood back to admire it, Fern wrapped her arm around Gran's shoulders and tipped her head to Gran's. "Thanks, Gran. I love you."

Gran patted her cheek. "I love you, too, but we're nae done yet." Gran tucked a hand through her arm, and they joined others walking toward the group gathered on the cliff top at the farthest point. Merlin and Raven stood a head above the rest of the people, and Gran made a beeline for them. Merlin reached out to briefly clasp Fern's shoulder, then Beri slipped into place on the other side of him. His face was red, but instead of the grin she'd expected, only one side of his mouth tipped up halfheartedly.

Geez, what had happened during that *word* with Sir Humus?

No one was talking now, so she peeled her gaze from Beri. A few stragglers ran to meet their families in the crowd that mostly faced east. A salty breeze rose off the water, making the evening balmy, and far below, the sea rolled and shimmered. The clear eastern sky had purpled, not quite dark enough to see stars. Fern turned to look over her shoulder where a lighter sky surrounded the sun—blues, pinks and a line of orange near the horizon.

"Look," someone called, "it touches."

The bottom of the sun dipped to the water and began melting into it, quicker than she thought possible. Someone else called to turn around. The sky was lightening on the eastern horizon, and the edge of the moon broke over the water.

A cheer went up, sending an excited rush across the group, catching Fern up with it. She didn't dare look away from the steadily growing orb. It appeared huge, three or four times the size of the setting sun and, as it rose, so did her excitement. Energy hummed in her. She felt like dancing, but with the ceremony starting, she needed to look like an adult. Though no one had said exactly when in it would begin, so...she stretched up onto her toes and bounced a bit.

People fell silent. Had they seen her jiggling? She glanced to one side, then to the other. Every single person, uh, *wizard*, was aglow. Gran shone yellow green, Merlin was rusty brown, Raven his chestnut brown and Beri the emerald green she knew so well.

The other colors varied—peachy-oranges, azure blues and deep reds—and appeared in clumps where families stood together. She easily recognized Willow's family's gold magic.

Fern stole another look at Beri. Nice. The way his energy

moved and quivered had her up on her toes again. *Whoosh—* she lost control. Her green shimmied like a garter snake streaming through the tall grass, with no chance to catch the tail because you couldn't tell where it was. She tried to pull it back, but it wasn't going anywhere else. Now the only energy missing from their family group was, sadly, Mom's sage.

The rising moon broke free from the water. Another cheer went up, and fireworks shot from wizards' hands.

Was there anything they couldn't do with this energy?

She put up her hand to try it, but Gran caught her wrist. "It's time, lass," she whispered.

Several elders joined them in walking to the cliff's edge, the huge moon hanging over the sea beyond. The council members formed an arc, and Fern and Gran faced them, their backs to the sea.

Gran said, "Take out your mother's gift."

Her hands shook while she loosened the drawstrings on the leather pouch, and it didn't help that they still glowed. She tried collecting the energy, but it raced even more wildly.

"Take your time," said Sir Humus.

At last, she had Mom's glass cradled between her palms.

Sir Humus stepped forward and put his hands over her head. Loudly, he called out, "Who presents this wizard before the Summer Fourth Moon Council Gathering?"

"I, Lady Lark, present this Windborne youth, Fern of the Meadows, heir to Lady Heather, Witch of the Meadows. She bears a gift from Lady Heather showing her support and approval of this presentation." Then, in a softer voice, Gran added, "Now, Fern," and nodded encouragingly.

Fern visualized sending up the tower of light. The racing

strands in her palms wouldn't cooperate. They glowed more brightly—proof something was happening, but not what she wanted. Fern framed the image again. Her magic scattered. How could she have bonded so well to her ratna and not be able to do this?

My plants helped.

"'Twould be better if you had your ratna," Gran murmured, "but remember you've done this without it, on my knee."

She had. Yet now the excitement from earlier seemed all wrong. What was she doing standing here in front of these people, trying to prove herself with only two-day-old magic? It was no use. They'd have to dismiss her until another fourth moon, when she'd be better trained in magic and could show that her mother really did approve.

A hand clasped her shoulder, and another slid under her hands.

Fern turned. "Mom," she whispered in relief. "You made it."

"Just, I see. Those jewelers were a pair of gabby old hens. Now, Fern, draw a breath and settle yourself."

Wiping the wet from one eye, she gave her mom a little smile and took the breath. Calmness spread over her. Mom could show her approval since she was here.

Mom's next words were totally alien to their life in Colorado. "Very good, my meadowsweet. Now take your magic in hand."

She wasn't going to help? "I, uh... Mom!"

Mom cocked a brow at her.

Fern's eyes flickered between her mom and grandmother standing shoulder to shoulder. They both had the don't-mess-with-me look.

Okay, she had come to the island on her own. She'd started learning about plants on her own. Had a job. Earned her own money. Could cook and clean, when she felt like it. And she'd gotten her magic on her own. She'd found the seeds and also figured out how to put magic into them and then used her plants to put magic into the land.

She had to do this, too, if she wanted a life on the Isle of Giuthas. The wind changed, coming from the south and carrying the scent of pine, damp soil and wildflowers— everything she loved. The enclave might be old-fashioned and have difficult people to deal with, but what community didn't? Gran had promised they'd work together on the changes, and Fern planned to start with the policy about exiling nonmagical kids from Giuthas.

Closing her eyes, Fern drew in another breath. She pulled her loose energy to her core and stilled it. She slowly released it to her channels, then to her hands. Something else seemed to be happening, but she was afraid to look. *Fill and mix*, she directed the magic. The glass hummed warmly against her palms, and as if from afar in a dream, she saw her magic flowing upward.

An appreciative murmur rose in the crowd behind her. She opened her eyes. A light tower glowed in her hands. Not as high as the one Mom had made, but it shone steadily.

Woo-hoo! I did it!

Mom squeezed her shoulder. "Hold it while we complete the ceremony."

To one side of her, Gran raised a tower of her yellow-green light. On the other side, Mom gestured to someone in the crowd before raising her tower. *Wow.* Mom outdid herself—the sage tower rose above Fern's head. Another light tower appeared on the other side of her mom's. A rich, rusty brown, Merlin's face in its glow. When a smaller, chestnut brown one appeared, she wasn't surprised to see Raven.

But the furry, gray guinea pig cradled in the crook of his arm did surprise her. How had Hilda gotten here?

Her whole family stood with her. Her family. Fern blinked away tears as she held her hands and energy steadier than her heart felt.

"Step forward, Fern of the Meadows," said Sir Humus.

She did, carefully balancing her light tower, and his booming voice rang out, "Who presents Fern of the Meadows for the position of heir to the Witch of the Meadows?"

"I, Lady Heather, her mother and Witch of the Meadows."

"I, Lady Lark, her grandmother."

"I, Mister Merlin, her father," he boomed, strong and proud.

"I, Master Raven, her brother."

A sharp *squeak* pierced the quiet—Hilda—and laughter twittered across the crowd before Sir Humus asked, "What say you, council members?"

"Aye," rang a chorus of voices.

"Do you accept this position?"

Fern swallowed. They'd practiced this line. "I accept responsibility for the Meadows for the Windborne of the Isle of Giuthas. I share this gift and burden of all it entails with my family and will do my part to see it prosper."

"Thus, let it be known upon the rising of the Grain Moon at the Summer Fourth Moon Council Gathering in the Season of the Meadows that Fern is now heir to the Witch of the Meadows. Welcome, Mistress Fern."

The people roared their approval, exploding more wizard fireworks, the largest and loudest from Raven, who shot his tower into the air like a rocket.

Its explosion evaporated Fern's magic, leaving the glass mound in her hand. It glowed brightly, sage energy swirling with just a touch of spring green.

She held it out to her mother.

Mom slid an arm around her waist and shook her head. "No, sweet, you put it away to keep. You brought your magic together really well tonight. I think you're on the way to being able to handle mine. Isn't she, Mum?"

"Aye, more than you realize, Heather. You did brilliantly, dear, just brilliantly." Gran patted her cheek and bustled behind them to speak with her council cronies.

Mom kissed her, and Fern held her close to whisper, "Thanks for asking Merlin and Raven to also stand up with me tonight."

"I wouldn't have had it any other way. They're our family. We'll work on bringing that together again as well."

She had time to whisper, "Thanks," before Raven thumped her on the back.

"Way to go, Fern," he said. "I knew you could do it." With a squeal, Hilda squirmed from Raven to Fern to snuggle at her neck. Merlin hugged her and even put an arm around Mom to draw her close for a moment, which earned him a startled smile.

Then everyone surrounded them and wanted to hug her, shake her hand or just say congratulations.

Everyone except the person she wanted most to see. Beri.

39

Almost Everything She Could Ask For

After the ceremony, well-wishers greeted Fern. She shook hands while her parents and Gran introduced her to what seemed like every islander. Beri slipped through the group—talking to Mom over on the side, listening solemnly to Sir Humus, head bent in deep conversation with Raven. Never did he speak with Fern. It seemed impossible, but...

Is he avoiding me?

The wizards wandered off to the glowing-domed displays, and musicians brought instruments to a spot nearby. Food was set out, and the fire in the circle was lit. At last, only Mom, Merlin, Gran—holding Hilda—Raven and Willow were left.

Where was Beri? He'd disappeared.

"It's so exciting for you, Fern." Willow hugged her again.

"I'm glad I could be here," Mom said. "Sir Humus says I missed a demonstration of your ratna bonding across the Meadows? I canna believe it, but he may have said it was *spectacular.*"

Raven put an arm around her shoulders. "I must say, she owes me some credit. If it hadn't been for me slipping her tips, she'd never have shown those old-timers."

"No way!" Fern shrugged him off with a laugh. "Well, maybe one or two, but all tips came *after* I had the seeds, so no credit for that. But thanks," she said, and Raven dipped his chin in answer. Suddenly, that wasn't good enough. She hugged him. After a stiff second, he hugged her back, and then everyone was close and talking about how wonderful the ceremony had been. Even Hilda squeaked and wriggled in Gran's arms.

Mom leaned over to pet the guinea pig. "Mum, it isn't like you to keep a pet. Why is this little animal living with you?"

"Remember my cousin Scallop of Tern Bay? She thought I was lonely and found Hilda at one of those human places she frequents, an animal rescue center. After I saw how clever she is, I couldn't refuse."

"I thought the same when I crossed to Hillux and the rascal chastised me for not being with Fern." Mom stroked Fern's cheek, her eyes suddenly shiny. "I'm glad I was here. Your magic has been so long coming, it's lovely to see."

Raven was laughing. "I daresay I've seen some that wasn't *lovely*. Dad? Even though she got the bond done, you still need to train her up."

"Aye, Merlin is the wizard to handle that. Do you not agree, Heather?" Gran said. "Especially with you so busy with your art."

Everyone stopped talking. Under Fern's arm, Mom stiffened and turned her gaze on Gran.

What did Gran think she was doing, laying out the old battle just when everything was going so well?

In the silence of their tight circle, Hilda ground her teeth, making a chittering sound of displeasure. Mom wrenched her gaze down to the guinea pig. So did Gran. Then, like magic, Mom seemed to melt. Her features softened, and her slender frame leaned into Gran's.

What had Hilda *said*?

"Right, then." Gran threw her hands up. "No more secrets *or* grousing. I did give Heather my blessing *and* admit that on occasion I have bragged about my daughter's talent. Time to celebrate. Lad, come help me sequester my wild animals so I can settle my sweet piggy into a bunch of lush grass. She's earned it." Gran took off, and Raven followed.

Merlin cleared his throat. "I need to check our display. Perhaps you can stop by later, Heather?"

"I promised Mimosa a visit," Mom said. "But I'll make it brief." Her gaze flicked to Fern, then back to catch Merlin's. "Walk me there?"

Oh, this looked good. Fern hated to interrupt, but caught Mom's hand. "Can you wait a sec? You, too, Willow?" Fern tugged Mom aside and dipped her head to whisper, "I'm assuming you didn't come here until after the jewelry-store owners left. What did the gabby hens decide?"

Mom grinned and gave her a thumbs-up.

"Yes!" She hugged her mother. "You did it."

"Yes and no," Mom whispered. "I've got the job, now to create it. Not a word about this until I sort it out."

"You're gonna tell Merlin?"

"I don't know." She sighed. "Keep your fingers crossed for me."

Mom and Merlin walked toward the displays, their multi-colored glows lighting up the dark like a fair. The space between her parents grew narrower, and *perhaps* their hands joined.

"Aw, wouldn't it be nice if they got back together?" Willow sounded wistful. "I know Raven would like it."

"I would, too. But I'm not so sure about my mom."

"She doesn't miss having a partner to share things with? Or living in a world with magic?"

Fern shrugged. "She really does hate gardening and has always loved throwing herself into art. She's in her own world when she's doing it. Nothing makes her happier."

"How can this be? Mam says that Merlin and Lady Heather were a perfect energy match. When I'm with Raven, I'm a-flush with energy and happiness. The way you must feel with Beri. How can making art compete with that?"

"You'd have to watch her flamework glass to understand. Can you help me find Beri?"

"Raven will know where he is." Willow stared off into space, listening for a moment. "He's gone down to the beach, east side."

Together, they strode to the cliffs. The climbing moon cast enough light for them to see a figure walking on the narrow strip of sand below.

"It's Beri," Willow said with assurance, pointing with her peregrinator. "Let me take you down."

Fern closed her eyes. Stillness surrounded them, replaced by the close roar and the damp spray of the ocean. She blinked, eyes adjusting to the moving white waves on one side of her and the looming black cliff on the other. Up ahead, Beri strode along the firm sand.

Willow winked and disappeared.

Jogging, Fern caught up to him. It would be romantic to be walking *with* him on this beach. "Beri?"

He turned, frowning the moment he saw her.

Fern's confidence wavered. "Hey, I wanted to talk to you." She reached a hand.

He drew back. "If another person sees green flames, I'll—" His face twisted, and she held her breath while he looked everywhere but at her. "I have tried to sort this and canna. Each person has a different opinion, and none have time to discuss it with the others, so they order me to wait. But I canna just *wait* while seeing you within reach to...touch."

Her hand dropped, and so did her heart. Neither could she.

"They've accepted my personal plans, but those with you..." Beri dug into the wet sand with his toe. "Sir Humus says 'tis not proper for me to be flinging myself at the heir to the Witch of the Meadows, and Merlin agreed."

Of all the crazy—

"You didn't *fling* yourself."

Wet sand flipped from his boot. "I asked you to show me your energy," he said in exasperation.

"You had to because *I* never would have known what to do. I'm approved and could do what I did because you helped me." But he'd said something else. "Merlin doesn't want us to bond?"

"He won't say." Beri's gaze shot to hers. "Duffy came up while I spoke with Sir Humus and withdrew her prebonding request. I told Merlin that and that Salm's had his way with you—"

"*What?* How could you say that?"

He looked confused. "You said naught happened even when he kissed you. Salm didna deny it when I spoke with him."

"Right, but do you have to say it using those particular

words? *Had his way with* me?"

"You wish me to say it another way?"

"Please! My mom will think—never mind, just say he kissed me."

"Merlin insists 'tis only fair for you to meet the unbonded lads in the settlement between sixteenth and twentieth year. I canna cross him."

"Just how many do I need to meet? Because Gran told me I better not kiss anyone else. She told me to prebond with you."

Beri practically jumped he jerked so quickly. "She did? Lady Lark told you to prebond with me?"

She nodded. "So who has the final word?"

A grin spread across his face. "Lady Lark." Then he sobered again. "I suppose. Lady Heather mentioned a word with Merlin, too. Spells, 'tis difficult dealing with multiple parent figures."

"No kidding." *Mom knows what I want. Merlin doesn't.* "Call Raven to get Willow, please."

"Uh, aye?"

It didn't take long for Willow to return. Fern clasped her hand. "Please take me back."

Willow looked like she wanted to ask why, but she pereported Fern to the cliffs.

"Where will I find Merlin?" Fern asked.

"The first place I'd look is in the wildlife display. It's the forested one with rocky bluffs."

Must be in the part of the circle she hadn't seen. Fern set off, Willow skipping to keep up, until Fern noticed. "Sorry. Thanks for your help."

"So it didn't go well talking to Beri?"

"It went fine. Why do you say that?"

"You left him there without a word."

Fern whacked her head and jerked to a stop. Geez, she had. What a stupid thing to do. "Please send a message through Raven. Tell Beri I'll be back."

Willow was silent while they approached the displays. Fern recognized the tall, rusty-brown dome as Merlin's.

Willow sighed. "Beri says he'll wait for you."

"Nice."

"Forever if he has to."

Wow. They exchanged grins, then threaded their way into the fire circle.

"Oh, there's Merlin with—" Willow pulled up short.

Sir Humus.

And the men had seen them. Merlin raised a finger in a "wait" signal and ended his conversation. He didn't look especially happy, and Fern's heart sank. What now?

"Good luck," Willow whispered, and she ducked into the Forest display.

Merlin's arm came across her shoulders. "We need to talk."

Her stomach twisted, but she drew a breath and nodded.

He steered her out of the circle and back toward the cliff she'd just left. The moon was climbing above the waves, trailing a stunning rippling light, and she ached to be back on the beach, walking hand-in-hand with Beri.

Merlin dropped his arm and faced her. "Fern, this is one of the happiest days of my life. I don't wish anything to ruin it or to separate us in any way, but things with you are happening faster than I can keep up. Earlier, I heard reports of flaming with Beri. Now, Humus has additional news regarding Beri that involves you. These are things I don't know how to handle with a daughter. Perhaps I should hear your side. You and Beri?"

Her palms were sweaty. Again. At least the light was dim enough for him to not detect a blush. "I like him. A lot."

Merlin looked away.

What did that mean? They hardly knew each other. Telling Gran had been different. They had a history, and Fern had known Gran would listen to all her reasons and understand. With Merlin... Who knew? This could be all wrong.

No, it wasn't *all* wrong. This was her dad, and she needed to give him a chance to understand. "I-I might even love him, but I need more time to be sure," she added quickly. "That's what prebonding is for, right? He's the one I want to try that with."

Merlin—her *dad*—tentatively put his hand on her shoulder. "That makes me very happy to hear. If it were any other boy you had feelings for... Truth be told, I'm not sure what emotion was running through my body when I heard you were seen flaming with a young man. Fern, I've just gotten my daughter back. It's selfish, but I was hoping to get to know you myself," he mumbled in a choked voice.

She hugged him, which felt right. "I want that...Dad. I do."

"Heather wants the same with Raven. We canna promise anything, but we'd like to share some family time."

"Time for the four of us would be wonderful." *Before there are the six of us*, she wanted to add, but decided not to push her luck. Fern eyed him hopefully. "But isn't Beri family?"

"Aye, Beri is. And he tells me you are the one for him."

"Yeah," she whispered. Fern heaved a sign and immediately wished she hadn't, because Dad turned her to face the

350 | LAUREL WANROW

moonlight and studied her like Lady Mimosa had.

"Something's still wrong," he said.

"I guess it's nothing. I was just thinking tonight's so special and I can touch everyone except the one guy whose hand I want to hold," she said wistfully.

"Not kiss him?" Her dad jostled her a little.

"Nah, we already got in one really good kiss. That'll hold me for a day. Right?" She stopped a teasing smile from forming.

"Should." He looked thoughtful. "This *is* a special occasion, Fern. I haven't given you a gift to acknowledge it."

"That's okay, Dad. Having you in my life is the best gift. And I really appreciate your help in smoothing over this personal stuff."

"Do you lock away your energy when you touch Beri?"

She glanced sideways to gauge if this was a good thing but couldn't tell. "Yes. Or I don't touch him."

"And still you are flaming," he said kindly. "Would you like your magic to stay secure so you can hold hands with Beri?"

She sighed. "Yeah."

Dad's grip on her shoulders tightened, and more than his fingers touched her. His energy swept through her channels and sped to her closed-down core, wrapped itself around hers and sealed it over with a little click, all before she had time to blink.

He lifted his hand and stepped back. "We call this a quash, when a parent locks down the magic of a young'un, a technique to keep everyone safe if someone gets out of hand. You may touch Beri now. 'Tis my gift to you."

"I—uh..." The quash felt weird, but what he said totally

caught her off guard. "Really? All I like?"

He fixed her with a look. "Within reason, you ken?"

"Oh, I ken." Fern laughed. "But what about Beri? He had an equal part in those flames."

He shrugged, and his wings appeared. "Let me see if the lad would like a gift, sort of an extension of yours." He stepped to the side of the cliff and jumped.

Fern gasped. Wings spread, her dad soared in a long glide down to the beach and out of sight. She paced a circle while waiting. He wasn't gone long. Dad flew up, Beri right behind him, his freckled face grinning.

They drew in their wings, and Merlin clasped Beri's shoulder for a few seconds. Then with a wink, he said, "Have fun, you two," and walked away.

Without discussing it, they strolled past the musicians and out to the end of the bluff, where they were quite alone.

Perfect. For her anyway. "So you can't use any of your magic?"

"Nary a spark." Beri took her hand, and they both stopped.

"Sorry. It must be strange for you." *Like a punishment?* she wanted to ask, but she didn't want to take her hand from his.

Nothing happened. Magical, that was. His fingers felt warm and strong, and he stroked his thumb over the back of her hand. A fire ran up her arm and down her spine, a feeling that had nothing to do with magic this time. At least not that kind.

"Oh, I am nae sorry," Beri said breathlessly. He leaned in until their noses were all but touching, and his spicy scent drowned out the isle's sea-salt and pine scents. "Merlin suggested we keep secret that 'tis due to a quash. Let people believe you have the control you have shown creating your bond."

"What about you?"

He grinned. "Passing the fifth of my trials has put me in the unique position of having first choice of any available habitat when I turn eighteenth next month. Yet I am so distracted by you tha' I told them, 'No, thank you.'"

"You...turned down a habitat?"

He shrugged one shoulder. "Can you keep another secret?"

She laughed. "Are you kidding? I've skated through my entire time on Giuthas on secrets, and I'm collecting more."

He looked so serious that she squeezed his hand. "I want someone to share secrets with. And to have no secrets from. You're my trial for that."

Beri's lips turned up slightly at the corners, in that I've-got-a-secret smile. She tugged his hand. "What?"

"I've requested a *rumspringa* break. A gap year, you called it," he said. "They want to settle in the new wizards, but Merlin says they will agree to it, either when the isle stabilizes or by my birthday, whichever comes first. He will see to it."

Oh. Disappointment flooded her. Fern dropped her gaze to their twined fingers. "Where do you plan to go?"

"That is the secret. Most people will think I am exploring Windborne enclaves and academies in between helping in the Meadows in a prebonding trial with you. But I approached Lady Heather and asked to apprentice to her."

Fern's gaze shot to his.

"She agreed, if I would be an exchange student at Boulder High." Beri searched her face. "I didna know of such a thing, but have agreed and gotten the approval."

"To go into the human world?"

"You asked if I feel strange, and I must!" He laughed. "I wish to spend time getting to know your life there. And you."

"But you can't use magic there." She bit her lip and lifted his hand in hers. "It'll be like this all the time."

"Spells, Fern, it does nae matter." He pulled her into a hug. "*You* are worth losing magic over."

ACKNOWLEDGMENTS

The Witch of the Meadows is truly the book of my nature-geek heart. It's been through many versions, originally as my first NaNoWriMo novel in 2007 named Meadow Magic. After revisions, I submitted to the 2009 Lone Star Writing Contest under the title Wildflowers and Winged Boys—and won my first contest! The story sat while I worked on others.

I still loved Meadow Magic so pulled it out again. While working on it this time, my original critique partners from all those years ago provided plotting advice and a new title. Huge thanks to Karen, Jessica and Jen for sticking by me!

My thanks go out to fellow writers at CritiqueCircle.com for critiques as I ran it through the queues, especially Susan, Andy, Lord and Memy. Thanks to my beta readers, Rebecca and Sabrina.

Forever thanks to my critique partners, Michelle, Jason, Karen and Allison. These folks have read again and again, making the story shorter, clearer and stronger!

And of course, thank you to my family who have put up with my agonizing over every detail: Bill, Em and Theo. I love you.

ABOUT THE AUTHOR

Before kids, Laurel Wanrow studied and worked as a naturalist—someone who leads wildflower walks and answers calls about the snake that wandered into your garage. During a stint of homeschooling, she turned her writing skills to fiction to share her love of the land, magical characters and fantastical settings.

She's the author of *The Luminated Threads* series, a Victorian historical fantasy mixing witches, shapeshifters and a sweet romance in a secret corner of England.

When not living in her fantasy worlds, Laurel camps, hunts fossils, and argues with her husband and two new adult kids over whose turn it is to clean house. Though they live on the East Coast, a cherished family cabin in the Colorado Rockies holds Laurel's heart.

Visit her online and sign up for her new-release newsletter at www.laurelwanrow.com.

Made in the USA
Columbia, SC
27 August 2018